Business from 9 to 5,
and romance...

AFTER
HOURS

AFTER HOURS

A FIRST TIME FOR EVERYTHING
by
Jessica Steele

LOVEKNOT
by
Catherine George

FIRE BENEATH THE ICE
by
Helen Brooks

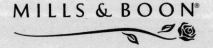

MILLS & BOON®

*MILLS & BOON and MILLS & BOON with the Rose Device
are registered trademarks of the publisher.
Harlequin Mills & Boon Limited,
Eton House, 18-24 Paradise Road, Richmond, Surrey, TW9 1SR*

AFTER HOURS
© by Harlequin Enterprises II B.V., 1999

A First Time for Everything, Loveknot and *Fire Beneath the Ice* were
first published in Great Britain by Mills & Boon Limited
in separate, single volumes.

A First Time for Everything © Jessica Steele 1990
Loveknot © Catherine George 1988
Fire Beneath the Ice © Helen Brooks 1995

ISBN 0 263 81542 0

05-9910

*Printed and bound in Great Britain
by Caledonian International Book Manufacturing Ltd, Glasgow*

Jessica Steele lives in a friendly Worcestershire village with her super husband, Peter. They are owned by a gorgeous Staffordshire bull terrier called Florence, who is boisterous and manic, but also adorable. It was Peter who first prompted Jessica to try writing, and, after the first rejection, encouraged her to keep on trying.

Her first book was published by Mills & Boon® in 1979 and since then Jessica has written 65 novels, published in more than 20 languages. Luckily, with the exception of Uruguay, she has so far managed to research inside all the countries in which she has set her books, travelling to places as far apart as Siberia and Egypt. Her thanks go to Peter for his help and encouragement.

A FIRST TIME
FOR EVERYTHING

by

JESSICA STEELE

CHAPTER ONE

IF SHE were to be truthful, Joss owned, she didn't feel very much like going out that Monday evening. She could not have said why particularly it was that the Beacon Theatre Group had no appeal that February night, though, as she poured herself a second cup of coffee, she didn't think the dull and gloomy weather had very much to do with the way she was feeling.

Silently she sipped her coffee, and a few minutes later she carried her used dishes from her dining-room and through to her smart cream and pale green kitchen, knowing that she would go out. It wasn't in her nature to let anyone down, and Abby, her closest friend, was at present smitten with Fergus Perrott and, for some reason, seemed to need her along to boost her confidence.

Joss set about tackling her washing up, reflecting that Fergus had not asked Abby to go out with him yet, but that these new and frequent visits to the Beacon Theatre Group—an offshoot of the Beacon Oil Sports and Social Club—seemed to be paying dividends. She was sure she had seen a gleam of interest in Fergus's eyes last Friday as he'd watched Abby during rehearsals. All three of them worked for Beacon Oil at Beacon House, London—she and Abby both on the secretarial side, while Fergus worked in Personnel.

Thinking of last Friday, Joss pondered that she must have been feeling a bit like today's weather then—or maybe started to feel in the need of something more stimulating than her present job, for she had realised that she had been only half joking when she'd asked Fergus then if his department had been notified of any interesting secretarial vacancies.

'Finding the Audit Department too dull?' he'd queried.

'It—has its moments,' she'd replied, 'but it's not as challenging as it once was.'

'There's nothing more challenging just now than a transfer to Costing,' Fergus had told her.

'I think I'll stay where I am—"Costing" doesn't sound very much different from "Auditing",' she had answered, being unable to see anything likely to stimulate by the switch.

Leaving her neat and tidy kitchen, Joss went to get ready to go and pick Abby up. They had known each other for three years now. The whole time in fact since, at twenty years old, Joss, with her feet well and truly on the secretarial ladder, had started work at Beacon Oil.

In an attempt to lift her glum spirits, Joss tried to count her blessings. She had a good job—a very good job, she reminded herself. True, she had worked exceedingly hard to get on, and as a reward for being industrious she had been promoted several times in her three years at Beacon House. She now worked for Mr Edwards, head of the Audit Department, and she knew without false modesty that he thought well of her.

The work she did was of a confidential nature and had, at one time, stretched her abilities. But, having worked for Mr Edwards for a year now, she no longer felt stretched.

A short while later she left her apartment, telling herself that she must not allow herself to get discontented. She was well paid for her labours; the high salary Beacon Oil paid her made the expense of buying her small but smart flat and running a car just affordable.

She and Abby took it in turns to use their vehicles, and as Joss drove along to her friend's home she attempted to make herself believe that it was just 'February' that was making her feel so unsettled. Maybe everyone felt the way she did during the second month of the year. Somehow, though, she didn't feel convinced.

Joss had only joined the theatre group at Abby's bidding and, aware that she had no acting ability, she was quite pleased to sit sewing or whatever else was required while Abby and the rest of them got on with it.

'He's not here!' Abby's hushed but disappointed wail as they entered the hall they were allowed the use of brought Joss rapidly away from her own thoughts.

'Perhaps he's out the back somewhere,' she tried to cheer Abby, not seeing anything so special about Fergus Perrott herself, but sympathising with Abby, who clearly did.

'I'll bet he's not,' Abby said, looking to an outer door as if hoping that Fergus would walk through it.

As it turned out, Fergus was not there, but they were half an hour into rehearsals and Joss, acting as prompter, was about to give Abby a line she had missed when, glancing up, she suddenly saw that Abby had not so much forgotten her lines, as had had them taken momentarily out of her head by the sudden arrival of Fergus Perrott.

'Sorry I'm late, everyone,' he boomed, and excused himself, 'Had to work late.'

'Aren't we the busy one!' commented a man next to Joss whom she knew only as Larry.

Though she had to hide a smile she couldn't help but agree that, with all of them working for the same firm, Fergus had made it sound rather as if his job was of more importance than anyone else's.

When a short while later there was a general break

while the producer went into a huddle with Abby and a few of the others, Fergus came over to Joss and Larry moved away. Joss noted the considering look Fergus gave her, but she thought he was still out to impress when he said after a dramatic moment, 'Ah, Josslyn, are you still looking for a job you can get your teeth into—something that's a little different?'

About to tell him that she had changed her mind, she opened her mouth—then hesitated. Suddenly, as it registered that, although she was only ever called Joss, he had called her Josslyn, she realised that he must have taken a peep at her personnel file. If he was so busy that he had to work overtime, then he wouldn't have time to waste on checking her file, would he? Not unless, she perceived, he had some good reason to check on her and her capabilities and any other notes made on her record with the company over the last three years.

So, 'I could be,' she said after some moments of deciding that it didn't seem that he could be speaking purely for effect.

'I'm sure you will be when I tell you...' Fergus began, and soon had Joss looking at him wide-eyed and incredulous as he revealed how a telex had been received from Beacon House, Cairo, late that afternoon stating that one top grade secretary would be returning to England, and requesting that another top grade secretary be sent out immediately.

Joss's mind was on the instant a seething mass of questions, but since one of her most heartfelt desires had always been to see the Pyramids at Giza, which she knew was not so very far away from Cairo, all she could gasp was, 'Cairo! You're offering me a job in Egypt!'

'It's only a temporary job,' Fergus hastened to tell her, and went on to explain how delicate negotiations were going on in Egypt with regard to a contract for the refining of great quantities of crude oil. 'The present secretary out there must have gone down with a bug or something,' he continued, 'which reminds me, you'll have to check up with our medical department tomorrow about jabs and things you'll need before…'

'Just a minute!' Joss stopped him before he could go racing on, while at the same time she tried to hold down an inner and growing excitement at the very thought. 'How long's temporary—and what do I do afterwards?' Suddenly some of her excitement faded. It was all very well to go rushing off to the Middle East at this quite terrific opportunity, but what about when the temporary job was over? Since she had a sizeable mortgage on her flat she just couldn't dash off without giving a thought to how she could meet those monthly mortgage repayments when she got back.

Fergus, it seemed, had an answer for everything. 'Mr Edwards will welcome you back with open arms, you know he will,' he declared, and Joss's feeling of excitement started to soar again.

She went home that night with her head spinning from the question and answer session she'd had with Fergus, and let herself into her flat and went over everything in her mind again.

The contract which Fergus had spoken of must be almost agreed upon, she mused, because according to him her stint in Egypt would only be for a month or so.

Which, she reflected as she went into her kitchen to make herself a hot drink, was so much the better from her boss, Mr Edwards', point of view. She thought that perhaps he might not be very keen to let her go, but maybe he wouldn't mind so much if it was only for a month— an absence of not much more than her annual holiday really, when he would have had to get someone else to do her work.

She mustn't start thinking of it as a holiday, she brought herself up short, having had other things to spend her money on since going in for flat purchasing, and a holiday being out of the question. Pulling her thoughts away from anything remotely connected with holidays, and burying such thoughts of how at last she was going to have the chance to see the fantastic, stupendous, mind-boggling Pyramids of Cheops, Chephren and Mycerinus, Joss tried for calm.

For a moment, several moments in fact, she had been uncertain that Fergus had the power to offer her the temporary job in Cairo. He was fairly high up the Personnel tree, she knew that, but the doubt had niggled so that she just had to ask, as tactfully as she could, 'Er—has Mr Grazier sanctioned your offering me this…'

She realised that perhaps she hadn't been as tactful as she had hoped when Fergus got on his dignity and told her grandly, 'As it happens, Mr Grazier is at present sunning himself somewhere in India—in his absence I have full charge of the office.'

'He's on holiday?' she queried, and found that she had deflected his hurt pride when he replied that his boss always chose to depart from England's shores in February, and then went on to tell her to bring her passport into the office with her tomorrow because she would have to see about getting a visa.

Joss went to bed that night still trying to keep a lid on her excitement. Nothing had been settled yet, she tried to remind herself. Fergus had told her not to mention anything to Mr Edwards tomorrow until she had heard from him—which had again made her wonder if Fergus had as much clout as he would have her believe. She recalled how he had said that the telex had been received late that afternoon, and could not help but wonder then if his telling her to hang fire meant that Fergus had to first convince someone else in his office that she was the right person to go.

Suddenly then she became a little proud of herself. Why shouldn't she go? Beacon Oil were a company that worked worldwide. Staff, secretaries, were often being sent all over the globe—as in the case of the secretary who was returning from Cairo—so why not her!

She felt too excited to be ready to close her eyes, and a whole range of thoughts had gone through her head before Josslyn eventually went to sleep. Her thoughts had grown hazy as sleep claimed her, but one of her last waking thoughts was to wonder if maybe Fergus was keen for her to have the job out of some wish to impress Abby with the power of his position, or perhaps—since from where he stood it must seem that she and Abby were inseparable, for they did most things together—if he was anxious to have her out of the way in order to have a clear field with Abby.

That same thought was in Joss's head as she sat in her office the following morning. She was certain, having caught the way in which Fergus looked at Abby, that he was interested in her friend. And although, on the face of it, it didn't seem possible that a man of such self-importance should be backward about asking Abby for a date, Joss was prepared to consider that her theory might be right.

'Good morning, Joss,' Mr Edwards, tall, beaky and fatherly, greeted her when he came in, and Joss was suddenly overwhelmed by a feeling of guilt.

'Good morning, Mr Edwards,' she replied, and badly wanted to tell him right then about her discussion with

Fergus last night. Just in time, however, she remembered that Fergus had told her not to mention anything to Mr Edwards yet.

An hour later she was beginning to think that it was just as well she hadn't said anything to her boss—the way things were looking, there was nothing *to* tell him! Five minutes later, as she began to realise that it looked as though the temporary Egyptian job had gone to some other secretary, she began to feel a shade annoyed. She was as well qualified as most, and she must be jolly good at her job—or why else would she be holding down the responsible job she had now?

A minute afterwards, though, her phone rang, and suddenly, as Fergus Perrott said, 'You'd better see about getting your visa,' her annoyance abruptly vanished.

'You're… I'm going?'

'Didn't I promise you the job?' he answered smugly. But by then Joss didn't care how smug he sounded; she was going—going to Egypt! She was going—to see the Pyramids!

In actual fact her departure for Cairo was not as immediate as had been requested. Apart from her visa application and other formalities to attend to, she had to present herself for the various vaccinations thought advisable.

But it was someone in Personnel, however, who acquainted Mr Edwards with the fact that his secretary was being sent on loan to Egypt. They must have phoned through at the same time that she was speaking with Fergus, Joss realised—and have done their job most tactfully—for her boss did not seem too badly put out when, as she put down her phone after noting Fergus's lengthy instructions, Mr Edwards came into her office from his own.

'What's this I've just heard about you going to Egypt on some top priority, highly confidential matter?' he asked without preamble.

'Do you mind very much?' she asked him quietly.

'Yes,' he said severely, though he added, 'But as long as it's only temporary I'll do nothing to block you going.'

'I'll be back before you've noticed I've gone,' she promised, then set about doing the hundred and one things that suddenly presented themselves as most urgent.

By the time all formalities had been completed and her temporary successor initiated, the rest of the week had gone by. With arrangements made for her to fly out to Cairo on the following Monday, Joss spent the weekend with her parents at their home in Eastbourne and returned to London after lunch on Sunday to pack everything she had made ready in the evenings during the week.

The excitement that had been part and parcel of her since Fergus's phone call last Tuesday spiralled as her plane took off on Monday, churning away inside her throughout the flight.

None of that excitement had diminished when, having put her watch forward by two hours, she landed in Cairo a little after half past four that afternoon. By the time she had claimed her luggage and passed through passport control, it was nearing five, and Joss looked about for whoever had been sent to meet her.

It took all of five minutes as the arrival area emptied for it to dawn on her that whoever had been sent to meet her was late. When another ten minutes went by and no one had turned up, she found herself in something of a dilemma. What if the person who had been instructed to meet her had forgotten—or, worse, had been involved in an accident? It had gone five now and she had no idea if the Cairo office worked a nine-to-five day, but, as she saw it then, she considered that she'd be best employed in somehow getting to Beacon House with all speed.

She had no trouble in locating a taxi when she left the airport building, but had more trouble in getting the taxi-driver to take his eyes off her long ash-blonde hair.

'Can you take me to Beacon House, Cairo?' she asked him when she did gain his full attention and kept her fingers crossed that he could understand English.

To her relief he could, and not only that, but he seemed to know straight away where Beacon House was. With her luggage swiftly stowed away, the driver set off, with Joss hoping with all she had that she would not find the office closed when she got there.

If the worst came to the worst she could always book into a hotel overnight, she made contingency plans—though she prayed that it wouldn't come to that, and closed her mind to the possibility that February could be the height of the tourist season with all hotels fully booked.

Having decided what her plan of campaign must be, she took a moment out to notice the traffic. Horrendous was putting it mildly! As far as she could tell, traffic drove on the right, but with the proviso, or so it seemed, that one overtook on whichever side there appeared to be a gap. Her heart went into her mouth when it seemed to her that her driver took his taxi much too close to a man sitting astride a donkey which was taking a stroll down the main road. The donkey was unharmed, however, and as she twisted to look back to check, she saw that as well as being unharmed, the animal seemed oblivious to the traffic and the incessant blaring of car horns that went with it.

She forgot all about the donkey, however, when, facing the front again, she noticed that the taxi was slowing down. Her heart picked up a few agitated beats when the driver finally stopped outside a smart-looking glass-fronted building. Peering from the window of the taxi, she read with relief the embossed 'BEACON HOUSE' over the doorway, and turned back, intending to ask the driver to wait while she checked if there was anyone about—what she didn't need, if the office was closed, was to go wandering the streets of Cairo with her heavy suitcase looking for a hotel.

But the driver was already out of the car, she saw, and was round the back extracting her luggage, so swiftly she left the vehicle too, and went quickly to test the door of Beacon House. To her utmost relief, it yielded. She went in—the taxi-driver followed.

A man somewhere in his late twenties and of medium height got to his feet as she went further inside. 'Do you speak English?' she asked him.

Her relief was total when, with just a hint of a London accent, he replied, 'Most of the time—who,' he added admiringly, 'are you?'

But Joss had other things on her mind just then than embarking on flirty repartee with this representative of Beacon Oil who obviously liked what he saw.

'I'm the replacement secretary from England,' she told him, 'I've just come from the airport.' She saw that, for all he appeared to look momentarily stunned, he had a quick standard of recovery. For in no time he had taken her large suitcase from the taxi-driver and—somewhat to her amazement—had what seemed to her to be an argument with him in Arabic, and, all before she had got herself completely together, he had paid her taxi fare and had sent the driver on his way.

'Rule number one,' he told her as he turned back to her, 'never pay the first price they ask. In actual fact,' he went on knowledgeably, 'you should have agreed the fare before you got into his taxi.'

'How much do I owe you?' Joss asked him.

'Forget it, I'll claim it on expenses,' he told her. Then, smiling a welcoming smile, 'I'm Baz Barton.' He held out his hand.

'Joss Harding,' she told him, shaking hands, and went on, 'I wasn't quite sure what to do when there was no one at the airport to meet me...' She broke off as a door leading into another office opened and another man of about the same age and stature as Baz Barton—clearly attracted by the sound of voices—came through.

'Look what we have here,' Baz Barton addressed the other man in tones that hinted, to Joss's mind, that he was surprised to see her there at all! 'This is Joss Harding from Beacon, London,' Baz went on, 'Joss, the manager of Beacon, Cairo, Malcolm Cooper.'

'Glad to know you, Joss,' said Malcolm, extending his right hand.

'Weren't you expecting me?' she questioned, the question seeming to her to be one needing to be asked if one linked the manager's quickly hidden look of surprise with the fact that no one had been at the airport to meet her, not to mention that certain something in Baz Barton's tone just now.

'Last week we were expecting—er—a replacement,' Malcolm replied. 'London should have let us...' He broke off then, smiling cheerfully. 'But you're here now—and welcome. Now,' he swiftly got his thoughts together, 'when did you last eat?'

His question was not one she had been expecting, but as the excitement she had nursed over the hours settled down, she only then realised that she felt hungry.

'I had a meal on the plane,' she replied.

'Which was hours ago. Baz and I were going to have a bite any time now. Leave your case here,' he decided, and, checking his watch, he turned to Baz Barton and remarked, 'He won't be here for a couple of hours yet; we might as well go now.'

They were all three sitting in the coffee bar of a nearby hotel, and Joss was tucking into a cheese omelette that came complete with chips, before she learned more of the 'he' who was expected some time after two hours had passed.

As yet, she had no idea where she would lay her head that night, but she was in the company of two of her fellow countrymen, both of whom she assumed knew Cairo well from the way they were instructing her on the various do's and don'ts. Apparently, while it was 'not done' to try and get a reduced price in any of the recognised stores, it most definitely was 'done' to haggle in the bazaars. More, it seemed one risked spoiling the market traders' enjoyment if one did not enter the 'haggling' game.

With her anxieties abated now that she had traced the two Beacon 'locals', Joss, who—no matter how she was feeling inside—had earned a reputation for being unflappable, accepted that where she would lay her head that night was no immediate cause for concern. Malcolm, she realised, must be the man who was negotiating the contract for the refining of crude oil, so she would be working for him.

It was on the tip of her tongue to ask him what particular bug had laid his previous secretary so low that she had had to return home—he had already warned her about the water, stressing that she must not even clean her teeth with it. Suddenly, though, Baz Barton was voicing the opinion that it was a good job she had arrived that day rather than tomorrow.

'Why particularly?' she asked.

'Because we normally shut up shop at five and leave work for the day,' he replied.

Joss was about to refer in passing to her contingency plan of taking herself off to a hotel for the night if need be—and of presenting herself at Beacon House in the morning—when a stray strand of curiosity stirred.

'You had some particular reason for not closing the office at five tonight?' she queried.

'Too true,' Malcolm took up. 'Thane Addison rang just before you arrived...'

'Thane Addison!' Joss exclaimed. His name was legend back at Beacon House, London. She had never met him, of course, but she knew his name well enough. According to popular report, as well as having a seat on the board of Beacon Oil, Mr Thane Never-still-a-minute Addison was Beacon's chief anywhere-in-the-world troubleshooter. 'Is Thane Addison here—in Egypt?' she questioned, and started to feel quite excited again. Especially when she heard Malcolm's reply.

'Not only is he in Egypt,' he told her, 'but he's on his way to Cairo right at this very moment.'

'Wh-where's he coming from?' Joss asked when she had got her breath back.

'Alexandria,' she was told, and, as the meal ended, she learned that the reason why both Malcolm and Baz had still been on the premises when she had arrived was that Thane Addison had phoned to say he was on his way to sign some papers they had ready for him. While they waited they had decided to have a bite to eat nearby, after which they would return and be back at the office for when he arrived.

Joss returned to the office with them. By that time all daylight had gone and she was beginning to feel that she wouldn't mind at all if someone gave her some kind of a lead as to where she would be kicking off her shoes that night. But for the moment she decided not to say anything to Malcolm that might be of a problem nature—not that she could think of her overnight accommodation as being anything of a problem. But quite clearly Malcolm, as well as Baz, seemed slightly nervous of Mr Addison's visit— they could sort it all out when he had gone.

It was nearing eight o'clock that night when, with all three of them waiting in the outer office, Malcolm, who had been watching the window, suddenly shot to his feet. 'He's here!' he said, and as suddenly, Baz Barton had shot to his feet too.

It must have been infectious, Joss realised a moment later, because as the door into the outer office was thrust open she discovered that she was on her feet too. She acknowledged then that she was quite excited at the thought of meeting the much-talked-of Mr Thane Addison in person.

Within a very short while of the tall, broad-shouldered, fair-haired man's entering the room, however, Joss was no longer sure about how she felt. Thane Addison seemed to be somewhere around thirty-seven, she would have said, had an air of knowing what everything was about— and had a pair of piercing grey eyes which, she was soon to learn, never missed a thing.

He came in, briefcase in hand, nodded to both Malcolm and Baz, spotted her—and her large suitcase nearby—and stopped dead. Then, without waiting for either of the other two men to perform the introduction but—even as she formed the idea that he had quickly assessed who she was—fixing those piercing grey eyes on her wide brown ones, he was demanding coldly, 'Who the devil are you?'

Joss was unused to anyone talking to her in such a fashion, but she hadn't come all this way to have a slanging match on landing with one of the company's board members. So she drew her unflappable self out of hiding, and in clear tones told him formally, 'My name's Josslyn Harding. I'm the replacement for the secretary who returned to England last...'

'The hell you are!' he cut rudely across what she was saying. And, while she stared at him and had the hardest work to remain outwardly unflappable, he snarled, 'You're saying that they've disregarded my instructions entirely, and sent you as Paula Ingram's replacement!'

'I rather think,' Joss replied, as every muscle in her body tensed, 'that they have.'

That was not all she thought, for as his words 'my instructions' penetrated, all her excitement rapidly disappeared. All at once, even though she found the thought too incredible, she was gaining the most definite view that she had made a mistake in thinking that she had been sent here to work as Malcolm Cooper's temporary secretary. Suddenly, as she stared into the hostile eyes of Thane Addison, she received the most definite vibes that he was to be her new temporary boss!

Though, as cold steely eyes pierced into her, she suddenly had the most concrete feeling that the job wouldn't even last as long as temporary. Because, as she stared back at him, it startlingly began to dawn on her that, if she was reading the signs correctly, Thane Addison would soon be ordering her back to England—on the very next plane!

CHAPTER TWO

FOR how long she and Thane Addison continued to stare at each other, Joss couldn't have said. So taken aback was she by him, by his manner, and by the fact that it seemed that he was the man she had been sent to Egypt to work for, that she was oblivious to the fact that there were spectators present.

Thane Addison had not forgotten, however, though she was still staring into his cold steely eyes when he flicked his glance to the two witnesses, then commanded her harshly, 'Follow me!' In the next moment, without a by-your-leave to the Cairo office manager, he turned about and without checking to see if she was 'following' went striding into Malcolm Cooper's office.

It was Joss who closed the door after them. If he had anything tough to say, and from the look of him she guessed that he had, then she thought she would prefer not to have an audience.

'Who assigned you to this job?' he rapped before her fingers had time to leave the door handle.

'Fergus—Fergus Perrott,' she replied and, too late, she saw as his eyes narrowed that it might have been better had she replied 'Personnel'. 'He works in Personnel,' she added, hoping to make things better, but only to discover that—nobody getting up earlier in the morning than this man, apparently—she had only made things worse.

'This Perrott—he's a personal friend?' Thane Addison charged, and for the first time in her life Joss felt backed into a corner. She did not like the feeling.

'Yes,' she told the tall and aggressive-chinned man opposite her. 'But I got the job on merit, not through the "old pals" network.'

'You're sure about that?' he rapped.

Briefly Joss hesitated, and too late realised that the sharp-eyed man she stood before had noted that hesitation—even if she did rapidly follow it up with a positive, 'Yes, I am.'

'You were called to the Personnel department, were you?' he demanded, and Joss saw that here was a man who would get any truth out of you whether you wanted to reveal the exact circumstances or not.

'Does it matter?' she queried, her unflappable front sorely in danger of slipping. 'Fergus Perrott might have told me of the temporary vacancy because he and I were in each other's company that evening after the telex had come through...' Oh grief, she thought, realising that she was making it sound even worse than ever. 'But I've worked at Beacon House, London, for three years now, and he must have checked my personnel file and have seen that...' this was no time to be modest '...that I'm no slouch when it comes to being an efficient confidential secretary.'

For perhaps two seconds Thane Addison stared coldly at her tall trim self, then, rocking back slightly on his heels, he questioned, 'Does your super-efficiency include your being fluent in Arabic?'

'I... No... I...' she broke off, and knew positively that she would be going home on the next plane. 'Fergus didn't say...' she broke off as she realised she wasn't doing Fergus any favours—not that after this he deserved any, if what this man had said was true—and she supposed it was. 'I didn't know you'd asked for an Arabic speaker,' she said lamely, and started to feel a shade indignant suddenly as it occurred to her that, in the limited time available, Fergus would have been hard put to it to find a 'fluent' *and* 'top grade' secretary!

'Nor did he tell you, obviously, that I more specifically stated that I wanted a male secretary!' Thane Addison grunted, chips of ice glistening in his eyes.

'There must have been some mix-up over the telex,' Joss replied and, as she realised that she could say goodbye to the job for sure now, her indignation got the better of her. 'Though I think I should mention—in case it's some time since you last worked in Great Britain—that there's such a thing as the Sex Equality Act in force now. It isn't…' It was as far as she got.

'To hell with equality!' The chief troubleshooter at Beacon Oil blasted her eardrums, and suddenly the fact that anyone could roar at her so made Joss exceedingly angry.

'That's typical of men like you!' she erupted.

'You know nothing at all about a man like me!' he rapped back, ignoring the angry sparks flashing in her dark brown eyes. 'Nor will you!'

'I wouldn't want to!' she flared, reading into his last three words all the confirmation she needed that she wouldn't be staying. And, after having been so excited about this trip, she felt angrier than ever. 'It's no wonder to me at all,' she stormed on heatedly, 'that—that…' what was the woman's name? Paula Ingram, that was it. '…that Paula Ingram had to return home sick. The only wonder…'

'For your information,' he sliced thunderously through what she was saying, 'Paula Ingram didn't return to England because she was sick, but because I sent her packing when she went all female on me and let her emotions get in the way of her work.'

Joss was not sure that her mouth did not fall open as the import of what he had just said struck her. 'You *sent* her home?' she queried, her fury with him negated by her surprise. 'You—*dismissed* her!'

'That's what I said,' he bit back toughly.

'B-because of her—emotions?' Joss still couldn't quite believe what she was hearing.

'I was called in when negotiations with the Osiris Corporation started to foul up. I came to work—so did she,' he grunted, and tossed at her bluntly, 'The job I'm here to do is proving sticky enough without my having to contend with some female with over-active hormones!'

'Over-active hormones!' Joss repeated in astonishment.

'I don't know how else you'd describe some woman—without the least encouragement from me—taking it upon herself to declare her undying love,' he told her curtly.

'For you?' she exclaimed, and as her eyes went saucer-wide in her face, 'Paula Ingram told you she loved you?' she asked, aghast.

'And if you're half the confidential secretary you say you are, you won't repeat that outside of this room,' he pronounced, his jaw jutting at an aggressive angle again.

'As if I w...' Suddenly Joss halted. Was she imagining it or, despite her losing her temper, despite what had been said, was there an intimation there that he was going to allow her to stay to complete the job she had been sent to do?

'You hadn't better!' he did not wait for her to finish before threatening. 'Nor, if you've any interest in furthering your career with Beacon Oil, will you let your hormones get out of control while you're working for me!'

'My godfathers!' Joss snapped, her normally even temper on the the rampage again. 'I'd as soon...'

'I've enough problems in ironing out the difficulties which Yazid Rashwan daily puts in my path,' he strode straight over her eruption, 'without having to take time out to discipline another member of staff who takes it into her head to go all female on me.'

Joss had no idea at all who Yazid Rashwan was, but just then she was unconcerned with who he was. More particularly, she was staring at Thane Addison in absolute incredulity. The man was warning her off! This man was laying on the line that she was not to get any romantic ideas about him and was *actually warning her off*!

'I assure you, Mr Addison...' she began when she had her breath back. But again she broke off. Somehow, where once she had been certain she would be taking the next plane to England, she now somehow knew that—providing of course that she behaved herself—she was going to be allowed to stay. A swift memory of how she had always wanted to see the Pyramids at Giza sprang to her mind and, as a familiar dart of excitement speared her, she knew that—despite having to work for this brute of a man—she wanted to stay.

'Yes?' he queried curtly, having been watching her the whole of the time.

His query reminded her that she hadn't yet told him what she was assuring him of. 'I assure you,' she repeated, and unknowingly tilted her head a proud fraction, as she added, 'that oil would turn to water before you'd have need to discipline *me* on *that* score.'

Had she hoped to dent his ego a little, then Joss was disappointed. For he was singularly unimpressed as he grunted, 'Huh!' and then commanded her abruptly, 'Go and wait in the outer office.' She was on the way to the door when he added, 'Tell Cooper to come in.'

I wonder if he's ever heard of the world 'please', Joss

thought briefly, but by then she was telling Malcolm, 'Mr Addison would like to see you,' and Malcolm was wasting no time in getting to what was his own office.

'Perhaps,' Baz Barton said as the door closed on the two, 'I should have mentioned that Mr Addison wanted a male to replace Paula Ingram.'

'It's not important,' Joss swiftly slipped into her unflappable role to reply, though she was sufficiently curious to tack on, 'I didn't know that anyone else was aware of Mr Addison's request, though.'

'The telex went from here,' Baz explained.

'I see,' Joss smiled, and because she had one or two things to think about, yet sensed that Baz wanted to talk, she asked, 'Is there somewhere I can wash my hands?'

Having made her escape, she went over her interview with Thane Addison a second time. Very soon she was fuming again. Instant dismissal, to her mind, was one dickens of a way to discipline somebody! Poor Paula Ingram!

A few minutes later, though, Joss wasn't so sure that she felt so very sorry for Paula Ingram. To hear Thane Addison tell it, he had given the woman no encouragement whatsoever. So what sort of female, unencouraged, would suddenly declare undying love?

On thinking about it, though, Joss realised that she had been in an office environment for long enough to know that some women did occasionally imagine—entirely un-invited—that they were in love with a boss who some-times praised them for a job well done. Against that, though—Thane Addison! And what praise would he give? He didn't even know how to say 'please'!

Joss left the cloakroom having decided that she would probably work herself to a frazzle before Thane Addison would praise anything she did. It was only because he must by now be fairly desperate for a secretary that he had agreed to her staying at all, she suddenly realised. It was for certain that, while she didn't like him, he reciprocated that feeling of dislike in full measure.

All at once, though, it came to Joss that he didn't have to like her, did he? Only then did it dawn on her that the only reason he had not sent her packing was that—in a business capacity—he needed her. To wait for Beacon House, London, to send another secretary out—a male one this time—could take all of another week. Which meant that Thane Addison would use her, because it was expedient to do so.

At that point in her thinking Joss realised that she felt tired and weary and that she was grateful for the chair which Baz Barton indicated she should take while they waited for Thane Addison and Malcolm Cooper to finish their business in the other office.

'How was London looking when you left?' Baz enquired idly as they waited.

London, she thought wistfully, and tried to remember why she had been so eager to leave it. The Pyramids, she recalled, and smiled at Baz as she asked him, 'How long is it since you were there?'

She did not get to hear his answer, because just then the door to Malcolm Cooper's office opened and, briefcase in hand, Thane Addison came striding through. Joss saw his sharp glance go from her curving mouth and to Baz, then back grimly to her. She gained a clear impression from his grim look that she had just earned herself another black mark; the first for daring to be of the female sex, the second because he quite clearly thought she was passing the waiting time in having a light flirtation with Baz Barton.

'Come with me!' he commanded her curtly and, without a break in his stride, he headed for the outer door.

Both Malcolm and Baz dived to hand her her case, but Joss got to it first. Thane Addison was by then going out through the door, and, with no time to wish the other two individual goodnights, Joss called, 'See you!' and as fast as she could considering her handicap, with Baz holding the door open for her, she hurried after the man she was beginning to hate rather than merely dislike.

After a minute or so of charging after his departing back, however, she felt her temper start to fray and—working overtime that day—it came out yet again. Abruptly she stopped. Abruptly she thumped her case down and decided, damn him, enough was enough.

Her show of defiance proved to be brief, though, because just then the man up in front reached a sleek dark car that was obviously his, and he too stopped. Joss picked up her case again, and by the time she got to him he had the car door unlocked and was in the act of opening up the boot.

Unspeaking, he stretched out a hand and, as if it weighed nothing, took her heavy case from her and placed it in the rear compartment.

'Where are we going?' Joss questioned when after closing the boot he remembered such courtesies as to go and open the passenger door for her.

'Alexandria!' he clipped, and left her staring after him stunned as, plainly believing that she was big enough to get into the car by herself, he left her and went round to the driver's door.

Alexandria! Getting herself a little together, she seated herself in the passenger seat, and closed the door. By that time Thane Addison was in his car and was setting it in motion, and Joss saw that even at this time of night—and by then it was around eight-thirty—the traffic was still crazy.

She waited only to observe that he was not turning a hair as he drove into the car-horn-blaring nightmare of motorised confusion, and decided that he appeared to be more than capable of coping with anything, and that her questions were not likely to interfere with his driving. 'How far is Alexandria?' she asked coolly, having no idea if that city lay a few miles around the next bend or how far away it lay.

'About two hundred kilometres,' he deigned to toss in her direction.

Two hundred kilometres! Joss swallowed down the exclamation and by quickly dividing by eight and multiplying by five she reached the calculation that Alexandria was a hundred and twenty-five miles distant! It could take all of three or four hours to get there!

Wondering if she was ever going to get to bed that night, she choked back her astonishment that, unbelievably, she was now on her way to Alexandria and, striving hard to retain a cool note she commented evenly, 'I rather thought I'd be working in Cairo.'

'Complaining already?' Thane Addison grunted, and awakened in Joss latent ear-boxing tendencies.

She had far more control than to give in to the urge to set about him, however, though his—in her view—uncalled-for nasty remark left her deciding that she'd die sooner than volunteer another comment to the swine of a man. Lord, who could love such a man? Paula Ingram must be weak in the head!

For quite some while Joss silently fumed about the man she had the misfortune to be sitting next to, then gradually her anger subsided. Then it was that she noticed that they had left Cairo behind and were now speeding over a main toll road and that, apart from a parallel tarmacked road for traffic going in the opposite direction, they seemed to be driving through the desert.

Excitement flared up in her again, and momentarily vanquished any tiredness caused by being up at the crack of dawn and the ensuing weariness brought on by waiting at the airport, by travelling, and by waiting at Beacon House in Cairo. She was here! She was actually in Egypt! And she didn't care a button about the pig of a man driving this car. She was good at her job—and she would jolly well show him!

How Thane Addison had crept back into her thoughts again, she wasn't quite sure. But she pushed him out again and for some miles concentrated on the never-ending succession of large advertising hoardings to be seen in the cars' headlights.

Soon, however, the flashing billboards started to have a hypnotic effect and gradually her eyes began to close. Abruptly Joss jerked herself awake. But when tiredness joined forces with the weariness from her trials and tribulations of that day, suddenly the battle to keep awake was lost.

She drifted to the surface to discover that the car had stopped. She opened her eyes, and as she came fully awake, was instantly horrified to discover that she had either slipped or moved sideways in her sleep, and that her head was now resting, in supreme comfort—on Thane Addison's manly shoulder!

In the next split second she was sitting bolt upright and rapidly trying to decide if she should apologise for using him as a pillow, while wondering—in the light of Paula Ingram's so recently throwing herself at him—if he thought she was of the same inclination. As she got herself more of a piece, however, Joss's streak of unflappability began to stand her in good stead, so that she did not apologise but thought, by showing him some degree of coolness, to let him know that she'd as soon fall off the top of the highest Pyramid as fall for him.

So 'Where are we?' she questioned him aloofly, and very nearly lost all sign of being cool when, his lofty manner knocking hers sideways, he threw over his shoulder as he got out of the car,

'My apartment.'

Joss got out of the car too, and went to join him at the boot, from where he was extracting his briefcase and her suitcase.

'Why?' she questioned.

'What do you mean, why?' he challenged, and when she just stood and stared at him, he gave her an irritated look, then, his voice more an aggressive snarl than anything, 'It's gone eleven, and this is where I live,' he stated bluntly, 'and if you think I'm toting you around Alexandria trying to check you into a hotel at this time of night, then do *you* have another think coming!'

'You're saying that I'm staying *here*?' Joss questioned, but with her case in his grip he was already locking up the boot.

She did not thank him that, not bothering to reply, he led the way into the apartment block. To carry her case was the least he could do, in her opinion. She was glad, though, that from what he *had* said she was able to glean the knowledge that he knew she would have preferred a hotel to his hospitality.

Though why a man who'd had the gall to warn her off should then bring her to his apartment was beyond her. Most odd, she thought as they entered the building, and then wondered—was it odd, though? Perhaps she wasn't as wide awake as she had thought, but somehow, even to her weary self, it seemed quite credible that this swine who was now greeting the concierge in Arabic '*Masa'il kher*, Mustapha,' could be putting her to some kind of test.

Well, he needn't worry himself that she might try to join him in his bed that night, she thought in disgust, and strangely, as she went up some marble steps with him, she heard herself asking, 'Is there a Mrs Addison?'

They had reached a first-floor landing and he was inserting a key into one of the doors before 'I've a mother—in England,' he drawled arrogantly.

'I won't ask about your father,' Joss muttered, needled by his high-and-mighty arrogance, and so fed up with him and his manner suddenly—even if he was her boss—that she was feeling just scratchy enough not to care whether he had heard or whether he hadn't.

He had heard, though. But although she would not have been surprised to have something short, pithy and painful hurled back at her for her intimation that she doubted that he had ever had a father, suddenly, and to her utter amazement, she saw his rather well-shaped lips twitch.

She was still not quite believing that she had somehow reached his sense of humour when, his mouth setting in firm lines, all sign of his being remotely amused gone, 'I can be an even bigger bastard than you think I am, Miss Harding,' he threatened, 'so don't push your luck.' With that he opened the door, and they entered his apartment.

It was a roomy, spacious apartment, Joss saw, well furnished to the point of quiet luxury. It was a masculine apartment, though, with no sign of flowers or a woman's touch. She had an intuitive feeling that were Thane Addison to have a wife he would in all probability want her to travel with him wherever he went, and it was quite unthinkingly that she queried, 'You're not married?'—and wished she had spared her breath.

'Rest easy!' he rapped, once again the snarling brute she was getting to know. 'I never *ever*,' he stressed, 'mix business with *that* sort of pleasure!'

Several hot retorts rushed to Joss's lips. But, just in time, she bit them back. She was tired, and if he had driven from Alexandria to Cairo and back again within the last eight hours, then he must be tired too. But as she received the message that, while there was some space in his life for women—and the virile look of him backed that up—she had no need to lock her bedroom door that night, that thought triggered off another.

'Do I have a bedroom to go to?' she asked him coolly, since he had dispensed with the word 'please,' not seeing why she should resurrect it.

'I'd better show you over the place,' he said brusquely, and she received yet another message—that he didn't want her blundering into his room in the middle of the night looking for the bathroom.

Perhaps I'm being over-sensitive, she thought a moment later as he began to show her where the kitchen and other rooms lay. It was a well-fitted kitchen, and in keeping with the rest of the apartment, but she guessed, since he would be moving on once this job was done, that the flat most likely was company-owned and did not specifically belong to him, but was there for the sole use of Beacon's Oil's highest.

'Are you hungry?' it occurred to him to query once they'd done the rounds of the flat.

Joss shook her head. 'I just want my bed—I've been up since...' Her voice faded at his curt look, and, convinced that he was about to bite something to the ef-

fect of 'save me from complaining women,' she clamped
her lips together and went over and picked up her suitcase.

'Are you too tired to make up your own bed?' he
sarcastically wanted to know, when having collected linen
and a blanket he took her to one of the spare bedrooms.

'Goodnight,' Joss replied frostily, fuming again when
a moment later the firm closing of the door told her she
had the room to herself.

The swine of a man! she raged as she opened out the
sheets he had given her. My heavens, what an uncivilised
brute! she seethed, as she shook a pillow into a pillow-
case.

Having made her bed, she visited the bathroom across
the hall, washed her face and cleaned her teeth with the
bottled water provided and was heartily glad that she
hadn't again met her 'host'. She had seen enough of him
that day to last her a lifetime!

She undressed and got into bed, and relived everything
that had taken place since she had met him—and in no
time she was fuming again.

He'd actually warned her off! *He had actually warned
her off!* Starting to become more enraged than ever, Joss
fought to stay calm lest she go and seek Thane Addison
out to tell him there and then exactly what he could do
with his job.

Having attained a modicum of calm some five minutes
later, she remembered how, on the way here from Cairo,
she had determined that she was good at her job and that
she would jolly well show him. How the dickens, though,
could she show him how good she was, if at the first
hurdle she went running back to England?

She would stay, she wouldn't run, no matter how
insulting Thane Addison was, she decided—though she

couldn't think that he could improve on the insult he had already served her. She wasn't ready to go back anyway, she thought as sleep claimed her—not until she'd seen those Pyramids, anyhow!

CHAPTER THREE

HAVING slept soundly once she had got off to sleep, Joss awakened on Tuesday and, remembering that she was not in England but in Egypt, she smiled. Then she remembered *him* and her smile swiftly faded.

That he had actually had the unmitigated nerve to threaten dismissal—for that seemed to be his idea of disciplining someone—should she so far forget what a thoroughly detestable brute he was and fall in love with him, still irked her.

But she was there to work, not to lie in bed imagining pleasant fates that might befall him, such as falling down the stairs and breaking a leg or something of an equally charming nature—she wouldn't even offer him a temporary splint!

That for someone she hated Thane Addison was occupying so much space in her head seemed only natural to Joss as she pushed back the covers and reached for her robe. She couldn't hear him moving around, but she had a feeling that he was the type of man who survived on very little sleep.

She was proved right about that, in as much as that as she left her room and made for the bathroom, she discovered that he was already up and about—and showered too, she observed. For just as she went to open the bathroom door so he, robe-and nothing else-clad as far as she could make out from the bare hair-roughened chest and bare straight legs to be seen, came out. His fair hair was still wet and a few shades darker, she saw, and then noticed that as she was taking him in, he was taking in her robe-clad, tousle-haired self.

'Good morning,' she mumbled.

'Use the bottled water to clean your teeth,' he grunted, then they passed each other—she to go into the bathroom and he to go striding to his bedroom.

As Joss stretched out a hand to turn on the shower she saw that her hand was shaking from the encounter. Most odd, she deliberated, but then she was unused to hating anybody.

Back in her room, she quickly dressed in a lightweight business-looking two-piece and quickly applied the small amount of make-up that she wore. Then, knowing without a shadow of a doubt that wherever she slept that coming night it most definitely wouldn't be in this apartment, she quickly stripped the bed and folded the bedding. All that remained was to fasten her case and then go and find out what happened now.

Leaving her case for the moment, she took up her shoulder-bag and went looking for Thane Addison. She found him sitting in the kitchen. He was immaculately suited, wore a white shirt and silk tie and, she realised, was quite good-looking. He was already at work, she saw, and was scanning some typewritten notes which he held in one hand, while in his other hand he held a cup of coffee.

'There's coffee in the pot,' he looked up to inform her, seemed to approve of what she was wearing, then frowned and had gone back to the typed pages he held when he instructed, 'Make yourself toast.'

Because she was both thirsty and hungry Joss found the bread and popped a piece in the toaster and poured herself a cup of coffee. Silence reigned in the kitchen as she tracked down butter and marmalade.

Soundlessly she ate her repast. Without saying a word that might interrupt his concentration, she downed her coffee. He, she saw from the plate on the draining-board, must have finished his toast before she'd got to the kitchen.

He'd emptied his coffee-cup too, she noted, and, rather than just sit looking at him once she too had finished, she gathered up all the used dishes and washed and dried them. When she turned round, though, and took a glance in his direction, it was to see that he had ceased studying the papers in his hand, and was watching her!

'It's just that I've a tidy mind,' she told him shortly, not wanting him to think she was taking advantage of the domestic scene to get through any barrier he might put up.

'I'm glad to hear it!' he retorted grittily, and, taking up his briefcase from the floor beside him, he inserted his papers, snapped it to, then demanded, 'Ready?'

Joss knew from his tone that it was more than her life was worth to tell him no. And she went swiftly after him as, seeming now to be in something of a hurry, he went striding to the outer door.

At the door, however, he stopped so abruptly that she almost cannoned into him—only by a hair's breadth did she avoid a collision. Which, she would have thought, since this was clearly 'I hate female secretaries week', would have pleased him.

But not so. For, giving her a superior look from his much taller height, 'It was never my intention,' he drawled, 'to have you as my permanent guest.'

'What?' she queried, wondering what that had got to do with the fact that she had only just managed to keep from wrapping herself around him.

'Your case, Miss Harding,' he enlightened her stonily, 'your case!'

Pink colour stained her face as Joss remembered her suitcase in one of his spare bedrooms. Without a word she went to collect it, and knew then that she was going to have to develop a very thick skin if she was going to work for him for any length of time.

'Thank God it's only for a month,' she muttered when she got back to him, and again, didn't care a damn whether he heard or whether he didn't. Though, as she glanced at his still granite expression as they left his apartment, she knew that there was no amusing him this morning.

Without comment he took her case from her and in long, easy strides made short work—with not a broken leg in sight—of the stairs. Not deigning to run to keep up with him, Joss went at her own smart pace. Her suitcase was in the boot and he was just getting into his car when she reached the passenger's door.

It crossed her mind, as they started off, to query where they were going. But she was feeling just then that she would tear her tongue out before she would ask him anything. To her way of thinking, he could be taking her anywhere. Yesterday she had thought she would be working in Cairo, but today here she was in Alexandria. Would they be journeying for another three hours before she got anywhere close to a typewriter?

Leaving her fate in the lap of the gods, Joss brought her thoughts away from her temporary and cantankerous boss and where she might or might not end up that day, and took pleasure from watching the busy scene they were passing through.

The traffic in Alexandria was as horrendous as Cairo, she thought. They went in for horn-blowing just the same, at any rate. It was interesting to see the way Western dress merged quite happily with Middle Eastern dress, though. In the main it seemed that most men were dressed in Western style, with only the occasional man dressed in the shoulder-to-ground-length galabiyah. Joss saw several women shrouded all in black, and many more with their hair completely covered so that only their faces were to be seen. The sun was shining, and she felt it to be quite warm when, to her wonderment, she saw one man done up to the neck in muffler and overcoat!

She was in the middle of thinking how the man would never survive an English winter if he thought this was cold when all at once she became aware that Thane Addison had slowed down and seemed to be looking for a parking spot.

Naturally, being him, he found one without difficulty. When he left the car, so did she. Although her fury at his sarcasm over her case had simmered down somewhat, though, she was still feeling cross enough not to want to talk to him as she kept pace with him.

When he halted, she halted, then followed him into a set of offices that seemed much the same as the offices she had been in in Cairo yesterday. This, she quickly realised, was Beacon House, Alexandria. To her surprise, for she was past expecting anything normal of Mr Thane Addison, he introduced her round.

'This is Halima, who efficiently deals with the switchboard and any callers,' he introduced the pretty Egyptian receptionist. 'Miss Harding will be with us for...' he broke off and flicked his glance to Joss, then continued '...only a month, I think you said?'

'That's right.' Joss smiled at Halima as she extended her hand, and stayed cool in the knowledge that he had not missed her muttered 'Thank God it's only for a month' back at his flat.

Thane Addison then introduced a man who appeared out of nowhere at the sound of their voices, and who turned out to be Sami, the firm's Egyptian driver and general messenger. Then Thane was taking her into one of the other offices, and there she met a man of about thirty who was there to liaise with local Egyptian companies and who went by the name of Chad Woollams. 'Josslyn Harding,' Thane completed the introduction.

'Joss,' she shortened her name as Chad Woollams took her hand, and she cared not a light that her temporary boss was giving her a sharp look. In point of fact she was quite glad of any chance to show him that, while she was quite happy to let anyone use the more friendly shortened version of her name, she intended to be Josslyn, or preferably Miss Harding, to him for the duration of her stay.

'They never had anyone who looked half as good as you working at Beacon House, London, while I was there,' Chad Woollams offered with a warm smile.

'If you'll let Miss Harding have her hand back, Woollams, we can get on,' Thane Addison cut in sharply.

As if scalded, Chad Woollams let go of her hand. 'I'll see you,' he said bravely as Thane Addison took hold of her elbow and propelled her out—and into the next office.

The office next door housed Beacon Oil's Arabic-speaking, Egypt-stationed legal representative. Richard Maybury was a stocky man of about forty-four, who had a degree in English law, and a sound grounding of Egyptian law. He and Thane Addison, Joss learned, were working closely together on the contract which Thane had been brought in to sort out.

'Glad to know you, Josslyn,' Richard smiled as they shook hands.

Joss thought that to invite him too to use the shortened version of her name in front of Thane Addison might be overdoing it, so she stayed quiet, and, after a few minutes spent with the other man in business discussion, Thane took her to where she would work.

Her office was on the first floor, and was pleasant enough, being light and airy, and with an up-to-the-minute typewriter, similar to the one she used in London.

'My office is through this door here,' Thane told her, and went through to return a moment later with a handful of dictaphone tapes. 'A present for you,' he said, placing them down on her desk, and, with a look in his eye which she translated as saying 'that little lot should keep you quiet for a while', he told her, 'I have to go out,' and left her to it.

Joss was glad to see him go. At a guess, she thought, since Paula Ingram had been so unceremoniously sent packing, she probably had the whole of a week's work to get on with. Which was fine by her—at last she was about to start work.

An hour later she was deeply immersed in her task and discovering, somewhat to her surprise, that Thane Addison's voice on tape was quite pleasant—and that she rather liked the sound of it.

Clot, she derided; it wasn't that she liked his voice so well, but that she liked his way of working. For she could not fault anything about his crisp, clear sentences, and indeed found that she was most impressed that he could dictate great long tracts—a lot of it highly technical—with not an 'um' or an 'er' in sight.

Soon she was deeply immersed in her work again and had no idea that another hour had gone by until the door opened and Halima came in with a cup of coffee.

'I thought you might be ready for a cup of coffee, Miss Harding,' the pretty young Egyptian woman smiled.

Joss thanked her, and invited, 'Call me Joss,' and they spent a few minutes in friendly conversation, with Joss, who needed some Egyptian currency, discovering that there was a bank nearby.

'It will close at twelve-thirty,' Halima was just telling her when a buzzer she had switched on before leaving the switchboard sounded. 'I have a call!' she exclaimed, and swiftly disappeared.

Feeling she had earned a short break, Joss went to the bank, to return to her desk feeling much better for having more currency than the small amount she had been allowed to bring into the country.

She still had a lot of work to get through, however, and not having seen Thane Addison since his parting 'I have to go out' comment, she was soon pounding her typewriter again.

She was halfway through what she realised was a highly confidential document when the door opened, and was left open, as Chad Woollams came in.

'Lunchtime!' he told her as he came a little closer.

'Already!' Joss exclaimed, and, taking a disbelieving look at her watch, she saw that it was a quarter to one. 'Good heavens—the morning's flown!' she told him, feeling faintly staggered that a minute ago it had been eleven-fifteen.

'Then one can only suppose you're enjoying your work,' Chad remarked with a smile, and as Joss realised with a feeling of shock that she had enjoyed the work she'd done that morning and found it far more interesting and stimulating than the work she did for Mr Edwards back in England, Chad went on, 'I've come to take you to lunch.'

'Lunch?' she replied blankly, her thoughts still deep in the document she had been typing.

'You will lunch with me, won't you, Joss?' he smiled winningly.

Joss thought perhaps she would. But she never got to tell him so, because just then the man who she had evidence had the sharpest ears was suddenly standing in the open doorway, and it was he who answered for her.

'Miss Harding already has a lunchtime appointment, Woollams,' he told him curtly.

'Oh!' Chad spun round, startled. 'Er—I'll see you later, then, Joss,' he turned back to smile, but when Thane Addison stepped into the room and left the doorway free, he quickly left her office.

Joss didn't argue. Perfect secretaries—and that was what she was going to show him she was—knew better. She had not forgotten his 'You're sure about that?' comment when she had told him that she'd been given the Egypt job on merit and not via the 'old pals' network.

So, she asked, 'Have I got time to finish this page?'

'Depends how fast you type,' he answered curtly, and as Joss slammed into her typewriter, he came and picked up the work she had typed that morning.

Somehow she found his presence unnerving, but she typed through to the end of the page and, having managed to hold on to her nerve and complete her typing without the smallest error, she set the page down on the desk. Then, knowing she had no time to type anything else, she tidied up her desk.

She knew there was some comment about to break from Thane Addison as he handed her the typed pages he had been studying, though she very much doubted that she would be on the receiving end of any praise from him.

Nor was she, but she had to admit to a tiny feeling of

agreeable surprise when he drawled, 'Well, well, a secretary who can spell "kinematic viscosity"!'

'You should see how I handle the really difficult ones!'
Joss murmured coolly, and when the feeling of wanting
to smile almost fractured her cool front, she bent her head
and collected up the tapes he had given her. 'Do we have
a safe?' she asked a moment later when she had control
of her never-before-known peculiar sense of humour.

'There's one in my office, and Richard Maybury has
one,' Thane Addison replied, and signed for her to follow
him.

His office, Joss saw, was large, as was his desk and, as
she had that morning realised, his work load. Which therefore made it a little surprising that his desk-top was absolutely clear. His briefcase seemed to go most places
with him, she realised, suddenly spotting that he held it
in his left hand. He had, though, put his briefcase in the
safe and had turned to take the tapes and her morning's
typing from her when it occurred to her that he must carry
a lot of his work in his head too.

The tapes and the typing were locked in his safe when,
from his lofty height, he turned to look down at her, and
that was when Joss's curiosity got out of hand. Despite
her stubborn intention not to ask him what the lunchtime
appointment was that prevented her from accepting Chad
Woollams' invitation, she could not keep it back any
longer.

'Will I need to bring anything?' she questioned, and
found that Thane Addison had no trouble in following her
train of thought.

'We're having a business lunch, but you can leave your
notepad behind.'

They were in his car and driving through the hurly-burly of Alexandria's traffic when Joss asked him, 'Can you tell me what my role is during this business lunch?'

'Your *role*, Miss Harding, is that of my secretary,' he replied aloofly.

'I—see,' she said as levelly as she could, when in actual fact she suddenly felt again like boxing his ears—how this man had the most uncanny knack of rubbing her up the wrong way! She rather thought he did it on purpose—she knew she was his secretary, for goodness' sake! Refraining from thanking God again that the job was only temporary, she took a controlling breath. 'Perhaps, Mr Addison,' she went on, knowing for certain that they must be lunching with one other person at least—for anything he wanted to discuss solely with her about business could be done in the office, without his needing to take her out to lunch, 'perhaps there might be one or two matters which you might care to brief me about. Who, for instance…'

'Your brief, Miss Harding,' he clipped, 'will be to keep your eyes and ears open.'

Now we're getting somewhere, she thought. 'We're meeting someone from a British firm?' she queried, feeling, since he knew she couldn't speak Arabic, that she must be being instructed to listen carefully to what their English-speaking business person had to say.

'My lunch guest is Mr Yazid Rashwan,' he soon, confusingly, scuttled the logic of her thinking.

'Oh!' she exclaimed, and then, having not only heard Yazid Rashwan's name before, but having come across it several times in her work that morning, she was pleased to be able to identify him. 'Mr Rashwan works for the Osiris Corporation, doesn't he?' she questioned.

'Yazid Rashwan,' Thane Addison informed her, '*is* the Osiris Corporation!'

Joss opened her mouth, then fell silent. The Osiris Corporation was the company Beacon Oil were keen to sign a contract with, and she was lunching with the man who *was* the Osiris Corporation—whew!

The rest of the journey did not take long, and then her boss, who it seemed had told her all he thought she should know, was drawing up outside a large hotel which was lapped by the waters of the Mediterranean.

It was then, as Thane escorted her into the hotel, that she began to feel quite unexpectedly proud to be walking alongside the tall, good-looking troubleshooter-in-chief of Beacon Oil.

Because her boss was playing host to Mr Rashwan, they had arrived courteously ahead of him, and as they waited for him to arrive Joss started to feel very thrilled, too, that she had been included in this meeting.

What sort of business was to be discussed, though, she was interested to see. For, having witnessed herself that Thane Addison had deliberately left his briefcase back at the office, she began to conclude that—for all it was very much the wish of Beacon Oil to have a contract signed— it seemed that any business to be discussed would be done so very informally.

Yazid Rashwan, when he arrived, was a slightly portly man of about fifty. He was as smartly and as immaculately tailored as her boss, Joss saw. So too was the man who was about half Mr Rashwan's age, and who accompanied him.

'My friend!' Yazid Rashwan greeted Thane Addison warmly, and in perfect English. 'We have kept you waiting?'

'Not at all, Yazid,' Thane replied as the two shook hands.

'You know my son, Khalil,' Yazid included the young man with him. 'You do not mind that he joins us?'

'Of course not,' Thane replied smoothly, as he shook hands with Khalil Rashwan, then turned to introduce the slender woman by his side. 'Josslyn arrived from England yesterday to help me with my paperwork,' Thane went on easily, and, quite peculiarly, Joss felt her heart skip a ridiculous beat to hear, from the sound of it, that he intended to use her first name.

'Miss Ingram is no longer here?' Yazid queried.

'She had to return to England rather urgently on a matter unconnected with her work,' Thane told him easily.

'Am I not to be introduced to Josslyn?' Khalil Rashwan suddenly butted in, his eyes making a meal of Joss's face and ash-blonde hair.

'Do not be impatient, my son,' his father smiled, but his son was impatient, it seemed, for, not waiting for anyone to introduce him, he took hold of her right hand.

'I am Khalil Rashwan,' he told her, and as he shook hands with her, in the same perfect English as his parent, 'My father sends me to other countries very frequently to further my knowledge of the oil industry, but I am pleased that I am in Egypt at this time.'

Joss was a little nonplussed to know quite how to deal with this man who was still holding her right hand. But her cool unflappable manner stood her in good stead as, retrieving her hand, she replied non-committally, 'Your work must be very interesting.'

'Shall we find the dining-room?' Thane Addison suggested, and as his glance skimmed over her without lighting particularly on her, Joss knew she had somehow earned herself another black mark.

Because he was an admirable host, however, the meal-time passed without anyone but her being aware that she had somewhere, it seemed, put a foot wrong. She decided to put it to the back of her mind and concentrate on the business in hand. Though, although both Osiris and Beacon were mentioned, as far as she could tell, nothing of a very specific nature to do with the contract—which was what this business lunch was all about—was discussed.

Not, she had to admit, that she caught everything that was being said, because Khalil Rashwan, who had seated himself next to her, seemed to have no interest in business and would often make some comment to her while the other two men were in easy conversation.

'Did I hear that you arrived only yesterday?' he questioned as the four of them sat drinking an after-lunch coffee.

'Yes. I...'

'But you can have seen nothing of Alexandria yet?' he butted in, and promptly declared, his warm gaze fixed intently on her brown eyes and creamy skin, 'I will attend to that straight away!'

Joss strove hard not to blink at the young man's open enthusiasm. He might well have been a couple of years older than she, but he seemed to her to be a couple of years younger. She was conscious, however, that she must do nothing that might offend him, though she was unsure if Thane Addison—from a business point of view—would approve or disapprove if she accepted what she thought was an invitation from Khalil—who had already told her that she must use his first name.

'Actually, Khalil,' she told him lightly after some moments, 'I'm here to work.'

'But you cannot work all the time!' he exclaimed at once, and decided on the spot, 'I will show you some of Alexandria this afternoon.' He broke off, paused only briefly, then went on enthusiastically, 'This afternoon I will take you to the Greco-Roman Museum.'

Starting to feel uncomfortably that she stood a grave risk of offending Khalil, Joss glanced at Thane. Had she hoped that he might step in and help her out, however, she would have been sorely disappointed. Though she had prior warning that she was wasting her time in looking to him for direction, when she caught the cool way he met her glance.

She could, none the less, have done without what she considered his sarcastic, snide remark, as he told her evenly, 'You mustn't neglect your education, Josslyn.'

'There!' Khalil straight away seized on what he saw as her boss's permission. 'We have finished lunch. We will go now and…'

'I'm sorry, Khalil,' Joss interrupted him quickly, speaking instinctively and not giving herself time to think, 'but I have a great deal of work waiting for me at my desk. It's impossible for me to go with you today. Thank…'

'Tomorrow, then,' he interrupted her quickly, and while she was getting over the way he was insisting on being her guide at some stage, he was getting to his feet. 'I'm sure that my father and Thane have matters to discuss which do not concern us—shall we take a walk outside?'

As Joss saw it, there was little she could do but agree. For all she knew, Khalil Rashwan might have been told to accompany his father for the precise reason of getting Thane's secretary out of the way so that the two men could have an off-the-record business discussion which might benefit both companies. Yazid Rashwan was smiling approvingly anyway, she observed, and although a quick glance at her boss showed that Thane was not smiling, neither was he commanding her to stay exactly where she was.

'That would be pleasant,' she told Khalil lightly, and excusing herself to the two men, she left the table and went with Khalil from the hotel, which stood in isolation but with the grounds and attractive pink and white minareted building of the Montazah Palace standing very near by.

Joss had been wondering what she should talk to Khalil about, but she need not have worried, for he did all the talking necessary, though it was true, most of his talk took the shape of questions. Even though his questions were mainly about her life in England.

'So you have no special man friend in England?' he recapped as they strolled in the hotel grounds.

'I more often go out with a group of friends,' she replied, and got him off the subject when she noticed a car parked at the hotel that had been decorated with ribbons and bouquets of flowers. 'Is that a wedding car?' she asked him.

'Yes,' he replied, but did not have the interest she had in the romantic sight of flowers decorating the bumper, bonnet, boot and roof, while pom-poms of white ribbons adorned door-handles and wheel-hubs.

They were making their way back to the entrance when Thane Addison and Yazid Rashwan suddenly appeared. Joss made it to Thane's side just as he was shaking hands with Yazid. She made her own goodbyes and, feeling rather relieved that she had come from the business lunch without having committed herself to go to the Greco-Roman Museum with Khalil Rashwan tomorrow, she went quickly—to keep up with Thane's stride—to his car.

She was in the passenger seat and Thane was driving away from the hotel when she wondered if he had actually conducted any business with Yazid Rashwan. She considered the matter for a moment or two, then decided that as

Thane Addison's secretary—albeit temporarily—she should naturally show an interest.

'Were you able to bring negotiations any nearer to a satisfactory conclusion?' she opened her mouth to make the interested business enquiry—and wished she'd kept her mouth closed.

'You're that concerned?' he snarled back at her for her trouble.

'What's that supposed to mean?' she enquired, heated in a second.

'From where I was sitting, you were more concerned in encouraging the overtures of Yazid Rashwan's son!' he barked toughly.

'I was not!' Joss protested vehemently. 'All I did was try to be polite. To…'

'He couldn't take his eyes off you!'

'I didn't do anything to…'

'You don't have to do anything,' Thane Addison abruptly cut in again. 'It's the way you look!'

'I can't help the way I look!' she snapped, and was ignored for her trouble.

Swine! she fumed, and glared at him. She looked away when, his jaw jutting aggressively, he showed himself impervious to her ire. They were nearly back at the office when it occurred to her to wonder if there might not have been some sort of back-handed compliment in his comment, 'It's the way you look.' She shrugged the thought aside. As if she cared! The man was a monster.

'Hello, Halima!' she greeted the receptionist cheerfully when with Thane Addison striding in front of her she crossed the reception floor.

'Hello, Joss,' the other girl smiled, and Joss went up to her own office and cared not that her boss had gone in the direction of Richard Maybury's office.

That was to say that as far as she was concerned he could go to hell and the sooner the better—but not before he had unlocked his safe and given her back the work she had been in the middle of.

Expecting that he would come up to his office at any moment, Joss fumed about him for a while. Wretched man, she thought irately, then remembered that he still had her case in the back of his car and that she had no idea of where she would be camping out that night. Not that she'd ask him—she'd be damned if she would!

Fifteen minutes went by, and when she realised that in all that time, and with loads of work to be done, she had done nothing but twiddle her thumbs, she was of the opinion that this was ridiculous.

In the next moment she had the phone in her hand and was asking Halima if Mr Addison had gone out.

'He's in conference with Mr Maybury, I think,' Halima answered, and before Joss could tell her not to, 'I'll put you through,' she said, and efficiently did so.

'Joss Harding here,' Joss said when Richard Maybury answered his phone. 'Is Mr Addison with you?'

'Just a minute,' he replied, and the next she knew was that her taciturn boss was on the line.

'Addison,' he announced.

'Josslyn Harding,' she replied, keeping her tones as level and as courteous as she could. 'May I have my work from the safe, please?' she requested, and hated him some more when without another word he put the phone down on her.

Ignorant pig! she railed, and got up and went to look unseeing out of the window. She was still there when she heard his footsteps on the stairs. She heard him go into his office by another door, and saw no reason to move until the door connecting their two offices opened and he came through with the work she had given him to lock away before lunch.

'Thank you,' she said politely, and found her politeness wasted when, without comment, he strode out.

That man! she thought, enraged, and took her fury out on her typewriter. Fortunately she was an accurate typist, so that even in her temper she achieved quite a lot of error-free work that afternoon.

She had a break for a cup of tea at about four o'clock, but, knowing that she had a lot of last week's work to catch up on, was soon busy at her typewriter again. She hardly thought it was out of consideration for her and the backlog she had to cope with that Thane Addison had not given her any dictation that day. He'd probably give her a double helping tomorrow, she realised—if in fact he wasn't somewhere right at this moment dictating another load on to tape.

When a moment's weariness took her and she paused to stretch her back, the thought again occurred—where would she be sleeping that night? She started to type again, and was still of the view that she was not going to ask, when it suddenly struck her that, stuck away up here the way she was, being a new member of staff, she could easily be forgotten! For all she knew, Thane Addison could have finished discussing legal matters with Richard Maybury, and could have left the building hours ago!

Joss was on the point of being certain that everyone would leave Beacon House that evening without giving her another thought, and that she would be spending the night locked in where she was, when suddenly the door opened.

Without so much as a grunt Thane Addison came over and took a look at the vast amount of typing she had got through. Then, 'You've done enough for today,' he told her. 'Clear your desk.'

Striving hard to hold down some sarcastic comment to the effect that he should watch it, that he had almost given her praise, Joss began to tidy her desk. Since there were only seven minutes to go before five o'clock, she didn't thank him either for his intimation that she could pack up for the day. Though on reflection she realised that he would probably, either here or at his apartment, be working on into the evening. She doubted anyway that his working day stopped at five.

Having handed to him anything that had to be housed in the safe that night, she was busying herself putting the cover on her typewriter when he came back into her office.

'Ready?' he questioned.

For answer, Joss picked up her shoulder-bag. She had no idea where they were going, but unless he was taking her to some meeting or other—and his 'You've done enough for today' remark rather precluded that—she guessed he was taking her to her new abode.

She was still of the view that wild horses would not make her ask him, and, having taken her lead from his taciturn manner, she determined that unless she had something very necessary to say, she would say nothing.

Having expected that she would be staying in some quite decent but moderately priced accommodation, the amazement she experienced when he stopped the car outside a newish and luxurious-looking hotel loosened her tongue. When he got out and began to extract her case from the boot, she too got out of the car.

'I'm staying here?' she asked in astonishment.

'We can't have Khalil Rashwan thinking we're paupers when he comes calling,' he drawled, nastily, she thought.

Tilting her chin an angry fraction higher, Joss clamped her lips shut and went with him into the hotel. Apparently she was expected, so she guessed then that, had she thought to ask Halima if she had any idea where she would be staying, there was a good chance that Halima would have been able to tell her that Thane Addison had contacted this hotel at some time during that day.

Thane Addison waited only to see that she was checked in without any hitch—and she refused to be grateful to him for that—then he was telling her, 'Sami will be on hand to collect you in the morning and to bring you back in the evening.' Then he was gone.

Her room was excellent, but any pleasure she might have found at being so housed faded as she recalled Thane's sarcastic comment, 'We can't have Khalil Rashwan thinking we're paupers.'

Deciding to put Mr Thane Addison and his acid tongue from her mind, Joss set about unpacking and, since Beacon Oil very definitely weren't paupers, she decided a little room service wouldn't break them. She phoned down and ordered a pot of tea.

The tea had arrived and she was in the middle of writing an 'everything's marvellous' letter to her parents, who would worry themselves silly at any hint that her life was not a bed of roses, when the phone suddenly rang.

Expecting it to be a wrong number, Joss went to answer it, and got the shock of her life to hear Khalil Rashwan on the other end. She was still in the throes of wondering how on earth he had managed to find out which hotel she was in, when she realised that he was asking her out to dinner.

'Oh, I'm sorry, Khalil,' she told him pleasantly, 'but I've not long checked in here, and I've one or two things I must do.'

'We can dine in the hotel, if you're tired,' he pressed eagerly.

'Actually, I'm not awfully hungry,' she told him, quite liking the man, but not sure that she cared to be pursued so assiduously. 'I ate a big meal at lunchtime,' she reminded him.

'Very well,' he agreed at last, then went on to state, 'I shall look forward to showing you the Museum tomorrow as we agreed. Shall I call for you at your office?'

Just at that moment Joss could not in truth remember if she had agreed to go to the Museum with him the next day, or if she hadn't. But, since his father *was* the Osiris Corporation, and since she didn't know that Khalil might report back to his father that someone from Beacon Oil had broken their word to him, she could see nothing else for it.

'That would be nice,' she replied, not really seeing how a secretary's breaking an agreement could in any way affect the agreement Thane was trying to reach, but not wanting to be the one to put the smallest spanner in the works. 'Is one o'clock all right?' she asked Khalil, and put the phone down a few minutes later knowing herself committed, and hoping against hope that the Museum could be 'done' in an hour—her lunch hour.

She had only just picked up the pen she had put down and had written no more than half a line when to her surprise her phone rang again. Warily, hoping that it was not Khalil ringing again for some reason, she went and picked the phone up—then got another shock.

'Who were you talking to just now?' Thane Addison demanded. And when, stunned, she was wondering how on earth he knew she had been speaking to anyone, he went on shortly—she not being swift enough in her replies, apparently—'Khalil Rashwan rang wanting your address. Are you dining with him?' he demanded to know.

For all of two seconds Joss was ready to let Thane Addison run for an answer. But that was before she realised that, with the negotiations he was conducting proving so troublesome, maybe he had a right to keep his finger on every pulse.

So, thinking that, in view of his remarks about her encouraging Khalil at lunchtime, it would please him, she began, 'No, I refused…'

Abruptly, she was interrupted, and Thane was sounding not pleased at all when, 'You haven't offended him?' he rapped.

'Of course I haven't!' she flared, angry that he thought she couldn't handle things better than that. 'I'm seeing him tomorrow…' she went to go on to illustrate how Khalil couldn't have been offended. But the line was suddenly dead. Thane Addison had crashed his phone down.

'Swine!' muttered Joss as she snapped her phone back on its rest. From where *she* was sitting, it seemed she couldn't do anything right—no matter which way she jumped!

CHAPTER FOUR

Joss breakfasted on croissants, jam and coffee the next morning, then returned to her room to check her appearance. She wondered fleetingly if she should take with her the leather zip-up document wallet which she had packed at the last minute, and decided it would do no harm. She might never need to use it, but it would take up little space if she left it in the office—that way she would be ready for any eventuality.

At half-past eight she left her room and took the lift to the ground floor. Thane Addison had told her that Sami would collect her, but naturally it would never have occurred to His Grumpiness to tell her at what time.

Pleasingly, however, the first person she saw as she made her way to the automatic glass outer doors was Sami. 'Good morning!' he beamed happily, and as she smilingly replied to his cheerful greeting, 'Shall I carry your briefcase?' he enquired helpfully.

'I can manage,' she smiled, and as he escorted her to a smart-looking car and held the passenger door open for her, her smile extended deep within her. She was in Alexandria, and suddenly she was feeling very good about it.

The feeling was doomed not to last. For one thing, although they reached the office unscathed, Sami was not the cool driver that her boss was. Joss wryly considered that car horn manufacturers in the city must do a roaring replacement trade. She had heard of people driving on their brakes, but in Egypt, it seemed that everyone drove on their car horn.

Thanks to Sami's driving, however, she was at the office well before nine. 'Thank you, Sami,' she told him as, trying to look as though she had never tensed up once in the certainty of a collision, she got out of the car.

'I will be here for you at five o'clock,' he promised with a wide grin.

What could she do under the threat of such a treat? 'Thank you,' she murmured again, and pushed her way into Beacon House.

'Good morning, Joss,' Halima, as ever smiling, greeted her, and as Joss went over and exchanged a few pleasantries with her, the outer door opened and Chad Woollams came in.

'Say you'll have lunch with me today,' he addressed her without preamble.

'I've only just had breakfast!' she laughed.

'I know, but I've a feeling that I've got to get in early if I'm to have the privilege of your sole company.'

Chad's brash manner amused her. She had come across his type before, and knowing him to be completely harmless, she felt in no way uncomfortable. 'Sorry, Chad,' she smiled at him, 'you're not early enough—I've a previous appointment for lunchtime.'

She was on her way up the stairs when he recovered sufficiently to call after her, 'What about dinner tonight?'

'What about lunch tomorrow?' she called back.

'You're on!' he grinned, and she rather gathered that she had walked straight into that one.

She had the trace of a rueful smile on her face when she entered her office, but she straightened her expression at once the moment she saw through the open communicating door that Thane Addison was first in.

She remembered the bad-tempered way he had slammed the phone down on her the evening before, and was in two minds about giving him the courtesy of a greeting. Then he looked up from his work, and she suddenly found herself staring into his piercing grey eyes.

'Good morning,' she said coolly, and turned away to go to her desk.

She had stowed away her document wallet and her bag when she noticed that the work she had last night put away in the safe was now on her desk. Quite clearly she was meant to get on with it with all speed. She did.

The communicating door remained open, and when at eleven o'clock Halima brought in a tray containing two cups of coffee, Joss took a break. Halima took a cup of coffee in to Thane Addison and returned to Joss's office, but, unlike yesterday, she did not seem disposed to stay for a chat.

Joss sipped her coffee after Halima had gone and then, having collected several queries during her two hours of work, she took her business queries, and a personal one of her own, into the adjoining office.

'Is it convenient for me to see you with some queries?' she enquired, as finding a clear space on his desk she put down some completed confidential and faultless typing.

'What's your problem?' he asked and, encouragingly, sounded civil enough.

In no time at all he had dealt with every one of her business queries. But when Joss did not at once move away, he gave her a cool look of enquiry, and she sensed that he was impatient to get on.

'Something else worrying you?' he clipped uninvitingly.

'Not worrying, exactly,' she replied quickly, and guessing that his mood was not going to sweeten in any way for being kept hanging about, 'It's just that Khalil Rashwan is calling for me at one to take me to a museum, and I'm just not sure if I'll be able to make it back to the office for two o'clock.'

She saw Thane Addison's face darken, and knew that she was about to receive the sharp edge of his tongue at any minute. Surprisingly, though, he must have bitten back any acid remark. His, 'What do you expect me to do about it?' however, held acerbity in full measure.

'Nothing!' she replied in a heated moment—then gained control of a temper that this man had to do very little to unleash, and added in a dignified way, 'That is, I was wondering if I might have an extended lunch hour? Naturally,' she went on quickly, 'I shall work late to-night.'

For about five seconds he leaned back in his chair and grey eyes pierced steady, unflappable brown ones, then, 'Naturally you will,' he agreed. And, as she gathered from that that she had the extended lunch hour she had requested, he stretched out a hand to take up the completed work she had given him, and drawled, 'You're a fast worker, Miss Harding.'

Joss returned to her desk knowing full well that the man she at present had the misfortune to be working for had not been complimenting her on the speed of her output, but on the swiftness with which she had got herself a date with the son of a man who *was* the Osiris Corporation.

She again slammed into her typewriter and, the work she was then engaged upon being of a less tricky nature, she found that her thoughts were wandering. Looked at in that context, she supposed Khalil Rashwan could be termed as something of a catch. Not that she was interested in him that way. He was a pleasant enough man, but in her view, though older in years, not mature enough for her.

Why her thoughts should suddenly grasshopper on to Thane Addison suddenly, she had no idea. But all at once she discovered that she was thinking that Thane too could be termed as something of a catch! Grief! she thought in the next second—as if she was interested in *him*!

At half-past twelve she took some more work in to him, the last of anything of a confidential nature, and was certain that—for all his eligibility—she pitied any poor woman who was so soft in the head as to be interested in him.

'Have you plenty to get on with when you do make it back?' he had the nerve to ask when she was about to return to her office.

Swallowing down a snappy 'I'll make it last', Joss managed to stay calm. 'I think I'm about halfway through the backlog,' she said as evenly as she could.

'Shouldn't like you to get bored,' he drawled, then stood up, and was towering over her as he added, 'I'm going to lunch now—I may not be back before you.'

'Bon appétit!' she bade him, and as he cleared his desk, in a suddenly cross frame of mind she returned to her office.

She did not look up when she heard the door from his office into the corridor open and close—she hoped he never came back. Which, she realised some minutes later, made it most odd that she should then start to think about how she had previously received the message that there was some space in his life for women. For suddenly she was remembering that he had told her on Monday night, 'I never *ever* mix business with *that* sort of pleasure.' She tied that in with the fact that he had gone to lunch early and had indicated that he would be late back. Her brow wrinkled crossly as she found herself wondering—was he then having an extended business lunchtime or a pleasure-filled one? Would she in fact see him at all that afternoon?

When Joss made ready to leave her office at one, she was little short of astounded to realise that she had spent quite some time in speculating about Thane Addison in an out-of-work context.

As if she cared, for crying out loud! she scorned, and went down the stairs to find Khalil Rashwan was already in reception waiting. 'Josslyn!' he beamed, stepping over to her.

'Hello, Khalil,' she replied, and in a friendly way she extended her right hand.

That was a mistake, for again he held it longer than necessary. However, once she had retrieved her hand and they were outside Beacon House, he was attentively showing her into the passenger seat of his opulent car and was talking of taking her to lunch.

'I'm afraid I haven't time to lunch *and* visit the Greco-Roman Museum,' she told him, as firmly as she felt she could in the circumstance of not wishing to offend him.

'But you must eat!' he protested. 'And I have reserved a table…'

Wondering at what time she would get back to her office, Joss compromised for a snack lunch, and Khalil agreed—the only complication being that no one seemed in any hurry to do anything. Khalil, certainly, seemed to have all the time in the world, and the smart restaurant to which he took her seemed to be of the belief that their clients would rather linger over even a snack meal than rush at it. It was therefore nearly two when they left the restaurant.

Relieved to be in the car and on her way to the Museum, Joss discovered that her relief was a little premature. For, having thought when Khalil stopped the car that they had arrived at the Museum, she discovered that he had brought her to a little park.

'Where...?' she began to question.

'I thought you might like to see Pompey's Pillar,' he smiled, and escorted her up a good many steps to the tall monument that looked to be somewhere in the region of about ninety feet high.

'Er—thank you,' said Joss, and because she felt that he was really putting himself out for her enjoyment, she delved into the far reaches of her mind to try and remember if she'd ever heard of Pompey or his Pillar. 'Pompey—Julius Caesar's rival?' she dragged out of some dark corner to query.

But Khalil, smiling as ever, was shaking his head. 'No,' he told her, and furthered her education by telling her that the high granite monument was erected much later than Pompey's time, in honour of the Emperor Diocletian. They spent about ten minutes in wandering round the little park, where a carpet of small and bright yellow flowers spread out and mingled with artefacts of other centuries.

When at the end of that time Khalil announced that they would now go to the Museum, Joss, who had been battling not to look at her watch, was much relieved again.

She forgot about time for a while once they had entered the Museum, however, finding that the relics from Alexandria's Greek and Roman past were most interesting. Slowly they wandered from section to section, taking in sarcophagi, statues, reliefs and paintings as they went.

They were in a section which housed a vast coin collection, however, when Joss glanced at her watch and saw with astonishment and some alarm that she had already extended her lunch hour by one and a half hours.

'It's half-past three!' she exclaimed to Khalil, unable to conceal a little of her agitation.

'The time worries you?' he asked, and looked as though it was of some concern to him that she must not be worried.

'I have my work to do,' she told him, and glanced about for the exit.

'Thane Addison is—um—a slavedriver?' Khalil queried as, realising that she was now desirous of returning to her office, he escorted her from the building.

'Oh, no,' she replied to his question, realising that, for all that their conversation had nothing to do with the contract which Thane was there to negotiate, she was still a representative of Beacon Oil—her first loyalty, therefore, since she wouldn't be here but for her job, being due to them.

They were in Khalil's car and he was driving her back to Beacon House when she began to wish he had not mentioned Thane Addison's name—for the brute of a man now refused to be ejected from her mind.

If he was a slavedriver, then he drove himself just as hard, she had to admit. Though she thought it was fair to say that she drove herself pretty hard without anybody's help—and she enjoyed being busy. In actual fact, though, save for giving her those tapes yesterday, Thane had left her pretty much alone while she caught up, which couldn't, she mused, be called slavedriving in anybody's book.

That was, she mused, until one remembered—when she had more than enough to do—his 'Have you plenty to get on with?' remark before lunch. In remembering that remark, however, Joss was soon remembering her thoughts about *his* extended lunch hour.

Khalil was pulling his car up near Beacon House when

Joss began to think that, depending on how Thane's 'lunchtime' had gone, she might not see him again that afternoon. And suddenly, and most strangely, she discovered that she did not know how she felt about that.

How very peculiar, she thought a moment later, and as Khalil walked with her to the door of Beacon House she shrugged away as ridiculous any absurd notion that she should feel anything at all where *that* man was concerned.

'May I dine with you tonight?' Khalil asked as she thanked him for lunch and for showing her a little of Alexandria's antiquities.

Joss thought briefly of how Beacon Oil commanded her loyalty, but then set that against the problems she might be storing up for herself later—she was here for a whole month, for goodness' sake!

'I'm sorry, Khalil,' she told him, half fearful that she might have Thane Addison breathe fire and brimstone if she offended Khalil and put the skids under the deal Thane was trying to do with his father. 'I've something else I must do tonight,' she added quickly—and felt enormously relieved when, although he looked a shade downcast, Khalil accepted her refusal without offence.

'I expect it is often this way for you,' he murmured sadly, then promised, 'I will telephone you.'

Joss said hello to Halima as she went in, and discovered that she felt sorely tempted to enquire if Mr Addison had returned from lunch. She pushed the question down, however, and decided that she hoped he had not returned, and that he would stay out for the rest of the day.

Which made it most irritating to her that her heart should hurry up a crazy beat when, going into her office, she saw through the open communicating door that Thane Addison was seated behind his large desk.

'I didn't expect to be this late—I'm sorry,' she braved

the scowling look of him to enter his office and deliver the apology she felt was due.

'That makes two of us!' he grunted sarcastically, making her wish she'd let him run for his apology. 'Bring your shorthand pad in!' he ordered.

My stars! Joss thought when an hour later she reeled out of his office—and she'd denied that he was a slavedriver? She took herself back to her desk and hoped with all she had that she would be able to read back the masses of quick-fire dictation she had taken down in the last sixty minutes.

If she had worked strictly to the time she had taken out then she would have finished work around seven that evening. But her fingers were still flying over the typewriter keys at seven-thirty.

Thane Addison was working late too, but, finding the work she was doing for him totally absorbing, Joss was completely unaware of the time. She had just come to the end of a page and was in the act of removing it from her machine when she became conscious that he had left his desk and had come to stand in the doorway.

He appeared to be studying her to some degree, but, staying cool, she looked back at him. He filled the doorway, she noted, yet he had not an ounce of spare flesh. In fact, she saw, he was quite something of a man. Astonished at the way her thoughts were straying, for she could not remember taking so much detailed note of any man before, she hastily averted her eyes. At the same moment, he moved forward.

'You can leave the rest of that until the morning,' he told her.

Joss glanced at her watch, then flicked her glance at him. 'Is that the time?' she gasped.

'Why—going somewhere?' he challenged, his tone instantly aggressive, accusing almost.

'Not tonight!' Joss said hotly, instantly nettled, and indeed, she felt so annoyed that she cared not just then that he was her boss, as she added pointedly, 'Since I've been here I've discovered that there are occasions when I prefer my own company to anyone else's.'

She did not suppose she had offended him; in her view he had too thick a hide for anything she said to dent him. Though quite what she expected him to answer, she did not know. But she was glaring at him hostilely while he stared arrogantly back when, as if against his will, the corners of his mouth started to pick up.

Staring at him, she was as amazed as she had been once before when she had thought she had seen evidence that her tart tongue had amused him. But, as before, all sign of him being remotely amused was soon gone, and as he had done yesterday, he commanded, 'Clear your desk,' and returned to his office.

Five minutes later Joss had her desk cleared and, with the work she had placed in her desk drawers—it not being so confidential that it needed to be put in the safe—she had nothing to go into his office for.

Which therefore made her feel most awkward when she went slowly across her office carpet and waited while he secured his briefcase. Then he looked up. 'Er...' she said hesitantly, then took a grip on herself, 'Sami's gone for the day, I—er—suppose?' she made herself ask the question.

For a second Thane Addison looked back at her unspeaking. Then, 'You can find your own way to your hotel,' he told her arrogantly, 'or,' he added, and a mocking light had suddenly come to his eyes, 'take a lift in my company.'

Quickly, her lips twitching, Joss turned away. She had not expected it, but *he* had amused *her*. She hoped he hadn't noticed.

There was no chance of her lips twitching the next day. Thursday morning was busy to the point of being frantic, with Thane Addison, in Joss's opinion, being at his intolerant worst. To her mind, if he was out to disprove any outrageous rumour that he might have a sense of humour, then he couldn't have done a better job.

She was glad when it was lunchtime and she left her office to meet Chad Woollams in the reception area to go for a bite of lunch. But no sooner were they seated in a restaurant than she discovered that she was not the only one to feel the cutting edge of Thane Addison's tongue that morning.

'All I said was "Good morning" and he came down on me like a stack of coal,' Chad complained.

'For just saying "Good morning"?' Joss enquired.

'Well, I suppose he did have an axe to grind,' he admitted, honestly if reluctantly. 'He's laboured like stink to restart negotiations with Osiris when they got stuck in the mire. What he didn't need was for me to drag my feet and not contact Mr Ismail...'

'Mr Ismail?' queried Joss, the name somehow familiar as if she had typed it recently. 'Seif Ismail?' she remembered.

'The same,' Chad confirmed.

'Isn't he one of the Osiris Corporation's legal representatives?' she asked.

'They don't come much higher,' he told her. 'Unfortunately, I was up to my eyes in it yesterday when Mr Addison came back from a meeting and told me to fix up a meeting between Seif Ismail and Richard Maybury to discuss some legal snarl-up.'

'Oh dear,' murmured Joss, seeing for herself that Thane Addison, following up any morning greeting with a question of when had Chad arranged for the meeting of the two legal representatives to take place, would blow his top to be told that Chad had done nothing about it. Especially when Thane was working his socks off over this deal. 'You've—er—arranged the meeting now, I take it?'

'Are you kidding?' Chad laughed, starting to cheer up. 'Within two minutes of Mr Addison's chewing me up and spitting out the pieces I'd got Sami driving me over to Osiris to see Mr Ismail personally. He and Richard are meeting this afternoon. I guess you could say,' he opined after a few moments silence, 'that when Thane Addison wants something done—he gets results.'

'Will he get the agreement he wants with Osiris, do you think?' she asked.

'If *he* can't pull it off, then nobody can,' Chad replied, and spoke for some time of the many hurdles that had had to be overcome to get negotiations so far forward that the legal representatives of both companies, who had been working in an advisory capacity from the beginning, were now about to be brought into contact with each other. 'I can't see what other stumbling blocks will crop up,' he commented, 'but the whole thing's been fraught with one obstacle after another.'

Hence Mr Thane Addison, troubleshooter-in-chief, being called in, thought Joss as she and Chad left the restaurant and returned to Beacon House.

Thursday afternoon was no easier than the morning had been, and Joss returned to her hotel that evening hoping against hope that Khalil would not take it into his head to telephone. All she wanted to do was to put her feet up and recharge her batteries. She didn't think she had even sufficient energy to find a tactful way to tell him she didn't want to go out with him.

However, Khalil did not telephone her, and Joss went to bed to sleep soundly, and to start work on Friday and to have the day as hectic as the day before. Khalil did phone that night, but by then she had come up for air.

'I made myself not telephone you last evening, because I do not want you to get tired of me,' he told her with such charming honesty that Joss felt drawn to like him more than she had so far.

'Oh, Khalil,' she said softly, and was to regret that her tone must have been a shade warmer than she had meant it to be, because after that, it seemed that he was never off the phone.

She declined his invitation to go out with him on Friday night, and on Saturday accepted an invitation from Grace Maybury, Richard's wife, to go to their home for dinner. She was glad, therefore, that when Khalil phoned and asked her to dine with him on Saturday evening, she was able to truthfully plead a previous dinner engagement.

'Then you must dine with me tomorrow,' he insisted.

Joss thought about it for a moment, but couldn't really see any reason why she should not dine with him. He was a pleasant enough man. 'Could we dine in my hotel?' she asked, her mind on the gruelling day Monday might turn out to be, and how it might be an idea if she had an early night on Sunday.

'Anything you say!' he replied jubilantly, but he still rang her on Sunday to check that she had not forgotten.

Joss took to Grace Maybury when she dined with her and her husband on Saturday. And her dinner with Khalil went much better than she had anticipated. True, she would have preferred that he had not attempted to take possession of her left hand while she was trying to eat her rice, fish and jacket potato, but he'd soon got the message when she looked at him solemnly and quietly told him, 'I need that hand, Khalil.'

Sami was there to drive her to Beacon House on Monday morning, and Joss metaphorically squared her shoulders as she went into the building, to be ready to tackle anything Thane Addison might throw at her that week.

As seemed to be his habit, he was there before her and, for once, was quite civil as he bade her, 'Good morning.'

Someone's had a good weekend, she found herself thinking, quite sourly, she realised, so she brightly answered 'Good morning,' saw that his eyes were on the upward curve of mouth, and felt momentarily glad that some friend had once told her she had a beautiful mouth. Then she bent to stow away her shoulder-bag.

By the time she had done that, however, it was as if Thane Addison had decided he had been too civil, for, 'Come in here with your pad,' he was suddenly instructing coldly.

'One of these days he'll say "please" and I'll drop down dead,' Joss muttered as she went in. She took a seat and stared at him with sweet, innocent eyes when, going on past performances, she realised that he had probably picked up her mutterings on his never-miss-a-thing antennae.

He made no comment, however, but, as if he was bent on paying her back for her sauce, his dictation over the next forty minutes was, she would swear, more rapid than ever. Only just by the skin of her teeth managing to keep up with him, Joss couldn't have been more gratified when the phone in her office rang, and he broke off.

'Shall I go and answer it?' she enquired prettily, knowing full well that Halima would ring Thane's office for her if she didn't answer her own phone.

'Here!' he snarled, and, lifting his receiver, he pushed it at her.

'Hello, Halima—were you ringing me?' she asked when Halima came on the line.

'Mr Rashwan is calling you,' Halima replied, and as Joss realised that it would be Rashwan junior, not senior, Halima was putting him through.

'Josslyn?' he enquired.

'Yes. Hello, Khalil,' she answered, and saw Thane Addison make a short angry movement. Clearly he did not care to have his time wasted while she took personal calls.

'Josslyn, I am devastated,' Khalil began soulfully, and, while all she wanted to do was to terminate the call, he went on to tell her that since having met her he had forgotten he was scheduled to fly to Japan today. 'I thought it was next week,' he told her, and went on at some length about how, now of all times, it was entirely the wrong time to go.

It was entirely the wrong time for him to ring too, Joss saw as she flicked a glance at Thane and caught the icy blast of his angered gaze.

'Er—how long will you be away?' she asked Khalil when he paused for breath.

'A week—perhaps two,' he complained.

'Then I shall still be here when you get back,' she told him quickly, ready by then to say anything to get rid of him.

'You promise?' he questioned urgently.

Oh, help! Joss thought, and as Thane gave her a fierce look and seemed ready to snatch the phone out of her hand at any second, 'Yes, I promise,' she said recklessly. Recklessly, because she was of the opinion just then that Thane Addison with his tendencies towards instant dismissal might be giving way to those tendencies at any moment. Shortly afterwards she told Khalil that she must go, and said goodbye to him.

'I trust you didn't terminate your call on my account,' Thane Addison offered with grim sarcasm.

'Khalil—Khalil Rashwan, he's leaving for Japan for a week or two,' she excused Khalil's call.

'Oh, good,' Thane drawled mockingly, then, his voice changing to granite, 'Perhaps now,' he said harshly, 'I might look forward to having your full and undivided attention during office hours.' And before she could retaliate that she considered his remark most unfair, he was straight away picking up from where he had left off in his dictation, and she was having to push her pencil at the gallop to catch up with him.

The rest of that Monday flashed by, with Joss so busy that she came to the firmest conclusion that she had had it easy working for Mr Edwards. Which fact made it a puzzle to her that, when Sami drove her back to her hotel that night, she should feel she would not have changed that day for a day back with Mr Edwards.

What that signified exactly, she had no idea, when after her dinner that night she went up to her room. Did it mean that she was so masochistic that she actually enjoyed working for that swine Thane Addison? He certainly kept her on her toes, but... Joss gave it up, and went to bed.

When Khalil Rashwan rang her at about three o'clock the next afternoon, she thought he had not gone to Japan after all. That was until he told her that he was phoning her from Japan!

'Was there something in particular you rang about?' she queried, thinking that to be calling from so far away must mean that his call had something to do with business.

'I rang particularly to hear your voice, Josslyn,' he told

her warmly, and as Joss thought 'grief!' and that this situation looked to be getting out of hand, she was heartily
glad that Thane Addison was out on a business meeting.

'That's very nice of you, Khalil,' she told him as evenly
as she could, then went on to tell him, using all the tact
at her command, that she would prefer it if he didn't ring
her at her office.

The only trouble with that, she discovered as the week
went by, was that Khalil took to ringing her every evening
at her hotel. However, by the time Friday arrived she had
grown more adept at tactfully handling the warmer of his
comments.

By Friday, too, she was more adept at her work in
Egypt, and felt more in the swing of what was trying to
be achieved with the Osiris Corporation. The pace in that
direction was starting to hot up, she realised as that Friday
morning she sat at her typewriter finishing off a very
rough draft of a contract which Richard Maybury and Seif
Ismail had been in consultation over. She had started on
the rough draft yesterday afternoon, and had worked late,
but because there were so many pages of it she had not
been able to complete it.

In actual fact, she was only coming to an end at twelve-
thirty. Taking the last page out of her typewriter, she
checked it over for mistakes, found none, and felt it
couldn't be very much longer now before Thane Addison
had reached his goal.

Collecting up the many sheets of the draft outline, she
went into the other office, and as Thane looked up, she
handed him the neat bundle of work.

'Is that all of it?' Thane enquired.

'Yes,' she replied, and felt a glow as he flicked through
the pages, then said,

'You've done well.'

'I try,' she murmured drily.

'Then try to get me Yazid Rashwan; if he's free this afternoon I'll take this…' He broke off, something in her sudden change of expression stopping him. 'So what do you know that I don't?' he asked quietly.

Not a lot, she rather thought, though she did know that Yazid Rashwan was many miles away from Alexandria. 'Mr Rashwan's in Luxor,' she replied, and saw from the way Thane leaned back in his chair and steadily eyed her that he wanted more than that.

'And from where did you learn that titbit?' he enquired when she wasn't very forthcoming. 'Or should I say from whom?'

'Khalil told me.'

'He's back from Japan?'

Joss shook her head. 'He phoned…'

'When?' rapped Thane, and, dropping the work she had just given him down on his desk, he stood up, everything about him aggressive.

'Last night,' Joss told him quickly, then started to get cross herself—for heaven's sake, there was no need for Thane Addison to look the way he did! He should know by now that she wasn't likely to give away anything that was confidential to anyone!

'He phoned you last night, from Japan?' Thane demanded.

'Yes, he did!' she replied defiantly, refusing to be browbeaten.

From the narrowing of his eyes she knew that he neither liked her tone nor what she was saying. Nor did she like the cold thoughtful look that came to his eyes. 'It's not the first time he's rung you from Japan, is it?' he demanded.

'He rings every…' her voice faded as she saw the sudden jut of Thane's jaw. Then, 'No, it isn't!' she said shortly.

'In fact, he rings you at your hotel every night,' Thane documented, his aggression now out in the open. 'Every night, since you gave him the encouragement of promising to be here still when he gets back!'

Joss blinked at him in astonishment that he should remember so accurately the details of what she had said on that one and only phone call she had taken from Khalil in his presence. Then, 'I wasn't particularly encouraging him,' she tried to deny.

'I don't know what the hell else you'd call it!' he snarled, adding fiercely, 'But perhaps that's all right with you. Perhaps you don't mind that he's out to bed you! That his pursuit of you means...'

'It's not all right with me!' Joss cut in, outraged. 'I'm doing all I can to walk a middle line between not offending the man who's the son of the man you've said *is* the Osiris Corporation, while my paramount wish is to stay loyal to Beacon Oil. On top of that, I quite like Khalil, but,' she continued when a muscle jerked in Thane's temple, 'I've no intention whatsoever of going to bed with him.'

Thane took a pace away from her as she stormed to an end. Then he turned back and told her harshly, 'I'm not having all the effort I've put in on this job ruined by your telling Khalil Rashwan, in anything but diplomatic terms, to cool his ardour.'

'It won't come to that,' Joss replied as coolly as she could.

'Huh!' he scorned. 'If you really believe that then you're more naïve than you've a right to be.' Then, clearly not believing she was naïve at all, he thought for a moment, then came to a decision that left her little short of gaping. 'You'd better tell him when next he rings that, in his absence, you've become smitten with—me. Tell him…'

Joss's gasp of incredulity caused him to break off, and as astounded as she was by what she had just heard, she was nevertheless quick to erupt, 'I'll do nothing of the kind! Why,' she went on heatedly, even though it had nothing to do with what they were discussing, 'I don't even like you—much less fancy you!' she told him, and went to swing away from him.

She had reckoned, though, without the fact that Thane Addison did not care for people walking away from him in the middle of an argument. She was made to realise that fact, however, when he caught hold of her arm and swung her back to face him.

'Who the hell wants you to?' he roared, and all at once, as a sudden gleam entered his eyes, she realised that some new thought had just come to him when he breathed, 'Though to prove a point,' and the next she knew was that Thane Addison was hauling her into his arms.

Shock kept her motionless for about two seconds. That was all it took for him to have her close up against his body, and to place his lips over hers.

It was the feel of his warm, well-shaped mouth on her own, though, that startled Joss into an awareness of what was happening. And suddenly, she went wild. She aimed a kick at his shin, and missed. She tried to get a punch to his shoulder, only to find he had somehow pinioned her arms down by her sides. She twisted her head this way and that, and finally she managed to pull her head away from the close proximity of his.

'Let go of me!' she yelled, and when he wouldn't she tried to land another kick to his shins. That one missed too, and before she knew it, he had recaptured her mouth.

For perhaps another minute she fought to get free, then all at once, and quite unexpectedly, a new and different emotion from the outrage she had been seething with began to spurt into life. And she stopped fighting.

Quite when she began submitting, she did not know. Nor did she know quite when, instead of meekly submitting, as the fire he was igniting in her started to burn, and flame, she began to respond.

Indeed, she was barely conscious that she had begun to respond to the urges of her body until, with her body pressed close up against his, and with her arms wrapped tightly around him, she suddenly came to realise that it was he who was breaking their kiss, and not she! That it was he who was pushing her away from him—and not she who was pushing to try to get away from him.

Which, when it did dawn on her, left her more astounded than ever. Her unruffled front was well and truly routed and she was left in no way able to cope when, as his arms dropped to his sides, he mockingly surveyed her.

'Point proven, I think, Miss Harding,' he drawled. 'You don't have to like a man, much less fancy him. You turn on—without such niceties.'

Joss had been through several sharp emotions in the last ten minutes. She was suddenly visited by another— the emotion of violence. With her self-control shot, she had no chance of harnessing that violence, and in a flash her right hand had arced through the air.

Her hand stung from the impact of striking him a furious blow on the side of his face, but she was entirely unrepentant. Tossing her head in the air, she stormed back to her desk, snatched up her bag and sailed out of her office, and out of the building. The swine—she hoped it hurt!

CHAPTER FIVE

HALF AN HOUR later Joss was seated in a nearby hotel with a cup of coffee in front of her, and she was still fuming. It was lunchtime, but she was too furious to eat. How dared he? The pig of a man! She was glad she had hit him!

Another half-hour went by, during which time she had ordered another cup of coffee, and had hotly determined that he could keep his job. She didn't want it, she was going straight back to England. She might not have seen the Pyramids yet, but, Pyramids or no Pyramids, she was leaving.

When ten more minutes had passed and she had made no move to get going 'straight back to England', Joss realised that she had cooled down considerably from being so blazingly furious. She was still angry with Thane, but as another five minutes ticked by she started to think more with her head than with the heat of outraged emotion.

It was then that she began to realise that, by walking out on her job, she would be playing right into Thane Addison's hands. He'd just love that, wouldn't he? He'd had a down on female secretaries before she'd arrived. He'd just love to telex London and tell them to send another secretary out, doubly stressing this time that he insisted on a male.

Inside another two minutes Joss was thinking, like hell she'd leave! She thought back to how she had once determined she would stay—no matter how insulting

Thane Addison was. And although she thought he could not get more insulting than to intimate, the way he had in his 'You turn on without such niceties', that she was anybody's, Joss started to dig her heels in. She wouldn't run, damn him. She was good at her work, she knew she was. Although this, she thought, as she got up, paid her bill and left the hotel, was a matter unconnected with her secretarial skills.

A taxi cruised by, a taxi which would have taken her to her hotel. She ignored it. She was not going to slink back to Beacon House, London, with her tail between her legs. No, she would not!

Halima was busy with a call on her switchboard when Joss, with her head tilted at a defiant angle, entered the Beacon Oil building. Joss smiled in her general direction and, with her heart suddenly banging against her ribs, went up the stairs to her own office.

The communicating door between the two offices was now closed, and as she reached her desk and stowed her bag she had no idea whether Thane was in or not. It did not take her very long to find out, however, for no sooner had she referred to her notepad and begun typing some work which had been held in abeyance while she typed the rough draft of the contract than the dividing door opened.

Stubbornly she refused to look up, but carried on with her typing. When the door closed again and Thane Addison did not come forward she guessed he was standing with his back against the door just watching her, and her fingers fumbled and she stopped typing.

Hoping to hide the sudden turmoil of her emotions under a cool front, she raised cool eyes and looked at him over the top of her typewriter. Instantly her glance was caught and held by him, and as an unbidden memory returned of the way she had pressed herself to him, had wrapped her arms around him—and had responded to his kisses—warm colour stained her cheeks.

She knew that his all-seeing glance had not missed the sudden flare of pink in her normally creamy skin, but all at once Joss was unconcerned with the irritating fact that, when she hadn't blushed in years, her blushing facility had chosen that moment to reassert itself. Because, when she had been too furious to consider the matter before, she was suddenly recalling how Paula Ingram was said to have thrown herself at Thane.

True, she doubted that Paula had attempted to fracture his cheekbone the way she had when she had hit him, but at that precise moment she started to get the feeling that the decision of whether she returned to England or stayed on in Egypt did not rest with her. She had been under no illusion before but that she would suffer the same ignominious fate as Paula Ingram if she ever came all 'female' over him. Again Joss recalled the way she had wrapped her arms around him, and suddenly she was certain that, like Paula, she was going to receive her marching orders.

Being certain of that, however, she still felt a very nasty jolt to see Thane Addison straighten from his casual stance by the door, and to hear him begin coolly, 'You'd better get back to your hotel and pack. I've—'

'That's most unfair!' she erupted hotly, immediately furious and on her feet as she refused to let him finish, and with no chance to hide the emotion she was feeling. 'You started it!' she raced on. 'I hit you because you—you…because of what you so vilely said,' she spluttered in her rage. 'You deserved it. You—' This time she wasn't allowed to finish.

'Whether I deserved your losing control of your fiery temper is neither here nor there!' he roared over the top of her voice, then commanded her toughly, 'Go and get your belongings together—'

'You swine!' Joss cried, the fiery temper he had spoken of outraged, as she slammed into her desk drawer for her bag. 'You utter swine!' she went on as she raced for the door.

She had the door open, but did not go through it. For suddenly he was speaking again, and all at once there was mockery in his voice. 'Cut the flattery, Miss Harding,' he drawled, 'or I may change my mind about the apartment I've found for you.'

Astounded, her jaw definitely dropping, she closed the door and turned back to him. 'You've found me—an apartment?' she asked, her temper flown, ashamed as she realised that if she'd let him finish what he'd started to say instead of going off half cocked, she'd have had no reason to lose her temper.

'Go and pack,' was his answer.

Joss moved into the furnished apartment which Thane had found for her that Friday night, and spent Saturday and Sunday thoroughly enjoying her new abode. Hotel living was all right as a stopgap, she mused, but her apartment was cosier and much more like home.

There were moments, though, when she would stop in the middle of being thrilled to bits to be in her new home, to feel overcome with guilt at the quick way she had wrongly assumed what she had.

She had been wrong to accuse Thane of being unfair, she acknowledged, totally wrong. She had seen enough by now of the way Thane worked to know that he was about the fairest person she had ever come across. He would not have needed her reminder that 'he had started it' to know that it would be unfair to dismiss her for something which he had instigated. And she, she realised a little unhappily, should have known better.

In her defence, though, she had been upset, and he was the cause. That still didn't make it right, she owned honestly, and accepted that he was due an apology from her for having so unfairly thought what she had.

In facing honestly that she owed him an apology, however, Joss found that she could not as honestly take out her reactions to Thane's kisses and dissect them. He, and his expertise, must take the blame there, she decided, and swiftly turned her thoughts to the fact that as her stay in Egypt could not be for much longer now, for the short remainder of her stay Thane had moved her out of the hotel and into an apartment.

She doubted that it would bother him one way or another that she might be happier living in an apartment, but realised, when thinking about it, that since in every thriving business all expenditure had to be accounted for, even for the short time remaining, it was probably more economical for her to switch from an expensive hotel and into furnished accommodation.

Joss hadn't given thought to how she would get to work, but, thinking that there was no time like the present to find out, she left her apartment at her usual half-past eight on Monday. She smiled at the concierge as she passed him, and went into the outside sunlight—to see none other than the faithful Sami.

'Good morning, madam.' He beamed his gentle smile.

'Good morning, Sami,' she greeted him cheerfully, and so started a week where Halima told her that Mr Addison was already closeted with Richard Maybury in conference, and where when she reached her office, her first telephone call of the day was from Khalil Rashwan in Japan.

'Why didn't you tell me that you were checking out of your hotel?' he asked at once. 'I have been trying to reach you by telephone!' he exclaimed, and sounded quite distraught.

'I moved into an apartment on Friday,' Joss told him cheerfully, having by then discovered that Khalil had a tendency to be overdramatic, but soon settled down if she didn't take too much notice.

'Then you must give me your telephone number at once,' he declared.

'I…' Joss broke off, as only then did it dawn on her that she couldn't remember having seen a phone in the apartment. 'I don't think I've got one,' she told him. When later the call was ended, she put the phone down, knowing that for the short time she would be there, there seemed little point in doing as he'd requested and having a phone installed at her apartment immediately.

From there a week followed where Khalil, while apologising for ringing her at the office, still rang her most days—having a few more dramatics one day when he fretted that he would not be back in Egypt as soon as he'd thought. Joss went out for a meal with Chad Woollams one night during that week, and learned that he was recently divorced and trying to cover the fact that it still hurt. While at the office, she started to feel a definite 'buzz' in the negotiating department.

Not that things were going without a hitch. So many amendments had been made to the rough draft which she had typed that the whole thing had to be done again.

When that week rolled to a close, she felt exhausted, but as if she at last had something to get her teeth into. She quickly recovered, however, and was glad to repay Grace and Richard Maybury's hospitality by having them to her apartment for dinner.

And then, before she could turn around, it was Monday again. 'Hello, Sami,' she greeted the Egyptian driver as she left her apartment, and by the time she reached her office she was geared up to start another week.

She had no sooner reached her office, however, than Thane Addison came through the open communicating door. He looked at her for long unspeaking moments, and then, just when she was expecting to get her ears singed for something she had done or had forgotten to do, 'Good morning,' he grunted, then told her, 'I've got to go to Cairo.'

'I'll find something to do,' she murmured, knowing that she wouldn't have to look very far, though lord knew where the vast amounts of paperwork she daily got through came from.

'Hmph,' he grunted, his sense of humour clearly very Monday-morningish, and was halfway back into his office when he stopped, turned around, looked at her, then told her, 'Stop looking—you're coming to Cairo with me.'

Joss had been on the Cairo to Alexandria road before, only then it had been late at night. This time when Thane drove the reverse journey from Alexandria to Cairo, it was daylight, and she was able to see, with the sun shining brightly overhead, that it was indeed desert on either side of the two parallel roads.

Occasionally there were signs of greenery, and now and then quite a bit of vegetation, but only to soon change to desert again. The journey was uneventful, however, with Thane as far as she could gather concentrating his thoughts on business matters and preferring her to be silent. He had very little to say to her at any rate, but she didn't mind that. Somehow all seemed right with her world, and she experienced a feeling of contentment.

That feeling of contentment was still with her when

they reached Beacon House. She was pleased to see Baz Barton again, who, after respectfully greeting her boss, suddenly beamed her a smile and seemed delighted to see her.

'Joss!' he cried, and asked, 'How goes it?'

'Cooper in his office?' Thane Addison cut in crisply before she could answer, and before she knew it she was whisked into Malcolm Cooper's office and the door was closed, and they were getting down to business.

In actuality, Joss couldn't have said that she considered her presence very necessary at the meeting between Thane Addison and Malcolm Cooper, but, remembering how on her first day of working for him he had told her to keep her eyes and ears open, she absorbed as much of the highly technical talk as she could, and took notes whenever she was requested to do so.

When later on Thane became fully occupied in sifting through some complicated figure work with Malcolm, Joss went from the office to see if there was any coffee going. It was then that she met Oma, Halima's Cairo counterpart. Oma spoke English every bit as well as Halima, but, with Baz Barton wanting to monopolise Joss, Joss did not get much of a chance for a conversation with her.

'Chad Woollams has all the luck,' he told her at one point.

'Why?' she asked innocently.

'He's based in Alexandria,' he replied, and at her look of enquiry he told her, 'So are you.' He grinned, which caused her to have to smile, and then the door to Malcolm Cooper's office opened and Thane stood there.

She caught his disgruntled look, and for a moment she thought that something had been amiss with the figures he had been looking at. She realised, when he went striding to the outer door and held the door open for her, that it wasn't that he was disgruntled but that he must have a lot on his mind.

'Bye!' she called to Oma and Baz, and to Malcolm who had followed Thane out. Then she went quickly to where Thane was standing. We're coming on, she thought; at one time he wouldn't have held the door open for her but would have left her to sprint after him.

That, or have snarled 'Come!' or some such order, she thought whimsically as they reached his car and she stood waiting for him to unlock it. Such whimsy, however, brought a smile to her face.

Though she had no idea that she was smiling until she heard Thane sharply challenging, 'Something amusing you?'

On any other day, such fierceness would have made her rise up swiftly. But the strange feeling of contentment was still with her, and for once since she had known him Joss felt not the smallest inclination to flare up in return.

So, meeting the fierce glare of his look serenely, she suddenly smiled. 'I had coffee,' she told him. 'You didn't.'

'Get in,' he grunted as he turned his key and all four doors unlocked.

Joss bent her head to 'get in', but not before she had glimpsed that his mouth, though looking severely repressed, was definitely trying to pull upwards at the corners.

They had been on the Cairo to Alexandria road for about an hour and a half when Thane pulled off the road and turned into a modern single-storeyed restaurant. And Joss could not have been more pleased about that. Not for herself, but for him. It was, in her opinion, more than time he had a rest.

'Hungry?' he asked, as he escorted her into the restaurant.

'Yes,' she replied truthfully, for by then it was way past lunchtime.

To her pleasure, however, instead of getting back into the car and continuing on their way once their meal was eaten, Thane suggested that they stretch their legs by taking a short stroll along the paths which separated neatly kept lawns. She paused for a short while when they came to a small budgerigar aviary, and was pleased when Thane did not seem impatient to move on. From there they moved to look at some hens which were kept in an immaculate wire-netted enclosure which was complete with house and run.

It was as they strolled back to the car, however, that Joss realised, without being able to put her finger on any specific reason why, that she was quite enjoying the day. Which in turn caused her to realise that, with Thane being at his most affable since she had known him, it was more than high time that she apologised to him. Her apology for accusing him of unfairness when he had never meant to dismiss her was long overdue. Not that she would apologise for hitting him, she thought without heat, as he started up the car and they got on their way again. He had deserved that.

'I never did—er—say—I was sorry,' she began while the idea was upon her, though having not realised, as she faltered, how difficult it was to bring the subject up.

'For your having had a coffee back in the Cairo office and leaving me to die of thirst?' he queried, and she loved that note of humour in his voice.

'No,' she owned with a laugh, and was serious when she added, 'for thinking you unfair.'

'Apology accepted,' he said lightly, and Joss's feeling

of inner contentment expanded. She was not quite sure how she felt, however, when, clearly having thought back to what had triggered off her accusing him of being unfair—she having hit him for his remarks, and what had led up to those remarks—he enquired casually, 'Is Khalil Rashwan still ringing you every evening from Japan?'

His voice had remained light, Joss noted, as she told him, 'No,' and added, since he obviously didn't know, 'There's no phone in the apartment you found for me.' She was on the point of realising that he could not know that Khalil rang her most days at the office, since by pure coincidence he had been elsewhere when those calls had come through, when after sifting through her reply, he suddenly had another question.

'He knows you've checked out of the hotel, though?' he asked, his tone abrupt, all lightness suddenly gone.

'He rang me—at the office—when the hotel told him that I no longer lived there,' she was forced to confess.

'So he's taken to ringing you *every day* at the office?' Thane barked, and as storm clouds threatened, every bit of Joss's feeling of inner contentment vanished.

'Not every day!' she answered sharply, and, since she felt that she had done nothing wrong, 'But most days!' she told him defiantly.

'A fact which you were going to keep to yourself!' Thane snarled.

'It's got nothing to do with work!' she erupted.

'Yes, it has!' roared Thane, and while the only complaint she could see he had cause for was that she was taking those calls on the office phone during office hours—and surely nobody was that mean-minded these days?—he was telling her curtly, 'While I'm in charge of this Egyptian project I want to know everything that goes on. If I'm to have facts down to the nth degree at my fingertips, I want to know every time anyone from Osiris makes a move. Your first loyalty, Miss Harding,' he told her harshly, 'while you're employed by Beacon Oil, is to me!'

'You *are* unfair!' she exploded, not taking kindly to being so trounced. 'Khalil and I are just—friends. Work doesn't come into it!'

'Don't be so bloody stupid!' Thane thundered. 'He's the son of the man who runs Osiris, isn't he?'

Joss didn't answer. Feeling furious to be called stupid—bloody stupid at that—she stared out of the side window. From then on until they reached Alexandria, she said not another word.

By then, though, she had simmered down as she remembered that Yazid Rashwan had, more than once, effectively gummed up the works of getting final draft contract details agreed upon. She knew that Khalil was his only son, and very dear to him. Which made her wonder then—as Thane all too clearly had wondered— whether, should Khalil have cause to complain about her for some unknown reason, might not his father—even at this late stage—change his mind about what was a multi-million-pound deal.

It was something of a pill to swallow that for a second time she had unjustly accused Thane of being unfair, but as he parked his car near to Beacon House Joss could not bring herself to apologise. She was still smarting from being called bloody stupid. Besides, she had apologised once that day—once, in her opinion, was enough.

She was still of that opinion when Sami drove her back to her apartment that night. Nor was she feeling in any friendlier frame of mind towards Thane Addison when Sami drove her to the office the next morning. Though when, included this time, she went with him to a meeting with Yazid Rashwan to take any notes that might be required, she could not help but admire Thane as she witnessed at first hand the way he dealt with each sticking point as it cropped up. Somehow she had imagined a troubleshooter to be a person who went in there with guns blazing, but it wasn't like that at all. There was no doubting that Thane could be tough when the occasion demanded it. But she was staggered to witness his seemingly endless patience, his willingness to take apart piece by piece the tiniest obstacle. Thane's diplomacy, too, was of the highest, she saw—that diplomacy being much in evidence when he himself refused to yield ground.

All in all, Joss clearly saw that morning why Thane Addison had been sent in when all other efforts had failed. When at the end of that meeting a definite breakthrough had been made, she could not have been more thrilled.

She spent that afternoon taking down page after page of highly confidential matter. She felt then that she could forgive Thane anything that, after losing his temper with her the way he had yesterday, he still obviously trusted her—and her loyalty. For not only had he taken her with him to that meeting this morning, but he was now quoting figures to her which any competitor would give their eye teeth to get hold of.

Knowing that her work was wanted urgently, she worked late that night, but had still typed only half of it when at eight o'clock Thane, who was also working, came into her office and told her briefly, 'That's ample for today.'

She spent all Wednesday morning in finishing off her typing, and, while being aware that the document was not fully complete, she handed her typing to Thane, who then summoned Richard Maybury to his office. When at four o'clock Thane called her in, he was alone, but had the work she had handed him before him. It was clear to her then that he and Richard Maybury had been sifting through it with a fine-tooth comb.

'Can you work late again this evening?' he asked, the fact that he had *asked* a plus, even if she was fully aware that he'd have something caustic to say if she replied that she couldn't.

'Of course,' she told him promptly, and, sensing that it was connected with the work she had laboured over, 'Is there something wrong?' she asked seriously, though she did not see how there could be, since she had double-checked her work.

'Couldn't be more right,' Thane answered, and over the next couple of hours he dictated material which was to be inserted into the work she had been engaged upon.

Joss, who by then knew the concise way in which Thane constructed his business sentences, knew immediately that he had asked, and taken, Richard Maybury's legal opinion on certain of the clauses. But the whole of the while they were working, a picture was building up, so that at the end of that two hours Joss, whose intellect had not stayed idle, had started to tingle.

So much so that when Thane had dictated the last full stop, she had grown quite excited. She tried to remain calm, and thought she might have succeeded, but she could do nothing about the shining look of elation in her eyes when, raising her head, she just had to say, 'That's it—isn't it? The contract, I mean! You've done it! You've...' Her voice faded as she caught his intent glance on her.

Then he was leaning back in his chair and telling her, 'True,' and all at once he smiled the most wonderful smile and suddenly, crazily, Joss wanted to kiss him. Then Thane was flicking a glance at his watch and, telling her to make two copies, was adding, 'And now I must make tracks for the airport.'

'Airport?' She gave herself a mental shake and asked in surprise, 'You're—meeting a plane?'

'I'm catching one—I'm flying to England,' he told her, and all at once her heart plummeted—he had finished his work; he wasn't coming back!

'You—er—must be exceedingly pleased at what you've achieved,' she hoisted her unflappable front aloft to tell him, and knew unbounded pleasure suddenly when, after pausing for a moment, he smiled a second time.

'I won't consider my side of the job done until I see Yazid Rashwan's initials next to mine on that preliminary contract,' he told her, indicating the work she had in her hands. He was on his feet when he told her that Richard Maybury was working late too, and would give her a lift home. Then, having thought of everything, it seemed, he was giving her face a steady scrutiny and telling her, 'See you when I get back,' as he went striding to the door. At the door, however, he turned, looked at her again, then said quietly, 'Bye, Joss.'

For an age after he had gone, Joss stayed staring at the door he had closed after him. She knew that she was going to miss him, but it was not until several minutes later that she was able to pull herself together and to realise that to think for one moment that she was going to miss him must surely mean she had been out in the sun too long.

She finally left Thane's office and returned to her own where, glancing down at the new dictation he had given her, plus amendments and insertions to the contract, she realised that it totalled up to two days' work. She had better get started.

The next hour flew by, but she had barely dented her workload when Richard Maybury came up to tell her that he was calling it a day. 'Can I put my work in your safe?' she asked him as she began to get her papers together.

'Of course,' he replied, and a short while later, with her confidential work locked in his safe, he gave her a lift to her apartment.

It took Joss a long time to get to sleep that night. Again and again as she closed her eyes she would find her thoughts on Thane Addison, who was winging his way through the late night on his five-hour flight to England. Most oddly, as she assumed that he probably had a board meeting to attend in the morning, she wondered if he would get a chance to catch some sleep on that flight.

A moment later she was asking herself, good heavens, what did she care? In any case, she had worked for the man—he was superhuman—he probably didn't need any sleep.

For a while she forced her thoughts away from him and dwelt instead on the man who had posed many difficulties for Thane on the road to reaching this preliminary contract stage. She had been working in Egypt for just over three weeks now, and if she had gleaned anything in that time it was that, for all Yazid Rashwan had not made reaching agreement easy, having at last reached agreement over the contract, he would stick to it. He was the same type of man of honour as was Thane Addison, and though small changes might later be made before the main contract was drawn up, once both men had set their initials to the preliminary agreement both, she felt, would consider its major content binding.

Thoughts of Yazid Rashwan and of how everything would work for the mutual benefit and future prosperity of both the Osiris Corporation and Beacon Oil were far from Joss just before sleep at last arrived. For by then she was longer able to keep at bay the memory of the crazy and most extraordinary emotion that had taken her when, realising what Thane had pulled off, she had experienced the urge to kiss him.

Grief! He'd have loved that, wouldn't he? She could just see him now, telling her, as he had told her within the first half-hour of their meeting, something about having enough problems '…without having to take time out to discipline another member of staff who takes it into her head to go all female on me'. Joss pulled the covers over her head and went to sleep.

Thursday was a day where she typed herself to a standstill. Friday was very much the same, and she finally pushed her typewriter back from her at around three o'clock. She then set about checking and rechecking the contract she had just spent two days in getting into shape, and forgave herself for her feeling of pride as she finally placed the impeccable end result in a folder of thin cardboard. Then the phone on her desk rang, and it was Chad Woollams.

'Haven't you got a home to go to?' he joked.

Swiftly Joss looked at her watch. She saw that it was ten past five. 'Tell Sami to hang on,' she replied, 'I've just got to give Richard something for the safe, then I'll be ready to…'

'Sami's still here, Richard isn't.'

'He isn't?'

'He said something about Grace wanting to take a trip to Aswan this weekend, so he shot off early,' Chad explained.

Joss thought for a second—there were two safes in the building, but she had a key to neither. I knew I'd brought that leather document wallet with me for something, she mused. 'I'll be with you in five minutes,' she told Chad, realising that he was waiting to lock up. Putting down the phone, she opened a drawer in her desk and took out the leather document case that, in four weeks of her working in Egypt, had not had an airing.

Perhaps she was being over-cautious, she contemplated when, with the bulging wallet in her hand, she left her office. The likelihood of any of their competitors forcing entry into Beacon House seemed remote, but industrial espionage was a fact in big business and not fallacy, and she hadn't broken her back setting down specific details and figures only to have them stolen. As an added pre-caution, as well as the two copies of the contract, her notes and shorthand notepad were in the wallet too.

Once Sami had dropped her off, Joss made her way up to her apartment and relaxed with a cup of tea. Then, feeling somewhat revived, she went and had a shower and washed her hair. She decided to let her hair dry naturally and ran a comb through it, and, clad in her housecoat, went into her kitchen and made herself a snack.

She had eaten her meal and cleared away, and was in the throes of wondering if she should write another letter home while considering that since there couldn't be very much more for her to do in Egypt now that she would probably arrive in England before her letter, when some-one rang her doorbell.

She knew with confidence that none but the most presentable would get past the concierge, and so, checking only to see that the housecoat she had on was securely fastened, she went and opened the door a tiny way. And, as her heart started to race idiotically as she saw Thane so unexpectedly standing there, she pulled the door open wider.

'Th…Mr Addison!' she exclaimed. 'When did you get back?'

His answer was to study her from the top of her newly washed blonde head to the tips of her mule-clad but otherwise bare feet. Then he smiled a slow smile, a warm smile, then drawled softly, 'I agree—it is time you used my first name.'

'Come in,' she invited, and suddenly became conscious that her newly washed hair was fluffy, and that she hadn't a scrap of make-up on, and that she needed a moment— or several—to get herself together.

Having turned away from him, she turned back to look at him as he followed her into her sitting-room. He seemed strangely dear to her then, this tall, broad-shouldered, grey-eyed man, whom she was beginning to acknowledge she had missed seeing this last two days.

But while she was busy in stoutly contradicting any ridiculous notion that he was dear to her, or that she had missed him, for goodness' sake, she saw that his eyes were travelling around her sitting-room.

'You're quite settled here?' he enquired when his eyes had done a full circuit and had come to rest on her face.

'Oh yes,' she replied, refraining from telling him that she wouldn't have a chance to settle and that she'd be back in England before too long. Though, since this was the first time that he had bothered to put the question at all since he had found her the apartment, she gave him a friendly smile and said, 'Can I offer you a drink?'

It was a cause for relief that he opted for a cup of coffee; her alcohol supply was less than limited. She left him in her sitting-room while she went into the kitchen, and cogitated on whether she should go and change out of her housecoat. She made the coffee wondering if he would think her stupid if she did change—since he was only going to stay for as long as it took for him to drink his coffee. She then got totally cross with herself to think that when she had always been in charge of herself, and able to make positive decisions, she should suddenly, for some obscure reason, have turned into such an indecisive creature.

When she took the tray of coffee into her sitting-room she was still clad in her housecoat and, having given herself a brief lecture, was decidedly in charge of herself.

As yet she had no idea why Thane had called, but since she felt that it could not have been to specifically ask her if she was settled there, she supposed he would tell her when he was ready. In the meantime she poured two cups of coffee, and, handing him one of them, enquired, 'How was England?'

'Raining,' he replied, and studied his cup for a second, then raised piercing grey eyes to look into hers and question offhandedly, 'Anxious to get back?'

'To the rain?' she laughed.

'To the man friend?' he answered.

'There's no one in particular,' she owned lightly.

'Fergus Perrott?' he queried, making her blink that he should have remembered Fergus's name after all these weeks.

'My girlfriend Abby is more interested in Fergus than I am,' Joss informed him, and somehow found herself telling him about the theatre group, her non-acting role in it, and how she had come to be in Fergus's company that night after the telex had come in from Cairo.

'How fortunate for us,' Thane commented when she had come to an end, and as she stared at him to realise that he must be saying, in a roundabout way, that he was pleased it was she who had been sent out to Egypt, he suddenly smiled.

Again Joss was taken by his smile, but she had just been reminded that he hadn't wanted a female secretary at all, and certainly not one who went all female on him. She decided then that the only way she had missed him was not having him around to bark out his commands over the last two days.

'Do I take it from that, that a female secretary isn't so bad after all?' she murmured, as she took a sip of coffee.

'Talking of work,' Thane easily ignored her question, 'Yazid Rashwan was on the phone to me as soon as I got in.'

'Everything's still all right, isn't it?' she asked urgently.

'Of course,' he replied, and with the confidence of a man who knew his job, and who also knew he had done his job well, 'Once Yazid and I have initialled that contract then as far as he and I are concerned—given that both our legal offices will make minor adjustments out of love of jargonese—the crude oil contract will be in the bag.'

Joss was about to ask if she should congratulate him now, when she suddenly remembered something. 'Oh, I've had to bring both copies of the contract home with me!' she exclaimed quickly.

'You have?' he queried, his grey eyes on her alive expression.

'I didn't have time to put them in the safe before Richard left tonight,' she explained, and felt warmed right to the core of her at Thane's reply.

'My fault,' he accepted full responsibility, and then, endorsing how much he trusted her, 'I was on my way to the airport when I remembered I'd meant to leave you the safe key,' he told her, which compliment made her forget her intention to go and get the document wallet for him.

'You were rather busy that day,' she excused his small lapse of memory in masterly understatement.

'*We* were,' he corrected, and the fact that he had not

overlooked that she had worked hard that day too made her feel good inside. Then Thane was going on, 'As I was saying, Yazid telephoned me a short while ago—he's invited us to his home in Luxor for a few days.'

'Luxor!' she exclaimed, and the contracts had gone completely from her mind as what Thane had just said penetrated. *'Us?'* she questioned, and all at once started to feel excited at the prospect. Though her excitement swiftly dimmed as she saw from Thane's sudden frown that she must have got it wrong somewhere. 'Not us?' she queried.

'I've agreed we'll go to Luxor,' he replied, a certain coolness starting to show in his manner, 'but have had to decline the invitation to stay in his home.'

'Had to?' queried Joss, not quite understanding why. 'Because—it wouldn't be right from a business point of view?' she queried, and received an irritated look for her trouble.

'Once that contract is initialled Yazid and I will both be on the same side businesswise,' he told her impatiently. Sarcasm had entered his tones as he added, 'In case you didn't know—his son will be home.'

The change in Thane from the good-humoured man he had been to the sarcastic brute he now was was as confusing to Joss as what he was saying. 'What's Khalil being home got to do with—?' It was as far as she got.

'Where the hell have you been all your life?' Thane blasted explosively. And while she sat and blinked at the sudden anger in him, 'Confound it, woman,' he roared, 'can't you see he's panting for you?'

'Of course he isn't!' she burst in hotly, only to be shouted down.

'Of course he is!' he barked. Then suddenly he quietened, and started to look a shade incredulous. 'You can't see it, can you?' he asked. And while Joss stared wide-eyed at him, 'Are you as innocent as you look?' he questioned, and when she had no intention whatsoever of confirming that for him, she then had more evidence that he was never content until all questions had been answered to his satisfaction. 'Saints preserve us...are you a virgin?' he demanded.

'What's that got to do with anything?' Joss suddenly erupted, not liking the feeling that she was being taken to task for something that was totally outside of business.

Watching him stormily, she saw his faintly incredulous look change to one of complete astonishment. She knew then that he had read all the confirming truth he needed in her reply. It was all there in his exclaimed, 'Oh, my godfathers!'

'And what am I supposed to gather from that?' she asked shortly, not liking him very much just then.

She discovered that he wasn't liking her very much either when, on his feet and clearly about to leave, he stayed to snarl angrily, 'For two pins I'd take your virginity myself, get that out of the way, then throw you to the wolves!'

'When I want that sort of a doubtful treat from you,' Joss retorted furiously, rocketing to her feet too in her rage, 'I'll let you know!'

Toe to toe they stood breathing fire at each other as hostilely Joss glared into the furnace of grey eyes in which she read that it would give him something of a pleasure to strangle her. Then, while she was feeling that she wouldn't at all mind setting about him, suddenly the humour of the situation got to her. At that self-same moment she saw Thane's lips twitch. Then, simultaneously, and while all the odds were against it, they both burst out laughing.

Who moved first as their laughter faded, she had no idea, but suddenly, as Thane looked at her, and as she stared quietly up at him, she found she was in his arms.

Gently he lowered his head and kissed her. Then his arms had fallen from her and he was going towards the door. 'I'll call for you in the morning,' he said as he reached it.

'You'll—call for me?' she queried, feeling somewhat bemused and not very clever in the brain department.

'I did say,' he murmured, 'we're going to Luxor.'

He had gone by the time Joss came out of her bemused state. Suddenly, though, a slow smile appeared on her face. She was going to Luxor—tomorrow—with him! Ten minutes later she realised that he had intimated that it might be for a few days. Joss thought she had better go and pack.

CHAPTER SIX

JOSS was up early on Saturday morning. Though she could hardly put the blame for that on the fact that she didn't know at what time Thane might arrive and might, if he intended to drive the five hundred or so miles she calculated it was to Luxor, call for her at the crack of dawn.

She had been wide awake when light started to appear in the night sky at about five-thirty and, having slept badly, she left her bed. She realised that the most probable cause for the fact that she had barely slept must be a little excitement. She had remembered during the night having read how, only recently, archaeologists had dug out some centuries-old statues from an underwater dig at the Temple of Luxor. And she was actually going to Luxor!

She was bathed and dressed in no time, and had remembered again Thane's gentle kiss on her mouth. But she didn't want to dwell on that. It had no special significance, anyway. Not that she had wanted it to have. Good heavens, it had been no more than a moment of empathy after their shared laughter.

Determinedly she put the memory from her, and decided it was more being told she was going to Luxor than Thane's kiss that had taken from her head every thought of giving him the copies of the contract. She cogitated for quite some while about whether she should pack the document case with the clothes she would take, but in the end she opted to carry it. It could well be that they would be going by train to Luxor, or maybe they would fly there. She had no idea which mode of transport they would use, but for security she decided she wanted that important leather wallet where she could see it.

When it came to what clothes she should pack, Joss had been in another quandary. The only suitcase she had with her was a large one—a trifle big for the 'few days' which Thane had spoken of them being away. On thinking about it, however, she saw no point, since she had plenty of room in the case, in not taking an item of clothing to cover every occasion.

She glanced round her apartment, took in the fact that it was neat and tidy to come back to, and sat down to wait for Thane, wishing she had thought to ask him at what time he would call.

It was half-past eight when, just as she had taken another look at her watch, someone rang her doorbell. Instantly she was out of her chair, and had taken a few steps towards the outer door when she suddenly stopped dead. Inexplicably, crazily, she suddenly felt overwhelmingly shy to see Thane again.

Grief! she snorted mentally, unable to remember ever feeling this way before. My giddy aunt! Just because he had gently kissed her! She was twenty-three, for goodness' sake!

Having given herself a swift and hurried lecture along the lines that she was not some awkward schoolgirl, Joss went to the door. As she remembered how amicably they had parted last night, a friendly smile curved her mouth as she pulled open the door.

'You took your time!' grunted Thane, and her smile swiftly departed, and she swallowed down the hot rush of words to tell him that if he felt like that about it he could go to Luxor by himself.

He was her boss, she remembered in time as she looked

up at his unfriendly, unsmiling, I-hate-female-secretaries face. It might be a Saturday, but she had never considered herself a strictly nine-to-five Monday-to-Friday secretary, so she stepped back from the door and picked up her case, document wallet and shoulder-bag. 'I forgot what time you said you'd be here,' she told him prettily, feeling fairly certain that he would recall that he had kept that piece of information to himself.

He gave her a cutting look and with a snide, 'Travelling light today, I see!' he wrested the large suitcase from her grip and went down the stairs, leaving her to secure her flat.

Joss was again thinking him a pig of a man by the time she joined him in his car. She'd be damned if she'd explain that at such short notice as last night she had had no chance to go out and purchase anything smaller in the case line, she fumed, as they drove away. In fact, she decided as a short while later she realised that they were making for the airport, she'd be damned if she'd say anything to the man.

That her silence throughout the drive to the airport bothered him not a scrap was obvious by the way he totally ignored her. Indeed, he had parked the car and had her case in one hand, his much smaller case in his other hand, while at the same time he effortlessly managed to hang on to his briefcase too, when he addressed her at all. And that was only to rap a terse, 'You've got the contract with you?' as he eyed her document wallet.

'Both copies!' she retorted, and, since he hadn't a free hand to receive it, she was—while stifling the urge to hit him over the head with it—still holding on to it when they entered the airport building.

They had some time to wait at the airport, for as well as airport security being very strict, their plane was late.

The flight to Luxor, however, was uneventful. Though with Thane burying his head in some paperwork extracted from his briefcase, Joss had time and space in which to wonder what happened in the night-time hours to turn him from the good-humoured man who had left her apartment last night to the bad-tempered brute he was this morning.

It didn't take her very long to find the answer. Nothing had happened. When had he ever been any different? Hadn't he always been the same: pleasant or nearly so one minute, then, without reason as far as she could see, coming on all stroppy with her.

Let him get on with it! she fumed, then fell to wondering, as she had during her wakeful hours last night, if he had really refused Yazid Rashwan's invitation for them to stay in his house on account of Khalil's being there. She felt sure that he must be wrong about Khalil panting for her, though that was beside the point, the point being—had Thane really risked offending Mr Rashwan by turning down his invitation to stay in his home? Had he really risked offending the Egyptian's proud honour?

Joss was still finding it incredible that Thane might have risked putting the contract he had laboured so hard and long over in jeopardy, as the plane started to descend at Luxor. From what she had witnessed, she had seen that both Thane and Yazid had a very great mutual respect for each other, a respect that bordered on friendship, so it wasn't so surprising perhaps that at the end of their work Yazid Rashwan should, from that feeling of friendship, extend the invitation.

Thane, in his business dealings, had a plentiful supply of tact, of course—not that he ever wasted any of it on her. The plane had landed when Joss realised that she must have got it wrong somewhere. For knowing Thane as she did, and the importance of this contract as she did, she felt certain that if it was a choice between risking the contract or risking her, then, to use his own charming expression, she'd be the one who would be thrown to the wolves.

Joss found Luxor a good deal warmer than Alexandria, and was glad she was wearing lightweight cotton clothes. She still had charge of her document wallet as, by taxi, she and Thane left the airport.

Luxor was as bustling and as busy as Alexandria, she observed, though a good deal more touristy. She wondered if she would have a chance to see the Temple of Luxor, but began to doubt it. She had been in Egypt nearly a month—and hadn't seen the Pyramids yet!

The taxi drew up outside a smart hotel, and, with Thane being such a terse brute, Joss was human enough to hope, when with supreme confidence he strode up to the reception desk, that they would tell him they were so busy with the tourists that there wasn't a room to be had.

They said nothing of the kind, of course. 'You have two rooms for me, name of Addison,' he told the receptionist. And while he went through the checking-in formalities, Joss realised that not only must he have telephoned in advance, but that men like him would always get a hotel room. Even if the hotel was so fully booked that the manager had to move out, Thane Addison would get a room, she thought sourly.

'I'll get a porter to take your cases up,' the receptionist said when the formalities were completed, and Thane turned to Joss.

'I've got a busy afternoon,' he told her shortly. 'Get yourself some lunch and...' He broke off, and as he seemed to study her face for a second, she caught a glimpse of something less harsh enter his expression—or thought she did, but knew herself mistaken when in the next second it vanished, and he was telling her crisply, 'We're dining at Yazid Rashwan's home this evening—you'd better rest this afternoon.'

Without a word Joss turned away and went with the porter. Thanks for telling me I look a wreck! she mutinied. She didn't want to *rest*, she didn't need to *rest*. Damn it, why did that man continually upset her so?

A moment later she was of the view that it wasn't that he upset her in particular, but that *he* would try the patience of a saint. She put thoughts of him out of her head when, not condescending to witness that his luggage was taken to his room, he had left her to do it.

'*Shokran gaezilaen,*' she thanked the porter, handing him the expected tip which she had discovered was very much part and parcel of the Egyptian way of life, and, observing that she and Thane had rooms next to each other, she checked that his smaller case was deposited inside one of them, and claimed the other.

Wretched man, she rebelled, and, Saturday or no Saturday, it was her considered opinion that if he was working, he should want her to work too—not *rest*!

That, though, was before she recalled that he hadn't said he was working but that 'I've got a busy afternoon'. Oh, to hell with him, she fumed, and, as visions of him having a busy non-working afternoon started to crowd her head, she rang room service. It was nearing three o'clock when she ordered an omelette and a salad, and decided to unpack.

Having newly discovered that they were dining at Yazid Rashwan's home that evening, Joss was pleased with her last-minute thought both in England and in Alexandria to pack one floor-length gown that would cover any formal, semi-formal, or just about any occasion. Shaking out the cream silk with its muted splodges of nasturtium, lemon and orange, she thought it would fit the bill nicely. The dress had a deep but decorous neckline from which a four-inch flounce fell in soft folds, those folds repeated where the material flared softly from hip to hem. Its sleeves were elbow-length and the cut was such that it showed off her slender waist admirably. Joss knew she looked good in the dress that appeared quite simple but had cost so much that, without the cheque her parents had given her for her birthday last year, she would have had to think twice about such self-indulgence.

Her unpacking did not take long, and she wandered out on to her balcony and for a while was lost in wonder at the view. For there across the road from her hotel flowed the lifeline of Egypt, the Nile. Watching, she saw a crowded ferry make its way to the other side of the river's bank, where lush green grasses and tall date palms formed a foreground to the majestic and arid red-gold Theban Hills.

Somewhat in awe of the magnificence before her, she stayed on her balcony, turning her head this way and that, just absorbing all that was spread out as far as the eye could see. Then the man from room service arrived with her meal.

Since there were a couple of rattan chairs and a table out on the balcony, there was no question but that the balcony was where she would eat. She had been sitting tucking into her meal for some minutes, however, while gazing at the date palm, still with a cluster of unharvested dates hanging down on a level with her balcony, when it suddenly occurred to her that since the date palm went way past her balcony, and since she was on the sixth floor, then, incredibly—how tall was this particular tree for heaven's sake?

She never did get to calculate the answer, for, annoyingly, as though determined to upset her, thoughts of Thane Addison and his cantankerous manner that day started to edge in.

Drat the man, she thought irritably, her moments of peace from him not long enough. But, her meal finished, her mood of happy discovery gone, she left the balcony and decided to change, deciding at the same time to thumb her nose to his 'You'd better rest this afternoon', and go out. When had it ever bothered him if she went on till she dropped?

While she was out of her clothes, however, she thought she might as well take a shower. And, having taken a shower, she looked at her nails which she thought could do with a tiny bit of attention before dinner that evening, and wrapped a housecoat around her prior to getting busy with emery board and nail buffer.

Quite what time it was when she yawned and decided to lie on top of her bed for a minute or two she had no idea. What she did have some idea about was that when she woke up it was dark outside. Swiftly she switched on some light, switched the light off again when she remembered about mosquitoes, then went to close the sliding door to the balcony. Only when she had the light on again did she go racing to pick up her watch.

Relief cascaded in as she saw that it was only seven o'clock. The few Egyptians she knew dined fairly late, so, although His Lordship next door had not given her any idea of what time she was to be ready, she didn't think he would come calling before eight. Just in case, though, she hadn't better hang about.

At twenty to eight, she had showered again, was dressed in her cream silk dress and had applied her make-up. A few minutes later she was re-checking that her long ash-blonde hair was all right when she heard what she thought was the door to the adjacent room opening and closing.

She knew her ears had not played her false when she heard someone walking by her door call a civilised greeting in passing, then heard Thane's voice reply, 'Good evening'.

Most oddly, then, her heart began to absurdly misbehave itself, but she had less than two seconds to pull herself together, because two seconds later there was a rap on her door. Joss took another second in which to look in her mirror again and in which to have a last-minute anxiety about the suitability of her dress after all. Then, going to the door, she remembered the document wallet she had walked away from Thane with and turned back to get it. Then she went and opened the door to him.

Then she forgot completely any nerves about whether her dress was suitable or not, because Thane, freshly shaven and in a dinner jacket, was something else again. Why her heart should suddenly start to race like an express train, as she looked at him, she didn't have time to analyse. But it did race, and she felt all at once too choked to speak as she saw his eyes go over her, starting at her shining hair and slightly flushed cheeks to skim over her breasts, waist and hips, and back up to her mouth, and finally his grey eyes pierced into her large brown eyes.

'W-will I do?' she enquired as coolly as her husky throat would allow.

'You look stunning—and you know it,' he told her sharply, which manner of compliment left her feeling a glow to hear him say she looked stunning, while at the same time she felt like boxing his ears that he should intimate that she had merely been fishing for compliments, or, worse, that she was conceited.

'Shall I bring this?' she queried coldly, holding up the document case as he stood back from her door.

'It would be rather pointless to come without it, wouldn't you say?' he drawled, and, leaving her room, Joss closed the door with a bang that resounded all the way up the corridor. Immediately she was sorry, but one of these days she was going to crown the swine!

Yazid Rashwan had sent a chauffeur-driven car to the hotel to pick them up, and, with Yazid's villa being some twenty minutes' drive away, Joss had time to get her rattled temper under control.

She still had the document case in her possession when a servant opened the door to the many-roomed, sumptuous home of the man who was the Osiris Corporation. Then Yazid Rashwan was there.

'My friend!' he greeted Thane warmly, and when the two had shaken hands, 'Miss Harding,' he easily remembered her name. 'Come and meet my wife.' And all three of them went to a graceful drawing-room where a charming and elegant woman of about fifty and who was dressed in a long black evening gown came forward.

'Welcome to my home,' she bade them both, though it was clear that she had met Thane before. Then suddenly Khalil Rashwan appeared.

'Josslyn!' he exclaimed as he came rushing forward to take both her hands in his. 'I have spent many long minutes in listening for the car to arrive—and then I missed it.'

'How are you, Khalil?' she asked him pleasantly, and might have asked him how he had found Japan, had his father not reminded him of his manners.

'You remember Thane, my son?' he enquired, and Khalil dropped her hands to go and shake hands with Thane.

'Please take a seat here, Miss Harding,' Yazid's wife smiled.

'Thank you,' Joss smiled back, and invited, 'Call me Joss, everybody does.'

'You never told me!' Khalil broke in as he quickly occupied the seat beside her on a luxurious couch.

'She doesn't tell everyone,' Thane commented drily.

Joss ignored him and was soon in conversation with Khalil's mother, who was soon inviting her to call her Noura, her first name. They spent quite some time in the pleasant drawing-room with conversation flowing easily, though with Thane, Joss observed, for all his outwardly urbane manner, giving her the occasional benefit of a steely look.

Seated as they were, no one else but Khalil, who was still right next to her, would have been able to witness Thane's cutting glances, but it didn't seem to bother Thane if Khalil saw or if he didn't. Not that Khalil seemed interested in looking anywhere but at her. Which, Joss knew full well, was what Thane's arctic glances were all about. Though from where she viewed it, short of insulting the whole family by suddenly coldly telling Khalil to go and sit somewhere else, she didn't see what she could do about it.

'How did you like Japan?' she got the question in when Khalil moved a few inches closer, and under cover of turning to address him she managed to move a few inches away.

'You were not there,' he said succinctly, and as Joss caught Thane's frown she started to hate Thane and began to wish she had never come.

She had some escape from Khalil's attentions when they went in to dinner. She was seated at the right hand of Yazid, and although Khalil was at the other side of her

with Thane sitting to the right of Noura around the cir-
cular table, there was some space between them.

'Seif Ismail is here in Luxor,' Yazid mentioned to
Thane during the main course of *lahma mahshiya*, which
was beef stuffed with cheese and served with sundry sal-
ads. 'I've suggested that he might call later this evening.'

'I think that's an excellent idea,' Thane replied lightly,
and Joss knew then that he had fully expected the
Egyptian lawyer to put in an appearance before the contract was initialled, and that indeed he would have been
surprised if he did not do so.

'Would you like more salad, Joss?' Khalil enquired attentively.

'Thank you, I've ample,' she told him, and later had
the same treatment when, as she finished a delicious helping of a pressed apricot pudding which had mixed nuts
and raisins in it, and went by the name of *mihallabiyet
'amar eldin*, he asked, 'Did you enjoy your pudding?'

'Very much,' she smiled.

'You would like some more?' he asked, and as Joss
politely told him that, delicious though it was, she had
had sufficient, she understood why it was that she could
not take him seriously, or take seriously Thane's belief
that Khalil was panting to get her into bed. For older than
her Khalil might be, but he seemed so young. Thane now,
with his sophistication... Abruptly her thoughts ceased.
Grief—what had Thane got to do with anything!

They had returned to the drawing-room and were drinking coffee when it was brought home to Joss that Thane
Addison had a great deal to do with *everything*. She realised that, possibly because they were the only two English
people in this Egyptian household, she was being over-
sensitive where Thane was concerned, but she was most
definitely feeling vibes of animosity coming from him.

While he and Yazid were getting along like a house on fire, all she was getting from Thane was a tight-lipped expression because she was again seated on the settee with Khalil.

Which, since it had been Khalil who had manoeuvred himself into a position next to her while his mother had been instructing the servants about something, was none of her making. In actual fact, she was starting to find Khalil just a wee bit tedious. She could not remember him being so—'cloying' seemed about the best word to fit, before he had gone to Japan, so had he changed, or had she?

Whatever the truth of the matter, she was starting to feel quite exhausted from the effort of fending off his attentions while at the same time, for fear of offending his parents who clearly loved and indulged him, maintaining a friendliness with him. She would not have minded at all had Thane suddenly declared that they must return to their hotel—indeed, she was more than ready to go—but she knew she was not going anywhere until *he* said so.

She grew hopeful that they would soon be able to leave, however, when a few moments later a manservant entered the room and said a few discreet words in Arabic which meant nothing to her, but which, having overheard Thane speaking the language on the phone a time or two, she knew he would understand.

It was out of courtesy to her, she realised, that Yazid said in English, 'Seif Ismail is waiting in my study—shall we adjourn, Thane?'

'Of course,' Thane said easily, and with a look over to where Joss sat he was on his feet. For one lovely moment she thought his look meant that she was to go into the study with them. But that hope died a death when, observing her slight movement as if she was about to rise, he stopped her by the quiet question, 'Have you got the contracts, Joss?'

She smiled at him, and as she bent down to the side of the settee where she had left the document case prior to going in to dinner, she wished she hadn't smiled. He'd only called her Joss so that the others wouldn't know that she wasn't exactly flavour of the month where he was concerned that evening.

Taking up the leather wallet, she was about to unzip it to remove the documents he needed, when he stretched out a hand and took the wallet from her. Then, with a courteous 'Excuse me, Noura,' to his hostess, he went with Yazid Rashwan from the room.

Although Yazid's wife could not have been more charming, the next hour dragged by for Joss. Had it been just she and Noura there, there would have been no problem. But, with Khalil wanting to monopolise her, Joss was very hard put to it not to be sharp with him. Which, she realised, made him think—since she wasn't verbally slapping him down—that she was encouraging him.

'You've been to England, I expect?' she smiled at Noura when a discreet glance at the watch on Khalil's wrist showed that the three men had been in the study for over an hour.

'Many times,' Noura replied, and they spoke for some minutes about the various parts of Great Britain that Noura had visited, until Khalil, having had enough of being ignored, even briefly, decided to chime in.

'Perhaps you will show me around England the next time I make the trip?' he interrupted to suggest. 'Though first,' he said eagerly, 'you must allow me to show you my country.'

'There's—so much to see,' Joss was replying tactfully

when, as his mother smiled indulgently, he caught hold of both her hands.

Several things happened at the same time then. With relief Joss heard sounds that told her that the business in the study was over. Then, as Khalil continued to keep tight hold of her hands and started to declare, 'You *must* allow me to show you, Joss. I will call...' all at once Thane was standing over them, and suddenly he was forcing Khalil to let go her hands by the simple expedient of pushing her document wallet at her.

Deciding that it might be politic to keep something in her hands, Joss hung on to the wallet as she took a swift glance at Yazid's face. He seemed well pleased, she saw, and, transferring her glance to Thane, she observed that he seemed equally well pleased. Sensing, though, that she was in his black books, she knew better than to meet his eyes.

'If my religion did not forbid alcohol, we would celebrate with champagne,' Yazid confirmed that all had gone well as he grinned to Thane. 'But, since champagne is out of the question, may I offer you some other refreshment?'

Tactfully Thane turned down the offer, then suggested that it was time that they returned to their hotel. It was another half an hour before Yazid allowed them to go and they shook hands all round, and another ten minutes, with Khalil coming out and seeing Joss into the car, before the chauffeur headed back to the hotel.

Joss's feelings were a mixture of relief to be away from Khalil, and a mixture of being exceedingly upset with Thane that, when she wanted to congratulate him most sincerely for all he had achieved, by his very uncommunicative attitude he had made it impossible for her to voice those congratulations.

She left him talking to the chauffeur when they reached

their hotel, and went swiftly to reception. 'Can I have my room key, please?' she asked the receptionist, giving her room number. Then, because it seemed petty not to do so, she asked for Thane's key too.

He was heading towards the desk as she turned round. Without a word she held out his key and stood bravely still while his grim glance flicked over her and the picture she made in her dress.

I wonder if he still thinks I look stunning, she thought sourly as he raised a hand and, without a word, took the key from her. It seemed that not only did he never say 'please', but that he had added 'thank you' to his list of words never to leave his lips.

Why that should bother her, she didn't know, but suddenly, and to her horror, she discovered that she was feeling quite weepy. 'Goodnight!' she said quickly, and went swiftly towards the lifts.

He had not answered her goodnight, nor had he followed her to where the lifts were. And that was all right by her, she thought, still having to swallow hard. She got into the lift and stabbed the number six button, and was sure she didn't care a light.

She was leaving the lift, however, when with a shock that threatened to make her knees buckle she realised that she did care! She cared very much. Suddenly—while starting to fume that she didn't know what was the matter with the wretched man that he should be so grim-faced when, after what he had achieved, he should be dancing a jig that his work was good as over—she halted.

All at once her heart gave a mighty lurch. And she knew then, with overwhelming clarity, that she didn't want it to be over! Then, like a bolt from the blue, she knew exactly what was the matter with *her*. She was in love with him! Oh, dear heaven, what utter madness!

CHAPTER SEVEN

SUNDAY dawned with Joss wide awake in her bed and knowing that she had done the unthinkable. She had done what Thane had more or less warned her not to do at their very first meeting—she had fallen in love with him.

Leaving her bed, she showered and dressed in light cotton trousers of pale lemon and topped them with a lemon T-shirt. Then, for something to do, she made her bed and tidied her room and, in need of escape from the four walls, though being careful not to make the smallest sound that would echo up the corridors and disturb other residents, she left her room.

She was not feeling in the slightest hungry, but was glad that the hotel's restaurant opened very early to serve breakfast. 'Good morning, madam,' a smiling waiter greeted her as she went into the restaurant.

'Good morning,' she replied, and went and helped herself from the self-service stand to a glass of *karkade*, a pleasant fruit-tasting drink made from dried hibiscus petals.

There was ample space in the restaurant, and Joss sat down at the nearest table and reflected that things looked no better from down here than up in her room.

'Coffee, madam?' the waiter who had greeted her approached her with a coffee-pot.

'Thank you,' she accepted, but the coffee went cold as she sipped her *karkade* and thought of Thane Addison and of what a total idiot she had been to fall in love with him. It had been coming on for some time—only now, now

121

that she knew, was she able to realise that all the signs had been there, but she had been too blind to see.

Well, much good would being in love with Thane do her, she sighed. She had the example of Paula Ingram before her to realise that she stood as much chance of Thane reciprocating her feelings as of the Nile freezing over. Unlike Paula Ingram, though, Joss knew she would die rather than let Thane know how she felt about him.

Starting to feel a little agitated lest she had given away any hint that she was starting to care for him, Joss went through agonies, and owned that she was more than a little fed up.

In desperation she turned her thoughts from Thane, but only grew more fed up when thoughts of Khalil Rashwan entered her head. Somehow she just didn't feel like coping with Khalil today, yet she thought she wouldn't need any prizes for guessing that he was likely to be on the telephone more or less as soon as she got back to her room.

That was—if she was in her room! Suddenly, from being totally fed up, Joss suddenly started to rebel. Why should she stay in her room? It was Sunday, for goodness' sake!

In the next few minutes she had left the restaurant and was taking the lift upwards. She had no idea what Thane's plans were for her that day, but he had intimated at the outset that they would be in Luxor for a few days, so he couldn't mean them to fly back to Alexandria that day. But with the job she was there to do virtually completed as far as she could tell, she just couldn't see any good reason why she should stay around the hotel.

Getting out of the lift on the sixth floor, Joss went quickly and quietly along the corridor. As she went by Thane's room, however, the feeling of wanting to see him became so intense that she almost knocked on his door.

She was then absolutely appalled that her feelings for him should so dent her pride, and she went swiftly past his door to insert her key into the next-door room and hurriedly shut herself in.

Only when that mad moment of impetuosity had passed did she realise the strength of her emotion for him. How could she have gone to him—what if he'd glimpsed from anything in her expression how she felt about him?

The realisation that any such knowledge he might receive would for certain see him dismissing her on the spot gave Joss the stiffening she needed. Ten seconds later she had herself firmly under control as she picked up the phone and asked to be put through to his room. She checked her watch; it had just gone seven-thirty. Sunday or no Sunday, she saw no reason why Thane, the cause of her sleeplessness, should sleep on undisturbed.

'*Aeywae,*' answered a voice she would know anywhere, although he spoke in Arabic. That voice, alert and awake, let her know that he had probably been up and about for ages.

Her knees went weak. She sank down to sit on the bed, and gripping hard on to the phone as if her life depended upon it, she announced herself coolly, 'It's Josslyn Harding. I wondered what plans you have for today?'

Silence was her answer for a few moments, then, 'Why?' he questioned bluntly, and, loving him, at the same time she hated his aggression.

She took a long and steadying breath, then replied as evenly as she could, 'Because, if we're not going back to Alexandria today, and if you've no need of me, then I wouldn't mind the day off.'

She had spoken calmly and politely. His reply was harsh and rapid. 'What for?' he demanded, and one of the sudden bursts of temper which she had become subject to since knowing him immediately flared up again.

'Because I've been in Egypt four weeks tomorrow and I've seen nothing yet but airports and offices,' she retorted hotly, stretching the truth a little in her anger.

His reply was swift and harsh. 'Do as much sightseeing as you want—I've no need of you!' he hurled at her. With that his phone went down, and Joss's breath caught in her throat.

She tried to rally herself by remembering that he jolly well needed her secretarial skills, didn't he? But she knew she was only fooling herself. With or without her speedy and proficient-plus ability at the typewriter, he had no need of her. Any secretary would suit. Look at how easily Paula Ingram had been replaced.

Damn him, she refused to be downcast, and was about to charge indignantly from her room when suddenly her leather document wallet caught her eye. Heavens! she gulped, as she recalled how she had left the wallet and all the highly confidential matter it contained lying about when she'd gone down to the restaurant.

She went over to it, picked it up and had a silent battle on the subject of going and knocking at the next-door room, and handing the wallet over to Thane. Against that, though, why should she? He'd pushed it at her last night, hadn't he?

The matter was resolved when just then she heard the clear sound of him leaving his room and securing his door. For one panicky moment she thought he was coming to see her, and her heart started to race. Her heartbeats steadied down again, though, when she heard his footsteps moving away in the opposite direction.

Well, she jolly well wasn't going to wait around for him to come back from his breakfast, she decided, pride arriving to give her aggression a much-needed boost. Though before she went anywhere, pride or no pride, her efficient secretarial self surfaced. Unzipping the wallet, she checked its contents. She anticipated that there would be only one copy of the contract inside, and indeed would have been most surprised had the two copies she had originally put there still been there. But everything was as she expected, she saw with a touch of relief—her notes, her shorthand pad and one copy of the contract, now initialled by both Thane and Yazid.

Zipping up the wallet once more, Joss knew she would not leave it lying about now that she had remembered it. When she thought about it, she realised that it made no difference which of them had the wallet, she or Thane, for his room was a replica of hers, so she might as well hide the folder in her room as wait around for him to come back and take it to him. Besides, she wasn't feeling very friendly towards him just now.

Five minutes later she left her room and walked to the lift, knowing that the wallet which she had wrapped in the dress which she had worn last night, and which she had then put inside her suitcase and locked, was as safe as it was going to be.

She descended in the lift wondering if the responsibility of looking after that confidential document which both Thane and Yazid now considered binding had not made her a little paranoid. It was for sure that Thane had no such concern since he was probably, at this very moment, tucking in to a hearty breakfast.

With that thought, she stepped out of the lift, walked about five yards into the vast lobby, then had all the evidence she needed that if Thane had breakfasted, he had made short work of his breakfast. Because, tall, broad-shouldered and straight, he was now standing at the reception desk making some enquiry.

Feeling instantly fluttery inside, Joss had about a second in which to decide whether she was ready to pass the time of day with him in person or if she wasn't. She had intended handing her room key in, but he was standing more or less in the exact spot that she had been making for.

She hesitated, and halted, and it was at that moment that Thane finished his enquiry and turned and spotted her. Feeling frozen, Joss tried to compose her features as, casually, Thane strolled over to her.

What she had expected him to say she had no idea, but after the way he had not so long ago snarled at her, his tone was very much different from the tone she had expected. For, looking down into her face, he asked pleasantly, 'Off to take in the sights?'

'Yes,' she replied, and, with her heart pounding erratically just at the sight of him, she knew she should walk on her way—and yet she seemed powerless to do so.

'Where are you going to start?' Thane, instead of moving on as she fully expected, stayed to enquire.

'I'm—not sure yet,' she replied, her heartbeats racing into overdrive when suddenly he smiled down at her.

'Then maybe I'd better come with you,' he commented, and while not believing her hearing Joss just stood and stared up at him, 'That is,' he began, and she could hear definite chinks of ice entering his voice, 'unless you've arranged other company?'

Wordlessly, she shook her head, and when Thane suddenly smiled again there was no way she could prevent the smile that started somewhere deep inside her from coming out into the open.

'What are we waiting for?' he queried, and before she had in any way collected her breath he had taken her room key from her, deposited it at the desk and turned back to take hold of her arm. Then he was escorting her outside to where several taxis were awaiting customers.

Joss was still finding it difficult to believe that what was happening was actually happening, when she sat in a taxi beside Thane, heading for the Valley of the Kings.

Minutes later she had recovered a little to decide that, since it seemed that the gods had decreed she should have some small time with him, she would snatch at it with both hands. There was no way in which she was going to turn her back on this unexpected bonus. She was going to enjoy every moment of this time of Thane not barking at her, or being generally aggressive. She had a few happy memories of him. Simply—she wanted more.

'The place seems crowded already!' she exclaimed when some while later their taxi-driver pulled up in a car park.

'Word must have got around that in a little while the sun will be unbearable,' Thane replied, and as Joss realised that everyone seemed to have the same idea of getting to the towering sun-scorched hills early before the sun turned everyone into grease spots, he gave the driver a few instructions in Arabic and escorted her away from the taxi.

Joss had no idea if Thane had asked the driver to wait, or what he had told him. But how they got back was, just then, immaterial to her. She was here, in the Valley of the Kings with Thane Addison, the man she loved, and nothing else mattered.

She was happier than she could ever remember as together they first walked through an area where souvenir sellers were pressing anyone who caught their eyes to buy.

'For you, madam,' one man in a green galabiyah and wearing a white headdress implored, holding up a T-shirt.

'No, thank you,' she replied, not firmly enough, she realised.

'But yes, madam,' he insisted, and would have hung it over her arm had not Thane spoke a little sharply to him in Arabic.

She knew better the next time when a similarly dressed trader tried to press a green marble scarab into her hands. Quickly she thrust her hands into her pockets. Then, looking at Thane, she heard him laugh. It was a memory to store forever.

They did buy something before they had run the full gauntlet of the souvenir sellers, though. At least Thane did. 'Just a moment,' he murmured, and taking Joss by the arm he guided her over to where one cheerfully smiling Egyptian was selling hats. 'This one, I think,' he said, taking up a white cotton one. And before Joss knew what he was about, he had gone through the good-humoured game of bargaining for it, and had then paid for it and was turning to place it on her head.

Instinctively her hands went up to adjust it. 'Does it look all right?' she asked, and found she was having difficulty in breathing as, having invited his inspection, she found herself looking up into a pair of serious grey eyes.

'You've been told you're beautiful, of course,' he commented, his expression unsmiling.

But, while she was thrilled that Thane thought her beautiful, she didn't want him serious, not now, not at this time of her storing up happy memories. For 'serious' was only a few steps away from 'aggression', she felt. So she replied, 'Of course,' and grinned cheekily up at him. For a second or two he continued to survey her solemnly.

Then suddenly, to her immense delight, he grinned in return, and Joss's cup of happiness was full.

It was an upward climb to the tombs of the kings, but no one was hurrying. Roads had been made in the rocky sun-drenched hillside where not one blade of grass grew as far as Joss could see.

The hills were impressive, as too were the tombs that had been hewn out of the rock. 'Have you been here before?' she asked Thane as they stood in a small queue waiting to descend into the tomb of Rameses the Sixth.

'It's always worth a second or third visit,' he replied pleasantly, and indeed, Joss was spellbound when their turn came to descend the deep stairway, and to see the splendid wall drawings of over three thousand years ago.

They had to queue a second time when, having climbed up from what were the depths, they moved to the smallest tomb, that of Tutankhamun. There were excellent frescoes to be seen, and, while most of the artefacts had been transferred to the Egyptian Museum in Cairo, the golden sarcophagus that had held the mummified body of the young king was absolutely breathtaking in its splendour.

Joss blinked against the bright sunlight when she and Thane came out from the tomb, and she had no demur to make when he told her, 'Put your sunglasses on.' For once she was rather enjoying being bossed about by him.

With the day hotting up uncomfortably, however, they did not stay in the Valley of the Kings for much longer than to take in a couple of lesser known tombs and to generally absorb the atmosphere. Then Thane, with a glance at her fair skin, was suggesting that they returned the way they had come.

'We'll stop and quench our thirst somewhere less crowded,' he mooted, eyeing the large refreshment building where the world and all comers were milling about.

'Fine,' Joss replied, her heart lifting. Her time, this time, this special precious time with him, wasn't over yet, then!

The taxi-driver *was* waiting and, spotting them straight away, he immediately left a group of other drivers he had been happily chatting with and came hurrying back to his taxi.

Maybe it was because her discovery that she was in love with Thane had made her time with him so precious, but it seemed that time was going fast when, in next to no time, she was seated with him in the cool garden room of a hotel. She had half drunk the glass of lemonade in front of her, while Thane had all but finished his.

To her delight, however, he seemed in no hurry to escort her back to their hotel, but appeared to have all the time in the world as they discussed any topic that occurred to them. By unspoken mutual consent, it seemed, not once did either of them mention work. Though when she was positively itching to know more about him, it was Joss who was on the answering end of the questioning. 'Do you live at home with your parents?' he enquired idly on one occasion.

She shook her head and, taking another sip of her lemonade, revealed, 'My parents live in Eastbourne. I left home some years ago.'

'You have a flat?'

'A small one, but mine own,' she smiled, and took another drink of her lemonade when she observed that his glass was empty. 'At least, I'm buying it courtesy of a mortgage,' she added, and wanted quite desperately to ask him about his parents and if he had a flat, a house, or whatever. But suddenly nerves—which prior to her knowledge that she loved him had been non-existent—were starting to bite. What if he thought she was deliberately prolonging drinking her lemonade just to keep him in conversation? On that pride-threatening thought, Joss finished the rest of her lemonade.

Then, like music in her ears, she heard Thane enquire pleasantly, 'Where to now?'

'Um…' she hesitated, wondering if she should take up more of his time. But she loved him, and suddenly she could no more turn down what the gods were offering than fly. Perhaps she was being greedy, but she had been in Thane's company, his pleasant company, for a couple of hours now—and she wanted more. So she told him, 'I haven't been to a bazaar yet,' adding quickly, 'A proper one, I mean—not the touristy one.'

'I know exactly what you mean,' he smiled, and to prove it a taxi was soon dropping them off in a market place where she could see no sign of any other European.

Like a miser Joss stored up memory after memory, of galabiyah-robed men, and of women clothed from head to foot all in black. Of stalls of oranges and green bananas. Of dusty, sandy streets, of rush-woven baskets.

There were more attractive sights than the fly-smothered meat laid bare on an open-air butcher's table, but it all added up to an entirely fantastic atmosphere as far as she was concerned. The most gigantic cabbages she had ever seen were for sale from one trader, while opposite him a young man was selling a whole range of aromatic spices.

Then, to crown what was for her the most wonderful of experiences, they came to a part of the market where on the outside of a small building, and hanging high in the air, were rugs of many different hues and sizes.

'That one is just crying out to go home to my dining-room,' Joss told Thane a trace regretfully, and before she knew what was happening, he had put his hand on her elbow and was guiding her inside. And, all before she had time to observe that there were shelves and shelves of silks and cottons, a couple of stools had been conjured up out of somewhere, both she and Thane had a glass of tea in their hands, and the rug she had admired was laid out on the floor for their inspection.

The rug was larger than she had at first thought, but that was a point in its favour from her point of view. Though she had to own to a feeling of being swept along by the trader's enthusiasm, and she was glad of Thane's calming presence when, looking down at her, he enquired, 'Is it still crying out to go to your home?'

'It's beautiful!' she breathed, and raised gentle brown velvety eyes to his. For a second then, as without a word Thane stared into her eyes, she thought she felt a sudden tension in the air. Then nerves got to her, nerves that he might see her caring for him in her eyes, and swiftly she turned her attention back to the carpet. 'Truly beautiful,' she added, 'but I can't possibly buy it.'

Long moments of silence followed, and she thought Thane was not going to make any comment. But, just as she thought they would thank the carpet-seller for his tea, and leave, Thane remarked, 'I think you could get it for as little as sixty English pounds.'

'Honestly?' she exclaimed, and, her appetite well and truly whetted, 'But how will I get it home?' she queried, unable to see herself rolling it up and carrying it over her shoulder, no matter how hard she tried.

'Leave it to me—I'll show you a trick,' he teased, and she loved him, and after much haggling which embarrassed her slightly but which the carpet-seller, his assistants and in fact everyone else seemed to take thorough delight in, she bought the rug which it had never been her intention to buy when she had left her bed that morning.

Then Thane was taking her in a taxi to air-freight it back to England. She was still in a state of euphoria when he suggested lunch.

She was sitting across the table from him, however, when she realised why it was that he was being so kind to her that day. With the initialling of that contract, he was released from the stresses of his business problems for a while. Today he could relax and make the most of a well-earned break.

Which thought made her sensitive to him and made her want him to enjoy the day as much as she was enjoying it. So she put any reserves of shyness and pride aside, and chatted in friendly fashion throughout lunch, and discovered, without quite knowing how the subject had come up, that she was telling him about her hankering to see the Pyramids.

'You haven't seen the Pyramids yet?' he enquired, in some small surprise.

'I've been to Cairo twice,' she informed him, and just had to smile as she added, 'My boss is a bit of a slave-driver and...'

'Say no more,' he cut in, his eyes on the sweet curve of her mouth. 'If you'll permit me, I'll have words with him and see if we can't arrange for you to visit the Pyramids one day soon.' Joss saw the light of laughter dancing in his eyes, and fell deeper in love with him than ever.

When she had finished her meal and had begun to think that her day with him was over, however, she could hardly believe her good fortune that it seemed it was not!

'Have you had enough?' Thane enquired, and she was unsure if he meant to eat, or of sightseeing.

'You've been very kind,' she replied quietly.

'Which means that you'd like to see more, but that

you're afraid of encroaching on my time?' Thane guessed, giving her a heart-fluttering amicable look.

'Something like that,' she murmured, and absolutely adored him when he replied,

'After the way I've worked you, I think that to put myself at your disposal for the whole of today is the least I can do.'

They were on their way to see the Temple of Karnak, with Joss being of the opinion that of the two of them he had certainly worked the harder, when she wondered if he had grown to like her. He must like her, mustn't he? Or was it just a case of two English people who knew each other and, with nothing else pressing, were simply passing a day in each other's company?

At that point Joss realised how ready she was to gather up any crumb of a suggestion that Thane liked her. But, since he was never likely to tell her—and probably never gave such matters a moment's thought—she would be content with what she had and to do all she could to ensure that nothing should spoil this most wonderful of days.

That the Temple of Karnak was impressive was, she thought, an understatement. The place was alive with tourists, and as Joss walked with Thane through a corridor where ram-headed sphinx-like statues flanked either side of the walkway, she was once more in awe. There was much to see, for the complex of the temple was, as well as being magnificent, enormous. It housed the Hypostyle Hall, which was reputed to be the largest hall of any temple in the world. At one time it had been the religious centre of Thebes and a place where for two thousand years the Pharaohs had built their monuments.

All in all there was much too much for Joss to absorb in one visit, and she knew she would be foolish to try. So she settled for being content just to be there—and with Thane.

'You'll be exhausted if we carry on at this rate,' he teased as they came away from the temple, and while she thrilled to his teasing, she was positively overjoyed when he suggested, 'How about returning to our hotel for an hour or two, then coming back here for the Son et Lumière tonight? We could fit in dinner afterwards.'

Joss tried desperately hard not to instantly grab at his suggestion. 'That sounds very nice,' she accepted pleasantly, and was further delighted when he hired a horse-drawn calèche to take them back to the hotel, then—and she knew she was fooling herself, but by then she didn't care—just as if he couldn't bear to be parted from her, Thane proposed that they shared a pot of tea in one of the lounges before they went up to their rooms.

By that lovely time, it was already dusk. 'See you in an hour,' Thane said as they parted, and Joss went into her room and closed the door, unable to believe that, incredibly, she had spent a whole day with Thane with not one cross or harsh word passing between them.

She had a quick shower and wondered if it was because of her new-found love for him that she was not flaring up at the least little pinprick. Or was it on account of the fact that Thane had not delivered any barbed comments that day? Whatever it was, it was marvellous to have Thane in this relaxed and charming mood. She had never felt happier.

A slight dent was to appear in her feeling of happiness a short while later, however. She had changed into fresh trousers and opted to wear a lightweight sweater. She then decided that, since Thane had said they would have dinner after the Son et Lumière, an embroidered cotton shirt would be more appropriate. Time was running short when she exchanged the sweater for a shirt, and she was just in the middle of recombing her hair when for no particular reason she turned her head in the direction of the door, and for the first time noticed what she had been too much involved with her thoughts to notice before. Someone, at some time, had slipped a note under her door.

Swiftly she went and picked it up and opened out the missive to find it was from Khalil. Her spirits dipped as she read that he had been trying and trying to get in touch with her that day. Had she not realised that he would do so? he asked. Would she please telephone him the moment she received his letter? He would wait by the telephone until then.

Slowly Joss wandered over to the telephone. She did not want to ring Khalil, she admitted. But then neither did she want him to spend any more time waiting by the phone. Not that she truly believed that he was doing anything of the sort. But... Her thoughts suddenly ceased when just then she heard the sound of Thane leaving his room. In a flash she was over at her dressing-table, slipping Khalil's note into a drawer while at the same time she took up the comb and hastily tidied up her hair.

Then the buzzer at the side of her door sounded, and she went to answer it. Thane had changed too, and her heart beat crazily at just the sight of him as he looked into her face for several long moments. Then a lazy kind of smile crossed his features, a smile she found attractive and heartwarming, as he remarked, 'You'll need a jacket.'

'Won't be a moment,' she told him, and dipped back into her room to take a lightweight windcheater out of her wardrobe.

Thane had not spoken falsely about her need of a jacket, Joss discovered, for by the time they returned to the Temple of Karnak, something of a sandstorm was blowing up. She was most glad of her windcheater when the Son et Lumière proved to be unlike any sound and light show she had been to before in that they did not at first take seats to sit and watch. At first they stood, with hundreds of other like-minded patrons, held back by a rope until the rope was lowered and they were allowed to move forward through the area where the ram-headed sphinxes she had seen that afternoon still stood guard. They walked some way through tall majestic pillars on which were engraved in deep relief the tales of gods and kings. They then came to another roped-off area, and clear female and then male voices intoned over loudspeakers the story of ancient Thebes while lights played on walls and monuments.

Joss was totally entranced as that rope too was lowered and Thane took hold of her arm lest, in the crush of people surging forward, they got separated.

A swirl of wind caused her hair to fly and she closed her eyes as a shower of sand made straight for her. 'Have you got your hat with you?' Thane bent down to ask.

'My sun-hat?'

'This is no time for vanity,' he said, and in the darkness she was sure that he was smiling.

She smiled too, realising as she put her hand into her shoulder-bag that at one time she might have reared up at his remark—missing his humour entirely. A second later she was taking the hat he had bought her out of her bag and pulling it down on her head.

In all, she thought they walked around for about an hour, and although by then she felt decidedly gritty from the sand and in the most definite need of a bath, she would not have missed the experience for anything. Though she full well knew that a good deal of her pleasure stemmed from the fact that she was there with Thane.

He must be enjoying it too, she felt, because although he must be suffering too from the gritty effects of the sandstorm, he had made no suggestion to abandon the show, as a few people around them had.

The finale of Son et Lumière took place at the Sacred Lake, and it was here, facing the lake, that row upon row of seats had been installed. Joss spent the most blissful half-hour just seated next to Thane. The commentary passed her by as she gave herself up to the pure enjoyment of sitting next to him in the dark, where he was not likely to see the truth in her eyes, and of loving him.

'Enjoy that?' he enquired, once the performance was over and they, along with those that remained, made their way along the rows of seats to the exits.

'Wouldn't have missed it for anything,' she told him truthfully. 'How about you?'

'What's a bit of sand between friends?' he replied, and she thought, Oh, Thane, I do so love you!

'What indeed?' she laughed, totally enchanted by him—he had suggested that they were friends.

'I don't know about you, but I could do with a shower before we eat,' he said a minute or so later when, with everyone scrambling for taxis, the taxi they had arrived in drew up beside them.

Inwardly, Joss was laughing. Trust him to have transport organised, she thought, as they got into the taxi. 'That's one of the best suggestions I've heard all day,' she smiled, and leaned back contentedly. Unbelievably, her day with Thane was not yet over. Once they had returned to the hotel and washed the sand away, they would meet again for a meal.

'How long?' she questioned when at the doors of their rooms they were about to separate. 'Half an hour?' she suggested.

'You've a head start on most other women.' Thane looked back at her. 'Make it twenty minutes.'

Joss was still inwardly laughing when, inside her room, she hurriedly brushed the sand from her hair, then stripped off and got into the shower. Oh, how she loved him! There would be no time to wash her hair, she mused happily, but who cared, she'd put up with that for the chance of seeing Thane again so soon.

She was just stepping out of the shower, though, when, making her realise that she had spent longer than she had intended over her ablutions, she heard her door buzzer sound.

Blotting most of the moisture from her skin, she tossed the towel back into the bathroom and quickly reached for her housecoat. Head start on most other women or no, she was just going to have to beg Thane for those ten extra minutes.

'I'm not…' she began as she pulled back the door, but her voice tailed off, for it was not Thane who stood there, but Khalil Rashwan. A Khalil Rashwan who was looking most upset. Suddenly Joss sensed trouble. 'Khalil…' she said his name in some instinctive move to ward off what—she wasn't sure.

'Why did you not telephone me?' he asked her angrily.

'I—er—haven't had time,' she replied honestly, if, she realised later, not very tactfully.

'You had my letter, but you didn't have time…' Khalil choked, his face working. 'Did I not tell you that I would wait?'

'Yes, but—' she tried to get in to calm him down, but could see when he took a step nearer to her that she had made things worse, not better.

'I've waited all this day for you to call me!' he ranted as she quickly took a step back. Then as he took another step forward and she backed again, she discovered that they were both in her room and that Khalil was going completely out of control. 'Don't you know what is in my heart for you?' he cried, and before she could stop him he had made a sudden lunge for her and made a desperate attempt to kiss her.

Panicking wildly, Joss equally desperately tried to make sure that he did not kiss her. There were only one man's lips she wanted—anyone else's would be offensive. Saving her breath to help with her energy, she pushed with all her might to break the suffocating embrace of the arms he had about her. Then suddenly, through her panic, she heard a mighty roar—and it did not come from Khalil. For Thane was all at once there, and in no time she was free.

Not that Khalil let her go voluntarily, but when Thane caught hold of him, he had no other choice. She had thought Thane might be physically powerful. He proved it. As if Khalil weighed nothing, he plucked him away from her. Then, after letting fly with a stream of Arabic directed at Khalil, Thane let fly with his fist and sent him sprawling. Khalil was still sitting in a stunned heap, when with more unfriendly-sounding Arabic Thane went over and threw him out of the room.

Having looked on with horrified eyes, Joss didn't know what to do first, go and see if Khalil was all right, or thank Thane for coming in when he had.

The decision about what to do, however, was resolved when Thane slammed the door on Khalil and turned back to her. But when Joss opened her mouth to thank him, she was shaken to see that he looked in no mood to want her thanks. Just one glance at his enraged expression was enough to tell her that if he was furious with Khalil Rashwan, then he was doubly furious with her, and she somehow got the impression that she'd be better off not saying anything at all!

CHAPTER EIGHT

WORDLESSLY Joss stared at Thane's hostile and unfriendly expression, and her spirits sank lower than ever. How she had ever thought or hoped never to see him hostile with her again, she couldn't think, because, as if they had not exchanged one pleasant word with each other all that wonderful day, he was now looking at her with positive chips of dislike in his eyes.

'I warned you!' he rounded on her, his grating tone all the confirmation she needed that the wonder of the day had been one-sided only—dear heaven, had she been in a fool's paradise! 'I told you he was panting to get you into bed,' he snarled, enraged, 'yet you still had to encourage him!'

'I didn't encourage him!' Joss erupted; she might be hurting inside, but she was nobody's doormat. 'All I...'

'Of course you encouraged him!' barked Thane, his hands clenching and unclenching down by his side. 'Just as you encourage every man who comes within your orbit! You...'

'That's most unfair!' she flew in explosively. 'I...'

'Is it?' he rapped. 'Like hell it is! You've been giving me the green light all day, for one!' he told her thunderously, and as Joss gasped and just had to defend herself against that—even if she lied herself silly—he came up close to her, his jaw jutting at a furious angle.

'I've done nothing of the sort!' she retorted. She had backed away from Khalil, but she stood her ground as she told Thane heatedly, 'If you've imagined for a moment

142

that I've been giving you so much as a pale green light, then do you have one heck of an imagination!'

'Imagined it, did I?' he bellowed, and, clearly needled by her refusal to back down, 'We'll see, shall we!' he roared, and the next Joss knew was that he had hauled her into his arms and that his mouth was over hers.

'No!' She tried to push him away when she had the breath, but Thane was stronger than she, and furious into the bargain.

'Oh, but yes,' he grated, and claimed her lips again, pulling her housecoat-clad figure closer and yet closer to him, seeming to become the more enraged the more she struggled. 'Keep that up, sweetheart,' he told her harshly when next she managed to get her mouth free, 'and I shan't need any more encouragement!'

Abruptly, as the realisation flooded in that, instead of making Thane see that she didn't want his harsh kisses, she was only inflaming him to desire instead, Joss ceased struggling in his arms.

Thane kissed her again and, as he realised that she was no longer fighting him, some of the anger went from his kiss. Joss felt his kiss gentle out, and suddenly she found it impossible to just stand passive in his arms. She became vibrantly aware of him, of the freshly showered smell of him, and as all at once he pulled her that bit closer to him, suddenly she was leaning against him.

Time stood still for her as Thane kissed her and trailed kisses down her throat. In his arms was where she wanted to be—nothing else mattered. Her arms went up and around him, and her fingers went to his hair, still damp from the shower. 'Oh, Thane,' she breathed, and revelled in the feeling of closeness with him when he moved with her to lie down on the top of her bed.

Again and again he kissed her, and as a fire sprang to

urgent life within her Joss responded ardently to his every kiss. When he pressed himself to her, she responded by pressing herself against him.

Desire for him spiralled in her so that she almost cried out his name again. Then some faint memory stirred that she was naked under her housecoat when Thane slipped his hand inside the front opening.

She clutched him desperately when his fingers unerringly came to circle her left breast, but she had no objection to make when he parted the folds of her gown and gazed down at the hardened pink peaks of her swollen breasts.

When he bent his head to kiss each breast in turn, Joss, with shaky fingers, undid the buttons on his shirt. A sigh of pure satisfaction left her when, after a few minutes of tenderly stroking and caressing her, Thane lowered his hair-roughened naked chest over the top of her uncovered silken breasts.

'Oh!' she sighed, in rapture at feeling his skin against her skin, his warmth against her warmth. Then Thane was kissing her again, and suddenly she was in a mindless vortex of wanting. Nothing mattered but Thane and that they shared of themselves in the most intimate way that there was.

She wanted to tell him there and then, I'm yours, but shyness suddenly attacked from nowhere and, when she had thought she no longer had any inhibitions, she was all at once too shy to tell him anything of what she was feeling.

Those unforeseen inhibitions were to trip her up yet again a moment later when Thane, after unbuttoning her housecoat the rest of the way, began to lay aside the folds and moved his head as if about to feast his eyes on the rest of her uncovered body.

'I...' she gasped chokily, and instinctively made to pull the folds of her housecoat close to again. A moment after that, she had recovered from her shyness, and was ready to make a small apology for being so self-conscious—now of all times.

But her apology never made it. For suddenly Thane had stilled, and as she looked up into his face, as he stared down at her pinkened skin and into her large melting eyes, it was as though he had suddenly come to to remember how furious he had been with her.

Then, to her utter bewilderment, he had rapidly jerked away from her and, having left the bed, his fury had returned when, glancing back to her, he snarled, 'Do your buttons up!'

More in haste than dignity, Joss sat up and somehow managed to expose more of her full breasts. With trembling hands she hastily pulled the edges of her robe together.

'W-what did I do?' she asked, still in a no-man's-land, and sorely needing some guidance.

'Do?' he charged. 'Plenty!' And while she just sat there and stared in stupefied amazement, he turned before her very eyes into the man she had once hated but had thought, in her naïveté, that she would never see again. 'Thanks to you and your wanton behaviour you've ruined what has taken me months to achieve!' he berated her arctically.

'I...!' she gasped, and could hardly credit any of this. Though as a degree of reasoning started to enter her brain she realised that he must be referring to the fact that Khalil Rashwan would have gone home to his father nursing a swollen jaw. In a flash she was on her feet and holding her robe close to her, grabbing at what pride she could find to say hotly, 'It wasn't me who hit Khalil Rashw...'

'No—you were satisfied to lead him on—right up to your bedroom door!' Thane scorched her ears. And while she was swallowing that, 'Well, I've news for you, Miss Harding,' he told her acidly. 'Beacon Oil doesn't do business that way.' Shaken rigid by what he had just said, Joss momentarily lost her grip on her housecoat. She saw a pulse beat in his temple as her robe parted at her breast, but she was totally unprepared for the fresh shock of his curt, 'Consider yourself no longer in the company's employ!'

She was staring after him open-mouthed when, with that, he went towards the door. Before he could open it, though, she was rocketing outraged from her shock. Perhaps it had taken the shock of what he had just said to negate the other helping of shock he had dealt her. But whatever the cause, she was instantly furious, and not likely to keep quiet about it.

'You can't dismiss me!' she shrieked, more enraged than ever that he was daring to serve *her* with the same dismissal treatment he had served Paula Ingram. 'I resign,' she spat. 'You can take your job and...' Her voice faded as she realised she was talking to the air. Thane had gone and had slammed her door shut behind him.

How could he? The swine, the diabolical swine! Who did he think he was, to tell her that she was dismissed? How could a man hold her in his arms one minute, the way he had done, and then tell her in the next that she was no longer in the company's employ?

For all of five shattered minutes, Joss could think of nothing else. Then suddenly, as pride arrived in great all-consuming measure, she was galvanised into action. In no time at all, spurred on by fury and outraged pride, she, who had never in her life been dismissed from a job, was furiously throwing things into her case and getting out of there.

'Taxi?' asked a taxi-driver the moment she put her nose outside the hotel.

'The airport,' she told him and, handing him her case, she did not first agree the fare as some weeks ago Baz Barton had advised. To her way of thinking any price would be agreeable so long as it took her far enough away from that monstrous swine Thane Addison.

She was still in high fury when the taxi-driver handed her back her case at Luxor airport. Who the *hell* did Thane Addison think he was? she railed as she went to find out the chance of a flight to Alexandria.

A flight to Alexandria was out, she discovered, though the next plane out was a delayed flight to Cairo. She supposed the sandstorm must have something to do with the delay, but somehow she suddenly felt it more imperative that she get out of Luxor with all speed than to worry where her plane landed. She booked a flight to Cairo.

The plane had taken off, with her on board, before it occurred to her that perhaps she wasn't thinking very rationally. Because as her thoughts turned to the next step, that of taking a flight from Cairo home to England, she remembered that quite a few of her belongings were back at the apartment in Alexandria.

A few seconds later, however, she experienced a moment's rebellion, and suddenly she was of the opinion that any clothes and belongings she had in Alexandria could jolly well stay there. She was going home—to England.

Although Joss remained of the view that she would not return to Alexandria to pick up the remainder of her things, the rest of her rebellion was short-lived. She tried hard to stay angry by telling herself that Thane Addison really was a swine—where had his famous diplomacy been when he'd taken a swing at Khalil Rashwan? That was what she'd like to know.

It was the simple fact of a stewardess coming and bringing round cheese sandwiches that triggered a weakening in Joss's harsh thoughts. Only then did she remember that she hadn't had any dinner. Which memory brought on another memory, the memory of how she had been going to dine with Thane that evening, of her excitement, and of looking forward to him calling for her.

A dry sob rose up in her throat, she choked it back, and blinked several times. She wouldn't cry, she would not. Oh, how could he have acted towards her the way that he had? How could the fates have been so unfair as to allow her to spend such a sublime day, when they had waiting in store for her such utter misery?

The flight to Cairo took fifty minutes, and, having landed and collected her case from the carousel, Joss decided to go and see about a flight to England. Her thoughts were still on Thane as she went—this time, on how he had threatened her with dismissal at the very outset.

He hadn't dismissed her for falling in love with him— that he had no idea of how she felt about him was the only bright spot in any of this. No, what he'd dismissed her for was because she'd ruined his weeks of solid work, which had culminated in him and Khalil's father initialling that contract. Thane had…

Abruptly, her thoughts shut off. Suddenly as the words 'that contract' played back in her mind she stood stock still and let her case fall to the ground. Yazid Rashwan might in his anger tear up his copy of that initialled contract, but there was another copy of that document— and she had it—in her suitcase!

Feeling totally stunned, Joss picked up her case and

reeled to a chair to try and get her head together. Several thoughts began to crowd her mind at once then, one of them being that while Yazid Rashwan might well be furious with Thane for hitting his beloved son on the jaw, Yazid was still the same man of honour, wasn't he?

Even so, even if after due consideration he did not tear up his copy of the contract, she just couldn't pretend that she did not have Beacon's copy of that highly confidential document in her possession. Dismissed she might be, though she preferred to believe she had resigned, but no efficient secretary worth the name would just dump a document like that, no matter how they had been treated. Well, maybe they would, she thought a moment later, but not if they were in love with the swine who had dismissed them.

Joss faced the fact that she was feeling very confused. What she was not confused about, however, was that she did not want to see Thane again. Never would she forget his 'You've been giving me the green light all day'—nor the way she'd shown him just how much she hadn't been giving him the green light, by putting up no more than minimal resistance when he had taken her in his arms.

She turned her thoughts away from such a painful memory, but, much as she shied away from having to see Thane again, she realised that she could not return to England without handing that document over to someone.

Once she had reached that conclusion, the decision seemed made for her. She left the airport building in search of a taxi, and planned it out as she went. She would deliver that contract to Malcolm Cooper at the Cairo office tomorrow. She would ask Malcolm to let Thane know that he had it, and also ask Malcolm to keep it in his safe until Thane either called for it, or sent someone for it.

'Taxi?' a fatherly-looking Egyptian man enquired.

Joss, with her thoughts on making for some hotel, since she couldn't stay at the airport overnight, nor could she camp out on the office doorstep until someone arrived to let her in, gave the driver her case and unthinkingly said the first thing to come into her head.

'Giza,' she told him for her destination, and realised that her head wasn't so clear as she had thought. Though when the driver, without turning a hair, closed the door on her and started up his taxi, she shrugged and thought that a hotel in Giza was as good a place as any.

He seemed a talkative driver, and spoke English to some degree. But when at any other time Joss might have been ready to pass a few pleasantries with him, she was starting to feel used up. Talk between them therefore consisted only of her telling him that she wanted to go to a good standard of hotel, and of him replying that he thought he knew one which would suit.

'You are on holiday?' he did try, but lapsed into silence after her monosyllabic reply.

'No,' she told him affably.

It was just over half an hour later, when he pulled up outside a hotel in Giza, when Joss started to realise just how confused she must be. Because, when she had had the ideal opportunity back at the airport to book her flight to England, she only then realised that she had not done so.

'Thank you very much,' she told the driver as he carried her luggage inside the hotel, and, just in case she had hurt his feelings by being such a silent passenger, she gave him a generous tip.

'Enjoy your stay here!' he beamed, and left her to it, and Joss approached the reception desk with her fingers crossed that she would be *able* to stay here. With her mind so elsewhere occupied, she just hadn't given thought to the fact that they might not have a room to spare.

Her worry proved groundless, however, for regardless of the hour—for it was by then two in the morning—the very pleasant man on duty seemed not to be able to do enough for her. 'Of course, madam,' he replied, with his dark-eyed glance on her creamy complexion and ash-blonde hair. 'How long will you be staying?'

'For one night only,' she told him, and, since he seemed to want to be helpful, 'Is it possible for me to book a flight to England from here?'

'For you—I am sure,' he smiled.

Half an hour later, given a hiccup or two in the booking of her flight, Joss was shown up to a room on the third floor, her flight booked for that afternoon.

A glance at her watch showed it was half-past two, and although she felt weary but not sleepy, she supposed she had better get into bed. Unstrapping her case, she took out her toilet articles and nightclothes and then, what was now becoming 'that wretched contract' in her mind, she extracted her leather document case from the folds of her cream silk dress, and checked the contents. Everything was there, she noted, and she put the document wallet back in her case and closed the lid. Then she washed, changed and got into bed.

She put the light out—nightmare thoughts crept in. She put the light on again, and lay there wide awake, her head abuzz with all that had so catastrophically happened. She hadn't led Khalil on to that extent, despite what Thane said. It was Thane himself who had more or less told her not to offend Khalil. Oh, it just wasn't fair, it just wasn't!

She fell into a light doze, wishing she could hate Thane for longer than short bursts. But she loved him, that love seeming to be without pride. For even after the way he had spoken to her, she still loved him.

Joss drifted to full wakefulness twenty minutes later, and twenty minutes after that she made more determined efforts to get some sleep by turning out her bedside lamp.

Her sleep was a little deeper that time, and a little longer. Though it was still dark outside when at just after quarter to five she was wakened from her slumbers by the town's faithful being called to prayer by a disembodied voice echoing from a loudspeaker over the rooftops.

Joss sat up, glad of the company. Somewhere a dog barked and a camel made its presence known, and, by then so wide awake that she knew there was no chance of getting back to sleep again, she consigned herself to sit and listen.

All the while the prayers and chanting went on she was making gallant efforts to push Thane from her mind. When shortly after five the chanting stopped, she had no chance to concentrate on anything else, and Thane, Thane, Thane whirled round in her brain.

Which was why, when at fifteen minutes past five the telephone on her bedside rang, she was glad of the distraction—any distraction would have been welcomed. She picked it up, knowing in advance that someone must have booked an alarm call for five-fifteen and that the night porter, or whoever attended to such matters, must have got the room number wrong.

She had meant, when she spoke, to quote her room number, but what she actually said, her wide-awake tone belying that she needed any alarm call, was 'Hello?'

Then she almost collapsed with shock and thought that, with having Thane so much on her mind, she must have gone over the edge. Because the voice that answered was

the voice of the man she loved! Incredibly, it was—
Thane!

'Joss,' he stated evenly, 'I'd like to see you.'

Thane! He…! What…? She took a deep breath, and
suddenly her heart leapt—Thane wanted to see her.
'I'm…' she began, then, like lead, her soaring spirits
plummeted. Oh, what an idiot she was! Of course Thane
wanted to see her—though not her at all really. More precisely, he'd remembered that she had that contract, and
he'd have made contact with the devil himself in order to
have that contract he'd worked so hard on restored to him.
Pride, which she had thought had deserted her, then
charged to the rescue, and somehow she had made her
voice as cool as his had been as she told him airily, 'That
might prove a little difficult.'

He didn't like her tone, she knew he didn't, it was all
there in the one sharp word he rapped back at her. 'Why?'
he asked tersely.

'With you in Luxor and me in Cairo…' She broke off
as only then did the magnitude of what was happening
strike her. Heavens above—how on earth had Thane
known she had left Luxor—that she had flown to Cairo?
Or even, more astonishingly, which hotel she had booked
into?

'In point of fact, I'm not in Luxor,' his voice came
again when it appeared he thought he'd waited long
enough for her to finish what she had started to say.

'Y-you're—not?'

'No,' he replied shortly.

'You're in Cairo?' she guessed, hoping with all she had
that she was wrong, because it would really be much better if she did not see him again. Her way of getting that
contract to him was much the better idea.

'No,' he replied again, and for all of a second Joss

breathed a sigh of relief. But that was before he added coolly, 'I'm in Giza.'

Suddenly her hand was gripping tightly on to the phone. Thane was here—in Giza! All at once her hands went moist, then in contrast her throat went dry. And as she went to speak her voice came out sounding husky when she put the question which she was beginning to think she knew the answer to before she asked it. That question, 'Which—h-hotel?'

'The same one you're in,' he replied.

'The same...' she echoed, her voice fading—she was shaken, even if he had confirmed what she had started to suspect.

'I'm along the corridor from you,' Thane told her, his tone taking on a crisp note, when, businesslike and a man with never a minute to spare, he went on abruptly, 'I've a meeting at eight—is it convenient if I come and see you now?'

Now! His forthright question sent Joss, who had never before knowing him dithered in her life, into something of a dither. No, no, no, said her head. Oh, yes, said her heart. She remembered how he had been the last time she had seen him, his accusation that she had given him the green light, and never, said her pride. Against that, though, was the fact that he had laboured hard and long in pulling off that contract. What more natural than that he should chase after her to get it? It would only take a moment to hand it over to him; she didn't even have to say one single word to him.

'Well?' he barked shortly, clearly not liking to be kept holding on while she made up her mind.

'Quite convenient!' she snapped, and slammed the phone down.

She was glad to feel angry with him, although unfortunately she could not sustain that anger. In seconds after slamming down the phone she went absolutely haywire. There was no sign of the unflappable Miss Josslyn Harding then as, leaping out of bed, she didn't know what to do first—run a comb through her hair, get into her housecoat or get the contract Thane was coming for out of her case.

Before she had done more than button up her housecoat and extract the wallet from her suitcase, though, and all before she was ready, she heard Thane's light tap on her door. She supposed she should be grateful that he was considerate of the other residents. Thane being Thane, it wouldn't have surprised her if he hadn't taken out his frustration that she'd waltzed off with the contract by thumping on the wood panelling. Hastily, taking up the leather wallet as she went, she sped to the door before he should get fed up with waiting and start to do just that.

At the door, however, her nerve momentarily disappeared, and she had to take a very deep breath before she reached down to the door-handle.

Her deep breath was meant to be a steadying one, but it was a waste of time. For as soon as the door was open, and she stood faced with Thane, her colour flared and her legs went like jelly. Oh, how dear to her he was, she fretted, as she looked at the tallness of him, and observed that he was dressed in shirt and slacks. He seemed newly shaven, she thought, but there was a look of strain about his eyes that worried her. Those eyes, though, seemed to be dissecting every aspect of her face, but although she knew he had come for the contents of the leather wallet, he was making no move to take it from her.

As yet, neither of them had spoken a word, but suddenly, as her high colour faded, Joss saw unhappily that there was no need for words. Everything that had needed saying between them had been said.

Wordlessly she lifted the document case and pushed it at him. Wordlessly his eyes left hers and he glanced down at the wallet she was offering. Though when she thought it must be some relief to him that the company's confidence had not been broken and that he could rest easy now that he had retrieved the contract, he suddenly absolutely astounded her. For instead of taking the document case from her—which surely he must have recognised from having seen it before—he did no such thing. But, raising a hand, instead he pushed it back at her.

Even more astounding, though alarming was more appropriate, Joss felt, was the way he then unceremoniously pushed his way into her room, and as she stepped back he deliberately closed the door.

Then, with his eyes going over her from the tip of her tousled blonde head to the toes of her mule-attired feet, he took the wallet from her and tossed it on to the bed. 'I didn't come for *that*!' he clipped, and suddenly, as all at once she noted the dangerous glint in his eyes, her insides started to tremble. She did not know why then he had come, but she had never known him sound so tough— or so determined!

CHAPTER NINE

NEVER more did Joss desperately need some composure, but as she stared at Thane all she felt was one agitated mass of inner turmoil. Eventually, however, she managed to find her voice, but it was only a trifle as cool as she had wanted to sound. 'You—might have said. You could have saved yourself a visit.'

'I—wanted to—see you,' Thane replied, and although he could not be meaning anything personal, what he answered nevertheless caused her heart to beat faster.

'It—er—must have been important—for you to follow me from Luxor,' she retorted, still trying to sound cool but, with Thane now holding her stare and refusing to let her look away, having the hardest work in the world just to think clearly. 'Oh...!' she exclaimed as one clear thought did occur to her. 'You must have been coming to Cairo anyway, so...'

She broke off when he made an impatient movement, though he did not contradict that he had been planning to come to Cairo anyway, but agreed, 'It was important, and still is.'

Which, as far as she could see, just had to mean that he was there, despite what he'd said, in connection with that contract which now reposed on her bed. Managing at last to tear her eyes away from his, she glanced to the leather wallet, 'You're sure you didn't come for that contract?' she queried, never having known him tell a lie, but feeling too confused suddenly to find any other answers.

Having looked away from Thane, though, her glance

went shooting back at him when, after a second or two of silence, he told her quietly, 'I came—among other reasons—to apologise.'

The 'other reasons' passed her by. '*You*—apologise?' she queried in amazement, and then found the stiffening she needed, as sarcastically she requested, 'Pardon me while I faint!'

'Am I so bad?' he enquired.

'How long have you got?' she answered spiritedly, and was weakened again when, most surprisingly, she saw the corners of his mouth twitch. Swiftly she went in search of more stiffening. 'So what, *in particular*,' she found more acid, 'are you apologising for?'

His amused look had not stayed around very long, she noticed, for his expression was tough again as though her continued acid tone was starting to needle him. And, as she supposed she might have expected, it didn't take him a second to vanquish her tart tongue. 'Not for damn near seducing you!' he bit sharply, and as pink flared in her cheeks as she was reminded of how small her show of resistance had been once he'd taken her in his arms, he startled her by groaning, 'Oh, confound it, Joss, have you no…?' Abruptly, he broke off, and, even more startling as far as she was concerned, she could have sworn that Thane, who she knew put his signature to deals worth millions without turning a hair, seemed strangely—nervous. 'Look,' he said after a moment, 'can we sit down?'

'It won't take that long, surely?' she replied, loving him, hating him, but above all afraid of giving away the fact that her love for him made her hatred puny by comparison.

'You're not going anywhere for some hours yet,' he retorted, and somehow she had a feeling that he not only knew—when she had told no one—of her plan to be at

Beacon House, Cairo, at nine, but also the time of her flight to England that day. Which, all in all, made her realise that if he could know what thoughts went on in her head, she would be wise to be doubly wary of him.

Somehow she managed to shrug as though it was neither here nor there to her. But, needing to hide her expression from him for a moment, she turned and made for a pair of small easy chairs in the corner of the room, which were separated by a low table placed between them.

'You were apologising, I believe,' she murmured when they were both seated, hoping with all she had as his eyes rested on her that she looked more relaxed than she felt. How she wished there had been time to fling some clothes on—not that to merely hand over that wallet, as she had thought, had in her opinion necessitated getting her best outfit out of the wardrobe. She saw his eyes move to her tousled hair, and wished too that she'd found time to pull a comb through it.

'I *was* apologising,' Thane took up after several moments of not saying anything, but just looking at her. 'I was way out of line in accusing you of leading Khalil Rashwan on when—short of telling him to go and take a running jump, and given that dealing with his crush on you called for some tactful handling—you acted in the only way your loyalty to the company would have you act.'

Crazily her heart gave an upward leap that Thane should now speak to her in full understanding of the difficulties she had faced. Against that, though, was her hurt at the way he had laid into her. Was she such a pathetic creature that, having now received his approbation for her actions, she should smile sweetly and tell him to think nothing more of it? She had to live with herself, didn't she?

'In point of fact, I quite liked Khalil.' Joss at last found the cool note she had wanted earlier. She saw Thane frown, though whether from her tone or what she had said, she didn't know. But he wasn't backward when it came to cutting her off, for as she took a breath to go on he was rapidly there to have his say.

'It didn't look to me as though you were liking him too well when he made a grab for you!' he told her curtly.

'That was different,' she snapped, not too thrilled to have that thrown up at her. 'Well, thank you for your apology,' she went on swiftly, and, taking it that this interview was over, made to get to her feet.

She hurriedly sat down, however, when Thane rose too and stayed her by stretching out his hands to her hands. 'I haven't finished yet,' he told her. 'In fact, I've barely begun.'

'In that case—' She sank into her chair once more, nerves again starting to bite as she snatched her hands away from his tingling touch. She felt a mass of agitation again, and longed for calm as he retook his seat and eyed her levelly. 'Am I to assume,' she said swiftly, 's-since you haven't finished yet, that you regret dismissing me for leading Khalil Rashwan on—right up to my bedroom door, I think you said?' she reminded him, and felt heartily glad to find the tart edge she wanted was there. 'Beacon Oil don't do business that way, I think you also said,' she added for full sarcastic and non-doormat measure.

To her surprise, though, when she fully expected that Thane might have something much more wounding to throw at her in reply, there was not a trace of sarcasm in his answer. Indeed, he seemed to agree that she was right to say what she had. 'I deserve to have that slammed back at me,' he said quietly. Then, after a moment's pause,

'Though there were—extenuating circumstances,' he went on slowly. Then, without pausing to tell her what these extenuating circumstances were, 'Of course you're not dismissed,' he stated. 'You're far too valuable to the company.'

Conversely, Joss did not want to be valuable to the *company*—she wanted to be valuable to *him*. 'I'm still valuable to the company, even though I've lost you that contract?' she queried, trying hard to adopt an uncaring note.

'Lost it?' he questioned.

'I know we've still got our copy,' she replied snappily, throwing him an exasperated look, 'and I know that because of its content it's still a highly confidential document. But if Yazid Rashwan has torn up his copy...'

'What makes you think he'd do anything of that sort?' Thane cut in coolly, and at that, Joss lost control of her temper.

'You're impossible!' she exploded, and raced on hotly, 'And I quote "Thanks to you and your wanton behaviour you've ruined what has taken months to achieve"!'

'Oh, hell!' Thane swore softly, just as though it did not please him to have his remarks quoted back at him. Then, giving her a level look, 'I can explain all that,' he said, but did not do so, but went on, 'It might relieve your mind to know that before I left Luxor I took a phone call from a very concerned Yazid Rashwan.'

'Concerned?' she queried, and, her interest taken, she forgot that Thane had not explained the reason for his offensive remarks.

Thane nodded, then continued, 'Apparently Khalil went home and told him how with a few—sharp words—I'd turfed him out of your room.'

Joss recalled how Thane had let fly with something in

Arabic at Khalil, but that wasn't all she recalled. 'From what I remember,' she told him coolly, 'you hurled, rather than merely "turfed", Khalil out.'

'He deserved it!' he clipped.

'I hope his father appreciated that fact!' she retorted tartly, and was a little open-mouthed at his reply.

'He did,' he told her solemnly. 'His reason for ringing was to tell me how Khalil, while not realising how things were—with you and me—was trying to get—'

'Things between you and me!' she exclaimed, and wished she hadn't. She knew as well as Thane that there was nothing between them—not on his side, anyway—so all she'd done was to bring attention to something she was very much nervous of discussing lest she slipped up in some small way.

'You'll forgive me, I hope, Joss,' he said, his eyes steady on hers as she tried to cover the fact that just his using her first name had made her feel soft about him inside again, 'but, while helping Khalil on his way, I told him that—you were my woman.'

Blankly she stared at him. Even as her heart went wild inside her, she made gigantic efforts to keep her composure as she tried to reason why Thane, given the fury he had been in, should tell Khalil that she was his woman.

Her heart was still on a dizzy merry-go-round—until suddenly she lighted upon the answer. Immediately, her racing heartbeats slowed. Thane would do anything to save that contract. Even while he was furious, his clear-thinking mind would lose none of its sharpness where that contract was concerned.

'Naturally, you'd have to tell him something to excuse hitting him,' she said aloofly. 'Naturally, too...' His dark look made her break off.

'I didn't *have* to tell him…' Suddenly *he* broke off, and most peculiarly Joss thought he looked strangely nervous again. She dismissed the notion as idiotic, but observed that he took a long breath before going on. Then, as though all at once wanting it quickly out of the way, he told her swiftly. 'When Khalil Rashwan got his head back together he, according to Yazid, while trying to get over his disappointment that you were "spoken for", became fearful that he'd offended against some British custom, and might have ruined the hours of work his father had put in on the contract.'

Joss's mouth was definitely open as Thane came to an end. 'So Yazid Rashwan rang you, to check that *you* hadn't changed *your* mind about the contract!' she exclaimed when what he had just said had fully sunk in.

'That's about it,' he confirmed, and Joss gave him a disgruntled look of disgust.

'Huh!' she scorned. 'If you fell in a dung heap you'd come up smelling of roses!' She saw his lips twitch again, but she wasn't feeling very friendly to him just then— he'd no right to have so much going for him. 'You'll tell me next, of course, that, with the certainty that you hadn't after all lost the contract, you felt, since you'd planned to be in Cairo today for your eight o'clock meeting, that you'd be magnanimous and let me know, in person, that I wasn't dismissed after all!' Suddenly she discovered that this man was just *too* much, and that she had worked herself up into quite a temper. 'Well, I've news for you, Mr No-please-and-very-little-thank-you Addison, I wouldn't work for you or Beacon Oil now if…'

'For lord's sake! What did I say?' he chopped in, but Joss had spent hours and hours in mental torment over him, and she wasn't ready to cool down—not now that she had let go.

'You've said more than enough!' she erupted, and, not deigning to go again over the insults he had served her, 'Had Yazid Rashwan not telephoned you tonight—last night,' she hastily amended, 'to let you know that that contract was safe, you'd not have given me a second's thought. You certainly wouldn't have tried to contact me. You'd have left Luxor without giving me another thought. You'd have…'

'Hell's bells, will you shut up?' Thane roared, about the only way he could get in.

Joss blinked, but having been so rudely interrupted caused her to break her tirade, and then start to panic that she might, in all she had said, have somehow revealed the fact that, desperate for any crumb, she had wanted him to give her another thought.

'So?' she challenged belligerently.

'So,' he said harshly, 'if you'll let me get a word in edgeways, I'll tell you that of course I thought of you. Ye gods, woman, I'd been searching Luxor for you *before* Yazid's call came through!'

Astounded by what he had just said, Joss just sat and gaped at him. Then, 'You'd been—searching… *Before* Yazid rang, you…' Her voice tailed off.

But if her tone was much more subdued than it had been, then Thane's tone too was very much quieter as he told her, 'You gave me one hell of a fright lighting out like that.'

'I—d-did?' she questioned, and then, desperately trying to get herself of one piece, 'You surely didn't think I'd so taken your remarks to heart that I'd thrown myself in the Nile?' She saw his glance on her become a trace speculative, and again started to panic that she might have revealed that anything offensive he might have to say did have the power to wound her deeply.

To her relief, though, he made no comment on that score, but replied after a moment or two of just looking at her, 'No, I didn't think that,' and then opened up, 'After I—left you—your room, I took myself off for a walk. Many thoughts went through my head during that walk,' he told her, 'but suffice it to say that my first action on my return was to go to your room.'

'I—see,' Joss said slowly, and realised then that Thane must have cooled down on his walk and, having done so, must have then have been plagued by his innate sense of fairness—that sense of fairness making him decide to come to her room to apologise. 'But I wasn't there,' she went on, 'so you...' She broke off and looked solemnly into his steady grey eyes. Somehow she just couldn't credit that he had, as he'd said, been searching Luxor for her.

'So I began looking for you,' he took up. 'We'd been going to dine, I recalled belatedly, then I realised that, you being you, you'd probably rather starve than break bread with me again after the way I'd behaved. Which, to my logical mind, meant that since you had to eat that you would, in all likelihood, take a taxi to some other hotel rather than risk having to share the same air if I was eating in the hotel we were staying in.'

As she looked at him, her resistance to him began to crumble. By the sound of it, he had given her more than a moment's thought. 'I forgot that I hadn't eaten,' she confessed quietly.

'Oh, my dear,' Thane said softly, and straight away her heart was on a merry-go-round again. 'Were you so upset by me that...?'

'Grief!' she scoffed swiftly, and was unsure whether or not her bluff of being entirely unaffected by him had come off.

But Thane was going on, and that small moment of danger was past, as he continued, 'I took a taxi to check the most likely hotels, then returned to try your room again.' Joss's eyes were widening in her face as she heard the trouble he had gone to in looking for her. But it did not end there. 'Then, when you didn't answer your door, I went down to reception to enquire if anyone had seen you. It was then I was told that your room key had been handed in, and that one of them could clearly remember seeing you with your suitcase.'

'Good heavens!' Joss exclaimed in surprise. The hotel they had stayed in had been a busy one. 'With everyone coming and going all the time, you wouldn't think anyone would remember...'

'It was a male of the species,' Thane broke in, making her heart flutter. 'You're not so easily overlooked, Joss.'

'Oh,' she murmured, and knew her feelings for him were getting the better of her. 'So what did you do?' she made herself ask a little stiffly. 'After one of the hotel staff had said...'

'What would I do?' he questioned. 'I took the key and checked your room for myself.'

Her eyes went even wider at that. 'You—er—found me gone, my clothes gone?'

He nodded. 'But not a clue anywhere to where you *had* gone. I was in my room throwing my things into my case when Yazid Rashwan rang.'

'Ah,' said Joss, and thought then that she had the whole picture. 'You realised that you'd spent enough time searching for me and that if you wasted any more you'd miss your flight to Cairo?'

'At that stage,' he replied, his eyes nowhere but on her, 'I didn't know if I'd be flying to Cairo, Alexandria or where the hell I'd be flying.'

'But your meeting!' she reminded him. 'The meeting you said you have in Cairo at eight o'clock this morning.'

'I lied about that,' Thane owned, and as far as she could tell he didn't appear to look in the least bit sorry.

'You—lied?'

'What else should I do?' he enquired. 'I'd been lucky so far in finding you. When you answered your phone sounding wide awake, I decided that I hadn't been through what I'd been through just so that you should tell me you'd see me at a more civilised hour.'

All that he'd been through? Joss could only think he must mean the trouble he'd been to to track her down. Though, since it seemed that he had no appointment in Cairo that morning, surely it had to mean that he—had *purposely*—followed her to Cairo! Suddenly her heart was beating rapidly again, and she knew then that she wanted, most urgently, to hear everything he had to tell her. Because—and she owned that she was feeling more than a degree confused—surely, when Thane could have easily telexed her pretty well anywhere in the world to tell her that he considered her still in the company's employ, he had come after her personally, meant that there was more to it than that. Didn't it? She remembered the marvellous day she had shared with him—until Khalil had come on the scene—and she swallowed hard on a dry throat. Good or bad, she wanted Thane to tell her the other reasons why he had come after her.

'You—er—said you'd been lucky?' she questioned, her voice sounding suddenly husky despite all her efforts to the contrary.

'Thank God for that sandstorm!' Thane said on a heart-felt note, and when she just sat and stared uncomprehendingly he explained, 'But for the luck of that sandstorm affecting flying schedules, I wouldn't have a clue where you'd flown to. When I started asking questions at the airport it soon became evident that because of the readjusted time-tables, the only flight you could have taken in the time scale of your leaving the hotel had to be the one to Cairo.'

'Good heavens!' Joss exclaimed again, though her tone was fainter this time. It seemed incredible that Thane had done such detective work about her. 'So you really did fly to Cairo after me?'

'And spent most of the flight wondering if you'd cooled down sufficiently to remember that you still had the contract, or if you were too mad, still hating my guts.'

'I—er—' she murmured, and realised that to tell him she'd been more hurt than mad would not do at all. 'I didn't remember the contract until my plane had landed,' she told him, then all at once, as her logical thinking started to stir, her spirits hit rock bottom again. 'That's why you followed me!' she declared suddenly. 'You knew I'd still got the contract and…' She broke off, shaken, as she saw from the furious expression that crossed his face and knew she had just made him exceedingly angry.

'Have you not been listening to a word I've said?' he roared on an explosion of anger. 'To hell with that contract—it's got nothing to do with why I'm here, nor did I give it a thought when I was searching Luxor for you! In fact, had Yazid Rashwan not telephoned about it, I doubt if I should have remembered it at all,' he blazed on. 'The only reason it stayed in my head during my journey here,' he informed her furiously, 'was that, to my mind, so much hinged on your remembering that you still had it.'

'I don't see how,' Joss told him stiffly, not caring to be roared at by him or anyone else.

'Then try this!' he rapped toughly. 'I'd checked your

room pretty thoroughly when I was looking for you, but it wasn't until after Yazid's phone call that I realised that had you left that contract for me I'd have seen it—likewise, had you torn it to shreds and dumped it in your paper-bin, I'd have spotted it there too.'

'You thought I might have torn it up!' Joss exclaimed in astonishment, a little shaken to see that her surprised exclamation appeared to have neutralised Thane's anger with her. For suddenly he smiled.

'I wouldn't have blamed you,' he replied gently, and while her heart flipped and she did what she could in the way of getting herself under control from the havoc just his smile and his gentleness had created in her, he went on, 'To my way of thinking, it seemed a pretty safe bet that you'd flown to Cairo, but it was also a pretty safe bet that, since you hadn't hung about Luxor airport waiting for the Alexandria flight, you'd no intention of returning there. Which in turn had to mean that what you did intend to do was to take the first flight out of Cairo to England, when for all I knew you might disappear to stay with people I'd never heard of, when it could be an age before I could find you.' Joss stared at him incredulously—was he saying that he would have followed her to England? 'That was,' he went on, 'unless…'

'Un-l-less?' she prompted, in love with him, fascinated by the way his mind worked, but above all feeling so strung up that she wanted him to go on, and quickly.

For a moment or two Thane said nothing, but just rested his eyes on her as if just the sight of her made him feel good to be alive. Her heart was thundering against her ribs when he suddenly seemed to collect himself, then replied, 'Unless you'd remembered that most confidential of documents. I haven't worked with you these past weeks, Joss, without learning that as well as having a shocking temper...' he broke off briefly when she looked as though she was going to argue the point, but when her lips stayed firmly closed, however, he resumed, 'you also happen to be one of the most loyal and efficient working partners a man could wish for.'

'Now he tells me!' Joss, while thrilled at his 'working partners' terminology, found that this time she could not take what he said without comment.

'You shouldn't need telling,' he rebuked her, a trace of good humour lurking at the corners of his mouth. 'I scoured Cairo airport for you, Josslyn Harding,' he enlightened her severely. 'When I couldn't find you, I had to pin all my hopes on your sense of duty, to the company, if not to me, winning through.'

'You—er—calculated that if I remembered in time that I hadn't yet given that document back to you, I wouldn't leave Cairo until I'd made sure it was in safe hands?'

'I wanted to see you, dear Joss,' he told her quietly, and while her eyes went saucer-wide and her mouth went dry and she started to tremble, he added, 'Which is why I had to hope with all my heart that, having remembered the contract, you would feel you couldn't trust it to the post, but would take it personally to the Cairo office as soon as it opened.'

'You...' she swallowed hard when her voice came out sounding more of a whisper than anything else. 'You—um—thought that you'd—er—meet me at Beacon House when...' Her voice faded.

'It was my intention to be there before you,' Thane took up, his eyes never leaving her face. 'But that was before I realised that I was so impatient to see you that I couldn't wait that long.'

'You couldn't?' she choked, and just sat staring at him as he shook his head and then confided,

'I raced round several hotels in Cairo checking to see if you were booked in. Then I suddenly remembered how you'd had a yearning to see the Pyramids. It was a long shot, but I abandoned my attempts to find you in Cairo and tried Giza instead.'

'Well…!' escaped Joss on a stunned breath of sound. Then, her voice strengthening, she felt she just had to tell him, 'To be honest, I was a bit all over the place—and wasn't thinking about the Pyramids when I told the taxi-driver that I wanted to go to Giza.'

For some seconds Thane stared at her as if he had taken quite some heart from the fact that, for a good long while after their row, she had still been all over the place. But, instead of putting the onus on her to tell him why that should be, he smiled, that gentle smile she was beginning to love, and told her, 'It doesn't matter, I found you.' His smile faded as he continued, 'But having found you, having booked myself in—a few doors up from you—I discovered that I couldn't settle to wait until daylight to see you.'

'You w-were awake when the call to prayer started?'

'My dear, I hadn't been to sleep,' he told her. 'Nor, when I began to wonder if the noise had awakened you, could I find it possible to wait any longer. When I rang your room and heard you sounding fully awake, I was at one and the same time encouraged that—by the sound of it—you couldn't sleep either; only to know myself for a fool to think that anyone could sleep with all that chanting going on.'

Looking at him, Joss thought she would soon collapse under the strain of the tension she was suddenly under. Nervously she licked her bottom lip, and then she just had to ask, 'Encouraged—why, Thane?'

'Don't you know yet?' he asked quietly, and Joss grew

very afraid that she had got it wrong and that her normal intelligence might have led her into an entirely false avenue.

However, she did find enough courage to begin, 'If it's not the contract that's important to y-you…' when suddenly her voice failed her, and she could go no further.

Which was when Thane, that look of strain evident in his eyes again, manfully took over. 'If it's not the contract which is so important to me,' he said, his grey eyes holding hers and reading what they could from her tense expression, 'then what is so very, very important to me that I've hared from Luxor to find you must, my very dear Joss, be you.'

'Oh!' she exclaimed softly, wanting to cry, wanting to launch herself at him, wanting above all to be held safe in his arms and for him to tell her that she really could believe what he was telling her.

'What does that "Oh!" signify?' he asked, his tone suddenly gritty, and sounding very much as though he was bracing himself to hear the worst.

Joss swallowed on her dry throat. 'It means,' she told him nervously, 'that—I'm—scared.'

'Of me?' he exclaimed abruptly, clearly appalled that she should be afraid of him.

'Of what you're *not* saying,' she replied swiftly.

'Of what I'm not…' he began to repeat, then suddenly stopped, and then, letting go what seemed to her to be a long-pent-up breath, 'I've just been telling you—for the lord knows how long—that I love you very much, Josslyn Harding. Are you now going to tell me that you, whom I've seen fully and quickly grasp the most complicated of issues, haven't worked that out yet?'

'A woman—likes to have these things spelled out,' she

told him modestly, if shakily, as her heart pounded away so loudly that she was sure he must hear it.

'Likes?' he took up the one word. 'You wouldn't give a man such encouragement without meaning it, would you?'

Joss almost asked him what sort of a woman he thought she was, but a glance at his stressed expression told her that he was never more earnest. 'No,' she said simply, 'I wouldn't.'

His answer was to stand up. Then he held out his arms to her. 'Come over here and say that,' he commanded her softly.

Quietly she left her chair. 'Thane!' she breathed his name, and as he reached out for her and gently pulled her into his arms, it was all she said for quite some minutes.

Then, after long moments of holding her close up against his heart, of leaning back so that he could look into her face, and of then gently, and oh, so tenderly, kissing her, Thane put her a little way away from him, and while still keeping his hands on her shoulders, 'Oh, my darling!' he murmured, and for the first time since she had known him, he seemed choked, and lost for words. Then, 'I won't ask you how in the name of good fortune you've come to care for me, but since I shouldn't mind having it spelled out either—is there anything you want to tell *me*?'

It seemed totally unbelievable to Joss that he should need to hear her say that she loved him, but, remembering how not all that long ago she had been nervous to believe he was saying that he loved her, she breathed shakily, 'Oh, Thane, I do so love you!'

He gave an exultant cry of triumph, and suddenly she was back in his arms again and he was raining tender loving kisses all over her face. Many more long minutes ticked by as he held her close against his heart. Then gradually he pulled back from her again.

His eyes were devouring her loving face. 'The torment you've caused me, dear love!' he whispered. 'The jealousy I've known since you, ash-blonde and female, and not at all what I wanted, arrived in Cairo, and coolly told me you were the replacement secretary.'

'Jealousy?' she questioned, positively adoring him.

'We have so much to talk about,' he smiled, and, quite clearly wanting her as close to him as possible, he moved her with him and took her to sit with him in one of the small easy chairs—the only room available for her being—on his lap. Then, securing her in his arms, 'You can have no idea of how all at sea I've been about you, young woman,' he informed her mock-seriously.

'I haven't,' she admitted, then, sending him a smile which he seemed to relish, 'but I should like to,' she told him.

'Minx!' he accused. 'Adorable minx,' and to please her he related, 'We started off by rowing the day we met. I, with the recent example of Paula Ingram, and how a friendly look can be misread, before me, dared to warn you against taking a fancy to me. What, in my colossal conceit, I didn't take into account,' he freely owned, 'was that, far from falling in love with *me*, you should show a preference for someone else.'

Having learned a good deal more of Thane since she had worked for him, Joss did not consider him conceited at all. But, 'Khalil?' she queried.

'For one,' he replied.

'Who else?' she questioned in surprise. 'I haven't...'

'Chad Woollams, for another,' he told her astonishingly.

'Chad Woollams!'

'You can't be more surprised than I was.'

'But you'd no cause!'

'There was no cause either why I should feel so irritated when Woollams tried to flirt with you under my nose.'

'But you were—irritated?'

'Greatly,' he replied. 'As, too, I was mightily irritated to hear him inviting you out to lunch.'

Casting her mind back, 'That was the day you and I went to lunch with Yazid Rashwan,' she remembered—and was again incredulous at Thane's reply.

'I'd no intention of taking you with me that day,' he confessed. 'Only when it looked as though you might be lunching with Woollams did it occur to me that I had every need of you myself.'

'I was never intended to be at that lunch... You were—jealous!' she exclaimed, thunderstruck. 'That far back, you were...' Just as she found it impossible to believe, by the same token she could not finish.

'That far back I was denying that I was anything of the kind,' he told her with rueful charm. 'That far back I was getting so tangled up about you, I was denying every truth about the emotions battering at me but which were insisting on trying to get through.'

'What sort of emotions?' Joss just had to ask, and as Thane bent his head to her she was kissed so long and so thoroughly that she forgot her question.

'I've an idea I shouldn't have done that,' he teased as he looked down into her flushed face, and, although she had not raised any objection, he pulled back from her and asked, 'Where were we?' Helplessly, Joss shook her head. Thane laughed and pulled her close to him again. 'Oh, dear heaven, how I love you,' he told her, and his voice sounded gravelly in his throat.

'I love you too,' Joss whispered, gazing at him in wonder at all that was happening. 'I think we were talking about jealousy,' she remembered.

'Ah, yes,' Thane took up, cradling her to him. 'Jealousy, and how I was denying its existence even though there were countless instances when it was staring me in the face.'

'Countless?'

'Apart from Woollams, I was having to do battle against the green-eyed monster when Rashwan junior phoned me to ask for your address.'

'That was when I first arrived in Alexandria and you booked me into a hotel?' Joss queried.

'And I was sure I didn't give a damn who knew which hotel you were staying in—which of course was why I was as mad as hell when, with there being no reason in the world for me to phone you, I did so and found the line to your room was busy.'

'You rang back,' Joss remembered, 'and demanded to know if I was dining with Khalil, and I thought it would please you to know that I wasn't dining with him...'

'And it did, of course, and I didn't like that either—that it should please me. I, my dear love,' he told her, 'was starting to get very mixed up about you.'

'It never showed,' she said warmly, and was gently kissed.

'I apologise wholeheartedly now, for every time I've ever been the least bit disagreeable to you,' Thane said handsomely, 'but, in my defence, nothing like this has ever happened to me before—and I not only did not trust it, did not want it, but did not want to believe it either.'

'Was it so bad?' she teased, and was kissed again for her sauce.

'Murder,' Thane smiled. 'I barely knew you that afternoon you went to that museum with Khalil Rashwan, yet, when I'd returned to work and you hadn't, I discovered that I was concentrating more on listening for your footsteps than I was on the job in hand.'

'Truly?' she gasped in astonishment.

'Truly,' he replied, and added, 'I went home that night, and when I'd determined that you were nothing to me, what do I do but damn well dream of you? You, my little love, have given me one hell of a time!'

'Should I be sorry?' she smiled.

'Yes, you should!' he retorted. 'How dare you ruin my peace of mind by telling me not once, but twice, that you quite liked Khalil Rashwan?'

The second time was recently, when Thane had come to her room in fact, Joss remembered. 'When was the first time?' she enquired.

'Heartless woman, how can you have forgotten?' he charged mock-severely—then reminded her, 'It was more or less in the same breath as you categorically stated that you didn't even like me—much less fancy me.'

'Oh, Thane,' cried Joss, instantly contrite. 'Did I hurt your feelings?'

'Not so much,' he said cheerfully, 'because you also told me that you'd no intention of going to bed with him.'

'Oh!' she exclaimed suddenly. 'That was the night you kissed me and then had the nerve to tell me that I'd turn on without such niceties as having a liking for a man.'

'You've so much to forgive me for,' Thane said quietly. 'I didn't know then, of course, that you had never—so to speak—turned on for any man to the extent I accused you of.' Gently then he kissed her.

'You—kissed me like that—the night…'

'And regained my senses on Saturday morning to realise that I didn't at all like the hold one certain most beautiful blonde had on me.'

'Oh, Thane!' Joss sighed, but, recalling how grumpy he'd been the next time she'd seen him, 'So that's why...'

'Exactly,' he cut in, as if he was not liking the memory of the grim person he had been that Saturday morning. 'But to get back to the previous evening, that was the night that I discovered you didn't sleep around. Forgive the male chauvinist in me, my love,' he said softly, 'but I felt so good to know that—that it just seemed entirely natural that I should take you in my arms.'

By then Joss was ready to forgive him anything. 'That was Friday, the night you came to tell me we were going to Luxor,' she said dreamily.

'That was the night I returned from England and, when I could have easily sent a messenger to tell you to pack a case, while still denying that I'd missed you in the two days I'd been away, I found that I just had to come in person.'

'Because you'd missed me!'

Thane grinned, kissed her lightly on the nose, then confessed, 'That wasn't the only time, my dear one,' and, when she looked at him expectantly, 'I was refusing to believe it, of course, but—remember driving with me to Cairo last Monday?'

'Of course,' she replied. 'Though I can't say that—although I took a few notes—you needed me along on that trip.'

'I didn't—from a work point of view,' Thane told her, and at her look of surprise, 'But dammit, woman, I'd just spent an entire weekend not seeing you and—even if I wasn't admitting it—I'd missed you, and wanted a few hours in your company.'

'Oh—if I'm dreaming, never wake me up!' sighed Joss.

'You're not dreaming, beloved,' he breathed tenderly, and held her against his heart.

For some minutes they sat close in each other's arms and, after having been through a welter of unhappiness when she had flown away from him in Luxor, she asked, 'When did you know for sure that—about your feelings, for me?'

'You mean when did I pull my head out of the sand and finally admit that I love and adore you?' Thane smiled. Then, looking down into her lovely shining velvety eyes, 'Yesterday,' he told her, going on, 'Having told you I'd no need of you and that you could do as much sightseeing as you wanted, I was suddenly bedevilled by the notion that I wanted to show you the sights myself.'

'You!'

'Me,' he replied. 'Which was why I hot-footed it down to reception and waited for you to come out of the lift.'

'You were waiting…!' she began, flabbergasted. 'You were making an enquiry; you might have missed seeing me. You…'

'No chance,' he told her. 'I spotted you the moment those lift doors opened—and pretended I hadn't.' Joss was staring at him in amazement when, his expression going suddenly serious he went on, 'We were in the bazaar, and you were looking at that rug. You said, "It's beautiful," and as I looked at you I knew then that I'd never felt happier in my entire life, and that I was enjoying every moment of my time with you. It was then I could no longer escape the truth. The truth being that, having more or less told you at the outset not to fall in love with me— I'd fallen totally and irrevocably in love with you.'

'Oh, Thane!' Joss sighed ecstatically.

'I knew then, dear heart, why I'd felt such a dreadful pang when I'd had to leave you to fly to England on Wednesday.'

'You'd—er—been going to leave me the safe key,' she whispered inconsequentially.

'Can you wonder, with you, with parting from you so much in my head, that I should forget it?' he murmured. 'Though it wasn't until yesterday, Sunday, that I understood what had motivated my actions in taking you protectively to my apartment on your first night in Egypt, or accepted that jealousy was behind my immediately setting about finding you an apartment without a phone when you told me that Khalil Rashwan was in the habit of ringing you at your hotel of an evening.'

'Really? But—but I distinctly remember you asking me if he still rang me every evening.' Suddenly she was looking astounded. 'You—knew *then* that I didn't have a phone!'

Thane refused to look abashed. 'That didn't stop him ringing you at the office, did it! Nor me from trying to tell you how—with him being Yazid's son—I needed to know everything. I afterwards wondered who I was trying the hardest to convince—you, or myself.'

'You knew it was yourself—yesterday?' asked Joss, getting to like this feeling that Thane really, really did love her.

Gently he stroked his fingers down the sides of her face. 'Oh, yes, my darling,' he breathed. 'I knew as we took that rug to be air-freighted that, having never experienced such inner joy at being with another person, I never wanted that day to end.' He smiled tenderly as he added, 'What better way to prolong it than to take you to lunch?'

Blissfully, Joss sighed again. 'And then to Karnak,' she murmured.

'And in the evening, back to Karnak for the Son et Lumière.'

'It was all so beautiful, so heavenly,' she whispered.

'Only I and my giant-sized jealousy have to go and ruin everything when, while in the room next to yours, I hear Khalil Rashwan's voice as I'm dressing.'

'You—er—came in pretty quickly,' Joss recalled.

'And for my sins had my jealousy go into overdrive to see some other man dare to take you in his arms. Oh, my dear, dear love, are you ever going to forgive me for my words and actions after that?'

'For—hitting Khalil?'

'Huh!' scorned Thane. 'He had it coming! No, my darling, for not merely accusing you of giving me the green light all day—wishful thinking on my part—but for damn near seducing you, and then for going on to accuse you of wanton behaviour with Khalil Rashwan. Topping it all—by dismissing you.'

'Er—why did you?' she asked quietly.

'Dismiss you?'

She shook her head. 'Any of it?' she replied, and basked in the glow of his tender expression.

'I'd lost my head over you, dear love,' he told her gently. 'In the first instance, I just went over the top from rage at Khalil Rashwan's daring to lay a hand on you. Then, when in anger I took you in my arms, I started to lose control completely. But for your having a last moment of reservation in our lovemaking, I should have been lost,' he murmured gently. 'But when you did suffer a moment of—hesitation, it gave a chance for a little sense to penetrate my mind. I wasn't sure what the hell it was that I wanted any more, sweet love,' he breathed. 'But even in my tangled brain patterns, I somehow just seemed to know that it couldn't be that I should want to take you in anger.'

'You were gentle then,' Joss reminded him quietly.

'In that moment of a stray strand of sense returning, I was scared,' Thane told her.

'Scared—you?'

'Believe it,' he smiled. 'I wanted you—dear heaven, how I wanted you! Which was why I had to get you to hide your body from me. But even though you'd covered yourself up, the memory of your beauty was still haunting me. I was scared, Joss, that I might yet go on to make you mine. I needed some help.'

'Ah!' she exclaimed as she recalled how, given that she had known a belated moment's shyness, she would not have stopped him had he not torn himself away from her. 'You needed me angry, not—er—compliant.'

He nodded in agreement that she had worked it out correctly. 'I had to accuse you of ruining my work, of being wanton, but then, while still in panic and desperately wanting you, I started to fear that in the gentleness—which you'd spotted—I might have revealed my love for you. I confess, Joss, my normal logical thinking processes had totally deserted me when I decided that you would soon know I certainly had no love for you—were I to dismiss you.'

'Oh, Thane, my poor darling!' Joss crooned, able then to see how very desperate he must have been.

'You forgive me?' he asked.

'Of course,' she smiled, and reached up and kissed him, and all was silent in the room as they shared the solace of each other's lips.

'Did I ever tell you that I think you're truly beautiful, adorable, and that I love you with all the heart that's in me?' Thane questioned softly as their kiss broke.

Joss smiled up at him. 'I don't think so,' she laughed, then thought to question, 'If you were so set on my *not* knowing how you—er—felt about me, what...'

'What made me decide to tell you after all?'

She nodded. 'You said I'd given you a fright, lighting out the way I did. Was it that that—?'

'I'd decided before that to try and find out how things were with you and if I stood a chance,' Thane butted in. 'When I left you—your room, I went charging out of the hotel, seriously needing to get my head together. I must have walked miles,' he went on, 'before I suddenly found I was starting to get hooked on the notion that you—to have been the way you had with me—might, dare I hope, have some feeling for me. Could it be—that I had no need to hide how I felt about you? I grabbed a taxi as soon as I could and, in a sweat, returned to the hotel to find you.'

'But I wasn't there.'

'That was when the nightmare really began,' he smiled, then grinned and added, 'You started to get to me way back, Miss Harding, do you know that?'

'I'm sure it never showed, Mr Addison,' she beamed, and felt she wouldn't have been human if she hadn't asked, 'When exactly?'

'You're such a delight to me,' he said softly, and took time out to place a kiss on her nose, before he went on to reveal, 'I was driving to Alexandria with you—that day you arrived in Egypt when, out on your feet, your head began to droop until finally it landed on my shoulder. I was about to tell you in no uncertain terms to sit up straight, when suddenly I glanced at you—and the words just wouldn't come. Despite myself,' he owned, 'I found I was taken by the sleeping, innocent and vulnerable look of you, and—against all my inner convictions, and all before I know it—I discovered that instead of dropping you off at a hotel, which is what I fully meant to do, I'd— can you believe it?—driven you to my apartment. Is it any wonder,' he asked, 'that I was not only very much annoyed with myself, but with you too?'

'I wasn't liking you very much that night,' Joss smiled in understatement when she recalled how infuriated he had made her.

Thane smiled too, but his expression had gone serious as he began, 'My darling, I've explained everything I have because, after the way I've behaved to you, I've felt that you've needed to know how it is with me, and the depth of my love for you. But now, beloved little Joss, can I ask you to tell me when you knew that you—loved me?'

It seemed incredible to her that Thane should need re-assurance that she truly did love him, and need to know when. But willingly she obliged. 'I knew for certain that I was in love with you the night we went to dine at Yazid Rashwan's home.'

'The night I was such an unbearable swine to you?'

'My sentiments exactly.' Joss grinned, was kissed for her trouble, but was then allowed to resume. 'We'd been driven back to our hotel, and I was going up in the lift on my own when, in the middle of mutinying against you, I suddenly realised why it was that your changes of mood could so affect my mood.'

'Er—had it been coming on before then?' he fished openly.

'What can I tell you?' she laughed. 'It was all there in the fact that when I realised that agreement over that con-tract had been reached I wanted, without knowing why, to kiss you.' On impulse she stretched up and kissed him. 'Congratulations,' she murmured, and when he looked adoringly at her she coughed to clear a suddenly emo-tionally dry throat, and went on, 'I've since realised, of course, that when I was telling you that not only did I not like you but that also neither did I fancy you, I was deluding myself as much as you. Even then I think I was loving you more than hating you. But,' she came to a smiling end, 'if I'm honest, I think love for you must have started to stir in me on that very night you took me to your apartment.'

Joss laughed again when, in utter bliss at being in his arms, and the belief that he really did love her starting to firmly cement, Thane pressed, 'I want you to be honest.'

She began to feel even more secure in his love as she realised that, just as she had wanted to know all about the emotions that had raged in him about her, so it seemed that he wanted to know all about her feelings for him.

'Well, one of my reactions that night was to fight against the impulse to tell you what you could do with your job,' she revealed—but then owned, 'Though I've since wondered if I was deceiving myself when I decided that I'd stay just to show you, and stay because I hadn't seen the Pyramids yet—because now I wonder, did I stay because even then you had that something "special" for me?'

Thane looked deeply into her eyes, then, lowering his head, he kissed her long and satisfyingly. Then, pulling back, he moved her until they were both standing. Then, 'Talking of pyramids, my love,' he said tenderly, and added mysteriously, 'If my geography's right...' and took her with him to the sliding door.

He was holding her to him with one arm as he slid the door back and, with Joss entirely unprotesting, he took her out on to the balcony. Somewhere a cockerel crowed, and her glance went from the tall eucalyptus tree to her left to the faint pink in the dawn sky. Then Thane was moving to the back of her and was turning her to look to her right.

'Thane!' she gasped, and just could not believe it. Then,

'Thane!' she cried again in complete and utter wonderment. For there, so close that she felt she could almost touch them, were the three Pyramids of Giza! She opened her mouth again, but so absolutely astounded was she that no sound came.

Totally surprised and much in awe of the two large Pyramids with a smaller one to the left-hand side, all shrouded in the early morning mist but clearly discernible for all that, Joss remained completely speechless.

How long she stood like that she had no idea. But, safe in the haven of Thane's arms, she at last gave a sigh of utter contentment, and let her head rest on his shoulder.

That was when Thane came to her side and half turned her to face him. In sublime happiness she raised her eyes to his, and at the warmth in his eyes her heart started racing anew, and he cupped her face in his hands.

Then, after taking a deep breath, 'My dearest Joss,' he began quietly, 'because I travel all over the globe and am often away from England for months at a time, I've put all thoughts of marrying out of my head.' Her eyes were large in her face as wordlessly, her heart not merely racing but sprinting wildly, she stared up at him. 'Up until now, I've been quite content, indeed, have enjoyed my bachelor status,' he continued, 'and have always known that my job meant more to me than marriage. But that, my own, was before I met and fell so heart and soul in love with you.' He paused, and taking a very deep breath—with the Pyramids forming a backcloth—he watched every expression in her face, then said, 'So what I need to know now, my heart, given that without you nothing has any meaning any more, is—will you marry me—*please*?'

Her heart gave a further burst of energetic energy, and Joss swallowed hard. She felt so near to emotional, happy tears, but looking at Thane, loving him and, unbelievably, observing from his tense expression that he seemed to be in some doubt about her answer, she put a gentle hand to the side of his face. And then she smiled.

'Since you ask so nicely,' she whispered chokily, her feelings for him all there in her look, 'yes, I will.'

'My love!' he breathed, and with a heartfelt sigh he gathered her into his arms.

Catherine George was born in Wales, and early on developed a passion for reading which eventually fuelled her compulsion to write. Marriage to an engineer led to nine years in Brazil, but on his later travels the education of her son and daughter kept her in the UK. And instead of constant reading to pass her lonely evenings she began to write the first of her romantic novels, which was accepted and published by Mills & Boon® in 1982.

Since then, Catherine has written more than 45 novels and has had over 18 million copies of her books distributed worldwide. When not writing and reading she loves to cook, listen to opera, browse in antiques shops and walk the Labrador.

LOVEKNOT

by
CATHERINE GEORGE

CHAPTER ONE

THE crowded room simmered with tension. Eyes met eyes and slid away, and conversation diminished to embarrassed murmurs of conjecture as the wedding guests, far too many of them for comfort in the close confines of the register office, waited for the bride. The registrar's smile grew fixed and finally disappeared as he darted pointed looks at the clock on the wall, his occasional dry cough adding to the susurration of whispers and shuffling feet from those gathered together to witness the joining in marriage of Miss Delphine Wyndham and Mr Alexander Paget.

Alone in a sea of unrest, the bridegroom sat like a rock.

And had done for half an hour, thought Sophie Gordon, as the clock on the town hall chimed in confirmation. And Alexander had never fidgeted once. The sunlit room was stiflingly hot, but every sleek, fair hair on his head lay in place, his white collar pristine above the dark morning-coat, the gardenia in his lapel as fresh as the moment he'd arrived. Alexander, as Sophie knew better than most, aimed as nearly as possible for perfection in all things, which made it all the more unbelievable that Delphine dared flout his well-known views on punctuality.

5

No man, surely, deserved to wait so long—and so publicly—for his bride to put in an appearance. Sophie was startled by a sudden pang of compassion. Of all the feelings she had harboured for Alexander Paget over the years, compassion was certainly a first, in spite of the links between them. Owing to the friendship between their respective parents he had inevitably been around all her life, sometimes in the background, occasionally to the fore. Once, briefly, she had even agonised in the throes of puppy-love over him. That, at least, had died a natural death from sheer under-nourishment, she thought, amused. Alexander had been so insufferably superior in his college days that her teenage adoration had soon veered in other directions.

Alexander played a prominent enough role in her life currently, it was true, because for the past few years she had been his secretary. A very good one, too, in her own opinion. Only a wife knew a man better than his confidential secretary, and in her own case, reflected Sophie, probably not nearly so well.

Sophie stole a glance up at her father to find him eyeing the bride's mother with professional concern. The lady sat twisting her doeskin gloves into ruin, her face deeply flushed beneath the brim of her hat.

'Hypertensive,' murmured Dr Gordon, *sotto voce*.

'Hardly surprising,' answered his daughter in kind, brows raised as she caught the eye of Edward Peregrine Paget, cousin and best man to the bridegroom. Perry kept twisting round in his seat to look towards the door, as if he hoped the bride might have materialised there when his back was turned. Fat chance, thought Sophie. When Delphine Wyndham makes her entry not a soul will be left in doubt.

When, at long last, the door did open, all heads but one swivelled as if jerked by the same string. But expectancy changed to surprise as, in place of the bride, her father stood in the doorway, beckoning urgently to Perry, who nudged Alexander and went with him from the room, closing the door on the buzz of comment which broke out an all sides. Mrs Wyndham sagged against the relative seated next to her, and Kate Paget, Alexander's stepmother, turned round to the Gordons, her attractive face worried.

'Something wrong, do you think, David?'

Dr Gordon smiled reassuringly. 'Delphine's probably held up in the traffic.'

Or she's broken a fingernail, or laddered a stocking, thought Sophie without charity. Delphine Wyndham would think nothing of keeping a room full of people waiting while the vital adjustment was made.

While the guests waited speculation very plainly ran riot through the room, some of it anxious, some of the faces agog with an avid curiosity, Sophie noted with disgust. She felt most concerned for Kate Paget, who tensed visibly as Alexander and Perry came back into the room. The bridegroom spoke privately with the registrar, then turned to face the assembled company, his green eyes frozen in his good-looking face.

'I apologise to you all for the long wait,' he said
with courtesy. 'I regret that there will be no
wedding ceremony after all. Delphine, I am told,
has changed her mind.'

There was a piercing wail as Mrs Wyndham collapsed in the arms of her companion, and Dr
Gordon sprang up at once to assist, Kate Paget
close behind him. It took some time to restore the
distraught woman to some semblance of composure, while the deserted bridegroom waited,
immobile, his face devoid of emotion. Sophie
stayed in her seat, well out of the way, pitying
Alexander from the bottom of her heart. All this
would be so horribly novel for him. He was
accustomed to a life amazingly free of the trials
and tribulations other, lesser beings had to bear.
She viewed him dispassionately, trying to see him
with the eyes of a stranger. He was a very fit,
attractive specimen of his sex, she conceded; tall-
ish, slim, muscular, with thick, sleek hair only a
little darker than the flaxen fairness of his youth.
Nor were his assets confined to the physical. A successful architect in a respected firm established by
his grandfather in the town of Deansbury,
Alexander had a name and professional reputation
known to everyone. Sophie found it hard to credit
that even Delphine could have been so heartless as
to leave a man like Alexander at the altar. Not, of
course, that the table in the register office was anything like an altar, in spite of the flowers someone
had arranged so tastefully. But the principle was
the same. Wherever a jilted bridegroom was left
could only be described as the lurch.

After the weeping Mrs Wyndham had finally been escorted from the room by her nearest and dearest, Alexander turned once more to the remaining guests.

'Although the wedding itself has been cancelled, a perfectly good meal is waiting to be eaten at the Deansbury Country Club, as arranged.' He smiled very slightly, beginning, at last, to show visible signs of strain. 'Forgive me if I make myself scarce. Under the circumstances I could only be the spectre at the feast. Perry here will take over for me, and on behalf of Mr Wyndham and his wife I urge you all to take advantage of their hospitality.'

'It was quite horrible,' Sophie told her grandmother over lunch next day. 'I never dreamed I could feel so sorry for Alexander.'

'Why not?' asked Cecily Wainwright with interest.

Sophie thought for a moment. 'Well, you know Alexander, Gran. He never seems in need of sympathy, let alone pity. He forges through life without a hitch. Even I can appreciate what a good catch he is for a girl—clever, successful, plenty of money——'

'Not to mention extremely attractive,' added her grandmother. 'Delphine Wyndham's reasons for crying off must have been very powerful.'

'Greed, I suppose.'

'And incredibly bad taste if she went off with that Foyle person.'

'Ah, but Terry Foyle is Delphine's Dr Frankenstein, Gran.' Sophie grinned wickedly.

Mrs Wainwright wagged an admonishing finger, but agreed there was truth in what Sophie said. Without Terry Foyle's consummate skill with a camera, Delphine Wyndham's rise to top modelling fame would never have been so meteoric, in spite of her looks and amazing waist-length black hair. The dynamic little East-Ender had transformed mere prettiness into every man's dream of erotic beauty, resulting in an offer from an American cosmetics firm to the pair as a package, a contract Terry Foyle had come chasing hotfoot to Deansbury to wave in front of Delphine's nose at the eleventh hour on the very day of the wedding.

'No contest,' said Sophie. 'Alexander and Deansbury had no chance against Terry Foyle and the Dreamgirl Corporation of LA.'

'So Delphine's flown off to the City of the Angels—most inappropriate.' Mrs Wainwright looked at Sophie questioningly. 'And how is Alexander?'

'Bearing up with fortitude.' Sophie's eyes danced as she told her grandmother how the jilted bridegroom had actually gone off to Greece after all, just as originally planned for his honeymoon. His passion for ancient ruins would be indulged to the full, even if those of the flesh were likely to go unfulfilled.

'Sophie!' Mrs Wainwright tried hard to look shocked, but was evidently much struck by Alexander's practical outlook. 'But surely not at the honeymoon hotel!'

'Oh, yes. Alexander was quite unshakeable

about it, according to Aunt Kate.'

Mrs Wainwright applauded his common sense, and reiterated her scorn for any woman addle-brained enough to desert such a level-headed bridegroom. Sophie, on the other hand, looked forward to Alexander's eventual return to Deansbury with mixed feelings, certain his mood was bound to be black in the extreme.

'Delphine's so gorgeous,' she said with gloom. 'Alexander's bound to be like a bear with a sore head when he gets back to work. Though why he imagined a girl like that would settle down to connubial bliss in Deansbury I'll never know.'

'Probably he just hoped she would, darling. Men can be very naïve in some ways.'

'Naïve! Alexander?' Sophie hooted. 'He's the shrewdest man I know. Delphine must be the one miscalculation he's ever made in his life.'

The two women went out into the garden after lunch to enjoy their coffee in the sunshine and catch up on family news. Both of them looked forward to their fortnightly lunches together. Sophie, in particular, relished the peace and quiet of the comfortable house where her mother had grown up, enjoying the contrast to her life at home. Here at Greenacre she could almost revert to carefree childhood again, whereas in Deansbury she ran the Gordon household and looked after her father and brothers in the time left over from her job with Paget & Son, Chartered Architects.

'When are the twins getting back from France?' asked Mrs Wainwright.

'Wednesday, I think.'

'Whereupon you, I assume, will be presented with a lovingly hoarded supply of dirty laundry.'

Sophie laughed. 'I'd prefer that to endless name tapes. Before they take off for Edinburgh I've got dozens of the wretched things to sew on.'

'I hope the university knows what it has in store,' commented Mrs Wainwright, and cast a keen look in her grandchild's direction. 'And what will you do with yourself then?'

Sophie looked startled. 'Do?'

'Now Tim has gone out to herd sheep in Australia, and Mark and Matthew will soon be setting Edinburgh alight, it seems to me that your presence in your father's house is not as essential as once it was.'

The thought was by no means new to Sophie. It had never left her over the past months. But apart from less food and laundry to cope with she foresaw very little change in her life. There was still her father to consider. And as a doctor David Gordon relied on her more than other fathers might have done in their particular circumstances, if only because he needed her in the house to answer the telephone on the two nights a week he was on call. When she said as much Mrs Wainwright looked disapproving.

'Don't you ever long for a life of your own, Sophie? I can't help feeling Louise would be up in arms if she could see the trend your life has taken lately.'

Louise Gordon had gone off by coach on a Christmas shopping trip to London shortly after Sophie's sixteenth birthday. The coach had crashed in fog in a pile-up on the motorway, and David Gordon and his four children had been left without the mainstay of their lives. Louise's father had suffered a stroke at the news and Cecily Wainwright had been torn apart by her loyalties to both her stricken husband and her grandchildren, forced to stand by while Sophie, the eldest, changed overnight from a carefree schoolgirl into housekeeper and surrogate mother to her brothers, studying for her A-level examinations and subsequent secretarial course at the same time as learning to manage the household. Dr Gordon had employed a woman to help clean the house in the beginning, but when the lady eventually retired Sophie elected to manage alone, since by that time Tim was away in Cirencester at Agricultural College, and Mark and Matthew old enough to help a little. And, if sometimes she longed passionately for solitude and privacy, only Cecily Wainwright ever really knew how much.

'I think it's high time you left the nest yourself,' the latter said trenchantly.

'Oh, so do I,' Sophie agreed, 'but I can't just take off and leave Dad. Besides, where would I go?'

Before Cecily Wainwright could make any suggestions the telephone rang, and she went off to answer it, leaving Sophie to her daydream of a place of her own. Somewhere, anywhere, just so long as it had no importunate men demanding food and clean shirts when all she longed for was time to herself after her daily stint at Paget & Son. She loved her father—and her brothers; felt closer to them than most girls perhaps, due to their particular situation. But secretly she hankered after space and time to herself. And the latter was slipping by. Almost twenty-four years of her life had been spent within the confines of Deansbury and the family circle. Even her job had been tailor-made for her, decided for her by others. The moment her secretarial course was completed Alexander had been conveniently in need of a secretary and that had been that. She was handed over to him like a parcel, and everyone had told her repeatedly how very fortunate she was.

'Not Dad, was it?' she asked, as her grandmother returned.

'No. David, I assume, is being spoilt to death by Kate Paget, as is usual in your absence.' Mrs Wainwright smiled rather smugly. 'In fact it was young Sam Jefford, and I've asked him round to tea.'

'Then I'd better be off.' Sophie scrambled hastily to her feet.

'Nonsense. Do something to your face and comb your hair while I wash these cups. Or are you going out with Julian this evening?'

Sophie had to admit she was not, and carried the tray into the house, learning that Sam Jefford was an estate agent in Arlesbury. Mrs Wainwright's manner was so elaborately casual, her granddaughter eyed her with suspicion. 'And how come you're pally with an estate agent, Gran?'

'I'll tell you when you come down.'

Sophie knew better than to argue, and ran upstairs to make the necessary repairs, brushing her brown, shoulder-length bob to smoothness and adding a touch of lipstick to the curves of her wide mouth. She eyed her rounded face dispiritedly, contrasting it with Delphine's high cheekbones and slanting gold eyes, remembering with gloom the narrowness of the other girl's hips, her enviable lack of bosom. Sophie had no illusions about her own dimensions, which Mrs Wainwright alluded to firmly as rounded, but Mark and Matthew in rather less complimentary terms.

When Sophie rejoined her grandmother in the garden, that lady wore the look of someone harbouring a gulty secret.

'Is there something you're keeping from me, Gran? Not ill or anything, are you?'

Mrs Wainwright shook her well-groomed head. 'No, dear, I am not ill. I intend selling Greenacre, that's all.'

Sophie stared at her dumbfounded. 'You're giving up this house? Oh Gran—*why*?'

'It's getting too much for me. The garden in particular, now that help is so hard to find these days, and too expensive if one does. I'm not getting any younger, you know.'

Cecily Wainwright was seventy-five, but even in the bright afternoon sunlight looked much less than that, and Sophie told her so, with an emphasis designed to hide her own dismay.

'I've rattled around in this place like a small pea in an oversized pod ever since your grandfather died,' went on Mrs Wainwright, 'and I'm tired of it.'

'Are you buying something smaller?'

'No, darling.' Cecily Wainwright turned a smile of pure mischief on her granddaughter. 'I'm moving into Broad Oaks.'

Sophie's jaw dropped. 'Broad Oaks! But that's a—a——'

'Home for the elderly. I know. I visit my old friend Anne Morton there regularly, and I've had both the time and the opportunity to decide I'll do very well there myself. I can take some of my own furniture if I wish, I'll have a room and bathroom to myself, pleasant communal sitting-rooms if I want company, Anne just along the hall—and I'll take the car, of course. I can go off on trips and have you to lunch just as before, I promise you. But at Broad Oaks I shall have the added bonus of being waited on hand and foot.'

Sophie sat trying to recover from the shock. 'You look far too young for—for Broad Oaks,' she said, after a while. 'Dad will be surprised.'

'David and I are not famous for seeing eye to eye about anything,' said the lady who had been strongly opposed to her daughter's marriage to an impecunious young doctor thirty years earlier. 'But in this case I think he'll agree I'm taking a very sensible step.'

'Why don't you come and live with us?'

'David Gordon and myself under the same roof! Be realistic, child.'

Sophie agreed ruefully that her grandmother was right, then looked up as a car turned in at the gate. 'Is this your estate agent, Gran?'

'Ah, so it is.' Cecily Wainwright smiled with pleasure as a man came across the lawn towards them. He was only a little above medium height and looked rather thin to Sophie, who was used to the burly physique of the Gordon men. Sam Jefford had reddish hair and brown eyes which lit his fine-featured face with charm as he greeted Mrs Wainwright, who introduced him to Sophie, and left the two young people together while she went indoors to make the tea.

Sophie hid a smile, used by now to her grandmother's incessant matchmaking tendencies, and asked the visitor if he lived in Arlesbury.

'I do, indeed. Above the shop now, in fact. I occupy a flat over my premises in Quay Street.'

'Right on the river? How lovely.'

'The place isn't really straight yet. I haven't been in the flat long.'

'You're new to the area, then?' commented Sophie.

He looked embarrassed. 'No, not really. I used to live on the outskirts of the town. Had a house there, but I've just put it on the market.'

'You're in the right line of business for that, then,' said Sophie, hoping to put him more at ease. There was a silent pause, then she got up. 'I'll pop in and help Gran. Shan't be long.' She ran into the house to forestall Mrs Wainwright's effort to heft a loaded tea-tray. 'Hey—give me that. Ladies about to be institutionalised shouldn't go round carrying heavy loads.'

Mrs Wainwright looked cross. 'Why did you leave Sam alone?'

'He seems a bit shy. I thought he'd be better if you came back.'

'He's been going through a bad time, poor boy.'

'Ill?'

'No. Divorced. Acrimoniously, if what I hear is true.'

'The Arlesford jungle drums?'

Mrs Wainwright gave her grandchild a withering look as she shooed her out into the garden, bringing up the rear with the cake-basket used for afternoon tea at Greenacre since time immemorial.

To Sophie's relief Sam Jefford relaxed a little over tea, chatting easily as he praised the moist, crumbly fruitcake and light-as-air scones.

'Wonderful,' he said, as he accepted a second cup of tea. 'Home-made cakes don't feature much in my life.'

'I trust you don't subsist on beans on toast,' said Mrs Wainwright disapprovingly.

'I'm a takeaway man, I'm afraid.' Sam Jefford changed the subject hastily by informing Mrs Wainwright her house would be advertised next day, both in the newspapers and his office windows.

Sophie whistled. 'So soon? Will it take long to sell, do you think?'

He shook his head, smiling. 'Five minutes, at a guess. Perfect decorative order, four bedrooms, idyllic garden and five minutes on foot from the golf-course. Can't lose.'

The talk grew general for half an hour or so, then the visitor got to his feet regretfully. 'Time I was off, I'm afraid. Some homework to do. My secretary's only part-time these days. Pregnant, you know.' He smiled at them. 'You wouldn't happen to know of an efficient secretary on the hunt for a job, I suppose?'

Mrs Wainwright's answering smile was sphinx-like. 'It's just possible I might, Mr Jefford. I'll be in touch with you.'

When she came back to Sophie after seeing the visitor off, Mrs Wainwright sat down with an air of purpose. 'Well?' she demanded. 'Did you like him?'

'He's very nice, Gran.' Sophie grinned. 'Match-making again?'

Her grandmother failed to rise. 'Never mind Sam Jefford. You're the one I'm concerned about, Sophie. I know how much you secretly long to do as all your friends have done, to leave home and gain your independence. Have a place of your own.'

Sophie shrugged. 'Just pie-in-the-sky for me, Gran.'

'Not necessarily.' Mrs Wainwright gazed across the lawn, towards the massed shrubs and trees which marked the boundary of the property. 'I've heard the tenants of Ilex Cottage are moving out shortly, you know. It's very small, and needs doing up, but if you fancy the idea I could arrange for you to have it. Of course, I know Arlesford is no more exciting than Deansbury, but at least it's somewhere different,' she went on. 'Now the boys are off your hands, Sophie, surely David can get a housekeeper and let you lead your own life at last.'

Sophie's eyes glistened at the mere thought. 'Where is the place, Gran?'

'In Church Row.'

Sophie knew the house, the last of a row of what had once been almshouses near the church, in a narrow walk overhung with trees, and very, very private. She came back to earth with a bump. 'Arlesford is thirty miles from Deansbury,' she reminded her grandmother. 'Too far to commute. For me, anyway.'

'Give up your job!'

'I can't, Gran. Especially since Delphine's just walked out on Alexander—I couldn't do the same.'

'Nonsense. Secretaries are no more irreplaceable than brides.' Mrs Wainwright's mouth curved in a very smug smile. 'Use your head, child. I rather fancy you wouldn't have to look far for a job in Arlesford, now, would you? Sam Jefford needs someone very soon, by the sound of it.'

Sophie thought furiously. The idea was tempting. Very tempting indeed. If she could just manage to break her father into the idea gently. Persuade him that her aim was independence rather than desertion. Then she'd be off and running. She shied at the thought of hurting him, but at the same time it was unbearable to think of letting such a golden opportunity slip away.

'You could take whatever you wanted from here to furnish it,' said Mrs Wainwright coaxingly. 'You must make the break some time, child. And, after all, if you decide to marry Julian one day, your father will have to let you go, won't he?'

'Marry Julian?' Sophie shook her head emphatically. 'No chance of that!'

'I just don't understand your generation! If you

feel like that about him, why do you encourage the boy?'

'"The boy" is thirty years old going on fifty, and needs no encouragement, I assure you,' declared Sophie. 'Julian Brett is perfectly happy in his museum, has private means from his mother, and if he wants to spend some of them on entertaining me now and then, who am I to complain? At the very least it means I occasionally eat something I haven't cooked!'

'And I always thought the way to a *man's* heart was via his stomach,' retorted Mrs Wainwright. 'How unromantic you are, Sophie!'

'Yes, I know.' Sophie slid down on her knees and buried her head in her grandmother's lap. 'Bad-mannered, too,' she said with a stifled sob. 'I haven't even thanked you for giving me such a wonderful, wonderful present. And I am going to live in Ilex Cottage, I am, I am—somehow.'

'That's better,' said Mrs Wainwright huskily. 'Now get up. Your tears are ruining my skirt.'

CHAPTER TWO

'CECILY'S going into a home?' Dr Gordon stared incredulously.

'That's right.' Sophie waved him towards the dinner-table. 'Sit down or the food will get cold.'

'It would have been too much to expect her to consult *me* as to her choice, of course,' he said acidly. 'I *am* a doctor. In this one solitary instance I feel I might have been deemed sufficiently knowledgeable to advise her.'

Sophie chuckled. 'How you two do go on. *I* suggested she came to live with us,' she added wickedly, and laughed out loud at her father's expression. 'Don't worry. Her reaction was very similar to yours.'

Dr Gordon was relieved enough to admit that his mother-in-law's choice of domicile was an excellent one, and changed the subject to talk of the Pagets and the débâcle of the wedding that never was, giving it his opinion that Alexander, though undoubtedly better off without someone like Delphine, was nevertheless a great deal more shattered by her desertion than he had allowed anyone to see on that unforgettable day.

'I'm sure he was,' agreed Sophie. 'How Delphine had the nerve to do it I don't know. I'd never have had the bottle.'

22

'To leave someone waiting at the church—more or less?'

'Exactly. She wouldn't have been the first bride to change her mind, but at least she could have been civilised about it—given Alexander time to cancel everything.'

Dr Gordon's agreement was wholehearted, and they spent the rest of dinner time talking about the twins' return home from their holiday in France, and their almost immediate departure again for Edinburgh.

'It's going to be very quiet without them,' said Dr Gordon pensively, and Sophie's heart sank as she cleared away. It hardly seemed the right time to broach the subject of Ilex Cottage.

Later she brought out a pile of towels and bedlinen waiting for name tapes, and began sewing at a furious rate while her father watched a documentary on television. It had been a wearing day at the office. Perry, who was Alexander's junior partner, had talked incessantly about Delphine's calumny, and by the time Sophie left for the day she was utterly sick of the subject. Fortunately she managed to leave on time and arrived home early enough to make her father's favourite casserole for dinner, with the idea of putting him in a receptive frame of mind for the news that she was contemplating leaving home.

Sophie stitched and snipped, her mind going round and round in the hope of finding a painless way of stating her case. She glanced up at times to find her father equally preoccupied, staring into space rather than at the television, which probably meant Monday at the practice had been hectic, as usual. And every so often Sophie stared into space herself, lost in dreams of the cottage in Arlesford, her eyes lambent with yearning as she imagined herself there, all on her own, with no one to please but herself. She could eat off a tray—a practice much frowned on by Dr Gordon—look at whatever programmes she liked on television. Perhaps not even have a set at all. She sighed heavily. If only there were some way of achieving her object all sublime, without hurting her father in the process.

Sophie snipped off the thread on the last name tape and folded the last bathtowel neatly on top of the pile, aware suddenly that the television was off and her father was staring at her with unaccustomed concentration. She tensed. What now? The look on her father's lined, distinguished face was unsettling.

'Sophie,' he said abruptly, 'have you any thoughts about marrying Julian?'

There seemed to be altogether too much interest in Julian Brett from her loved ones all at once for Sophie's liking.

'Julian's just a friend, Dad,' she said firmly. 'I go out with him mainly because he's not in the least interested in marriage.' To her surprise her father, instead of looking relieved, looked even more troubled. 'Something wrong, Dad?' she asked gently.

Dr Gordon got up, pushed aside the pile of linen and sat down by Sophie on the couch, putting his arm round her and drawing her close.

'Hey!' said Sophie, much alarmed by such unusually demonstrative behaviour. 'What's up, Dad? Something wrong?'

David Gordon drew in a deep breath, plainly

steeling himself to say whatever it was he had to say. 'Sophie, I want you to know how much I appreciate what you've done for us all since—since your mother died. I know you gave up all thoughts of college and career to look after me and the boys——'

'But I never *had* thoughts of college—or a career!'

He brushed this aside. 'Nevertheless I realise what an effort you've made and I want—*we* want to know that your place is with us always, for as long as you want it.'

We? Us? Sophie's eyes were like saucers. 'What *are* you trying to say, Dad?'

'I'm making a right hash of it,' he said wretchedly, 'but I'm trying to break it gently that for some time now, pet, I've been thinking of getting married again. Now I don't want you to feel you're in the way or anything silly like that . . .'

'Married?' breathed Sophie incredulously.

He nodded unhappily. 'But Kate and I agreed——'

'You're going to marry Aunt Kate?' screeched Sophie.

Her father hugged her to him convulsively. 'But it needn't make any difference, I swear. Please don't get upset, sweetheart.'

Sophie pushed him away, beaming all over her face. '*Upset,* you silly old thing! I'm thrilled to bits—I think it's wonderful!' And she gave him a smacking kiss to prove it.

Dr Gordon mopped his face with a handkerchief, letting out a sigh of relief. 'That's why I asked if you intended marrying Julian, Sophie. You've been going out with him for so long, I wondered if you'd put him off because you couldn't leave me.'

'Oh, my beloved father, just wait until I disabuse
you of any such ridiculous idea,' said Sophie, almost
incoherent with euphoria as she proceeded to tell him
all about Ilex Cottage, putting him in the picture at
long last as to how much she wanted a little place of
her own.

Sophie went round on a pink cloud all her own
after hearing her father's news, unaffected even by
the miniature mountain of dirty clothes which
marked the homecoming of Matt and Mark.

'It's wonderful news,' she told Kate Paget over
lunch at the Singing Kettle. 'I can't think why you
haven't got together sooner.'

Kate's humorous dark eyes were frank. 'The time
wasn't right. Your father wasn't over Louise. Not,'
she added quickly, 'that in one way he ever will be, I
know.'

Sophie assured Kate that Louise Gordon would
have approved strongly. 'Mother liked people to be
happy.'

'So do I. Which, I may add, brings me to the
subject of your proposed move.' Kate's eyes
twinkled. 'People will think your wicked stepmother
has turned you out in the snow!'

Sophie giggled, then plunged into news of the
cottage, and how she intended to paint and decorate
it herself before taking on the job with Sam Jefford.
'Gran made sure the job was mine the moment she
heard about you and Dad, of course!'

'Cecily's a born general—but I'm very fond of her.
She sent me flowers and a very graceful letter, which
I thought was a very nice gesture since I'm marrying

her daughter's husband.' Kate sobered. 'Alexander's the one least likely to be overjoyed about your departure, I fancy.'

'Do you think so?' Personally Sophie doubted it. 'I'll work a month's notice *and* train up my replacement. Unlike other ladies I could mention, I have no intention of leaving him in the mire!'

Nevertheless, as the day of Alexander's return grew nearer Sophie's pink cloud gradually evaporated. She saw only too clearly that a man newly returned from a solitary holiday that should have been a honeymoon was unlikely to receive her resignation with joy, if only for the sheer inconvenience of replacing her. The day he was due back Sophie made a special effort with her appearance to boost her morale, and arrived at the office a good half-hour earlier than usual, only to find Alexander had beaten her to it. He was already installed in his office, going through the day's post.

'You're back,' she said idiotically. 'Have you had a good holiday?'

The instant the words left her tongue she regretted them. Idiot! How could he have had a good holiday under the circumstances? A slow tide of colour rose in her face as Alexander looked up at her with one eyebrow raised in the sardonic way she had hated when she was younger.

'Good morning, Sophie. Yes and no.' He smiled very slightly. 'Yes, I'm back, and no, I did not have a good holiday.'

He looked tanned but tired, with dark smudges beneath his eyes. Otherwise he seemed much the same as usual. He stood up to look at some drawings on the frankly antiquarian drawing-board which had served his father and grandfather before him, then shot a look at Sophie, who was hovering unhappily, unsure whether to retreat or stand her ground.

'Go on,' he encouraged. 'Aren't you going to ask me why?'

'No,' she said shortly. 'I have enough sensitivity to realise why, strange as it may seem. I'll come back later if you're not ready to go through the mail. I've got plenty of work left over from yesterday.'

'The others kept you busy, did they?' He sat down behind his desk, clasping his hands behind his head. 'Have they found anyone for the draughtsman's job, by the way?'

'Perry has some candidates lined up for you to see today.'

'Good. Stop fidgeting and sit down, Sophie.'

Sophie did as he said, wondering how soon she could tactfully raise the subject of her resignation. 'How are you, Alexander?' she asked quietly.

'As well as can be expected, I think describes it. I was a fool, of course, to keep to Greece.' His eyes gleamed unseeingly as he stared at her. 'At the time I just needed to run like hell, I suppose, and my bags were packed and the tickets in my pocket, so I kept on going. My mistake was in going alone.' His eyes focused on her suddenly. 'Would you have come, Sophie?'

She suppressed a shudder. 'No fear!'

'Wise girl.' He shrugged his shoulders in the superbly tailored grey jacket. 'Ah, well, it's water under the bridge now. Besides, I hear there's another wedding in the offing.'

Sophie looked at him searchingly. 'Do you mind?'

'Good God, no—I'm delighted. Can't think why the two of them haven't joined forces long since.'

'I must go round in blinkers. The idea never even crossed my mind.'

'And do *you* mind, Sophie?'

Her smile was so incandescent, Alexander blinked. 'Mind? I think it's too marvellous for words.'

He shook his head. 'And there was Kate, afraid you'd feel pushed out into the cold; wicked stepmother syndrome and all that.'

Sophie straightened her shoulders, fixing her dark eyes on him with such intensity, his own narrowed in surprise. 'In actual fact I'm only too delighted to be pushed out. I hadn't intended telling you yet, Alexander. I was going to let you settle in first, but you may as well know now——'

'Don't tell me you're going to marry Julian Brett,' he said sharply.

It was Sophie's turn to blink. 'No. I'm not. I don't know why everyone's in such a hurry to marry me off to Julian these days. We're just friends. Really. He buys me dinner every so often, nothing more.'

'He's been buying you dinner, to my knowledge, for years, Sophie.' Alexander looked at her quizzically. 'It's generally held to be an aisle-job as far as you two are concerned.'

'I have no intention of getting married. To Julian or anyone else.' Sophie's smile was wry. 'Marriage, as I see it, is one long round of cooking, cleaning, shopping—not to mention children who need endless name tapes when they start school.'

'My God—is *that* how you see marriage?'

Alexander eyed her askance. 'You didn't have a word with Delphine on the subject, by any chance? If so, I'm not surprised she walked out on me.'

'I was never on close terms with Delphine.' Sophie looked him in the eye. 'My friends don't indulge in her type of behaviour.'

There was a nasty silence.

'I'm sorry,' she said at last, not really meaning it. 'I suppose I shouldn't have said that.'

Alexander shrugged. 'Please don't apologise. You obviously feel strongly about it. I take it you would not, under the same circumstances, leave it until the last moment to inform your bridegroom you'd changed your mind.'

'Absolutely not. However, since I'm never going to have a bridegroom the occasion is unlikely to arise.' Sophie took in a deep breath. 'But while we're on the subject, Alexander, I consider what Delphine did was barbarous. I know you and I don't always see eye to eye, but believe me, that day my heart bled for you.' She realised her mistake at once. Alexander's expression grew dauntingly forbidding as he turned to the pile of correspondence in front of him.

'How kind, Sophie. Nevertheless, don't waste your sympathy. I'm not likely to pine long. Women are replaceable—even women as beautiful as Delphine. Now, shall we get on, please?'

Smarting from the rebuff, Sophie seethed for the entire hour they spent together on the accumulation of post. She was on her way out of the room when Alexander called her back.

'Weren't you in the middle of telling me something, Sophie?' he reminded her.

'Oh, yes.' Any compunction Sophie had felt beforehand was long gone. 'I'll confirm it in writing, in the usual way, but I thought you should know I'm leaving, Alexander. I'll work the normal month's notice, of course.'

Alexander sat back in his chair, rolling a gold pen between his fingers as he looked at her. 'I feel like a sinking ship,' he murmured after a long, uncomfortable interval.

'I resent the implication, Alexander,' she said tartly. '*I'm* not ratting on you. I'm perfectly willing to find and train up a replacement before I leave.' Her eyes flashed. 'As you remarked not so long ago, women are replaceable. And I, in case you've never noticed it, do happen to be a woman.'

Alexander subjected her to a comprehensive survey, his eyes travelling very slowly from the crown of her shining dark head to the tips of her small black shoes and back again, lingering longest on those curves which reinforced her statement beyond question.

'So you are, Sophie,' he said eventually. 'I'm glad you brought it to my notice.'

Affronted, she turned on her heel and made for the door, but once again he called her back.

'Why, Sophie?'

She turned reluctantly to face him. 'Why what?'

'Why are you leaving me?' His eyes looked unexpectedly bleak. 'I thought this was the ideal set-up for you in your particular situation.'

'Is that why you originally gave me the job?' she demanded.

'No.' Alexander hesitated. 'To be completely honest, I gave you the job because Kate wanted me to.'

'Not because you thought I'd make an efficient secretary,' said Sophie tonelessly.

'No. But I was fortunate. You proved to be a *highly* efficient secretary.'

Sophie stared at him stonily. 'In which case I assume you'll be willing to give me a reference.'

Alexander smiled. 'Since we're soon to be related, won't that smack of nepotism?' He regarded her steadily. 'Besides, I very much want you to stay. If it's a question of more money——'

'Nothing like that,' she said quickly. 'I'm moving out of the district.'

He got up and strolled round the desk. 'Am I allowed to ask where?'

'Of course. Arlesford. Gran's given me a cottage there.'

Alexander bent to pick up a paperclip. 'The one in Church Row?'

'That's right,' said Sophie, surprised. 'You know it?'

'Yes.' He laughed a little. 'I might have known the fair Cecily had a hand in all this. What a lady. If she'd been a few years younger I'd have married *her* instead of making a fool of myself over Delphine.'

Sophie laughed, relieved that Alexander looked less hostile, and told him about her grandmother's bombshell about entering a residential home, and how she'd bulldozed Sam Jefford into giving Sophie a job. 'I'm sure the poor man must have been afraid to say no. He's stuck with me whether he wants me or not.'

Alexander took the pile of letters from her and laid them on the desk, surprising her considerably by taking her hands in his, his eyes very serious as they held hers. 'I've no doubt at all that Jefford wants you, Sophie. He'd be a fool if he didn't, and I know damn well he's no fool. He's too successful for that.'

'You know him, then?' Sophie tried to pull her hands away, but Alexander's long fingers tightened.

'Slightly. Before—before I went away I put him on the track of finding suitable premises for our new branch office.'

'Oh. Small world.' Sophie smiled briskly and pulled out of his grasp. 'I must get on. Perry will be after my services any minute. Do the others know you're back, by the way?'

Alexander nodded. 'I got in touch with both Perry and George Huntley last night.' He handed her the mail. 'Would you do me a very large favour, Sophie?'

She eyed him warily. 'If I can. What is it?'

'Will you come with me for a bar snack at the George at lunch time? To celebrate our parents' nuptials,' he said quickly, as she opened her mouth to refuse. 'And not just that,' he added. 'To be honest I'd very much appreciate a little moral support for my first appearance in public since that God-awful day.'

It was a new experience for Sophie to find Alexander Paget coaxing her for her company. She found she quite liked it. It was rather enjoyable to see the self-sufficient, infinitely superior Alexander waiting rather tensely for her consent.

'Why not?' she said casually.

Gratifying though his answering smile might have been, thoughts of lunch with Alexander filled Sophie with foreboding. All morning, even while she worked with her usual speed and concentration, she was dogged by the prospect of running the Deansbury gauntlet in company with her boss. Normally Alexander's lunches were working affairs, periods spent making the contacts vital to the success of a private firm of architects in a world where competition was fierce and the biggest plums fell to the most competitive bidders. Paget & Son were consistently successful in the Deansbury area, due partly to their long-established name in the field, partly because the firm's work was unfailingly excellent, and not least because of the charisma of Alexander Paget, who was universally respected as a man of integrity coupled with a very individual flair. Today, thought Sophie, sighing, all the world and his wife would be eager to express their sympathy over Alexander's recent experience. Hardly a tempting prospect.

In actual fact the occasion was less trying than Sophie had expected. The George, a popular place with business people at lunch time, was thronged with people pleased to see Alexander in circulation again. And all of them, to Sophie's surprise, seemed to take her own presence for granted. Due to the closeness of their respective families Sophie and Alexander were often present at the same family occasions, but Alexander had never actually taken her out to lunch before, or anywhere else, for that matter. He was very attentive, she found, also sensitive to her urge for seclusion, since he seated her in a corner with her back to the room, in a chair which gave her a view of the river outside the windows instead of a sea of curious faces. Sophie chose a glass of white wine and a small salad, refusing Alexander's pleas to try something more exciting.

'No, thanks.' She gave him a cool little smile. 'I rarely eat any lunch at all, except for an apple.'

He frowned. 'Why not?'

'Because I cook what my father calls "a proper dinner" every evening, and if I ate lunch as well I would be even rounder than I am now,' she informed him bluntly, flushing a little as, for the second time that day, Alexander made a leisurely examination of her person, which was clad as usual in garb suited to her job. Sophie made a practice of wearing tailored skirts and shirts to the office, concentrating on quality and cut rather than quantity, and today the skirt was black and straight and the shirt crisp white cotton dotted in black. Her legs were her main vanity, and she invariably wore fine, dark stockings and classic shoes with high heels to compensate for her lack of inches.

'You're not very tall,' said Alexander at last, 'but otherwise I'd have thought you were a very satisfactory size and shape.'

'That's not what you used to say!' said Sophie with feeling, then took a sip of wine, annoyed with herself.

He grinned. 'Well, you *were* rather on the roly-poly side at one time, admit it! But you grew out of that long ago.'

'Only on the outside, Alexander! Inside, due to
your relentless teasing when I was at the vulnerable
stage, I still feel fat.'

'My God! Is *that* why you treat me with . . .'
Alexander thought for a moment. 'Reserve,
perhaps?'

'It used to be downright hostility.' She smiled
reassuringly. 'But I've mellowed with time.'

'Thank the lord for that.'

At first Sophie found it difficult to enjoy a meal
interrupted so often by well-meant expressions of
sympathy, but on each occasion Alexander cut short
the embarrassed friend by introducing Sophie
whether she knew the man or not, and she grew
almost used to it after a while, rather surprised when
they were eventually left in peace.

'Thank God you came with me, Sophie,' said
Alexander, sighing. 'You've been a great help.'

'Perry or George would have done just as well.'

Alexander shook his head, looking more relaxed
now the initial ordeal was over. 'Perry was rushing
off to meet the latest conquest for lunch, and George
went out on that house inspection the other side of
Gloucester earlier on. Besides,' he added with a
sudden gleam in his eyes, 'neither Perry nor George
happens to be a beautiful girl. And a poor, ill-treated
male like me needed the company of just such a lady
very badly today. Does that sound very chauvinistic?'

'No. Only natural, I suppose. But I'm not
beautiful,' said Sophie.

Alexander frowned. 'Who says?'

'My mirror. Not only am I not beautiful,
Alexander, I'm neither blind nor equipped with rose-

coloured spectacles!'

At that moment yet another sympathiser came to their table to clap a hand on Alexander's shoulder. 'Sincere condolences, old chap,' said the man solemnly, nodding politely to Sophie before he took himself off.

'You'd think I'd suffered a bereavement,' said Alexander savagely.

Sophie regarded him thoughtfully. 'Haven't you?'

He pushed away his half-eaten lunch. 'In a way, I suppose.' He leaned his chin on his hand, looking up at her. 'I suppose the basic truth is that I just never got to know Delphine well enough. She was always flitting about the globe on those modelling assignments of hers, so we spent very little time together if one counts it up in hours. Fate plays some funny tricks, doesn't it, Sophie? If Delphine's family hadn't moved to Deansbury last year I'd never have met her at all.'

'Did she intend carrying on with all the travelling after—afterwards?'

'She insisted she was tired of it. Swore she fancied settling down.' Alexander's smile was crooked. 'I deluded myself she meant it.'

'I could never see what you and Delphine had in common,' said Sophie frankly.

He reached across the table and took her hand. 'To be candid, we had one thing in common which rather overshadowed everything else.'

Sophie coloured and tried to take her hand away. 'No boyish confidences, please, Alexander.'

'Hold on! I was merely trying to explain.' Alexander's grip tightened as he leaned closer. 'For your ears only, Sophie, to be perfectly truthful I'd have settled very happily for a less permanent relationship, but, believe it or not, Delphine held out for a wedding ring before she'd let me into her bed.'

Sophie stared. 'You mean . . .?'

'That's right, sweetheart. I was allowed to kiss, to touch as much as I liked, but nothing more. Not until I'd signed on the dotted line.' Alexander's laugh was bitter. 'To put it in a nutshell, I'm not only a laughing stock, but I'm suffering—and I do mean suffering—from frustration. Plus the knowledge that I've behaved like several different varieties of fool over Miss Delphine Wyndham. All of which are new experiences, I may add.'

Sophie eyed him in consternation, unsure how to express her sympathy without making things worse. 'I don't think you're a laughing-stock, Alexander,' she said carefully. 'How could you be? You're a very popular, respected man in Deansbury. I'm sure no one has even considered laughing at you.'

His eyes softened. 'Thank you, Sophie.'

She looked away. 'And you're certainly not a fool. I imagine any man would have done the same for a girl as beautiful as Delphine.'

'So I'm not a laughing-stock, and I'm not a fool. That disposes of two of my problems.' Alexander put a finger under her chin. 'Have you anything to recommend for the third?'

It slowly dawned on Sophie what Alexander meant. Right here in the bar of the George he was, she realised, making some kind of proposition, and, amazingly, she wasn't as angry as she might have expected to be, if ever she'd imagined such a situation arising between them. Not that she would have done in a million years. If their relationship had been slightly more than just employer and secretary from the beginning, it was only because their families had always been friends. Added to which, Alexander had been a such a tower of strength to the boys when their mother died. Sophie regarded him absently as she remembered his patience when the twins, particularly, followed him round like puppies during the time when their father was so shattered. She herself had turned to Kate Paget for comfort, as was only natural, and had never felt as close to Alexander as her brothers did.

'You're very quiet,' he commented, breaking into her thoughts.

'Alexander,' she said tentatively, 'I would have thought this particular problem would have been, well, lessened while you were away.'

'I fully intended it to be.' He smiled crookedly. 'But the other people in the hotel were couples, of varying sorts, and the thought of purchasing a lady's favours—with all the dangers and drawbacks entailed —put a temporary damper on my baser male urges.'

'Were there no other possibilities?' asked Sophie, rather surprised to find she wasn't embarrassed.

'None I cared to pursue.' Alexander released her hand. 'I apologise, Sophie. Forget everything I said.' He looked uncharacteristically contrite. 'I wouldn't blame you if you blacked my eye for even implying you might——'

'Restore your male ego to its former complacency?' Sophie finished for him acidly as she rose to go.

'Not exactly.' He held her jacket for her. 'I think I was just asking for comfort.'

'And I happened to be nearest, I assume.'

'Exactly,' he agreed lightly, and took her by the elbow to steer her through the crowd. 'And possibly dearest, too,' he said in her ear. 'After all, Sophie, you and I are *very* old friends. I was on your particular scene a damn sight earlier than Julian Brett!'

CHAPTER THREE

SOPHIE fully expected to feel awkward with Alexander after their lunch together, but he soon made it plain he felt no regret at having confided in her. In fact, Alexander now behaved towards her as though she were a woman with feelings and opinions to be considered, rather than just little Sophie Gordon who was so efficient and familiar he hardly noticed she was there half the time. These days he was charm itself, and she viewed the charm with suspicion, certain he had an ulterior motive for it. If she hadn't known him better Sophie could have sworn Alexander was pulling out all the stops to make her reconsider her resignation. Not that she had much time for conjecture, since Paget & Son were busier than ever, with the necessity for a new branch growing more urgent by the day.

'I wish your chum Jefford would hurry up and find something in the way of premises,' said Alexander irritably.

'He's not my chum,' Sophie replied.

Alexander smiled in his old, superior manner. 'Better beware, Sophie, when you work for him. He's just divorced his wife, and lonely men are dangerous beasts.' He squeezed her waist unexpectedly as he held the door for her, and Sophie, her arms full of files, was helpless to prevent him.

'I say,' said Perry sternly, cannoning into them from the opposite direction, 'would you two mind doing this sort of thing somewhere else, please? There are young, innocent draughtsmen about, you know.'

Alexander's cousin was in his late twenties, with a shock of blond hair a great deal less disciplined than that of his senior partner, and wide blue eyes which gave the lie to the razor-sharpness of the mind behind them.

Sophie included both men in an irritated glare and made for her office, wishing, not for the first time since Alexander's return, that he would revert to his former, pre-wedding-day self, to the time when his attitude towards her had been a lot more impersonal. And a lot easier to put up with, in many ways. She felt on edge most of the time lately, she realised, and put it down to the fact that she was up to her ears at home as well as the office. It was because the twins were leaving home for Edinburgh, she told herself firmly, and applied herself to the task of compiling a short-list from the applications received in response to the advertisement for her own replacement. Alexander flatly refused to have anything to do with it.

'Just weed out three or four from the bunch and I'll see them all on the same day,' he said indifferently. 'Otherwise I don't want to know.'

'But, Alexander, tell me if you want someone young and attractive, or would you prefer mature and reliable——'

'I want *you*, Sophie. But since you're hell-bent on deserting me I don't care a damn who you get in your place, just so long as the woman's literate and can type—and make decent coffee.' Alexander turned from his drawing-board to find Sophie frowning at him in disapproval. 'On reflection,' he added, 'don't get someone too glamorous. George Huntley's blood pressure is suspect and Perry, as you well know, has a very low threshold when it comes to your sex.'

Sophie glared at him. 'I see. You want someone unlikely to disturb you males with her physical charms. Thanks a lot, Alexander. In all the time I've worked here not a soul has ever made the slightest attempt to make a pass at *me*—which should tell me something!'

'My God, I should hope they haven't. They'd have had me to contend with!' He laughed and took her by the shoulders, his eyes teasing. 'Didn't you realise everyone was given the "hands off" instruction right from the word go as far as you're concerned, Sophie, from Perry downwards? I won't include George because he's happily married and wrapped up in his children. The rest know only too well they'd have me to answer to if they started chasing you round your desk.'

Sophie bit her lip. 'Oh. I see.'

'By the way, I almost forgot,' he said casually, 'I took a message for you while you were out to lunch. Brett can't make it tonight. Asked me to apologise for him.'

'Oh, right. Thanks.' Sophie nodded, undismayed.

'Aren't you disappointed?' said Alexander curiously.

'No.' Sophie's dark eyes lit with laughter. 'He was taking me to see some earnest foreign film at the Arts

Centre.'

Alexander shook his fair head in wonder. 'Good God! And you don't mind missing such a treat? How noble, Sophie.'

She chuckled. 'Don't be unkind. Julian's a very nice man, really. It's just that some of his tastes are a little—well, esoteric, that's all.'

Alexander's eyes glinted. 'Esoteric? What *do* you both get up to, may I ask?'

'Don't be disgusting!' she snapped.

He wagged a reproving finger. 'Now, now, Sophie. All I meant was poetry-reading, board-games and so on. Nothing naughty.'

Sophie flushed bright red and dived for the door, but Alexander caught her before she reached it and held her lightly.

'Sophie,' he said softly, 'let me take you out to dinner tonight, instead.'

In the time it took for Sophie's colour to subside her mind worked at a furious rate. She was highly suspicious of this new Alexander, the one who'd taken to teasing her and touching her and generally making it impossible to ignore that lately his attitude towards her had taken a decided U-turn. He was missing Delphine, she reminded herself, and behaving in the main with exemplary stoicism about it. Nevertheless, Sophie couldn't rid herself of a nagging suspicion which grew stronger by the day. Preposterous though it might seem, she was beginning to believe Alexander had elected to seek balm for his wounds from the last source she would ever have expected. Her own.

'Well?' he prompted. 'Will you, Sophie?'

'I can't,' she said. 'I'm cooking dinner for Dad and the boys as usual. I wasn't meeting Julian until later on.'

Alexander released her and stood back, still regarding her in the same unsettling fashion. 'Just a thought. Some other time, perhaps, before you finally shake the dust of Deansbury from your shoes.'

'Yes. Lovely.' Sophie smiled brightly and retreated to her office, which was small and cramped, but blessedly private, with a door she could shut on the rest of the workforce at Paget & Sons.

'Kate's coming round after dinner,' announced Dr Gordon, as the family gathered round the table later that evening. 'Thought we'd thrash out a few plans for the wedding.'

Matthew Gordon, large and dark like his father, received his plate with interest. 'What's this?'

'Beef olives.'

Mark, who was a carbon copy of his brother, gave a loud whistle. 'Touch of the *haute cuisine,* no less. Special occasion?'

'No. I got home early for once, and thought I'd try something different.' Sophie tasted her own portion cautiously. 'Hm. The garlic's a bit violent.'

'It's very good,' her father assured her, then grinned. 'Cast-iron defence against vampires, too.'

Sophie apologised, laughing, but the twins were enthusiastic. Their sojourn in France had given them a taste for the exotic and they ate heartily. Not, in their sister's opinion, that they ever did anything else.

'All our name tapes on?' asked Matt.

'Of course, O Master. Everything's ready for the off. And if you unpack anything else and wear it I'll throttle you,' warned Sophie.

Dr Gordon scrutinised his daughter's tired face. 'Busy day today, love?'

'Very. On top of the usual stuff, I'm trying to find someone to replace me. Not many of the applications are very promising so far.' Sophie felt dispirited, wondering now why she'd been ambitious enough to cook such a complicated meal at the same time as finishing off the twins' ironing.

'How's Alexander?' asked Mark. 'Pining for the tasty Delphine?'

'How would I know?' said Sophie shortly.

'Alexander's not the type to show his feelings to the world at large,' observed her father. 'Though Kate is amazed at how well he's taken it.' He fixed his sons with a peremptory eye. 'You two, by the way, can do the washing up. Sophie's going out with Julian.'

Sophie disabused him of this idea, and braced herself for the usual barrage of teasing over Julian, who'd never managed to win her brothers' approval. Ignoring them with the ease of long practice, she went to sit with her father, leaving the pots and pans to the noisy ministrations of the twins while she curled up in a corner of the sofa to watch the news. She thought half-heartedly about tidying herself, but decided against it, thinking Aunt Kate was unlikely to mind a shiny nose and faded old denims just for once.

'Something worrying you, pet?' asked Dr Gordon. Sophie smiled absently, her eyes on the screen.

'No, Dad. I'm fine.' She turned to look at him. 'I'm off to look at the cottage on Saturday, by the way, and since it's my Sunday at Gran's and the twins will have gone by then, I thought I'd stay the night at Greenacre.'

'Of course, pet.' He looked up as the doorbell rang. 'Kate, I expect.'

'I'll go,' yelled Matt from the kitchen, and to Sophie's consternation could be heard exclaiming in delight as a familiar voice greeted him at the door.

Alexander, it seemed, had decided to accompany his stepmother.

Kate came into the room to be kissed by David Gordon, her eyes apologetic as she gave Sophie a hug. 'I know you've been stuck with my son all day, too, love, but Alexander volunteered to drive me over. It's a bit foggy tonight.'

Alexander sauntered into the room, smiling, looking rather different from the sober-suited architect of the day in a yellow polo shirt and khaki cord trousers, Mark and Matthew hot on his heels as usual. He greeted Dr Gordon and Sophie with the air of a man confident of his welcome.

As he had a right to be, conceded Sophie, trying to be fair. They were all fond of Alexander, she told herself firmly, her brothers more than herself, of course. Indeed, Mark and Matthew seized on him at once, talking their heads off in unison about their eagerness to be off to Edinburgh, and Sophie retreated into her sofa-corner while her father poured drinks.

'You won't know what to do with yourself with those two off your hands, Sophie,' said Kate, joining

Sophie.

'Bliss,' agreed Sophie. 'How those boys eat! I'm sure Tim never ate so much when he was their age. Dad told you Tim wrote to say how pleased he was about the wedding?'

Kate nodded, her eyes warm. 'You've all been so good about it.'

'And why wouldn't we be?' Sophie smiled wickedly. 'I'm not losing a father, after all—only gaining a very lovely stepmother. Plus another brother to add to my tally,' she added deliberately.

Alexander looked up sharply. 'What was that?'

When Kate repeated Sophie's comment, he looked unamused. 'While I,' he said drily, 'seem to be losing out all round—first a bride, now a secretary.'

Sophie hugged her drawn-up knees, wishing she were somewhere else, but Matt bridged the awkward little silence with his usual blithe disregard for sensitivity.

'We were thrown by the news, Alexander. Who'd have thought Delphine would play a dirty trick like that? Pretty foul, if you ask me.'

'But no one has, Matthew,' said his father, 'so let us forget about the incident in question—my apologies, Alexander—and talk about Kate and me instead.'

Alexander held up his hand promptly. 'Could I, as son and giver-away of the bride, make one request, David?'

Dr Gordon nodded good-humouredly.

'Do you intend marrying in church?' Alexander's flexible mouth turned down at the corners. 'I know it's not up to me, of course, but I'm sure I speak for

Kate as well as myself when I say I don't think I could face another session in Deansbury Register Office!'

There was sympathetic laughter as David Gordon assured him the wedding would certainly be quiet, with only immediate family and one or two friends, but quite definitely in church.

'Aunt Kate,' said Sophie a little later, while the men were engaged in a discussion, 'are you inviting Gran?'

'Of course, love.' Kate looked surprised. 'Why? Do you think she won't want to come?'

'No, no. I'm sure she'll be delighted. I thought maybe you wouldn't care for the idea.'

Kate patted her hand. 'I wouldn't exclude her for the world. You can tell her this weekend that an official invite will arrive as soon as I get them printed.'

'What are you two whispering about?' Alexander joined them, making Kate move up so he could wedge himself between her and Sophie. 'Girlish confidences?'

'No. We were talking about Gran.' Sophie retreated as far as she could, but Alexander promptly moved with her, so that she was trapped.

'Ah, the divine Cecily,' he said, putting an arm along the back of the sofa. 'Hers was just one of several calls I had this evening after you went, Sophie.'

Sophie frowned at him in surprise. 'Gran phoned you? Business or pleasure?'

'A little of each. She asked me if I'd do a house inspection on the cottage in Arlesford before you move in, and of course I agreed. I wouldn't dare do otherwise!' He laughed into Sophie's surprised eyes, and moved his arm to hold her shoulders lightly. 'She said you were going to see the place on Saturday and suggested I go with you to look over it for dry rot or rising damp. So the survey is business, your company the pleasure.'

Sophie shifted restlessly, aware that the twins were taking great interest in the location of Alexander's arm. 'Are you sure Saturday's convenient? It seems a bit unfair to encroach on your weekend.'

'Not at all. There's nothing I'd rather do.'

'I'm relieved, Alexander,' said Dr Gordon. 'Since Sophie's set her her heart on living in that poky little cottage, I'd be glad to know the place is fit for human habitation.'

The telephone rang and Mark rushed off to answer it, returning to say Julian was on the line for Sophie. She scrambled thankfully from her corner, glad to escape. After listening patiently to a few minutes of Julian's apologies and suggestions for another evening out, she got back to find the twins had gone off to the local to meet friends, and in their absence Alexander had offered the bridal pair the Chantry, which was the house left to him by his father, and which he currently shared with Kate.

Sophie looked at him in surprise, well aware that he had intended living there with Delphine. Kate's original plan had been to move in with a widowed sister when Alexander married, but under the circumstances she had stayed on at the Chantry.

Alexander smiled. 'It's rather a spur-of-the-moment decision, but I've been given the option on a house I've had my eye on for some time, so I thought David could take over the Chantry with Kate.'

Kate took Sophie's hand in hers. 'David and I have been mulling over where to live ever since we decided to join forces. Even though none of you will be living with us permanently, I'd still like a house where there was a room you could each call your own. Tim included, when he gets tired of his Aussie sheep. Alexander's solution seems perfect.'

Dr Gordon nodded with enthusiasm. 'I'll put this one on the market immediately, then between us Kate and I should see Alexander's not out of pocket on the deal.'

Sophie looked at Alexander curiously. 'Where is the house you have in mind?'

'Oh, didn't I tell you?' he said casually. 'Your future boss has been very busy on my behalf. He's secured a house in Brading for me, and at the same time found the exact office premises I've been after for the firm.'

Sophie felt distinctly nettled. It was the first she'd heard of it. 'How fortunate. Are the premises large?'

'Slightly smaller than the Deansbury offices, but more than adequate.'

'Whereabouts in Brading?' asked Dr Gordon with interest.

'The house is at the end of Cheynies Lane. I did the original plans for it years ago when my father was alive. River frontage, very private, just what I want.' Alexander paused, smiling, while Kate looked down with sudden interest at a loose thread on her sleeve. 'But the office premises aren't in Brading after all, Sophie. Sam Jefford snapped some up in Sheep

Street in Arlesford.'

'Arlesford!' Sophie looked from Alexander's bland smile to Kate's uneasy face. 'Did *you* know about this, Aunt Kate?'

'Not until tonight.'

Sam Jefford, Alexander informed them, had rung just before he left the office. Some office premises had just come into his hands, and since they were right in the commercial centre of Arlesford he advised snapping them up immediately.

'And the house in Brading?' asked Sophie coolly. 'Did that come on the market today, too?'

'Er—no, not exactly. I went to see Jefford some time ago, actually. I'd been given the nod that Willow Reach might soon be up for sale.' Alexander smiled warily. 'I thought I'd kill two birds with one stone, vet your future employer at the same time—make sure he was a suitable type for you to work for.'

Sophie was so incensed at this, she never even noticed when her father led Kate from the room. She sprang up, eyes flashing, infuriated by the thought that her new life in Arlesford looked like being less free of the old one than she'd imagined.

'How very busy you've been, Alexander—downright interfering, in fact!' She battled to keep back tears of sheer temper. 'Why does everybody think I'm incapable of running my own life?' She dashed a hand across her eyes impatiently. 'Gran heard of the cottage—which is wonderful, I know, but then even *she* couldn't leave me to find my own job. She even organises you to go over the cottage with me. While you, Alexander Paget, have the sheer cheek to take it on yourself to check up on Sam Jefford's pedigree, not to mention the amazing coincidence of his finding premises for you in the very town where I intend to live. There were other premises, Alexander. I write your letters, remember. Perry's too. You could have had a place in Gloucester——'

'Too much competition.'

'Or Bristol——'

'Too expensive.'

Sophie's eyes flashed dangerously. 'I see. It just had to be Arlesford.'

'It was, I swear, sheer coincidence, Sophie.' Alexander moved nearer, but she backed away, her eyes dangerously bright.

'Even Dad seems to have some crazy idea of marrying me off to Julian Brett!' She paused, sniffing angrily. 'Perhaps it's not such a crazy idea. Julian, at least, doesn't try to run my life for me.'

Alexander's face darkened. 'None of us is trying to run your life, Sophie. We just want to take care of you, that's all—keep a friendly eye on you.'

'Oh, yes? And if all had gone to plan, and you were now living happily ever after with Delphine, would you, personally, still be so damn eager to keep an eye on me? Doesn't all this sudden rush of feeling stem from the fact that you've been thrown over by one woman and I just happen to be on hand as convenient target practice for that wounded ego of yours?'

Alexander had been standing with his hands in his pockets, but at her last words he removed them quickly and grabbed her by the shoulders, pushing her over to the mirror to stand close behind her so that she could see their reflections together; Alexander, his thick fair hair lying close to the classical shape of his head, his eyes glittering like a tiger's between his thick, dark lashes. And there's me, thought Sophie dismally. Hair like a bird's nest, eyes swollen, nose red, and tastefully attired in one of the twins' shrunken sweatshirts.

'If,' said Alexander, in a chillingly soft voice, 'transient physical comfort was my sole aim, Sophie Gordon, don't you think I might have chosen a lady just a trifle more suitable—from a purely male standpoint?'

The words acted on her like a cold wind, drying her tears like magic. She shrugged free of his hands. 'How stupid of me. You're right, of course. I'm a complete idiot.'

Alexander moved towards her, but Sophie flinched away.

'Don't——' she said sharply, and Alexander stepped back, his face set in grim lines.

'You mistook my meaning,' he said urgently, then cursed under his breath as Kate came in with Dr Gordon.

'Finished fighting, you two?' she said gaily. 'I've made some tea.'

With enormous effort Sophie managed to smile, aware all at once that her head was pounding. 'I wonder if you'd all excuse me? I don't feel very marvellous—must have been the garlic.' She swallowed hard, gave a stifled moan and fled upstairs to part violently with her dinner, then stripped her clothes from her shivering body and crawled into bed, like a small animal burrowing into its nest for shelter.

CHAPTER FOUR

SHEER willpower forced Sophie out of bed next morning to face her father over the breakfast-table.

'You look like something the cat dragged in,' said Dr Gordon, and took her pulse. 'Let me see your tongue.'

Sophie stuck it out obediently and Dr Gordon took one look, told her to put it away and gave her back her hand.

'Let me ring Alexander and tell him you're not up to going in today.'

Sophie yearned to succumb to such temptation, but somehow held firm. 'No, Dad. Too much on. Anyway, it was only the beef olives.' She shuddered. 'Never again.'

Dr Gordon looked sceptical. 'The rest of us managed to survive them unscathed. Kate was very worried about you. She popped up to take a look at you before I drove her home, but she said you were asleep.'

Sophie had been lying low, not asleep, but instead of saying so seized on an interesting point. 'Why did *you* drive her home?'

'Alexander left once you went off to bed. Said he had some work to do, so I asked Kate to stay on for a while.' He smiled at his wan daughter. 'Must have been quite an argument you two had, since you rushed off to throw up and Alexander rushed off to his drawing-board. Just like the old times, in fact, when you two argued about everything. I thought you were both past that stage long since.'

'Alexander seems to imagine he has some right to interfere in my life.' Sophie drained her teacup thirstily. 'Sees his role as Big Brother, not stepbrother.'

'When you were together on the sofa last night I received the distinct impression that Alexander didn't see himself in the light of your brother at all.' Dr Gordon got up, patting her head before collecting his medical bag. 'And don't flash those eyes at me, pet. I'm only a poor benighted father trying to bring up his daughter the best way he can.'

Sophie grinned at such blatant bathos. 'Oh, go and minister to someone else. I'm fine. Or I shall be after I've drunk a gallon of tea.'

Rather to her own surprise, Sophie was right. By the time she'd drunk the teapot dry she felt sufficiently restored to do battle with her appearance, and achieved a creditable result with extra blusher and eyeshadow, plus the morale-lift of a new cream silk shirt striped in black, with a black satin bow tied under the cream collar. Worn with her usual trim, black skirt and slender-heeled shoes the effect was both efficient and pleasing. Nothing, however, helped with the sinking feeling in her stomach at the prospect of facing Alexander. Sophie felt neither of them had emerged from the previous night's encounter with honours, and wished fervently she could leave her job at once, instead of keeping to her promise to train her own replacement.

By the time she reached the premises of Paget &
Son in the market square Sophie had worked herself
into an unprecedented state of nerves, only to find
that Alexander was not, as was his custom, at his
desk before she arrived. Perry called from his own
sanctum instead, which was unusual. Punctuality in
the mornings was not one of Perry's strong points.

'Alexander told me to remind you he's in court all
day today,' he announced, his face concerned as he
looked at her more closely. 'I say, Sophie, you feeling
rough, love?'

'Stomach bug,' said Sophie briefly, privately
delirious with joy that Alexander had elected to go
straight to court instead of coming first to the office
as he usually did. She felt better at once, and settled
herself thankfully to work through the day's mail
with Perry instead. Lunch was a cup of tea taken
alone in her office, while she just sat doing nothing at
all until her lunch hour was over, much of the time
spent in resisting the urge to type her notice, leave it
on Alexander's desk and never darken his door
again. Which was a pretty impractical move, Sophie
reminded herself, since they would soon be linked,
however loosely, by the marriage of their respective
parents. She worked with a will during the afternoon,
comforted by the prospect of a morning off next day
to help get the twins away on their journey to
Edinburgh. She was grateful for any breathing space
she could get before confronting Alexander again,
and went cold all over every time she thought of the
way Alexander had made it so crystal-clear that any
amatory intentions on his part had been the product
of her own imagination.

When she arrived home Sophie was relieved, and touched, to find that the twins had organised their own farewell dinner, in the shape of many and varied dishes from the local Indian takeaway, neither of the boys backward in disposing of their queasy sister's share of the spoils. When they'd taken themselves off for a final carouse down at the local pub, Sophie took her father's advice and went early to bed after a supper of toast and tea, and woke next day in better shape to cope with the frantic last-minute chaos as her excited brothers packed their old transit van ready to set off for the delights of Freshers' Week at Edinburgh University. Sophie felt a sharp pang as the battered van finally rolled away down the drive, taking her young brothers on the first leg of adulthood. She was glad of her father's arm around her as they turned back into the house.

'We'll miss them,' said Dr Gordon gruffly, and Sophie smiled, determinedly cheerful.

'But far fewer shirts and plates to wash!'

When Sophie arrived at the office after lunch Alexander was there right enough, but too preoccupied to pay attention to his secretary. Builders were in and out of the office all afternoon as he worked through a list of them, systematically vetting which of them were most suitable to tender for construction of a large superstore on the outskirts of the town.

Since Alexander was fully occupied, Sophie took the opportunity of writing to the four most promising aspirants for her own job, requesting the chosen ladies to attend for interview the following week. She was obliged to interrupt Alexander once to collect his diary to make sure which day was best, but he barely acknowledged her discreet murmur of apology, and Sophie withdrew quickly, more than content to keep as low a profile as possible. When it was time for her to leave Alexander was still tied up with the last of the builders, and she waited a while, reluctant to interrupt him again. Eventually, even though it was Friday evening, she decided to take the unusual course of going off without informing Alexander, said goodnight to Perry and left for the weekend with a sigh of relief.

Sophie woke with a start the following morning to repeated rings of the doorbell. She peered at her clock, bleary-eyed, to find it was eight-thirty, which meant her father would already have left for his Saturday-morning surgery. Yawning, she dragged a dressing-gown over her pyjamas and went down-stairs, expecting to confront the postman. Her jaw dropped when she opened the door to find Alexander smiling at her as he jogged energetically on the spot. He looked depressingly fit and fresh in a black tracksuit and running shoes, his hair only a very little ruffled by his daily morning run.

'Morning, Sophie. Thought I'd check what time you want to start for Arlesford,' he said cheerfully.

Sophie felt murderous. She dragged her dressing-gown closer round herself, horribly conscious of the spectacle she presented. 'I'm going on my own,' she said acidly.

'Don't be silly. Cecily told me to escort you, so escort you I shall.' He smiled kindly, as though she were a fractious child. 'Not still peeved with me, are you, Sophie? Run along, there's a good girl. I'll be back for you in an hour.'

Before Sophie could voice her objections Alexander was off, making for home at a pace that tired Sophie to watch. Irritably she banged the door shut and went upstairs to shower, fulminating, not for the first time recently, over her beloved grandmother's autocratic ways, and convinced the last thing in the world Alexander really wanted to do was potter about in a chilly old cottage on a Saturday.

Nevertheless, Sophie was ready and waiting when Alexander's Mercedes roadster slid to a stop outside the gate exactly an hour later. By this time she felt more composed, largely due to the fact that her hair was shining, her face made up with great care to look as nature intended it to look, and she was wearing her favourite brown cords and cream wool shirt, with an apricot mohair sweater knotted loosely over her shoulders by its sleeves. Not of a mind to let Alexander think she was over-eager, she deliberately hid in her bedroom and let him ring the doorbell twice before going downstairs to let him in. Her greeting was coolly polite as she asked him if he'd care for coffee before they set off.

Alexander, dressed in ancient denims which clung lovingly to his long legs, wore a shirt rather similar to Sophie's, with a fleece-lined denim jacket slung over his shoulders. He assented with enthusiasm, settling himself on a high stool in the kitchen while she made instant coffee in yellow pottery mugs.

'I'm sorry about the other night, Sophie,' he said, taking the wind out of her sails. 'I think you totally misunderstood what I said.'

'I don't remember what you said,' lied Sophie

without turning a hair. 'I just wasn't feeling well. My dinner disagreed with me.'

'I was afraid the news about the new premises was the real culprit.' His smile was disarming. 'I promise you, Sophie, it was sheer coincidence that Sam Jefford happened to find the ideal place in Arlesford. I'm not trying to breathe down your neck, scout's honour. Not that the idea lacks appeal,' he added very deliberately.

Sophie scowled at him over her coffee. 'I wish you wouldn't say things like that, Alexander. You never used to. I preferred it when you treated me like part of the furniture.'

'Did I?' Alexander shook his head disapprovingly. 'No wonder you don't want to work for me any more!'

'You know that isn't the reason,' she said, exasperated. 'I just want a change. It's nothing personal.'

'Then if it's nothing personal, my little friend, what objection do you have to seeing something of me socially?' Alexander's handsome face wore an expression of such friendly reason, Sophie thawed a little.

'Well, none, I suppose,' she said with caution. 'If that's all you have in mind, fine.'

'Good.' He slid off the stool, and took her by the hand. 'Come on, then, let's go.'

The air held a tang of autumn, the leaves on the trees just beginning to turn along the sunlit minor roads Alexander chose in preference to the swift, busy bypass which linked Arlesford to Deansbury. Sophie relaxed in the luxurious car, not at all averse to a journey enjoyed in such comfort rather than in the bus she would have caught otherwise. And any traces of constraint she felt were soon dispelled by Alexander's matter-of-fact attitude as he weighed up the merits of the four applicants Sophie had lined up for the following week, then went on to discuss the possibility of winning the job of designing a large, luxury hotel on the river at Brading.

'Are you likely to get it, do you think?' asked Sophie. 'The competition's bound to be fierce.'

Alexander was optimistic. By a stroke of luck he had obtained outline planning permission for the owner of the land in the first place, which gave him an edge when the owner sold the land to the hotel chain. 'Fancy taking a look at the spot?' he asked. 'We'll still have plenty of time to look over the cottage this afternoon.'

Sophie agreed readily. Brading was a picturesque place, hardly more than a large village on the banks of the Avon, and very popular with people who commuted from it daily to Bristol and Bath and even as far as London. The site for the hotel was a prime spot, with riparian rights along a sizeable stretch of river. Alexander parked the car near a group of willows overlooking a view of trees and sunlit, slow-moving water, and cattle grazing on the watermeadows on the far side of the river.

'The hotel aims to be one of those places you can get away from it all for a restorative type of weekend break. Indoor heated pool, jacuzzis, gymnasium, landscaped grounds with tennis courts, as many of the original trees as possible.' Alexander's eyes gleamed as if he could see it all taking shape on his drawing-board.

'Sounds idyllic.' Sophie hesitated, then curiosity got the better of her. 'Is the house you're buying near here?'

Alexander nodded. 'Would you like to see it?' His eyes were indulgent as he smiled at her, and Sophie's answering smile was wry. 'What is it?' he asked quickly.

'I was just thinking how kind and brotherly you are today!'

'Yes,' he agreed smugly. 'I am, aren't I?'

Sophie laughed as he drove off, looking about her with interest as the car turned off on an unadopted road which led along the riverbank for a mile or so without sight of another house until it ended in high laurel hedges and tall wooden gates.

'This is Willow Reach,' said Alexander in a proprietorial tone. He helped Sophie out of the car then twisted the iron ring that served as handle and swung open one of the metal-studded gates for her to go through into a garden she gazed at in wide-eyed delight. The smooth green lawns and herbaceous borders were conventional enough, but her attention was caught immediately by an avenue of yews cut in fantastic shapes, thrones, flowers, birds and beasts of every description drawing the eye towards a grotto where beckoning stone nymphs balanced stone conch-shells above a marble-rimmed pool.

'The fountain needs repair, I'm afraid,' said Alexander. 'What do you think of my new home?'

Sophie tore her eyes away from the grotto and turned to the house, which was built of age-mellowed stone to a design which was strangely timeless.

Countless small panes of glass had been used to make up the windows which dominated the mellow rose-gold walls, and a wistaria-hung veranda ran along the lower half of the house to form a balcony for the upper rooms.

'This,' said Alexander softly, 'was the first house I ever designed, long before you came to work with me, Sophie.'

'It's quite lovely, but——' Puzzled, Sophie turned from the house to the garden, then back again. 'If you designed it the house must be new, of course, yet it doesn't *look* modern, and I just can't believe that the atmosphere in this garden was achieved in a few short years.'

'Clever girl,' he said with approval. 'The original house was left empty for years, then the owner died, and this part of his estate was sold by the heir. My father acquired it, knocked down some of the house, which was much bigger than this, but kept all the building material worth saving and gave me the job of not only designing a house to rise, phoenix-like, from the ruins of the old one, but to ensure it blended happily with the existing garden, once it had been cleared. When Father first brought me here I quite expected to find a princess fast asleep somewhere in the middle of it!'

Sophie wandered round the house, peering through the windows at empty light-filled rooms with gleaming wood floors. 'Do you have a key, Alexander? Can we go in?'

'Afraid not. I haven't actually signed the contract yet.'

They spent a peaceful hour exploring the delights

of the walled garden on the other side of the grotto, where apples and pears ripened on espaliered trees and the autumn sun was warm. Afterwards they strolled down to the small, private jetty, where a dilapidated rowing-boat moved languidly to and fro at its mooring. They sat on an old stone bench near a line of willows at the water's edge, and Alexander explained how luck had been with him the night he'd been invited to a dinner given as a farewell party for the couple who lived in the house.

'They had actually sold it, packed up and moved out, and were almost on the point of leaving for Australia to join their children, when the sale fell through.'

'So you jumped in.'

'I couldn't resist the opportunity. I got on to Sam Jefford with the speed of light, believe me, when they told me he was handling the re-sale.'

'When will you move in?'

'As soon as I can. I need basics like curtains and some carpets, and in any case I thought I'd wait until Kate and David's wedding before I move out of the Chantry.'

Sophie was very thoughtful as they went back to the car, surprised to find herself almost unwilling to leave the tranquillity of the hidden, dreaming garden. 'It's so beautiful here,' she said, as Alexander swung the heavy gate shut and twisted the great iron ring to secure it.

'Too quiet for some,' said Alexander.

'Delphine, you mean?'

'Can you imagine her tucked away from the world here?' His tone was derisory. 'She was unenthusiastic about living in this part of the world at all. She did her best to persuade me to set up practice in London, even go to work for one of the big international firms. Willow Reach was never meant for someone like Delphine.'

Sophie was in total agreement, unable to picture the very contemporary Delphine in that sleeping, secluded garden, glad the gold, predatory eyes had never looked in disparagement on the house that was Alexander's brainchild.

As they set off again Alexander suggested they lunch at an inn on the outskirts of Arlesford to give them energy for the task ahead.

'Energy?' said Sophie with suspicion. 'What am *I* expected to do?'

'Hold the other end of a tape, if nothing else.' Alexander ushered her into the comfortable restaurant bar of the Feathers, where a fire was burning in the large cowled fireplace, regardless of the sunshine outside. They ordered home-made meat and potato pies, free of garnish of any kind other than great crusty rolls and fresh farmhouse butter.

'No use asking for chilli con carne or pasta here,' said Alexander, as they began on their meal with appetite. 'The lady of the house makes everything herself, and believes in plain, homespun fare cooked with loving care.'

'Amen,' said Sophie reverently, mouth full. 'This is the first square meal I've eaten since those horrible beef olives.'

'Which made you so crotchety, I suggest you never cook them again.' Alexander grinned at her across his tankard of beer.

'You were the one who made me angry, telling me I looked too much of a fright to attract any man,' she countered, throwing down the gauntlet.

'Is *that* what you thought I meant?' he said blankly. 'Good God! Slight communication problem, I assure you, Sophie. I meant something very different.'

'Whatever it was, I don't want to know,' she said flatly. 'Let's keep things friendly. Draw a veil over Wednesday.'

Alexander seemed on the point of saying something, then shrugged and went on with his lunch, following Sophie's lead when she introduced more neutral topics. After a pleasant hour or so they went on into Arlesford where Alexander parked his car in a small car park near the river, not eager to risk leaving his beloved Mercedes outside Ilex Cottage, where only a narrow walk separated the houses from the churchyard.

'Cecily says the people next door have the spare key, which saves us driving out to Greenacre first,' said Alexander, as they walked up the steepish hill towards the church. 'You'll be able to meet your new neighbours.'

Sophie preferred to do this on her own, and insisted Alexander wait some distance away while she knocked on the door of the adjoining cottage. The elderly lady who handed over the key was friendly and very jolly, also unashamedly curious about the tall, fair man waiting along the lane.

'That your husband, dear?' she asked hopefully.

Sophie denied it firmly. 'No. Mr Paget's come with me to do a survey on the house,' she said, loud enough for Alexander to hear clearly, since Mrs Perkins admitted to being a little hard of hearing.

'You might have introduced me,' objected Alexander, as he unlocked the door of Ilex Cottage. 'Even if I can't count myself honoured enough to be your husband.'

'No point. You're hardly likely to meet Mrs Perkins again.'

The look Sophie received was quizzical as Alexander ushered her into the sitting-room, which looked bigger than anticipated.

'Because it's empty, I suppose,' said Sophie, delighted, and ran through into the tiny kitchen, which was fitted with a very up-to-date oven and refrigerator, to her surprise. After a rapid inspection of the neat little cupboards Sophie made for the stairs which led from a door in the sitting-room to a tiny landing between a cupboard of a bathroom and the solitary bedroom, which boasted a bow-window like the room below.

Alexander followed her up with more care, obliged to duck his tall head before entering the bedroom. He winced at the sight of the wallpaper which was, Sophie had to admit, somewhat arresting, with a design of roses and looping ribbon bows, and quite overpowered the proportions of the room. Alexander removed strips of paper in strategic areas to look for damp, but found nothing to cause concern. Then he swung himself up into the loft space and spent some time inspecting the roof from the inside with a powerful torch, while Sophie went back downstairs to indulge in much mental interior decoration. By the time Alexander joined her she had dispensed with the patterned wallpaper, painted the walls white, hung yellow and white chintz at the windows and set flowering plants in the deep window embrasure.

'Isn't it perfect?' she said blissfully, as Alexander ducked into the room, brushing cobwebs from his hair.

'I'm not certain about perfect, but as far as I can see the roof's all right and there's no sign of dry rot. You've got a bit of woodworm, of course—inevitable in a house of this age—but nothing that can't be treated.'

'So it's all right?' she pressed. 'Nothing to stop me moving in?'

'I'll see,' he said non-committally, and it was another two hours before he passed final judgement, confirming that the basic structure was sound, there was no sign of settlement anywhere, the drainage system was satisfactory, and only a few tiles on the roof would need to be replaced.

Sophie flung her arms round Alexander and kissed his cheek in euphoria. He laughed, returning the embrace with interest.

'If that's my reward for a survey, what would I get for a helping hand with the decorating?'

CHAPTER FIVE

SOPHIE leaned back against his joined hands, her eyes frankly calculating. '*You*, Alexander? Can you really paint and so on?'

'I'd have you know I'm the Picasso of the home-decorating world,' he said solemnly. 'And, as regards the "so on", I'm unequalled!'

'No, seriously! *Would* you help me do the place up?'

'I take it you're willing to put up with my company so long as I make myself useful!'

'That's right.' Sophie pulled free, laughing. 'Perry, too, if he can paint.'

'I claim sole rights or none at all,' said Alexander promptly. 'Including Julian Brett,' he added.

'Julian wouldn't know one end of a paintbrush from the other.' She eyed him uncertainly. 'Do you mean it?'

'I do.' He strolled over to the door to examine the lock. 'But I'd want something in return, of course.'

'Oh, yes?'

'Help me choose curtains and carpets for Willow Reach.' He looked up, grinning at the surprise on her face. 'I'm making Kate a present of the stuff at the Chantry, naturally. Besides, Willow Reach has a very definite personality all its own. I want to please it with my choice.'

Sophie smiled. 'You talk as though the house were a person.'

'Since I designed it, I'm entitled to my feeling of affinity, Sophie.' Alexander glanced at his watch. 'Time we were off. I'd better deliver you to your grandmother at the gallop. I'm due back in Deansbury by seven.'

Cecily Wainwright ignored Alexander's refusal of tea. 'Nonsense,' she said, holding out her hand to let him kiss it as he always did. 'Ten minutes won't deter the lady waiting for you, I'm sure.'

Alexander surrendered, laughing, settling himself next to Sophie on a couch in the drawing-room while Mrs Wainwright plied him with Earl Grey and anchovy toast and demanded details of the condition of Ilex Cottage.

'It's charming, Gran,' said Sophie, her eyes shining with enthusiasm. 'I'd never seen inside one of those cottages before. It's so compact and cosy, and with the right curtains and a few coats of paint——'

'Yes, yes, darling, spare us the details.' Mrs Wainwright laughed. 'Delighted though I am to know you approve, it's Alexander's professional opinion I'm anxious to hear.'

Alexander supplied it succinctly, then slanted a smile at Sophie. 'My secretary will send you documented confirmation, of course.'

It was almost half an hour later before he rose to leave, and, sent by Mrs Wainwright to see him off, Sophie thanked him for giving her lunch and for taking her to Willow Reach.

'It was nice of you to give up your Saturday,' she said, as she walked with him to the car.

Alexander folded his long legs into the driving seat, then gave her a very straight look. 'No hardship, Sophie. And just for the records, I'm not really dashing off to an evening of riotous debauchery with a member of your sex.'

Sophie's chin lifted. 'Your social life is nothing to do with me!'

'Nevertheless I thought I'd let you know I'm dining with George and Sally Huntley, and, more significantly, Sally's uncle, who just so happens to be on the board of directors of the hotel chain concerned with the site in Brading.'

Sophie's pleasure at hearing this surprised her so much, her voice sharpened with the effort to hide it. 'Don't you ever do things because you simply want to, Alexander, instead of always with an eye to business?'

'Why, yes.' His eyes gleamed beneath lowered lids. 'That's precisely what I've been doing all day today, up to now. Goodnight, little sister.' And with a mocking salute he sent the roadster purring down the drive to the road.

'That's a strange expression,' observed Mrs Wainwright when Sophie joined her. 'Alexander teasing you again?'

'Yes.' Not that Sophie was very sure. The look in Alexander's eyes had been hard to identify. If he had been any other man she would have sworn he was making a very clear statement of intent. But he wasn't anyone else. He was Alexander Paget, who had known her all her life, and who, more to the point, had been on the point of marrying Delphine only a short time before. This sudden rush of interest smacked too much of the rebound for Sophie's taste. Besides, Alexander's role in her life had always been rather like an extra brother. Not, Sophie thought broodingly, that fraternal seemed the right description for Alexander of late. His attitude was very disturbing, not least because she felt sure his objective was balm for the wounds Delphine had inflicted. She found she quite badly wanted to know which was affected most—his pride or his heart.

Cecily Wainwright made no comment on her granddaughter's abstraction, turning instead to the forthcoming wedding while they ate a light supper. She was amused when Sophie confessed her surprise at her father's news. 'You must be blind, child. Kate Paget's been in love with David for years.'

Sophie looked at her grandmother in astonishment. *'Really?'*

'Oh, nothing untoward! Kate was Louise's closest friend all her life, even bridesmaid at the wedding. Then Kate surprised everyone by suddenly marrying Hugh Paget only a few weeks later, a man years older than herself, who already had a son.' Mrs Wainwright's smile was confidential. 'Personally I was always convinced it was because your father chose Louise. Though, to be fair, "chose" was hardly the word.'

'Mother always said she and Dad took one look at each other and that was that.'

'Nothing your grandfather or I said made any difference, certainly. People didn't just live together in those days, you know, but Louise would have gone off with David like a shot if we'd opposed the marriage.' Mrs Wainwright's smile was wry. 'So we

let her have her way. And then Kate married her
widower and I swear to this day she did it because it
meant staying near Louise—and David.'

Sophie stirred a spoon round and round in her
coffee-cup. 'I wonder how it feels to love someone so
much? I mean like Mother and Dad, and Aunt Kate,
too, if she's been carrying a torch all these years. I'm
not at all sure I want to feel so violently over anyone.'

'Have you never considered marrying Julian
Brett?'

Sophie sighed impatiently. 'No, dearest of
grandmothers, I have not. Julian's not the marrying
kind. And, before you begin to nurture any ideas to
the contrary, neither am I.'

'If you fell in love you'd probably think
otherwise,' observed Mrs Wainwright mildly.

'So I'll make sure I keep both feet on the ground.
If I ever detect even the slightest inclination in myself
towards falling in love, I'll run like hell!'

'Sophie!'

Sophie apologised and for the rest of the weekend
took care to avoid the subject, which was easy
enough, since all she really wanted to talk about was
Ilex Cottage. Her thoughts, however, were less exclu-
sive. Excited though she was about moving into a
place of her own, the look in Alexander's eyes as he
drove off kept intruding on her visions of solitary
bliss.

The following afternoon Sophie refused to allow
her grandmother to drive her home, unwilling to let
Mrs Wainwright drive sixty miles or so on a damp,
foggy day. 'I shall go by bus,' she said firmly.

'But it stops at every lamp-post on the way, child,

you'll be ages getting home.' Mrs Wainwright paused, interrupted by the doorbell, and sent Sophie to open the front door.

Alexander stood outside, smiling down at her. 'Hello, Sophie. Thought you might fancy a lift home.'

Sophie stared at him, nonplussed. 'Did you come all this way just to fetch me?'

Alexander nodded affably. 'Of course I did. I'm really quite an obliging sort of fellow, you know.'

'You must be, to drive thirty miles just on the offchance. I was about to catch a bus.'

'Wouldn't you prefer my car?'

Sophie regarded him with a suspicion Alexander obviously found very amusing. 'I wish I knew what you're up to,' she said at last. 'This sudden rush of attention on your part is very worrying. You must have some ulterior motive. Come on, confess. What is it?'

'Nothing sinister,' he assured her smoothly. 'It's all part of my plan to unite the Pagets and Gordons in one happy family. My motives, I swear, are of the purest.'

Mrs Wainwright's appearance put paid to further argument until greetings had been exchanged, offers of tea refused, and Sophie was in the Mercedes on the way home to Deansbury, when she returned to the subject with persistence, telling Alexander his change of attitude was making her uneasy.

'It's spooky,' she said frankly. 'I don't like it. You've always been the boys' ally, not mine. In fact you and I have never hit it off all that well at all, really. At one time we never managed to exchange

two words without disagreeing, then you moved into
your superior phase——'

'My *what?*' he asked, startled.

'Your superior phase—dating roughly from the
time you went off to college until, I suppose, right up
to your wedding day.'

Alexander threw her a narrow, frowning look,
then returned his concentration to the road, which
was half obscured by floating trails of mist.

'Superior,' he repeated. 'Is that how you've
thought of me all these years?'

'Yes. Not,' she added with brutal candour, 'that
you've occupied my thoughts all that much,
Alexander.'

'Why?'

'Why what?'

'Why *don't* I merit much thought from you,
Sophie?'

His voice was so toneless that Sophie eyed his
profile in surprise, wondering if he was annoyed.

'Well,' she began, sorry she'd ever embarked on
the subject, 'I suppose it's because you're so self-
contained and sickeningly successful at everything. I
mean, at school you sailed through exams, you were
cricket captain, head boy. And in adult life you've
always been well liked and respected, with your niche
in life all ready carved out for you in the family firm.
You just never seem to suffer from petty things like
the rest of us—I don't even remember your going
through the spotty stage, like Tim and the twins.'

Alexander's laugh was short. 'Which only goes to
show how effective those blinkers of yours are,
Sophie. You don't remember the spots because

you're years younger than I am, and my spots, if we must discuss them, just didn't register on you at the time. You probably failed to notice our respective parents were something more than just good friends because you've always been so wrapped up in your own particular form of martyrdom.'

Sophie shot upright in her seat. *'Martyrdom?'*

'That's right. I think you make rather a meal of the little paragon bit.'

There was a very tense silence in the car for some time as Sophie battled with the temper she rarely allowed herself to lose, because she knew from experience it did more harm to herself than to the object of her wrath.

'So that's how *you* see *me*,' she observed with hard-won calm. 'A sort of masochistic Cinderella, with handsome brothers instead of ugly sisters.'

'And I've decided to cast myself in the role of surrogate godfather,' he said casually. 'It's time you woke up to what's going on around you, Sophie —made the most of your life.'

'It's what I've been wanting to do for years,' she said, through gritted teeth. 'More to the point, it's exactly what I'm trying to do *now*, if I can ever manage to convince all of you I'm perfectly able to take care of myself.'

'You could have begun doing it some time ago if you'd ever woken up to the fact that David and Kate were only too ready to relieve you of your self-imposed domesticity.' Alexander reduced speed as he was talking, turning smoothly into a lay-by on the deserted road.

'Why have we stopped?' demanded Sophie,

alarmed.

'So you and I can have a little private chat.' Alexander turned towards her. 'Did you never realise that David hadn't the heart to hurt you by ousting you from your earth-mother syndrome until the need for it was past? Kate would have stepped in any time this past year or so, but she and David were afraid of hurting your feelings.'

'Not,' observed Sophie with feeling, 'a virtue one can attribute to you, Alexander Paget.'

'Which is probably why you and I disagreed so much when we were younger.'

'Very likely.' Sophie sagged in her seat, feeling utterly deflated. 'Why didn't you ever say anything, then, since you were so clued up about the entire situation?'

'Kate and David wouldn't hear of it. So, since it really wasn't any business of mine, I kept my mouth shut. And,' he added with candour, 'until just recently you weren't the constant focus of my attention. I was involved with Delphine by the time I realised how things stood with Kate.'

'Which meant you had no time to spare for irrelevant details like me.' Sophie managed a wry laugh. 'Not that I blame you. Delphine must have been an all-consuming interest.'

There was another of those silences Sophie had come to recognise as routine lately when alone with Alexander. This one was not thick with unspoken insults. It was surprisingly comfortable to sit alone with him in the gathering dusk.

'Delphine,' said Alexander after a while, 'was like an addiction, a habit I found hard to kick once it had begun. I never saw enough of her for my enthusiasm to pall, was never given enough physical satisfaction for my appetite to——'

'Sicken and so die?'

'Exactly.' Alexander's voice dropped several tones. 'Looking back on it, Sophie, I think I knew in one part of me that marriage with Delphine had no lasting chance of success.'

'The superior, above-the-belt Alexander. The rest of you wanted her come hell or high water, I suppose.'

Alexander sighed. 'Only, I suspect, because she flatly refused to let me have her.'

'You mean you might not have married her if she'd gone to bed with you as you wanted?'

Alexander was quiet for a moment. 'Sophie, I honestly don't know. Anyway, the question's academic—she didn't go to bed with me, and in the end she didn't marry me, either, so now I'll never know.'

'If she reappeared tomorrow and repented on both counts, would you have her back?' asked Sophie.

'I'd be tempted,' he said frankly. 'But I hope I'd have enough sense to refuse. She betrayed my trust, and, if I may descend to the purely selfish for a moment, she made me look like a bloody fool. I don't know that I'd care to lay myself open to a repeat performance. Not that the question arises. I received a suitably penitent letter from her a few days ago, saying how sorry she was and how she felt I was too wonderful a man to have a wife who was secretly hankering after the fame and success she's now all set to enjoy.'

Sophie pulled a face in the darkness. 'Would you think me excessively catty if I said Delphine should have told you all that a jolly sight sooner?'

'No, not in the least. I agree.' Alexander felt for her hand and held it. 'But Terry Foyle didn't turn up with the bait until the eleventh hour, unfortunately.'

'Are you still suffering from—from the addiction you mentioned?' Sophie asked diffidently.

'No. It was cured by that hellish wait in the register office. Not to mention my unilateral honeymoon. Both very efficient remedies, Sophie.'

'Then it sounds as though your pride, rather than your heart, suffered most.'

Alexander's fingers tightened on hers. 'I knew Delphine for too short a time to sustain any lasting hurt.'

'I thought it only took a moment to fall in love!'

'And about the same to fall out of it—if it's only infatuation.' Alexander raised her fingers to his lips and, to Sophie's utter astonishment, kissed them one by one. 'The more enduring emotions—friendship, affection, warmth—grow and develop all the time in the right kind of relationship.'

Sophie drew her hand away. 'Alexander, I don't——'

'Don't what?' he said softly, and slid an arm behind her to gather her close as he kissed her mouth.

There was nowhere, Sophie soon realised, to retreat in the seat of a car like Alexander's roadster. As his mouth met hers her head fell back against the double support of Alexander's muscular arm and the headrest, while his free hand held her head still, so that movement of any kind was almost impossible.

One of her arms was trapped between his chest and hers, her legs were confined by the steering column, and, when her free hand went up to pull at his wrist, it was like tugging at an iron bar. She decided her best plan was to stay perfectly still and unresponsive. He would soon grow tired of trying to kiss a lifeless dummy. The plan proved to be a total failure, since she found herself growing less lifeless by the second. Her responses, Sophie discovered, were bent on functioning independently of her brain. In fact, after only a few more seconds of persuasion from Alexander's expert mouth Sophie's brain gave up altogether, and her lips parted in abrupt surrender.

Alexander made a muffled, relishing sound deep in his throat, and joined both arms around her. A minority section of her brain revived fleetingly to warn her that all this was highly inadvisable, that it would be Monday morning all too soon, and the man kissing her with such unprecedented enthusiasm was also the man who would be waiting for her behind his desk when she arrived to work for him the following day. The last-ditch attempt failed, and Sophie abandoned herself to the wholly unexpected pleasure she was receiving, *and* giving, if the quickened tempo of Alexander's breathing was anything to go by. At the first touch of his tongue in her mouth her own curled against it in response, and Alexander gave a stifled groan and raised his head momentarily, but only to move his lips to her heavy lids, closing them with kisses that moved over her face and down her throat, lingering on the pulse he found throbbing there.

Suddenly there was a glare of lights and a braying wail of sirens as two police cars careered past, shattering the night with noise and lighting up the darkness for a few intrusive moments that brought Sophie back to earth with a bump. Before she had time to push Alexander away he was upright and in his former place, breathing very audibly as Sophie gathered her scattered wits. She was suddenly very angry—with him, with herself, and, most of all, she realised, mortified, with the police cars for interrupting them. She shivered, and Alexander breathed in sharply.

'I'm sorry, Sophie.'

Sophie was not pleased to receive an apology. 'For kissing me?' she demanded.

'Good God, no! How could I be sorry for something that gave me more pleasure than I imagined possible?'

This question found even less favour. Why should Alexander feel so surprised? Was it beyond the bounds of possibility that kissing Sophie Gordon could be such a pleasurable pastime?

'What exactly are you sorry for, then?' she asked.

Alexander recaptured her hand. 'Because we were interrupted, because I gave in to the urge to make love to you in just about the most uncomfortable place possible, because, more than anything, I think, I've known you so long and so well and have never made love to you before.'

'Aren't you taking my part in all this rather for granted?'

'Only in the light of your recent response, Sophie.'

'Oh.'

'Yes. Oh.' Alexander's voice grew husky. 'I never dreamed so much fire lay hidden behind that disciplined exterior of yours.'

Sophie's eyes widened. 'Disciplined? Me?'

Alexander squeezed her hand. 'Yes. No one could live the sort of life you do without discipline, Sophie.'

'It doesn't come easy,' she informed him drily. 'Not even to paragons like me. I have to work hard at it.'

'I realise that. It's why the disciplined front is what most people accept, instead of the other Sophie tucked away behind it.'

'The one who yearns to escape!'

Alexander's grip tightened. 'Are you sure that a cottage overlooking the graveyard in Arlesford is the best means of escape, Sophie?'

'It's the best offer I've ever had, believe me!'

'You could always marry.'

Sophie sighed. 'As I keep saying, *ad nauseam*, I, better than anyone, know what marriage means. No, thanks.'

'But you're talking about the daily bread of domesticity, Sophie. Marriage could, and should, provide a lot of butter—*and* jam.'

'Alexander, if you mean what I think you mean, all I've ever lacked is an actual husband who, perfectly naturally, would expect to take me to bed and make love with me on top of all the rest.' She shook her head fiercely. 'No way.'

Alexander laughed. 'So not only do you eschew the delights of domesticity, you're ready to dismiss the pleasures of the bed.'

'I won't miss something I've never had.'

The now familiar silence fell for a few moments,

then Alexander reached a hand to flick on the interior light so he could look hard at Sophie's face. She scowled at him crossly.

'Turn the light off! I feel like a sitting duck.'

Afterwards the darkness seemed denser than before. 'I wanted to see if you meant it, Sophie,' he said quietly.

'That I've never been to bed with anyone?' She chuckled. 'But that's strictly between you and me, Alexander. I don't want it spread around. Think how my reputation would suffer!'

'I'm surprised. And don't try telling me you're frigid, because I proved conclusively just now that you're not.'

'What's so surprising about it?' she asked defensively. 'You said Delphine wouldn't let you into *her* bed.'

'But that's because she was holding out for a wedding ring. I'm not gullible enough to believe no one had shared her bed before.'

'Yet you still wanted her!'

'Of course I did. I'm not antediluvian enough to expect a woman with Delphine's looks to be a virgin at her age. Nor,' he added, 'to be frank, would I have expected it of you, either, Sophie.'

Sophie thought this over, uncertain whether she was flattered or not. 'Because I'm twenty-three, you mean?'

He laughed softly. 'No. Because you're a very beddable lady, whatever age you are.'

'Oh, come on!' she said scathingly. 'Laying it on a bit thick, Alexander.'

'What do you mean?' The surprise in his voice was

so genuine, Sophie squeezed the hand holding hers.

'Put it this way. Remember I said you were superior? I have this little game I like to play, categorising people with a single adjective. You know yours. So my grandmother's is "autocratic", my father's "conscientious", Tim's "ambitious", the twins—being twins—share "exhausting", Kate's is "loving"—and so on. Am I boring you?'

'Not in the least! I don't really relish my own label, but go on. What I want to know is how you describe yourself.'

'My passport says it all, really. Hair brown, eyes brown, no distinguishing marks. In a word, "average".' Sophie paused. 'Or maybe "ordinary", because certain of my statistics are rather more generous than average.'

Alexander's utter stillness made her shift uneasily in her seat.

'So you're ordinary, are you?' he remarked very softly.

'Yes. Depressingly so.'

'Wrong.' He sounded so positive, Sophie fidgeted even more. 'There's nothing ordinary about your eyes, for a start,' he said, in a rather clinical manner. 'They're big enough and bright enough, God knows, and they smile even when your mouth stays all prim and proper, when you're trying not to laugh. Your nose turns up a little, it's true, but only enough to look endearing, and your mouth——' He paused. 'If I'm honest, it is a little on the wide side, Sophie, but it curves very temptingly, and now I give the matter thought, there's a fullness about the bottom lip——'

'OK, Alexander,' she said hastily, snatching her

hand away. 'No need to go on and on.'

He recaptured her hand and slid his arm behind her. 'I haven't finished yet.'

'Alexander——'

'Quiet,' he said sternly. 'I've only just started.'

Sophie wriggled frantically, but his arm tightened, keeping her still. 'Alexander, it's time we went home.'

'In a moment. I would just like to rid your head of this "ordinary" nonsense.' His voice roughened slightly. 'For one thing, as you say, there are certain things about you that are well above average, take my word for it.' And his hand released hers to move over the contours of her breasts, sliding over the thin wool of her shirt. He muttered indistinctly and brought his mouth down on hers. Sophie gasped, her breasts rising and hardening in response to the caress of his fingers. He took his arm from behind her, his mouth increasing its pressure so that her head fell back against the headrest as he dealt summarily with shirt buttons and the satin that lay beneath, pulling it down so that her breasts were pushed above it, bare and pointing, shamelessly offering themselves to hands that took loving possession of the silk-smooth fullness.

Sophie gave a smothered cry, trying to push him away, but Alexander caught her hands and pulled them wide, bending his head to take one of the swollen peaks in his mouth. Her body flushed all over with heat as his teeth grazed and his lips closed over a nipple, sending waves of heat knifing through her. Just as she thought she could bear it no more, Alexander returned his mouth to hers, kissing her parted lips with such demand that Sophie was vanquished.

When he raised his head at last, he said raggedly, 'Never say *ordinary* again, my modest little sexpot. It quite definitely doesn't apply.'

Sophie pulled herself together hastily and pushed him away, but her fingers trembled so much, Alexander was obliged to help button her shirt, his own hands gratifyingly shaky, she noticed. 'If I'm not ordinary, what am I, then?' she couldn't resist asking.

'If only one word is allowed, mine isn't an adjective.'

'Are you being rude?'

He cleared his throat as he switched on the ignition, turning his head to look at her before he drove off. 'No four-letter words, I assure you. The word that sprang to mind was "dynamite".'

CHAPTER SIX

SOPHIE was never enamoured of Monday at the best of times, but next morning she walked into Deansbury on leaden feet, deeply reluctant to face Alexander in the cold light of day. It was raining, and the pavements were treacherous with slick layers of fallen leaves as she trudged along her usual route to the market square, which was always fairly quiet at this time of day, with another half-hour to go before shops opened and the day got off to its real start. When she arrived at Paget & Sons Sophie put away her umbrella and hung up her wet raincoat, then fiddled with her hair and face until she could put off the evil hour no longer.

The encounter was less trying than expected. Perry was with Alexander, telling him about the new girl he'd met at a party, his blue eyes glittering as he waved his hands about to emphasise the importance of the occurrence.

'For God's sake, go away and channel your energies into some work. Dream up something spectacular to show the brewery for the new pub in Market Street,' said Alexander, looking up with a smile as Sophie appeared. 'Good morning, Sophie.'

'Good morning.' Her smile included both men and Perry gave her his usual spectacular grin before going off to do his cousin's bidding.

'It astonishes me that there are any girls left in the neighbourhood for Perry to discover,' said Alexander, and pulled the day's consignment of post towards him, plainly bent on getting on with the day at top speed, to Sophie's gratitude. The weekend might never have happened, she thought with relief, and concentrated on Alexander's voice, much comforted by the matter-of-factness of his manner. Indeed, apart from the hour they spent together each morning, she saw very little of Alexander that day or the next, since he spent most of the time in Arlesford, organising the new branch office.

'You won't forget the interviews today, will you?' she reminded him on the Wednesday morning. 'The first is at eleven.'

Alexander studied her broodingly. 'Can't wait to get away, can you?'

'I merely want to get things settled,' she said patiently. 'I've promised I won't go until the new secretary knows the ropes.'

'You haven't changed your mind, then?' He dropped his eyes to the pen he was rolling between his fingers.

Sophie backed away hurriedly. 'No, I haven't.' She returned to her own office quickly, uneasy at something in Alexander's voice, which was too reminiscent of Sunday's intimacy for her peace of mind.

Sophie had made a careful selection of candidates for Alexander's approval. The first girl was very pretty, but Sophie knew at once she would never pass muster because she had a shrill voice and ultra-long scarlet fingernails. The second candidate was innocent of nail-polish, make-up, and any attempt whatsoever to make herself attractive, however efficient she might have been, and Sophie mentally ticked her off the list as well.

Alexander strode into Sophie's office a little later and leaned his hands on her desk. 'Come and have lunch with me.'

'I've brought sandwiches.'

'Feed 'em to the birds.' The dark-lashed eyes took on a cajoling look Sophie associated more with the engaging Perry than his senior partner. 'Please, Sophie. Interviewing those women was a cold reminder that you'll soon be gone. Call it a working lunch if it makes you happier.'

Sophie wavered, then gave in. 'All right. But I'll meet you in the George in twenty minutes or so. I must finish this report first.'

Alexander's smile conveyed such genuine pleasure, Sophie felt flattered. And she wanted to have lunch with Alexander, if she was honest. After he'd left, whistling, she acknowledged secretly that she'd enjoyed lunching with him the previous Saturday. Her fingers halted in their flight over the keys. This new, attentive Alexander was a difficult man to resist, she found, her stomach muscles tightening as she thought, not for the first time, of the episode in his car. She had enjoyed his lovemaking far more than she cared to admit, even to herself, and put her responses down to the fact that she was a normal, healthy female, and Alexander was a very attractive man. Any woman would have behaved similarly under the same circumstances.

Even so, Sophie was in no way prepared for the surge of delight she experienced as she entered the bar of the George a little later and saw Alexander spring to his feet at the sight of her. His wave and smile was noted and commented on by all present, she knew only too well, as she made her way through the usual lunch-time crush to join him on the far side of the room.

'Tell me the worst,' she said, as she sipped the wine he had ready for her. 'I suppose I can write a couple of polite rejections to this morning's candidates?'

Alexander agreed gloomily. 'You suppose right. I didn't bother to send them out for a test because I knew damn well I could never stand either of those two round me all day and every day.'

'Perhaps one of this afternoon's ladies will be suitable.' Sophie gave him a mischievous smile. 'I should have asked for photographs. You could have chosen the ones you fancied most.'

Alexander refused to cheer up. 'Whatever she looks like, your successor will have a hard act to follow.'

Sophie felt startled. 'Why, thank you, Alexander. How kind of you to say so.'

'It's the truth.' Alexander looked up to meet her eyes. 'I shall miss you badly, Sophie. Won't you change your mind?'

'Is that why you asked me to lunch? To persuade me?' Sophie's tone was cold, to hide her sudden urge to give in and tell him she'd stay.

'No. I just wanted your company. Is that so hard to believe?'

Sophie wanted to believe. It was disquieting to find she wanted to believe everything Alexander said these days, not least the previous Sunday when he'd disagreed so gratifyingly with her own view of herself as Miss Ordinary. 'Sorry, Alexander. I didn't mean to be prickly.'

His smile brought the colour to her face. 'The most fragrant roses sport the sharpest thorns, don't they? You're blushing, Sophie,' he added.

'Is it any wonder?' she snapped, glad of the diversion as plates were set before them, and Alexander began to talk shop. For the remainder of their time together they discussed the new branch office, his ideas on furnishing Willow Reach, with a few minutes spent, inevitably, on discussing Ilex Cottage and how soon it would be fit for occupation.

'Not that I need wait for that before I move to Arlesford,' she said. 'I can always live at Greenacre if Mr Jefford wants me sooner.'

'Jefford can wait until I can do without you,' said Alexander flatly.

Sophie frowned. 'And how long is that going to be, may I ask?'

Alexander leaned his chin on his hand, his eyes almost concealed by his enviably thick lashes. 'That, Miss Gordon, is something I'm beginning to worry about a great deal.'

Her dark eyes opened wide. 'Surely another month will be long enough?'

'We'll have to wait and see,' he said cryptically, and helped her on with her coat.

The two applicants who arrived in the afternoon were far more promising, one an attractive young woman in her thirties, the other a very pleasant lady with grey hair and a no-nonsense look about her. Both women were sent out to Sophie's office to demonstrate their efficiency at typing, and after the second lady had taken her leave Sophie rushed into Alexander's office to demand a verdict.

'Well?' she asked. 'Any good?'

'Your eagerness is scarcely flattering,' he said acidly, 'but I suppose I must admit that both women were excellent.'

'So which one do you want?'

Alexander turned from the window to look at her broodingly. 'You know that already, Sophie. I want you. But since I may not have you, I think the most sensible choice is Mrs Rogers, the widow.'

Sophie ignored the sudden leap of her pulse at his first words in her relief to hear his approval of the pleasant Mrs Rogers.

'I'm sure she'll be excellent,' she assured him.

'And unlikely to find Perry chasing her round her typewriter, either,' agreed Alexander.

'*I've* never had any trouble on that score!'

'For reasons previously explained.' Alexander came swiftly round the desk to take her by the shoulders. 'I laid the law down originally for our respective families' sakes. Now——' He paused, looking down deep into her eyes. 'Now I think my motives might be altogether more personal.'

'Shall I go out and come in again?' asked a patient voice behind them, and Alexander relinquished a very hot and bothered Sophie to explain to Perry that a new secretary had been found.

'And is she young and nubile?' Perry gave Sophie an outrageous wink as she passed him on her way out.

'Sorry, old chap,' drawled Alexander. 'Grey-haired widow-lady with sons older than you.'

'Thank God for that,' said Perry piously. 'It'll be nice to come in here without having to knock first.'

Sophie fled, feeling the sooner she left Paget & Sons, the better all round.

Over dinner that night Dr Gordon reiterated his worries about Ilex Cottage as a suitable home for his daughter. 'I only hope you won't be too lonely there, Sophie,' he said, his eyes anxious. 'Silly, I suppose, but I can't help worrying. I shall miss you, pet.'

'That's what Alexander said, too,' answered Sophie, rather wishing she hadn't as David Gordon's eyes narrowed. 'But he won't for long, of course. We found a replacement for me today.'

'So you'll be able to fly the nest quite soon, then.' Dr Gordon went on eating his dinner, looking dubious. 'But Ilex Cottage won't be ready for a while, will it?'

'No, but I can lodge at Greenacre while I finish the decorating and make curtains, and so on. Dad— could I take my own bed with me, do you think?'

She was assured she could take anything from the house she wanted, and jumped up to hug him affectionately.

'Unless you'd like new things,' he said. 'I think I can spare the pennies for a few sticks of furniture.'

Sophie assured him Ilex Cottage would look odd with contemporary things. 'Gran says I can have one or two pieces from Greenacre, too, so I'll be fine. It's such a minute place I shan't need much.'

There were less disturbing encounters with Alexander for a while, since Sophie flatly refused to lunch with him more than once a week, and took to spending every weekend with her grandmother so she could get on with her home-decorating in Ilex Cottage, leaving Kate to show prospective buyers over the Gordon home. The sale had been put in the hands of Sam Jefford, rather to Sophie's surprise. He came to measure the house himself, and afterwards rather diffidently suggested a meal somewhere the following evening, since they would soon be working together. Sophie agreed, finding she enjoyed her evening with him more than expected. Sam Jefford was restful company, a complete contrast with either Julian or Alexander. Time spent socially with Alexander smacked of armed truce these days, full of unsaid words and fraught with the feeling that any moment he might brush aside the barrier she tried to keep between them. Julian, on the other hand, took her for granted, Sophie knew, and she was quite untroubled by the fact.

Consequently, Sam Jefford's eagerness to please was rather refreshing. Sophie suspected it stemmed from his recent harrowing experience of divorce. He was lonely and showed it. It was an interesting pastime to analyse the differences in all three men while dining with Sam Jefford, or during a trip to the theatre with Julian. It was disturbing, however, to realise that during any time spent with Alexander, in work or out of it, she never gave a thought to either of the other men. Or to anyone else. Which made Sophie sorry she had promised to remain at home with her father until the wedding. It was high time she was up and away. It just wouldn't do to go any further down the path she seemed to be travelling with Alexander these days, because she was con-

vinced that only heartbreak could lie at the end of it.
Once she had made the break and left Deansbury,
everything would be better, she told herself. On her
own in Ilex Cottage, she would be safe.

'I hear you've been seen dining with a new man
lately,' said Alexander one morning.

'Getting to know my new boss,' said Sophie.

'Not *too* well, I trust?'

'As well as advisable between employer and
employee.' Sophie met his cool green gaze serenely.

Alexander, who was dressed for London in a dark
overcoat and sober grey suit, gathered up his briefcase and strode to the door. 'For the first time I feel
pleased that you're leaving me, Sophie.'

She stared at him, affronted.

'No insult intended,' he assured her, with a distinctly tigerish smile. 'Since you seem to set limits on
professional relationships, I look forward to the day
when your relationship with *me,* Sophie, will be a
purely personal one.' He gave her a brief ironic bow
and departed for his conference, leaving Sophie completely routed.

Alexander's absence gave Sophie a golden opportunity to give Mrs Rogers a teach-in on the routine at
Paget & Sons. The new secretary was a quick study,
and showed signs of proving highly satisfactory. Her
keen sense of humour gave her a head start with
Perry, her interest in his children quickly endeared
her to George Huntley, while the young draughtsmen
and trainees were her slaves from the start because
Mrs Rogers brought batches of home-made cakes to
serve at coffee-time.

'One up on you, Sophie,' remarked Perry, mouth

full one day. 'Why have *you* never made cake for us?'

Sophie told him bluntly that no cake she made ever got past Matt and Mark, and now they were away she saw no point in adding to either her father's waistline or her own. Perry regarded the area in question and gave his opinion of her shape in terms that made her blush, adding that his wasn't the only eye in the office which took pleasure in dwelling on her charms.

'Only for God's sake don't tell Alexander I said so,' he begged. 'Himself is incredibly touchy where you're concerned these days. A touch of the green-eye, would you say? A scalp too many dangling at your belt of late?'

Sophie's dignified rebuttal was rather impaired by being called to the telephone to Sam Jefford, whose request for her company at lunch sounded untypically urgent.

'Is it all right if I go off to lunch a little early?' she asked reluctantly, self-conscious under Perry's mischievous blue gaze. 'Mrs Rogers will hold the fort for me.'

'Off you go, darling.' He wagged his finger. 'While the cat's away, and all that.'

Sam Jefford was waiting for Sophie in a quiet tea-shop well away from the market square, an establishment rarely patronised by the businessmen of the town. Sophie had chosen it deliberately, not happy about the ethics of lunching with her new employer in the George while she was still employed by Alexander. Not, she assured herself, that it was any business of the latter. Nor was her choice of rendezvous influenced by the desire to meet Sam

Jefford unseen by anyone she knew. But she was worried about what had brought him thirty miles to see her in the middle of a working day.

Her apprehension increased the moment she saw Sam. He wore an aura of uneasiness about him, despite the diffident charm of his smile.

'Hello,' she said cordially, as she joined him. 'What brings you to Deansbury at this time of day? Business?'

'Certainly not pleasure, Sophie.' He stared unseeingly at the menu.

'The Welsh rarebit's quite good here,' she said gently.

He pushed the menu aside. 'I'm really not very hungry. I'll just have some coffee, I think.'

Sophie smiled encouragingly. 'Snags with the sale of the house?'

'No.' He met her eyes with a desperate look. 'I've struck a snag in quite another area, actually. With my secretary.'

Sophie's heart sank. 'Oh, dear.'

He swallowed convulsively, staring down into the coffee the waitress put in front of him. 'I feel so bad about all this, but, well, you see the girl who works for me now——'

'The pregnant lady.'

'Quite. Well, I automatically assumed she would be leaving for good, you see. But she isn't. I mean, she doesn't want to. She wants to come back after the baby's born.'

Sophie regarded his downbent head in silence. 'You didn't know?'

He looked up miserably. 'I'm pretty hopeless

where women are concerend. It seems she expected to all along—she's not married, you see. She needs the job—even has a sister who'll fill in until she gets back.'

Sophie reached across and patted his hand. 'Don't worry, Sam.' She smiled a little. 'I'll find something else.'

He covered the hand with his own. 'Does this mean you'll stop seeing me now? Socially, I mean?'

'Of course not.' Sophie finished her coffee and stood up. 'Anyway, I'd better get back now. I'll give you a ring when I'm settled in Ilex Cottage. You can come round for a drink, or something.'

Sam Jefford followed her outside, looking forlorn. She smiled at him cheerfully, bade him a brisk goodbye and made her way back to Paget's, feelig forlorn herself. What on earth was she to do now? she thought in dismay.

Dr Gordon was very definite with his views when she told him later that the new job in Arlesford had fallen through. He strongly disapproved of his daughter's taking off to live alone with no job prospect.

'Since you've been in such a tearing hurry to organise your own replacement at Paget's,' he said forcibly, 'you'd better stay with Kate and me at the Chantry until you find yourself something to do in reach of Ilex Cottage.'

Sophie could have wept. Instead she swallowed hard on her response to this unusually dictatorial pronouncement and prepared herself for an evening devoted to answering the telephone, because it was Dr Gordon's night on call, with the added delights of preparing a casserole for the next day and tackling a pile of ironing, none of which came into her top ten of favourite occupations. Her father was called out before he'd had time to swallow his coffee, leaving Sophie alone to ponder bitterly on the irony of fate which gave out with one hand and took back with the other. Mrs Rogers had proved so instantly efficient that Sophie had taken the plunge and informed Perry she was leaving the following Friday, which meant only another week at her present salary. Alexander was a very fair employer who expected his pound of flesh, but also expected to pay generously for the privilege, and Sophie had amassed a comforting little nest egg. But it had been meant for such contingencies as new curtains and carpets for Ilex Cottage, not for tiding her over until, or if, she found a new job.

Sophie answered the telephone several times during the evening, sometimes to a worried patient, sometimes to her father, who usually called in to check where he was needed next. The list was larger than usual, enough to keep Dr Gordon occupied all evening due to the distances involved in reaching patients in outlying districts, and Sophie had prepared her casserole and was half-way through the ironing when the doorbell rang. She sighed, hoping it was not some patient local enough to call on her father in person, then stared in astonishment as she found Alexander on the doorstep, looking tired and pale, dressed in the clothes he'd worn to London.

'May I come in?' he asked.

'Of course.' Sophie fought down a surge of excitement at the sight of him and led the way through to

the kitchen. 'Do you mind if I carry on ironing?' she
said, glancing up at him curiously as she renewed her
attack on the pile of shirts. 'Something wrong,
Alexander?'

He watched her, the glare of the strip light striking
sparks of gold from his thick fair hair, and
emphasising the marks of fatigue beneath his eyes
and the silver-gilt stubble on his jaw.

'I called in at the office before going home,
Sophie. Perry left me a memo with various bits of
information, the most important of which was the
news that you're leaving next week.'

Fool that I am, thought Sophie. She nodded. 'Yes.
Mrs Rogers is an absolute marvel, so I couldn't see
the point of staying longer. She's coming in again a
couple of days beforehand for the changeover.'

'I see.' Alexander subsided on one of the tall
stools. 'Jefford's getting impatient, I suppose.'

Sophie folded a shirt carefully. 'Not exactly. It
seems I counted my chickens far too soon. Sam
Jefford came over to Deansbury today to tell me his
secretary wants her job back once her baby's born.
She's not married and needs the money. So, I shall
have to start job-hunting; very good for me, I
suppose. A new experience.'

Alexander slid off the stool and unplugged the
iron, then took her by the hands. 'I could offer you
an alternative, Sophie.'

She stared up at him in surprise, her pulse
beginning to race as she she met the molten gleam in
his green eyes. Her breathing quickened and she ran
the tip of her tongue over suddenly dry lips as the
hurried movement of her breasts drew Alexander's

gaze like a magnet.

'Sophie——' His voice was hoarse as he pulled her
against him and kissed her fiercely, one arm almost
cracking her ribs, his free hand moving over her
breasts as his tongue slid into her mouth. Sophie
yielded to him with a helpless moan, her arms sliding
under his jacket to hold him closer, and he flattened
his hand on the base of her spine, locking her hips
against his as he pulled her on tiptoe against him.

Breathing like a marathon runner, Alexander
picked her up and stood with her cradled in his arms,
his mouth demanding a response Sophie answered
without reserve. She locked her arms round his neck,
returning his kisses fiercely, submerged in her own
delirium, until at last Alexander gently lowered her to
her bare feet once more. Contact with the cold
quarry tile of the kitchen floor brought Sophie very
literally back to earth. Alexander smiled crookedly,
and smoothed her tumbled hair, touched his finger to
her swollen bottom lip.

'Why did I never dream you'd be so inflammatory,
I wonder?'

Sophie tried hard to control her breathing. 'I could
say the same thing,' she muttered.

'Then it's mutual? I'm not fantasising about
this—this explosion every time I touch you?'

'No,' she said grudgingly.

'You don't enjoy it?'

'I didn't say that.'

Alexander perched on the stool, drawing her close
to stand between his outstretched legs. Sophie
fidgeted, very much aware that neither of them had
recovered from their heated exchange. 'Sophie,' he

said quietly, 'I mentioned earlier I had an alternative proposition to make. Aren't you curious to hear what it is?'

Sophie bit her lip, almost certain she knew what he was going to say. The pieces of the jigsaw all fitted together so neatly. This sudden, newfound chemistry between them, her lack of a job, Alexander still smarting from his treatment at Delphine's hands. She was afraid it all added up to a proposal of marriage she didn't want. She wanted Alexander, it was true, but not Alexander on the rebound. She wanted, she realised with burning clarity, to go to bed with Alexander right this minute. Her body ached with frustration just from standing between the two rigid thighs keeping her prisoner. But Kate Paget's stepson could never ask Dr Gordon's only daughter to leap into bed with him—not without marrying her first.

'That's a very analytical look,' teased Alexander. 'Are you trying to guess what I have in mind?'

Sophie was unhappily certain what he had in mind. 'I think so, Alexander, but please—I don't want——'

'Hey!' He shook her slightly. 'Wait until you hear my proposition, at least, before you turn it down! Nothing sinister, I promise. I merely thought that now the job with Sam Jefford has fallen through you might care to carry on working for me instead.'

CHAPTER SEVEN

SOPHIE'S face went blank with astonishment, while Alexander's eyes narrowed to a very unsettling gleam.

'You *didn't* know what I had in mind, did you?' He put a finger under her chin. 'Sophie Gordon! Did you by any chance imagine I was about to request entry into your bed?'

'Yes,' lied Sophie faintly, weak with relief. Dear God, how close she'd come to making a complete and utter fool of herself. She offered up a silent prayer of thanks and gave Alexander a weak smile. 'Sorry.'

He shrugged ruefully. 'Don't apologise. If you were anyone else under these particular circumstances we'd be in bed at this very moment, finishing what we started. But you are your father's daughter——'

'And you're Aunt Kate's stepson,' Sophie finished for him.

'Which makes not a blind bit of difference to the fact that I want you like hell just the same,' said Alexander with intensity.

'But *why?*' Sophie's question was deeply curious. 'I'm just the same Sophie I've always been.'

'If I knew why, perhaps I'd be able to *stop* wanting you! I'm on a losing wicket, one way and another.

Knowing I can't have you makes me want you even more.'

'Just the same as Delphine.'

'Oh, no.' Alexander drew her closer. 'Not remotely the same as Delphine, since you mention it. For one thing, I was never allowed to make her untidy——'

'Spare me the sordid details!' Sophie struggled to wrench free, but his legs scissored to hold her prisoner as he jerked her against him.

'You brought it up. I'm just trying to make things clear.'

One thing was very clear to Sophie. Standing between his muscular thighs, pulled close to him as she was, it was impossible to ignore how much he wanted her. The hard, pulsing proof of it burned against her, right through faded denim and finest bespoke wool suiting.

'Alexander——' she gasped.

'Sophie,' he whispered in echo, and with a sudden show of strength lifted her off her feet and sat her on his lap, holding her still, ignoring her efforts to break free. 'I thought I wanted Delphine. God knows, she's beautiful enough. With you it's different. Very different.' The passionate sincerity of his voice quieted her as he cradled her against him, gazing down into her eyes as though willing her to see he was speaking the truth. 'You're *not* beautiful. But the way you look is a complete irrelevance. Sophie. It doesn't matter a damn whether you're dressed like this, or armoured in that no-nonsense stuff you wear to the office, or even with a red nose and swollen eyes like the night I made you so angry you threw up. I still burn with the same urge to pick you up and carry you off.'

'Where?' asked Sophie, fascinated.

His smile raised the tiny hairs all the way down her spine. 'I'm not sure—I rather think it's to my cave.'

The telephone interrupted the moment of danger, making them both jump. Alexander cursed and Sophie slid to the floor to answer it, unsteady on her feet from the effect of the new, uninhibited urges she had gone through life until recently believing were other women's prerogatives.

'Are you all right?' asked her father.

Sophie cleared her throat. 'Yes, Dad. Fine. No more calls.'

'Great. One more to go and I'll be home.'

Alexander followed her into the hall, shrugging into his overcoat. 'I'd better be off, hadn't I?' he said ruefully. 'Before I do, can I have an answer on the job question?'

'But, Alexander, you can't tell Mrs Rogers you've changed your mind—and you don't need *two* secretaries.'

'Ah, but I do. How about the new branch in Arlesford?'

Sophie's eyes lit like lamps. 'Oh, Alexander—do you mean it?'

'Of course I mean it! Why do you think I went out of my way to come here tonight?' he demanded, then smiled wryly. 'Which is not the whole truth and nothing but the truth, if I'm honest. I hoped I'd catch you alone.'

Sophie's eyes slid away from his. 'I could have been out.'

'Kate told me you always stay in when David's on call.'

'I might not have been alone.'

'True.' He shrugged and lounged against the newel post. 'To go on with what I was saying, you know Perry will run the branch in time, but in the beginning I'll need to get it off the ground myself. And I'll need an experienced secretary with me, one who can work on her own at times right from the start, since naturally I shall have to divide my time between Arlesford and Deansbury. In short, I need *you*, Sophie.'

Sophie threw her arms round him impulsively, tipping her head back to smile at him radiantly. 'I accept, Alexander—with gratitude.'

He smiled in mock-amazement. 'Why, thank you, Sophie. I'm not used to such appreciation from *you*.'

'While you've always had far too much from other women!' she said, grinning, then sobered. 'But I meant it, Alexander. I really am grateful. I was so miserable before you came because Dad had been laying the law down about my staying with him and Aunt Kate until I found a job in Arlesford. And I couldn't argue because he hardly ever comes the heavy father with me.' She pulled a face. 'I didn't relish the prospect of playing gooseberry to a couple of newlyweds.'

Alexander laughed, and bent to kiss her cheek. 'Well, now you won't have to. I told you I'd taken on the role of your guardian angel.'

Sophie looked at him thoughtfully for a moment. 'One thing, though. I really do want the job in Arlesford very much, but—how can I put it?—I

mean it must be on a strictly business footing.' She
flushed. 'Oh, lord, that sounds so big-headed. What
I'm trying to say——'

'Is that I must not presume on your gratitude,' he
said solemnly. 'No fun and games in the office, you
mean.'

'I wouldn't have put it quite like *that*. I'm just
asking that we work together as we've always done.'

'Of course. But on one condition. That you still let
me help decorate your beloved cottage.'

She laughed. 'Don't worry—I turn no one away
with paintbrush in hand.'

'Ah, but I insist on sole rights to the job.' And
with a glint of green eyes Alexander bade her goodnight and went off, leaving Sophie in such a state of
euphoria she had finished all the ironing and had a
tray ready with coffee and sandwiches when her
father eventually arrived home to hear the glad news.

Julian Brett struck the only discordant note in
Sophie's life in the days that followed, surprising her
not a little by his depression over her imminent
departure.

'But you've known for ages that I was going,
Julian,' she said, taken aback by his air of gloom as
they dined together in Julian's favourite Italian
restaurant.

Julian Brett was a slender man of thirty, with a
pale face and a lot of soft dark hair. He was the
curator of the Deansbury museum and lived with his
mother in a large, antique-filled Victorian house only
a stone's throw from where they were sitting at that
moment. He refilled Sophie's wineglass and leaned

back in his chair, studying her with lachrymose eyes.

'But I thought you were going to work for this Jefford chap,' he said.

Sophie drank her wine, feeling irritable. 'I told you it fell through, Julian. And if Alexander hadn't come to my rescue with the job at his new branch in Arlesford I'd have been forced to stay here until I found something else.'

'At least you'd have been safely under your father's roof,' he pointed out. 'And we could have carried on as usual.'

'Oh, really, Julian, the *status quo* may be the be all and end all of your existence, but *I* happen to yearn for change.'

'As I see it, Sophie, the only change in your life will be the fact that you live in that decrepit cottage instead of here.' His mouth thinned. 'Otherwise your working day will be dominated by Alexander the Great as usual!'

'Don't be feline.' Sophie frowned at him. 'You happen to like living at home with your mother, but I, love my family though I may, can't wait to have a little place of my own. All to myself,' she added, to remove any possible doubt.

Julian fiddled with his coffee spoon and cleared his throat several times before saying rather desperately, 'You could always have married *me,* Sophie.' He kept his eyes on the chequered tablecloth, which was just as well, since the blank astonishment in Sophie's face could hardly have been described as flattering.

'But Julian,' she said gently, 'you don't want to get married.'

'I don't want to lose you, either.' He looked up in

appeal. 'I mean, Mother won't live for ever, and you've never shown any signs of marrying anyone else. In fact you've always said you never wanted children, which is fine by me. Won't you at least consider it?'

Sophie could hardly believe her ears. 'But Julian—you're not in the least interested in having a wife!'

'I'm interested in having *you* for a wife, Sophie,' he assured her, with more urgency than she had ever heard in his voice. 'We could go on as we've always done. Mother would be pleased to have you move in with us, I'm sure. She gets lonely, you know, and she's quite fond of you. And there'd be no housekeeping to worry you—the Baxters have been with us for years.'

Sophie searched hard for a way to couch her refusal in suitably inoffensive terms. 'It's really very sweet of you, Julian, but you know better than anyone that I've never had marriage in mind—not even the kind you're proposing.' It hardly seemed charitable to tell him that the picture he painted of their future life together aroused a strong urge in her to turn tail and run out of the restaurant. Instead she enlarged on her appreciation of the offer, pointing out that Arlesford was only thirty miles away, that Julian could drive over and see her now and then once she was settled in at Ilex Cottage.

Julian looked at her aghast. 'My dear Sophie, you can't expect me to drive sixty miles or more in one evening just to take you out for a meal!'

Julian never took her out anywhere other than in Deansbury itself, in places where they could expect to encounter most of the upwardly mobile population of the prosperous town, Sophie reminded herself, resisting the urge to assault her escort with the Chianti bottle. It came as less surprise to her, therefore, than it would have to others to learn that by insisting on her move to Arlesford she had placed herself beyond Julian Brett's particular pale.

The following evening was a complete contrast. After Sophie's last day at the Deansbury branch of Pagets, the entire staff gave her a lively farewell dinner at the George Hotel, an evening much more to her taste than the one with Julian. Perry was on form, as usual, keeping the entire company entertained, while Alexander, as host, oversaw the smooth running of the evening in his own effortless way, attentive to Sophie in an understated manner no one took for anything different from usual. Only Sophie was conscious of an extra nuance; the added electricity which dated from the day of Alexander's return from Greece, something which seemed to grow and intensify each time they were alone together. All week at the office Alexander had been satisfactorily circumspect, apart from an occasional errant gleam in his eyes when they were alone, designed specifically, she knew, to give her an unnecessary reminder about the change in their relationship. But, as he sat beside her at the dinner-table, Alexander's thigh brushed Sophie's too often for coincidence, and each time the contact aroused a shock of response which surged through her entire body. The effort to hide it from the world at large filled her with illicit excitement, adding an edge to an evening she would have enjoyed to the full anyway, even without the added bonus of sitting close to Alexander.

He drank very little, she noticed.

'You're very abstemious tonight,' she commented in an undertone.

'For a very good reason. I'm driving you home.' He looked very deliberately at her mouth, then away from her suddenly flushed face to press Sally Huntley, his partner's wife, to more coffee.

At the end of the evening Perry sprang up to propose a toast, listing Sophie's attributes with his customary verve.

As everyone rose to echo the toast Sophie sat with a lump in her throat, her cheeks poppy-red and her eyes very bright, finding it hard to keep her voice steady as she got up in response to cries of 'Speech!' She thanked everyone for the exquisite jardinière, told them how happy she'd been at the Deansbury office, and how delighted she was at the prospect of keeping in touch by means of the new Arlesford branch. She turned very deliberately to Alexander. 'And last, but very definitely not least, I wish to thank our host for an evening I'll always look back on with immense pleasure.'

'That was a loaded remark you made at the end,' commented Alexander as he drove her home.

'I was just being polite!'

'I'm sure everyone else thought so. My own impression was different.'

'Do you deny you were—well, touching me under the table all night?'

'No. You said I was to keep my distance during office hours. Which I have,' he added virtuously.

'You didn't include social occasions in the taboo.'

'Then I should have. I was like a cat on hot bricks all evening!'

'You didn't show it.'

'But you knew very well how you were affecting me, didn't you?' she accused.

'The same way you were affecting me, I hope.' Alexander stopped the car a short distance from the house. 'There you are, Sophie. Home safe and sound.'

'Will you come in for coffee?'

'Is your father likely to be up?'

'Yes.'

'Then forgive me, but I won't. I'm not sure I can cope with more frustration tonight.'

Sophie stared down at her clasped hands. 'Then I'd better go in. Thank you for this evening and for bringing me home.' She reached up and kissed his cheek, and at once his arms shot out to hold her and his mouth closed hungrily on hers. When he raised his head he was breathing hard.

'I had almost persuaded myself I could let you go without doing that,' he muttered against her mouth. 'See what you reduce me to, Sophie Gordon— making love in cars like an importunate schoolboy.'

'I don't try to,' she whispered. 'I just can't get used to the fact that you—that I——'

'That two old friends like us should suddenly find they don't want to be friends, after all.'

Sophie drew away. 'Aren't we friends any more, then, Alexander?'

He gave a smothered laugh. 'Dammit, Sophie, surely it must be painfully obvious that I want to be

your lover, not your friend!' His voice grated as he
drew her back against him and began kissing her once
more, and for a few wild moments her arms went
round his neck, clutching him closer, then with
superhuman effort Sophie tore herself away, gasping
for breath.

'I must go in, Alexander. I can't stand much more
of this. I'm just not used to it.'

He caught her hand. 'I'm sorry, Sophie. I didn't
mean to break your rules. I promise I'll do my
darnedest to toe the line when you start at the new
office.'

Sophie squeezed his fingers. 'I was the one to
blame. I shouldn't have kissed you. I promise I won't
do it again.'

'Don't say that, Sophie——' He lifted her hand
and kissed the palm, turning her fingers over to cover
the place he'd kissed. 'Shall I see you this weekend?'

'Let's not make any prearranged plans,
Alexander.'

'Why not?'

Sophie found it hard to explain why not. It
sounded so pontifical to say she needed to leave
home and start her new life, distancing herself from
everything for a while before she could contemplate
Alexander in the light of a lover. Because that was
what he'd be if they saw much more of each other
alone, she recognised with honesty. And it would be
a very tricky relationship to maintain in secret, that
was patently obvious, when their lives were so closely
interlinked.

'Not yet,' she said with difficulty. 'It's too soon.'

'Too soon! We've known each other for twenty-

odd years. How well do you have to know someone
before you let them wine and dine you, for God's
sake?'

'Don't be angry, Alexander. If you must know, I
think it's too soon after Delphine.'

He let out a deep breath. 'Ah, I see. You still think
I'm on my ego-boosting trip.'

Sophie thought it over. 'I did think so at first, I'll
admit. Now I'm not so sure. Anyway, I still need
some breathing space.'

'Fair enough,' said Alexander, suddenly brisk. 'I'll
give you until our respective parents' wedding. After
that . . .' He paused significantly. 'After that I expect
a change of attitude, Sophie.'

'You mean you expect me to hop into bed with
you the moment my father's back is turned?' she
enquired acidly.

'No, I do not!' Alexander turned in his seat and
took her by the shoulders, shaking her slightly. 'All I
have in mind is an occasional dinner together or an
evening at the theatre. More or less what you've been
doing for years with Julian Brett——' He stopped
short, staring down at her intently in the darkness.
'Or is *he* the stumbling block? You prefer his
company to mine, possibly?'

The anger in his voice did wonders for Sophie's
ego. 'Nothing to do with Julian,' she assured him.
'He's not prepared to travel as far as Arlesford to
continue with our usual arrangement, you see.'

Alexander's shoulders shook. 'Good God! Not
that I'm surprised in a way. Brett's never been known
to take an interest in any woman other than you, as
far as I know. He doesn't come across as an importu-

nate lover.'

Sophie gave in to temptation. 'On the contrary,' she said casually. 'Last night he asked me to marry him instead of moving away.'

Alexander grew very still. 'Really?' he said, in a dangerously silky tone. 'And what was your answer?'

'The picture he painted of our future life together was madly attractive,' said Sophie with regret. 'Nevertheless I found the strength to refuse. As you already know, marriage has no place in my particular scheme of things.'

It was very gratifying to hear Alexander's explosive exhalation of relief.

'Thank God for that. Brett's not the husband for you, Sophie.'

Sophie was in full agreement, but saw no reason to let Alexander know it. 'I'm not in the market for any husband,' she said with emphasis, and opened the car door. 'Goodnight, Alexander.'

He jumped out to walk with her through the garden to her front door. 'It's going to be very strange without you at the office on Monday, Sophie.'

'In a day or two you won't notice I've gone,' she assured him. 'Besides, I start work at the new office the following week. Will it be ready by then?'

'Part of it, at least. We may have to dodge ladders and cans of paint for a while, but we should be able to manage.' Alexander watched while Sophie unlocked the door, then bent swiftly and kissed her hard on the mouth before striding back to the car. Sophie listened for a moment until she heard the car start up, then shut the door slowly before turning to find her father leaning in the kitchen doorway in his dressing-gown, watching her.

'Nice evening, pet?' he asked.

'Very nice indeed.' She smiled at him happily. 'Everyone was so kind; they bought me a lovely jardinière for the cottage. Oh, bother—I left it in Alexander's car.'

'He'll keep it safe.' David Gordon kissed her cheek affectionately. 'I thought perhaps you might be feeling blue after saying your farewells, but I knew Alexander would take care of you.'

'What *would* we do without him?' said Sophie mockingly, then returned her father's kiss and went up to bed, thinking she, for one, might be less preoccupied by constant thoughts of Alexander's lovemaking if he were to absent himself from their lives. Then she spent some looking at her bright-eyed reflection in the mirror, coming to terms with the fact that if Alexander were to go out of her life he'd leave a great big gap no one else would ever be likely to fill.

CHAPTER EIGHT

SOPHIE found her free week less free than she'd hoped. Most of it was spent in showing prospective purchasers round the house, a task she found she disliked. Her urge to live alone was as strong as ever; none the less she felt a pang every time she thought of strangers living in the house where she had grown up. It was a great relief when an offer for it came almost at once from the people she liked best.

'And,' she told Kate Paget afterwards, 'perhaps I can have a break from all this frantic housework now the place doesn't have to be inspection-perfect all day and every day!'

The quick sale meant Sophie could begin her new job in Arlesford with a free heart. She was to remain at home until the wedding, after which she planned to stay with her grandmother until Ilex Cottage was ready, and agreed meekly when her father told her she would be foolish to refuse Alexander's offer of driving her to and from Arlesford each day.

Secretly Sophie enjoyed the daily drive with Alexander, who was keeping nobly to his promise to maintain his distance until the wedding was over. She also found it both satisfying and challenging to work with him to set up the new branch, and quickly made her own impression on the office set aside for her own use. The building which housed the offices was old, with lofty rooms and corniced ceilings and more than enough space for the great leather-topped desk Alexander had run to earth in an antique shop. He brought his famous drawing-board from Deansbury, and a squabbed leather chair from his own study at home, and for the time being the elegant proportions of his sanctum were displayed to full effect, uncluttered at this stage by the samples of bricks and tiles and carpets that crowded every corner of the Deansbury offices. Sophie made the most of the peace and space while she could, knowing very well it was only a matter of time before the place was crammed with the overflow from Deansbury.

It was oddly intimate to work with only Alexander for company, with no Perry or George Huntley, or any of the others constantly in and out of her office with their demands. Sophie enjoyed it to the full, not letting herself think about the day when Alexander felt he could relinquish the Arlesford office into Perry's keeping and retreat to his proper place at the helm in Deansbury.

'You can't refuse to lunch with me here,' said Alexander the first day. 'I see no point in your marching off to the local coffee-shop while I eat a lonely lunch in the bar of the Unicorn.'

Neither did Sophie, who was happier to agree than she had any intention of letting him know. Now they were virtually alone together in the offices, give or take a decorator or two, their relationship had quite definitely embarked on a new phase. Sophie could no longer ignore the fact that she was growing steadily more addicted to Alexander's company. It amazed her to think she had once taken him completely for granted as a family friend, or even just as her boss, that she had never once been troubled by the disturbing feelings she now found intensifying towards him daily. All her life Alexander had merely been there, as much a constant in her life as her father or her brothers. Unless one took into account the very brief attack of hero-worship of Alexander at fourteen or so, which had been largely due to the violent envy of her friends the day Alexander collected her from school in the rather flash car he sported in his college days.

The first really deep emotion she had ever experienced towards Alexander, Sophie realised, had been her compassion for him the day he was jilted so publicly by Delphine Wyndham. From that day on it had somehow never been quite possible to resume the old taken-for-granted relationship with Alexander, mainly because he had emerged from the trauma of his bride's defection a subtly changed man. One who seemed to have woken up overnight to the fact that his efficient, familiar secretary was not only a girl he'd known all her life, but a woman with an attraction he was suddenly aware he reacted to strongly.

'I'm behaving excessively well, don't you agree?' he asked smugly over lunch towards the end of the first week in Arlesford.

Sophie laughed. 'An absolute pillar of rectitude!'

'Then let me take you out somewhere on Saturday as my reward.'

'No dice, Alexander. You said after the wedding. Besides, I'm spending the day with Aunt Kate, shopping for last-minute frivolities.'

Alexander, who was looking his spectacular best in chalk-striped grey flannel, sighed as he gazed at her across one of the small tables in the Unicorn's crowded bar. 'You're really going to keep me to my promise, then?'

Sophie nodded. 'You bet your boots I am!'

He eyed her morosely. 'And no doubt the most I can expect *after* the wedding is an occasional meal together. And if I'm very lucky, perhaps a chaste goodnight kiss.' His eyes kindled. 'How I wish we were strangers, Sophie, with no hordes of relatives to inhibit us.'

'By which I assume you feel hampered by the thought of Dad and Aunt Kate.'

'Not to mention the terrible twins!'

Sophie laughed. 'Imagine how disillusioned they'd be if they thought their hero had dishonourable intentions towards a lady!'

'The point being that the lady in this case is their sister.' Alexander grinned. 'It's not their illusions that worry me, believe me, it's their fists. Both of them would be down on me like a ton of bricks, howling vengeance.'

'Good lord, do you think so?' Sophie was much struck by the idea. 'In that case, perhaps you ought to know they've joined a martial arts club.'

Alexander groaned and put a hand over his eyes. 'Heaven preserve me. Your virtue is safe from me, I promise.'

'How disappointing,' said Sophie lightly. 'Come on. Time to get back to work.'

The day of the wedding was cold and showery, not

that the elements were the only factors to make the occasion very different from Alexander's ordeal. This time the ceremony took place in the beautiful Norman church in Deansbury, with flowers and candles and a bride who arrived to a triumphant paean of Bach on the first stroke of noon. The immediate family and a few close friends were the only guests present, and Kate looked so radiant that Sophie had to blink away a tear as she watched her father kiss his bride with moving tenderness.

Afterwards Alexander had organised a superb, catered lunch at the Chantry, and after it had been enjoyed, and the toasts drunk and speeches made, the happy couple set off for a honeymoon in the Bahamas. Sophie felt a decidedly sharp pang as the taxi rolled down the drive with her father and Kate waving through the window until they were out of sight. Cecily Wainwright, magnificent in mink coat and hat, intercepted the look in her granddaughter's eyes and led her back into the house.

'One always feels flat after a wedding. Drink some champagne,' she commanded, in her usual bracing way.

Sophie did as she was told, her eyes drawn to Alexander, who was laughing as Matthew and Mark regaled him with a catalogue of their exploits in Edinburgh. 'I feel as though a chapter in my life has ended,' she said forlornly. 'Does that sound fanciful, Gran?'

'Not in the least. Perfectly natural since not only are you moving out of your childhood home, but your father's acquired a new woman in his life. Not,' added Mrs Wainwright on reflection, 'that one could describe Kate as a *new* woman, exactly.'

'True.' Sophie downed a cheering draught of champagne, then steered her grandmother in the direction of the Vicar before going off to cope with a flurry of leavetaking as the guests began to depart. Even the twins, formal suits exchanged for their usual uniform of denim and leather, were bent on setting off for Edinburgh at once.

'The girls in the flat next door are throwing a party tonight,' said Matthew with anticipation as he kissed Sophie. 'We'll give you a ring at Gran's tomorrow.'

Once guests and caterers had gone, Alexander insisted on making tea himself while the two ladies relaxed in his drawing-room.

Mrs Wainwright looked about her curiously. 'Strange how things turn out. Kate will go on as mistress here after all instead of Delphine.'

'Let's forget about Delphine,' said Sophie flatly.

Mrs Wainwright chuckled. 'You consider Alexander's better off without her, I gather.'

'Someone mention my name?' asked Alexander, returning with the tray. 'Will you pour, Mrs Wainwright?'

The elegant old lady was only too happy to oblige, then shocked Sophie rigid by telling Alexander how fortunate he was to be rid of Delphine Wyndham. 'Stupid girl,' she added forcefully. 'Bad-mannered, too. Not done to make a laughing-stock of a fine man like you.'

Sophie glared at her grandparent, appalled. 'For heaven's sake, Gran!'

Alexander looked unruffled. 'I agree, totally. Now Sophie, here, would never dream of behaving like that, would you, Sophie?'

'Few people would!'

'Are you coming back with me in the Bentley, Sophie?' asked Mrs Wainwright, gathering up her gloves.

'She has a long-standing appointment with me tonight,' said Alexander, before Sophie could say a word. 'You haven't forgotten, Sophie, surely?' His eyes gleamed through his thick lashes. 'We arranged it some time ago.'

After the wedding, thought Sophie, taken aback to find Alexander meant it quite so literally.

'Splendid,' said Mrs Wainwright, rummaging in her alligator handbag. 'Here's a key, Sophie. If you're late, let yourself in. I'll probably be in bed. Weddings are so tiring at my age.'

Sophie went with Alexander to install Mrs Wainwright behind the wheel of the ancient Bentley she insisted driving in preference to the modern replacements David Gordon had tried to persuade her to buy over the years. In Cecily Wainwright's opinion the Bentley had more style, and the dignified vehicle continued to delight the inhabitants of Arlesford whenever Mrs Wainwright took to the road.

'Please drive carefully, Gran,' said Sophie anxiously.

'I always do.' Mrs Wainwright gave Alexander a smile. 'Bring her home safely, Alexander.'

Sophie had had quite enough of watching cars roll away from her by this time, and went back into the house with Alexander, feeling even more depressed.

'Will I do as I am?' she asked. 'Since you forgot to

mention any plans for this evening, I haven't brought a change of clothes.'

Because Dr Gordon had provided his daughter with a generous sum to spend on an outfit for the wedding, she had succumbed to the temptation of cashmere the colour of milk chocolate, the thigh-length tunic and brief straight skirt severely plain, unadorned by anything except the wide tortoiseshell bracelet on Sophie's wrist.

'Oh, you'll do,' Alexander informed her, after a long, leisurely survey of her person. 'But I'd like a minute or two to change, if you'll bear with me.'

'Of course.' Sophie took the tea-tray off to the kitchen, feeling ridiculously shy, to her annoyance, glad of a mundane chore like washing cups.

Alexander was back very quickly, his pin-striped Valentino suit replaced by heavy black jersey trousers, and zippered wool jacket over a white wool shirt.

'Right, then, Sophie. Let's go,' he said briskly.

'Where?'

'On a picnic.'

Sophie stared at him in amazement as he hurried her out of the house to the car. 'You've noticed it's almost dark, I suppose,' she said, as she slid inside. '*And* chilly!'

Alexander looked smug. 'I have. But it won't affect the picnic, I promise. Be fair. You *said* I could take you out occasionally for a meal. You didn't specify where.'

Sophie giggled suddenly, her spirits rising as they left Deansbury behind. 'A picnic will certainly be a change from Enzio's!'

'Julian's favourite restaurateur, I assume,' said Alexander scathingly. 'Where the socialites of Deansbury go to see and be seen. Nothing like that tonight, sweetheart. Just you and me.'

A tremor ran up Sophie's spine at the prospect, and Alexander, attuned to it instantly, placed a long-fingered hand on her knee. 'My sole aim is to cheer you up, little sister, I promise, because I could tell the blues were threatening a bit when your father went off with Kate.'

Sophie sighed. 'Yes. Human nature's very strange, isn't it? I've been yearning for my freedom for so long, and now I've been handed it on a plate, so to speak, I don't know quite what to do with it.'

'You'll soon adjust,' he assured her, and began to talk about the wedding.

It was some time before Sophie could pluck up the courage to ask the question which had been niggling at her all day. 'Alexander—was it all very painful for you today?'

Alexander drove in silence for a while. 'To be honest,' he said slowly, 'I did have cold feet about it beforehand. Quite unnecessarily, as it happened. The quiet, moving ceremony we witnessed in church today seemed to have nothing at all to do with my celebrated fiasco.'

'I was worried for you,' she said quietly.

'Thank you.' Alexander hesitated for a moment, glancing at her. 'But it was having you with me that made all the difference, Sophie. I wonder if you can understand that, already, the time with Delphine seems unreal to me, a kind of "brief gaudy hour", when a meteor hurtled into my life for a while, then out of it again. While you, Sophie, have always been there—glowing steadily; the lode-star every man needs in his life.'

Sophie took so much time to digest this that she failed to notice where they were until he halted the car. She peered up at him, eyebrows raised.

'Willow Reach, Alexander? Don't tell me, let me guess. We're having a barbecue in the garden!'

'God, no!' He laughed and left the car to open the big double gates before driving through.

To Sophie's surprise the lights were on in the house. 'Is someone here?'

'No.' He dangled a bunch of keys in front of her nose. 'Willow Reach is now mine, all mine. And the lights are on time switches, of course. You, Miss Gordon, are my very first visitor, but your picnic supper doesn't come cheap—you'll have to work for it.'

'Oh, will I?' Sophie followed Alexander as he unlocked the door and flung it wide before swinging her up in his arms and carrying her though into a large, square hall.

'What *are* you doing?' she said, her face scarlet as he set her on her feet.

He shrugged. 'It just seemed appropriate—all the talk of weddings, I suppose.'

'Then stop talking about them and show me round your house instead,' she said tartly.

Alexander was only too pleased to do so, his manner very proprietorial as he led her upstairs, through empty, beautifully proportioned rooms, fewer in number than Sophie had expected from the size of the house.

'When I originally designed it I made light and
space my priorities, rather than room-count.'
Alexander gestured towards the windows. 'Great
sheets of glass would have been entirely wrong for the
garden they looked out on, so I used small panes to
create a more cottage-like atmosphere.'

'It's perfect,' said Sophie simply, and ran a hand
down the mahogany rail which curved over wrought-
iron banisters of such intricate workmanship that
they could have been made of fine black lace. She
followed Alexander downstairs, through an elegantly
fitted kitchen, a sizeable dining-room, a graceful
drawing-room with beamed ceiling and shelved
alcoves flanking a white marble fireplace. Finally
they arrived at the door of a room Alexander
announced would be his study.

Sophie's eyes widened as he ushered her inside.
Unlike the rest of the rooms, it was anything but
empty. Piles of carpet samples were strewn about
next to swatches of curtain materials, rolled rugs
piled in one corner, canvases stacked in another, and
brochures everywhere, for everything from light-
fittings to bathrooms and colour-cards for paint. A
kilim rug made an oasis in the centre of the floor, and
on it stood the only item of furniture Sophie had seen
so far in the entire house, a rattan chaise-longue with
brown velvet cushions. She grinned at Alexander,
enlightened.

'I see, I see. *This* is where we picnic. But before
I'm fed I suppose my opinion is required on this lot!'

'Bullseye!' Alexander shrugged off his jacket, then
left Sophie alone to browse among all the fabrics, and
wonder about the quantity involved for the floors

and windows of this tranquil, graceful house.

Alexander returned quickly with a bottle of champagne and two glasses. 'I've had this chilling to the exact degree of perfection in anticipation of this very moment, Miss Gordon.'

Sophie kicked off her shoes and curled up on the chaise-longue with several swatches of curtain material around her, and held out her hand for the glass Alexander was offering. 'Pink champagne, no less,' she said appreciatively. 'To Willow Reach, Alexander; may you be very happy here.'

'Amen to that.' He drank deeply. 'Do you like the house?' he added casually.

'Who wouldn't? If a client ever needs proof of your flair, this house is a wonderful showpiece. Even inside, it just doesn't seem like a modern house. There's a timeless feel to it, as though it's always been here.'

'Probably because so much of the building material was salvaged, as I said when I showed you the garden, from the original house.' Alexander let himself down to sit cross-legged on the rug, then leaned over and refilled her glass. 'Willow Reach was built first time round to house the mistress of one of Charles the Second's courtiers. The gentleman's wife was rich and ugly and very jealous, so he built this house for his beautiful young mistress miles from anywhere, as it was then, with high walls instead of the present hedges, but the same fountain in the grotto in the garden. A secret place where he could be alone with his love, hidden from the world.' Alexander's expressive voice dropped at the last words, as he looked into Sophie's eyes. 'What are you thinking?'

'I was wondering what the girl did with herself while her lover was away at court. All those minutes and hours and days to be filled without him. How on earth did she pass the time?'

'Looking after her children, I imagine,' said Alexander prosaically. 'They produced quite a few, though oddly enough the gentleman was never blessed with a legal heir.'

'Poor rich, ugly wife,' said Sophie with compassion. 'Anyway, Mr Paget, sir, let's get on with the matter in hand.' She shook off the shadow from the past and knelt with Alexander on the floor, quickly engrossed in the colours and textures spread out all around them. His professional eye and her own natural flair for colour worked well together, and the time passed swiftly as they isolated a growing pile of possible choices. Two hours passed before a sudden rumble in Sophie's stomach reminded her it was a long time since the elegant wedding-breakfast at the Chantry.

'I'm hungry,' she said. 'Where's this picnic you promised me, slavedriver?'

Alexander sprang to his feet in remorse. 'Lord, I'm sorry, Sophie. Just stay where you are and I'll bring everything in.'

'Can't I help?'

'No. You've done enough today. Shan't be long.'

Alone, Sophie tidied her hair and stretched out luxuriously on the chaise, thinking about the girl who had lived and loved in the original Willow Reach. What was it like to be someone's mistress? she wondered. Surely a mistress never ironed shirts or cooked nourishing meals, or even knew how to thread a needle, let alone sew on all those endless name tapes? She rather fancied being Alexander's mistress. Her eyes narrowed as she pictured herself in expensive silk underwear, with hand-made lace, of course, and a satin peignoir falling open as she lolled on a chaise-longue like this, waiting for him to spend long nights of illicit passion with her, with never a hint of domestic chores to intrude on their bliss. Her eyes glittered darkly as she conjured up visions of weekends in Paris and Rome, holidays in Antigua and Bali . . .

'That's a very strange look in your eyes, Sophie!'

Sophie came to with a jolt as Alexander came back with a picnic hamper. She sat up hurriedly, smoothing her brief skirt into place, her cheeks hot.

'Daydreaming,' she said, and helped him set out their supper on the starched white cloth included in the hamper. Sophie fell to with a will on the delicious food provided by Alexander's caterers, with more appetite now for the slices of pink ham and succulent turkey breast, the smoked salmon and game pie, than she had felt for the wedding-breakfast earlier.

'Only cheese to follow, I'm afraid,' said Alexander. 'I told them to keep it simple, since it had to hang about for a bit.'

'It's wonderful,' said Sophie indistinctly. 'I'm starving. Probably because I wasn't in the least hungry lunch time.'

'I noticed.' Alexander put another slice of ham on her plate.

They made large inroads on the food, and afterwards finished off the champagne. 'Feel better now?'

asked Alexander lazily. He leaned back against the foot of the chaise-longue, his legs stretched out in front of him. Sophie lay on the velvet cushions, a little drowsy after the good food.

'I certainly do.' She sighed. 'This is such a lovely house, Alexander. You're a genius.'

'I know,' he said modestly. 'My picnic wasn't a bad idea, was it?'

'Inspired.' Reluctantly Sophie swung her legs to the ground and looked around for her shoes. 'Only now I'm afraid I'll have to ask you to drive me to Arlesford. I don't want to worry Gran by staying out late on my first night as her lodger.'

Alexander looked up into her eyes. 'May I have one kiss first? If you think back, I'm sure we decided a kiss now and then was acceptable.'

'*You* decided.'

He smiled, and drew her down gently into his arms and Sophie lay against him, her mouth parting beneath his so willingly that he crushed her to him with a groan, kissing her with a hunger she realised had been kept on a short rein all evening. Then, as abruptly as it had begun, the storm was over. His head lifted a little and his embrace relaxed as gleaming green eyes gazed down into heavy, slumbering dark ones. 'Does that count as one kiss?' he muttered against her mouth.

'I wasn't counting,' she whispered.

He drew in a long, shaky breath, then leapt to his feet, pulling her with him. 'Home!' he said firmly.

CHAPTER NINE

ON A cold November evening a few weeks later, Sophie thrust her paintbrush in a jar of white spirit and eased her aching back as she opened the door to the stairs.

'Coffee, Alexander?' she called.

'Five minutes,' he yelled back. 'Just giving the bedroom ceiling another coat.'

Ilex Cottage was very nearly ready for occupation. Sophie filled her new kettle in her minuscule kitchen, and took a deep breath of satisfaction, coughing a little as the paint fumes hit her chest. Cecily Wainwright had been keen to employ a professional decorator, but Sophie wouldn't hear of it, insisting the little house would be so much more her own if she did the painting herself. And the moment her grandmother learned who was giving a helping hand she said no more.

Alexander eased himself gingerly through the door at the bottom of the stairs, grinning when he saw Sophie sitting cross-legged in the middle of her uncarpeted floor with two mugs of coffee beside her.

'I'm trying not to brush against any of the paint-work,' she said, offering him a packet of biscuits.

Alexander let himself down beside her, flicking a finger at her nose. 'Paint-splash, Sophie.'

She eyed him critically. 'You should see yourself!'

Neither of them were acmes of elegance. Sophie was arrayed in dungarees and sweatshirt, with a peaked denim cap covering her hair, and Alexander wore a black running vest and tracksuit trousers, both garments liberally streaked with white paint.

'What a way to spend Saturday night!' commented Alexander as he munched hungrily.

'I need tomorrow for drying out. Then I can move in on Monday.' Sophie looked about her in triumph. 'All done! Isn't it perfect?'

'You're like a little girl with a doll's house.'

'I never had one, so probably that's why I'm so thrilled with this.' She drank her coffee, her eyes moving in all directions as she arranged furniture in her mind, finally focusing on Alexander, who was watching her with indulgence. She smiled sheepishly. 'Oh, I know it's a bit different from Willow Reach—the entire cottage would probably fit into your drawing-room. But to me this place is everything I've ever wanted.'

Alexander got to his feet and stretched, yawning as he looked at his watch. 'Come on, it's almost midnight. High time you were back at Greenacre.'

Sophie scrambled up, collecting the mugs. She looked over her shoulder at him as he followed her into the kitchen. 'I'm very grateful to you, Alexander. You've been so kind to me lately.'

He removed her paint-stained cap and slid his arms round her from behind, resting his chin on the top of her tousled head.

'Not only kind. Or haven't you noticed? I have also been quite remarkably virtuous and self-restrained, too.'

Sophie slid out of his hold, her eyes dancing as she turned to face him. 'I though maybe the paint was having an effect on your libido!'

He yanked her to him and kissed her, then shook her ungently. 'Don't push your luck, Miss Gordon. My libido happens to be alive and well, since you mention it. I'm merely biding my time.'

She sobered. 'Until when? And for what, exactly?'

Alexander's lashes veiled his expression. 'You'll know when the time comes.'

'Don't be infuriating—tell me!'

'No chance.'

Sophie felt it best to avoid anticipating his intentions a second time. She had been caught like that before, and only by the grace of God managed to avoid refusing a proposal of marriage Alexander had never intended making. This time, she could only think he must be waiting for her to move out from under her grandmother's roof before finally asking to share her bed.

It was a thought which preoccupied her a great deal over the next few days, all time she was settling in to her new home and helping her grandmother make the transition from Greenacre to the suite of rooms she was to occupy at Broad Oaks. Mrs Wainwright had insisted on overseeing the packing of her possessions, most of which she had been adamant over putting into storage for future use by Sophie and her brothers, and when the upheaval was finally over and the indomitable lady was at last installed in her new quarters Sophie was worried to see how tired her grandmother looked. She said so afterwards in no uncertain terms to her father and Kate, who had joined in the supervision of the move.

David Gordon exchanged a glance with Kate, then suggested all of them go to Ilex Cottage to see the finished result. When an admiring tour of inspection had been made the three of them sat with glasses of the sherry provided by Perry as a 'libation to the god of removals', and Dr Gordon explained to Sophie that Cecily Wainwright's heart was not as strong as it might be.

'When I heard she was moving herself into Broad Oaks I had a talk with her—behind your back, pet, I'm afraid.' He squeezed Sophie's hand reassuringly. 'Don't look like that! She'll last for years yet, as long as she takes it easy, with a regular professional eye kept on her. Your grandmother's a very sensible woman, and she's done the best possible thing under the circumstances.'

'I had no idea,' said Sophie with remorse. 'She never said a word.'

'And she won't thank your father for letting the cat out of the bag,' said Kate gently. 'So keep it to yourself, Sophie. Just go on as usual.' She grinned. 'You know how incensed she'd be if she thought David had spilled the beans.'

'Lord, yes!' Sophie smiled ruefully, and changed the subject by asking how they liked her colour-scheme. Kate was loud with her approval of the yellow and white curtains, and how well the dining-room carpet from Greenacre had cut down to suit the small room.

'I love the chaise-longue, too,' she added. 'Was that Cecily's?'

'No. Alexander donated it as a moving-in present,' said Sophie casually. 'Perfect there, isn't it?'

Except for the disquieting news about her grandmother, life was good for Sophie in the period following her move to Ilex Cottage. She saw less of Alexander, it was true, because Perry was now in charge of the Arlesford branch of Paget's. Nevertheless, in his role of senior partner Alexander visited the branch office fairly often, and followed his original plan of taking Sophie out for an occasional meal, or a trip to the theatre in Bath or Bristol, but he firmly refused her offers of a meal at Ilex Cottage by way of return.

'No, Sophie,' he said one night, as he saw her safely into the cottage. 'I'm giving you the breathing space you wanted, behaving like the virtuous family friend I'm believed to be. But frankly I don't think my virtue is so absolute as to survive an evening *à deux* with you, my lovely, neither here nor at Willow Reach.'

Sophie switched on a lamp then sat on the chaise, looking up at him in challenge. 'What if I don't *want* it to survive, Alexander?'

His mouth tightened as he gazed down at her. The soft cashmere of the suit she'd worn for the wedding outlned the curves of her breasts as Sophie clasped her hands deliberately behind her head, and crossed her legs in their gossamer dark stockings so that her skirt rode high above her knees.

'Sophie——' He stopped, running a hand through his hair as he flung away to the fireplace.

'Really, Alexander! I'm no Victorian maiden, likely to faint if you catch a glimpse of my ankles.'

'I can see a lot more than that!' He kept his back turned. 'I'm sure you've been told how beautiful your legs are hundreds of times, so just pull your skirt down and behave, Sophie.'

She sat up straight, addressing his broad shoulders. 'Perhaps I was wrong. Yet I could have sworn you'd changed towards me, Alexander. Lately you've been giving me the impression that you think of me as a bit more than just Sophie the family friend, or even Sophie the secretary. *Was* I wrong, Alexander?'

He swung round, his eyes glittering. He stared down at her for a moment, then caught her hands and hauled her up against him. 'You know damn well you weren't wrong.' He moved her hand to touch him. 'Does *that* feel as though I don't want you? Why the hell do you think I keep inventing reasons to interfere at the Arlesford office? Just to see you, my little friend! Perry gets bloody fed up with me, only he knows very well it's your neck I want to breathe down, not his.'

Sophie moved her hand delicately, exulting in his anguished groan as he crushed her to him and began to kiss her with all the urgency she'd been yearning for over the past weeks of impersonal friendliness. She'd been frantic for his touch, eager to breathe in the distinctive scent of him, feel the warmth of his body against hers. Her nerves were ragged with wanting him, and after a long, breathless interval Sophie tipped her head back, her eyes dilated as she gazed up into his.

'Take me to bed, Alexander,' she whispered, triumphantly certain he'd sweep her up into his arms. Instead his arms fell away and he shook his head, his eyes tight closed.

'No?' she said incredulously.

'I *can't,* Sophie!' The words were bitten out.

'Oh, God, not you as well!' Sophie turned away, hugging her arms across her chest.

'What the hell do you mean by that?' Alexander caught her by the elbow and spun her round. 'How many men do you ask to take you to bed, may I ask?'

'Only you, Alexander, only you.' Sophie's eyes flashed at him, humiliation and anger vibrating inside her. 'But don't worry. I won't again. Ever!'

He shook her hard. 'Listen to me, you little shrew. When you moved in here I had several requests from a number of people. Not couched in similar terms precisely, but all amounting to the same thing. Your grandmother, your father, Kate too; they all asked me to keep an eye on you, to take care of you, see you were all right on your own. Now maybe they intended me to check your pipes didn't freeze, or your drains didn't block. It's possible. But you know and I know that they meant me to see that no man gets ideas because little Sophie's living alone now. And I think they include me, Sophie, since I think I can safely say I *am* a man.'

She pulled free. 'Not merely a man, Alexander—

a paragon of perfection.' She put her hands behind her back, her eyebrows raised. 'Why not come clean? Admit I don't compare with Delphine in the sex department.'

Alexander gritted his teeth. 'For God's sake, what do I have to do to convince you I don't care a damn for Delphine any more?'

'Take me to bed and make love to me!' She eyed him defiantly. 'Why not? You've been here with me on several occasions lately, long enough to make love to me every time. Who's to know you haven't? Probably all the neighbours think we're lovers, anyway.'

'But we're not! And your family trusts me to see that we stay that way.'

'Then I think we'd better revert to our original relationship in future. Employer and employee.' Sophie quivered inside with wounded pride and something she assumed was sexual frustration. It was a new feeling. One that humiliated and hurt and spurred her on to lash out, to puncture Alexander's armour of rectitude.

'Our original relationship was also friendship,' he reminded her coldly.

'Then let's decide on a new relationship, with no personal feelings involved.' She went to the door. 'Thank you for dinner, Alexander. I won't say the evening was an unqualified success—but thank you just the same.'

'Does this mean I see you only at the office?' He stood over her, his eyes shuttered in his pale face. 'Can't we at least be friends?'

'I've had it up to here with men who just want to

be friends. It's very bad for a girl's self-esteem.
Goodnight, Alexander.' Sophie opened the door,
waiting pointedly. He gazed at her for a moment,
then grabbed her by the shoulders and kissed her
savagely.

'A pity to disappoint the neighbours,' he flung at
her, then strode off down the narrow walk, leaving
Sophie a prey to seething emotions as she banged
the door shut and stormed upstairs to bed.

'Bad night?' asked Perry next day, as Sophie
finished going through the post with him.

'No,' she snapped, then smiled apologetically.
'Sorry. Didn't mean to bite.'

'Don't mention it—just don't like to see you
down in the mouth.' Perry eyed her closely.
'Weren't you dining with my cousin and revered
boss last night?'

'Yes.' Sophie got up. 'Shall I make coffee now?'

'In other words mind your own business, E.P.
Paget, Junior Partner.' He grinned, his blue eyes
alight with curiosity. 'Don't tell me Alexander
came on a bit strong, Sophie! Shall Uncle Perry
slap his wrist for you?'

Sophie gave him a withering look and marched
back to her office without deigning to reply. Her
depression was acute. Her satisfaction over giving
Alexander his marching orders had lasted less than
the time taken to get herself to bed, leaving her
utterly miserable, and prone to looking up
hopefully every time her office door opened next
day. But it was always Perry, or Brian Harris the
young draughtsman, never Alexander. Each ring of
the telephone had her diving for the receiver, but it

was never the desired voice on the other end of the line. To her dismay even her delight in her new home was dimmed by her quarrel with Alexander, and as the days went by her evenings alone in the cottage began to feel lonely instead of peaceful. The rest of the week passed without contact with Alexander of any kind, professional or otherwise, so that Sophie was only too glad to accept an invitation to Sunday lunch with her father and Kate. She was helping the latter in the kitchen when she heard Alexander's voice in the hall. Kate's eyebrows rose as she saw Sophie stiffen.

'Didn't I mention Alexander was coming, love?'

'No, you didn't. How nice.'

It was not at all nice. The meal was an ordeal, since Alexander's manner towards Sophie was chillingly polite, and her reaction was to chatter nineteen to the dozen to hide her dismay. Kate and David Gordon, plainly worried by the constraint between their respective loved ones, did their best to keep the conversational ball rolling, but it was uphill work.

Sophie was deeply pleased to see Alexander looked haggard, as if lack of sleep was a problem they shared.

'How is Willow Reach?' she asked brightly. 'Everything done now?'

'More or less.' He met her eyes. 'The curtains you chose look exactly right, by the way. They were hung on Friday.'

'Oh, splendid. No—no, thanks, Aunt Kate, no pudding.'

'You haven't eaten much,' observed her father.

'Are you cooking proper meals for yourself these days?'

'Yes, Doctor, I am!' Sophie avoided Alexander's sardonic gaze and began a conversation with Kate on a televised opera they had both watched during the week, and shortly afterwards Alexander rose to go.

'May I give you a lift, Sophie? Arlesford is very little out of my way.'

'No, thanks. I'm staying to tea—if that's all right with you, Aunt Kate?'

Kate agreed with alacrity, and pressed Alexander to stay, but he took his leave with the air of a man desperate to escape.

'You two had a fight?' enquired Dr Gordon, while Kate was seeing her stepson off.

'Yes. Nothing to worry about.' Sophie smiled brightly and went off to help Kate wash up.

Sophie had refused Perry's invitations to lunch at the Unicorn right from the start, but next day he insisted she broke her rule. He was in jubilant mood and wanted to celebrate. Confirmation had just been received that the firm had won the Waterside Hotel job in Brading.

'Clever lad, our Alexander,' said Perry, as he brought their drinks to the table. 'Sorry for the delay, by the way. They're short-staffed.'

Sophie sipped her wine absently, her mind on the last occasion she'd been here. With Alexander.

'What's up, Sophie?' asked Perry affectionately. 'Anyone with half an eye can tell you and Alexander have called a halt to whatever's been going on between you. And,' he added, 'that neither of you is exactly happy about it.'

'There was nothing "going on", as you so delicately put it.' Nor likely to be, thought Sophie unhappily.

'Sorry—rather thought there was, myself.' Perry shrugged. 'I mean you've known each other forever, of course. But since that ghastly business with Delphine I fancy Alexander's a changed man in more ways than one. He fancies you rotten these days, Sophie, old family friend or not.'

'Nonsense,' said Sophie flatly, her heart leaping at the mere thought of being fancied by Alexander.

Perry put out a hand to cover hers. 'And I've seen Willow Reach. I know you helped choose a lot of the stuff there, so naturally I thought——'

'Well, you thought wrong.'

'So you're just good friends?'

'No, Perry.' Sophie swallowed hard, her eyes suddenly misting over. 'We're not even friends any more.'

'So *here* you are!'

Sophie jumped yards as Alexander's voice interrupted them. She stared up at him guiltily, her heart sinking at the look of icy disapproval on his handsome face as he loomed over them.

'We're celebrating,' said Perry, unabashed. 'What'll you have, Alexander?'

'Celebrating?' Alexander's voice grated, and Perry gazed at him, all blue-eyed innocence.

'The Waterside Hotel, of course, old chap.' He smiled benignly and went off to push his way to the bar.

'May I join you?' asked Alexander stiffly.

'Yes. Do.' Sophie swallowed some wine to moisten her suddenly dry mouth. 'Congratulations, by the way. You must be very pleased.'

'Thank you.' Alexander stared down at the table. 'Do you lunch here with Perry every day?'

'No. First time today, in fact. He insisted on celebrating your success.' Sophie looked away across the crowded bar, battling to keep calm.

'Is all well at the cottage?'

'Fine.'

'Good. How's your grandmother?'

'Much better now she's settled in. She's quite spoiled by the staff at Broad Oaks.'

Alexander put a hand out to touch hers. 'Sophie——' He bit back a curse as Perry came back, juggling three glasses.

'I ordered lunch for you with ours, Alexander,' he panted. 'Like a rugger scrum back there. Miranda's left. The blonde behind the bar,' he added, as the other two looked blank.

Sophie picked at her prawn-stuffed crêpe while Perry wolfed his steak sandwich then jumped up, saying he had an appointment. He pushed Sophie down into her seat as she rose to leave with him, telling her to finish her lunch like a good girl, and not to rush back to the office.

Alone together, both Sophie and Alexander gave up all pretence at eating.

'Alexander——'

'Sophie——'

They spoke together, then stopped short, looking at each other, and Alexander smiled for the first time.

'I can't stand it, Sophie. I've been bloody miserable since that night. Too much time to think in my empty house.'

'I've thought a lot, too,' said Sophie.

'Were any of the thoughts about me?' He took her hand in his under the table, stroking it with his fingers.

'Of course they were. Why were you so cold and distant to me yesterday?' she blurted.

'*I* was cold and distant? Good God—*you* were the original Snow Queen. One look from you and I had icicles on my roast beef!'

Sophie gave a choked laugh, then sobered as she found him looking at her with such intensity she gazed back wordlessly, as the pupils of his thickly fringed eyes dilated, holding her in thrall.

'I miss you, Sophie,' he said softly. 'All I can think of are those words you said.'

'Which words?'

'The request you made, my darling. If you could bring yourself to repeat it, I'd respond differently this time, I promise. I've decided I can't spend my life trying to please everyone but you and me.' He leaned closer, his hand tightening on hers. 'Ask me again, Sophie.'

'Here?'

'Yes. Here. And now.'

Sophie couldn't tear her eyes away from his. The noise and laughter all around them faded into nothingness. All she could see was Alexander and the hypnotic urgency of his gaze as he willed her to say what he wanted. She shivered, and his hand tightened on hers as she ran the tip of her tongue over suddenly dry lips. 'If I remember correctly,' she whispered, 'I said——'

'Alexander!' cried a high, fluting voice, shattering the spell. 'What a chase I've had, darling! I popped into your old office first, then I simply roared over here in Daddy's Jag to this new place, and some Brian person told me I'd find you in the pub. And here you are!' Delphine Wyndham stood over them, a fur coat slung over a gold jumpsuit. She turned the full force of her celebrated smile on the two people staring at her in frozen silence, her eyes narrowing as she looked from one rigid face to the other.

Sophie felt as though she were living through a bad dream as Alexander rose slowly to his feet, his face a handsome mask.

'Hello, Delphine,' he said quietly. 'Quite a surprise.'

'I'm back, darling,' Delphine announced blithely, the smile blinding as a ripple of intense interest ran through the entire bar. She preened, visibly lapping up the attention she was attracting, then turned to Sophie, who felt suddenly helpless, like a mouse transfixed by the predatory gaze of a sleek, black cat. 'He*llo*, Sophie—lovely to see you again. Still slaving away for Alexander, then?'

At which Sophie came to life and rose to her feet, gathering up her bag and scarf. She gave Delphine a composed little smile. 'Hello, Delphine. I'm sure you won't think me rude if I dash. Mustn't keep my boss waiting. I work for Perry in the branch office here these days.' She aimed the smile at Alexander's chin. 'Goodbye.'

'Sophie——' he said urgently, catching her arm as she passed, but she detached herself and began to push her way through the crowd.

''Bye, Sophie,' called Delphine, and laid a possessive hand on Alexander's arm. 'Now then, darling. Aren't you going to buy me a drink?'

Sophie fled blindly, bumping into Anna Mitchell, the wife of the proprietor.

'Sorry,' panted the latter. 'Utter chaos here today. God knows what we'll do tonight.'

'Do you need help in the bar?' asked Sophie urgently.

'Do we! Know anyone who could fill in for a night or two?'

'Yes. Me.'

CHAPTER TEN

SOPHIE'S offer, made on the spur of the moment, was a gut reaction to the shock of seeing Delphine. Brushing aside Anna Mitchell's thanks, she hurried away from the Unicorn, blind to everything but the expression on Alexander's face as he looked up to find Delphine smiling at him. He had stared at that exquisite face like a man in a dream, thought Sophie in misery. For herself the whole thing had been a nightmare, a brutal interruption of a moment which just possibly might have marked a turning point in her life.

The afternoon which followed was an experience Sophie hoped never to repeat. She spent it on tenterhooks, half hoping, half dreading Alexander might appear at any moment, Delphine in tow. All Sophie wanted was to be put out of her misery one way or another, but she was left in what could be loosely termed as peace. Perry never returned to the office after dashing off on a house inspection, and Brian Harris and his minions were deep in piles of drawings and prints for a new factory. It seemed an eternity before Sophie was free to go home at last, on fire with the desire to scrub herself from head to foot, feeling somehow that hot water and soap might wash away the humiliation of almost begging Alexander to be her lover, when he obviously still hankered after his Delphine. She could have kicked herself. Making a fool of oneself once was allowable. Twice was lunacy. Sophie sluiced water over her hair and face, mortified that she could actually have forgotten how beautiful Delphine really was. What man could look at such perfection without wanting to possess it? And Alexander, if he were to be believed, had never actually been granted the privilege. Which made it all so much worse. Men always, as Alexander had once informed her, wanted most the things they were refused. While she, thought Sophie, shuddering, had actually offered herself to him twice. *Twice*!

Sophie attacked her hair with dryer and hairbrush, then made a sandwich and crumbled it to pieces while she drank cup after cup of strong black coffee, pacing up and down her little sitting-room until it was time to set off for the Unicorn.

Monday evenings, Anna Mitchell informed her, were quieter than the rest of the week. Sophie was grateful for it since it gave her the chance to memorise prices, learn how to pull pints of beer and handle the optics, to wash and replace glasses, and generally accustom herself to the routine of the job. Frank Mitchell, the landlord, was a stalwart man with a pleasant but authoritative manner, popular with his clientèle. Sophie found him easy to work with from the start, mainly because she learned rapidly, and was quick on her feet. One thing he found hard to tolerate, Frank told her bluntly, was a barmaid who dawdled or spent too much time chatting up the younger male

customers. Sophie was astonished anyone ever had
time for chat with anyone from behind the bar of
the Unicorn, and went home at closing time feeling
very tired indeed. She could hear the telephone
ringing as she unlocked her door and burst into the
sitting-room just as it stopped. She glared at the
telephone in frustration, sure it had been
Alexander. She scowled. If he really wanted to talk
to her he would ring again. She went upstairs and
dawdled as long as possible while she undressed,
then lay in tense expectancy, sure the telephone
would ring again. It was only when it became
obvious at last that it was going to do no such thing
that she gave in at last and let herself cry her misery
into her pillow.

Perry was waiting when Sophie arrived at the
office next day.

'Morning, Sophie.' He handed her a note. 'I was
ordered to give you this before we start.'

Sophie thanked him, her mouth tightening as she
saw Alexander's familiar handwriting.

'I rang last night—repeatedly—without success.
I'm in court all day today, but I'll be at the cottage
tonight about eight. A.'

Sophie screwed the paper into a ball and threw it
in the wastebasket without comment, then applied
herself to the usual matters of the day, knowing
quite well that Perry was bursting with curiosity.
She made no attempt to satisfy it, and the
morning's post was dealt with and Sophie almost
out of his office before Perry succumbed to
temptation.

'Delphine's back, I hear,' he said, opening the

door for Sophie.

'Yes. You should have stayed yesterday.' She gave him a mocking little smile. 'You missed all the fun.'

Perry looked concerned. 'Look, love, I'm sure Alexander——'

'It's all right,' Sophie interrupted gently. 'Really, it is. Now I must get on.'

There was more to do than usual, to Sophie's eternal gratitude. She relegated Alexander's note to the back of her mind, refusing to lose her temper over the autocratic tone of his message. But as she took a break for lunch she allowed herself a small glow of triumph at a mental picture of Alexander knocking in vain on the door of her empty cottage later. If he wanted to see her, he'd have to find her first.

Sophie ran into Sam Jefford on her way to a snack lunch at the coffee-shop, and instead of avoiding her like the plague, as he had done on various occasions beforehand in the town, he stopped to speak to her.

'I hope you're settling in happily in Ilex Cottage, Sophie,' he said, smiling diffidently.

Sophie assured him she was, and fell into step with him as they walked along.

'Have you forgiven me?' he asked.

She laughed. 'If you mean about the job, of course I have.'

'I really felt very bad about letting you down, you know.'

Sophie felt touched. 'As it happened, it all turned out very well in the end, so please don't be embarrassed about it.'

Sam's face relaxed as he asked if he could buy Sophie lunch at the Unicorn by way of amends.

'No! I mean, no, thank you.' Sophie smiled brightly. 'I'm helping out there in the evenings for a while until they get someone permanent, so I'd rather steer clear in the daytime.'

When Sam suggested the coffee-shop instead it seemed churlish to refuse, and Sophie spent a pleasant interlude with him, her raw wounds soothed just a little by his rather touching efforts to please. Consequently she was late back at the offices, which were empty, except for a very unexpected visitor. Delphine Wyndham was enthroned behind the desk in Sophie's office, her gold eyes alight with malicious glee at the look on Sophie's face.

'Hello, Sophie,' she said, and got up, stretching as she pushed back the chair. She looked spectacular in the type of clinging, draped dress only the very slender could wear, with yesterday's fur coat suspended negligently from one shoulder, and, most eye-catching of all, the emerald engagement ring Alexander had given her prominent on her left hand.

'I happened to be passing, so I thought I'd pop in for a chat.' Delphine ran her left hand over her hair.

Just in case I'd missed the ring, thought Sophie. 'How nice,' she said coolly. 'May I offer you tea, or coffee?'

'No, darling, can't stay. I just came to put you in the picture, so to speak. Regarding our mutual friend.'

'You're a Dickens fan?' asked Sophie in mock surprise.

'What *are* you talking about?' Delphine sauntered to the door, then turned, lounging gracefully in the opening. 'OK Sophie. Let's get things straight. I'm back now. For good. So Alexander won't be in need of anything *you* have to offer, if I make myself plain.'

Sophie seated herself behind the desk, regarding her visitor with a serenity designed to hide the murder she felt in her heart.

'What a bitch you are, Delphine,' she said conversationally. 'I assume the LA contract fell through—or did Terry Foyle find a younger face for the Americans? After all, as models go, you're getting on a bit, aren't you?'

Delphine's face convulsed with a rage that obliterated its beauty. She leaned her hands on the desk and glared at Sophie. 'Little cow! How *dare* you? I know you've been dangling after Alexander all these years, but you can forget all that, Goody Two-Shoes. Delphine's back, and she's everything Alexander Paget ever wanted. And I do mean *wanted*. You, darling, just can't compete!'

Sophie shrugged. 'Don't panic, Delphine. You won't get any competition from me. A husband is not on my list of requirements. Run away and play with Alexander to your heart's content.' She looked at her watch pointedly, and drew a file towards her. 'Now, if you don't mind I have a lot to get through. I have a date tonight, and I'm rather keen to leave on time for once.'

Delphine backed away, disconcerted. 'Yes—well, as long as you know how things stand.' She drew the opulent fur around her, eyeing Sophie suspiciously. 'Who was the man with you outside?'

'Sam Jefford. Estate agent.'

'Did you have lunch with him?'

Sophie nodded, resigned. 'Yes.'

'Is he your date tonight?'

Sophie shuffled her papers pointedly. 'Not that it's any business of yours, but no, he isn't.'

Delphine shook her head blankly. 'I can't see what men see in you. I mean, you're not exactly a raving beauty, are you?'

'Perhaps it's the beauty of my nature which appeals. Now goodbye, Delphine.' Sophie turned away to her typewriter, wincing at the bang of the door as her visitor finally departed.

Sophie's mood was evil for the rest of the afternoon, half her mind on autopilot as she worked, the other half reviling Alexander Paget and Delphine Wyndham with impartial violence.

Stung by Delphine's insults, Sophie took great care with her appearance that night before setting off for the Unicorn. To bolster her much-tried ego she put on a black knitted dress livened up by a choker of giant silver and black beads, and was glad she'd taken the trouble when Frank Mitchell winked appreciatively at the sight of her.

'Very nice, Sophie. Just the thing to attract the punters.'

He was right. Sophie was run off her feet all evening, unlike the night before.

'Is it always like this on Tuesdays?' she gasped at one stage, as she polished glasses furiously.

'Tonight and every night,' Anna assured her. 'Don't knock it, love, it's business. And you're doing really well. Don't fancy giving up the day job and coming here on a permanent basis, by any chance?'

In Sophie's present mood it was a tempting thought. And if only Alexander were involved she knew she might have been rash enough to say yes. But there was Perry to consider, and all the others. And her feet. They would never stand it. She shook her head regretfully, then turned to a group of new arrivals with a smile.

'Good evening, gentlemen. What can I get you?'

Sophie shivered as she walked home. It had been stormy all day, but now the wind was at gale force, and clouds scudded wildly across a moonlit sky as she turned away from the lights of the town to make for Church Row. The wind howled demonically in the trees, funnelling through the narrow walk between churchyard and cottages, with a force that blew Sophie's hair in her eyes and bit icily through her raincoat. In a lull between gusts she halted, stiffening, sure she could hear footsteps. Telling herself she was tired, hearing things, she began to run the last few yards towards the cottage, her heart in her throat as the footsteps behind her quickened in pace with her own. As she reached her front door a hand caught her arm and she screamed as she spun round. Then the moon burst from the clouds to illumine Alexander's unmistakable fair head, and she glared up at him, almost beside herself with rage.

'What the hell do you think you're doing?' she spat.

'Where the *hell* have you been?' he demanded harshly in turn, ignoring her. He took her by the elbows. 'Didn't you get my note?'

Sophie shook him off. 'Oh, yes. I got your note.' She unlocked her door, then turned on him coldly. '*You* were the one who said you'd be here at eight, not me.'

Alexander opened the door and thrust her unceremoniously inside, his eyes glittering dangerously as he banged the door shut, then stood leaning against it, arms folded. 'I rang you at intervals all yesterday evening, until it got so late I assumed you must have gone off to stay with Kate. So I scribbled the note and gave it to Perry before I dashed off to court this morning. I should have taken time to couch it in more flowery terms I assume—beg you to deign to be in tonight. Where *were* you two nights running, for God's sake?'

Sophie shrugged out of her raincoat, her face flushed with anger. 'It's nothing to do with you where I spend my evenings.'

'My mistake. I thought it was.' Colour flared along Alexander's cheekbones, emphasising the white line round his mouth. 'I suppose this—this tantrum is because of Delphine.'

'Tantrum!' Sophie's eyes flamed at him. 'Just go, Alexander. Back to the loving arms of your faithful fiancée.' She spat the word at him, and Alexander came away from the door with a lunge, catching her by the hands.

'You're jealous!' His eyes gleamed with a triumph Sophie found unbearable.

'*Jealous?* Ha!' She tried to break free, but Alexander was ready for her and tightened his grip. 'Will you let me go?' she panted. 'I've had a long day and I'm tired, and I just want you to get out of here.'

'Who is he?' Alexander rapped.

Sophie glared at him. 'Who's who?'

He released one of her hands and brushed his fingers over her breasts with insulting familiarity. 'You're all dressed up for someone.'

Utterly enraged, Sophie dodged away and picked up the poker. 'Get out, Alexander Paget. Get out right now, before I do you an injury, you two-timing swine!'

'Sophie!' Alexander threw his hands wide in despair. 'What's got into you, for God's sake? OK, so Delphine turned up again. Is *that* the reason for all this?'

'Ten out of ten for observation! Now get out!'

'Look here, Sophie Gordon. I've been stuck in a car at the end of your lane for hours, just waiting to see you. I was getting bloody frantic by the time you turned up, and I'm not moving from here until you tell me what's eating you.'

'Then you'll stay here all night!' Too late, Sophie realised what she'd said. She retreated in alarm as Alexander advanced on her, his eyes narrowed to gleaming slits.

'With the greatest of pleasure. Give me that poker.'

'No!' Sophie swung it at him wildly, but

Alexander grabbed it in mid-flight, wrenching it out of her hand. He tossed it in the hearth and jerked her towards him.

'All right,' he said through gritted teeth. 'We'll leave the talking until afterwards.'

Afterwards? Sophie's mouth opened in protest but he closed it summarily with his own. For a split-second she yielded and his hold tightened, then she began to fight in earnest, kicking at him with high, slender heels, wrenching a hand free to grab at his hair, but Alexander was oblivious to it all. The beads broke and rolled in all directions, but he never lifted his mouth from hers, suffocating her protests, impervious to her flailing hands as he lifted her off her feet.

Sophie kicked and struggled like a wild thing, but Alexander merely man-handled her across the room and wrenched open the door to the stairs. Their ascent to the bedroom was violent and undignified, both of them coming into painful contact with the walls as Alexander stumbled inexorably upward, determined to deposit his writhing burden where he intended, on her bed.

The moment Sophie hit the quilt she scrambled up like an eel, but Alexander threw himself after her in a rugby tackle, catching her by the ankles and hauling her back along the bed. The clinging dress rode upward, displaying lace-topped hold-up stockings, and more, at which point Alexander lost whatever shreds of civilisation he had left. He groaned like a man in anguish and pulled her beneath him, his mouth hot on hers as his hand sought the warmth of a satiny thigh above the stocking. Sophie threshed her head back and forth, making choked sounds of protest, but Alexander's response was to straddle her with two muscular legs, one hand on her mouth as he struggled to rid himself of his jacket with the other. Neither of them heard the rising howl of the wind, both of them so locked in primitive sexual combat they were deaf and blind to anything but escape on one hand and mastery on the other. 'Let me go!' screeched Sophie, her voice unrecognisable as he took his hand from her mouth. Alexander's laugh was a deadly little sound, leaving Sophie in no doubt that, whatever he had in mind, freeing her was no part of it. At last he was out of the heavy leather jacket, and he leaned away a little to toss it on the floor. Instantly Sophie seized her chance, desperation lending her strength as she writhed free from his restraining legs and threw herself towards the foot of the bed just as the window blew in with an almighty crash and something hard and sharp connected with Sophie's head.

'Sophie!' Alexander's cry was agonised as he leapt for the light, his feet crunching on broken glass as he turned to see her sitting, dazed, in a heap of broken glass, staring at a bloody tuft of hair and skin lying on the pale yellow quilt. Wind howled through the room from the shattered window, and she lifted blank eyes to Alexander as he carefully cleared the broken glass away from her so he could lift her off the bed.

'Your face is cut,' she remarked.

'Never mind me.' His eyes glittered darkly in his chalk-white face. 'Are you all right, my darling?'

She nodded, then gasped as blood poured down her forehead and on to her hands and all over Alexander's white shirt, and suddenly there was a violent pain in her head and she began to scream as he lifted her in his arms and ran down the stairs at twice the speed of their recent ascent. Afterwards everything was a blur. Sophie was dimly aware through the pain and cold that she was in a car, then in a brightly lit room smelling of antiseptic, and there were nurses and young men in white coats, who took X-rays and gave her injections and did unspeakable things to her scalp with needles and thread and it all hurt unbearably, and then she was sick, and embarrassed and shivering when they cut the black dress off her and it stuck in places where bits of glass had speared her through the wool, leaving deep little cuts the nurses drew together with butterfly dressings, and finally, blessedly, she was tucked into bed and allowed to sleep.

When Sophie woke it was daylight and her father and Kate were standing beside her bed. She smiled gingerly, wincing as pain knifed through her head.

'I'm not going to say "where am I", because I assume I'm in Arlesford General,' she said hoarsely.

'Yes, pet.' Dr Gordon took her hand in his. 'How do you feel?'

'I've got a fair old headache, but I think I'm OK.' Sophie smiled at Kate. 'Sorry to give you a fright, Stepmama.'

Kate let out a deep breath. 'I'll overlook it this time. Don't do it again, please, darling.'

'How's Alexander? Is he all right?'

'A few cuts, otherwise fine.' Dr Gordon gave his daughter a wry look. 'I'm not sure why he was in your bedroom when the window blew in, but thank God he was there. You'd have been in a sorrier state altogether if that gash in your scalp hadn't been attended to at once, I assure you.'

Sophie's face turned from white to crimson then white again, and Kate pulled at her husband's hand.

'Go on, David. You'll be late for morning surgery. I'll stay with Sophie.'

'Kate's taking you home to the Chantry once you've been discharged,' said Dr Gordon briskly.

'Oh, lovely.' Sophie tried to smile. 'My own doctor in the house if I have a relapse.'

Later in the morning a very shaky Sophie stumbled into the Chantry with Kate, grateful for the latter's ministrations as she was installed on a comfortable couch, and fussed over a little. When Dr Gordon arrived at lunch time Alexander was with him, looking pale and exhausted, his cheek and temple decorated, like Sophie's, with butterfly plasters. After assuring himself his daughter was all right, Dr Gordon withdrew to the kitchen with Kate, leaving Alexander alone with the invalid.

'Is the cottage in a bad way?' asked Sophie, avoiding Alexander's eyes.

'Perry's checking the damage. I had to be in court again this morning. Another boundary dispute.' He sat on the edge of the couch and took one of her scarred hands in his. 'Are you really all right, Sophie? I thought they'd have kept you in hospital longer.'

Sophie smiled. 'Not for a mere crack on the head. It must have been some gale—Casualty had a very busy night.'

'So I gather.'

'How do you like my dressing? Rather chic—like a Sikh topknot, don't you think?'

Alexander leaned nearer. 'Stop chattering and let me apologise. I'm so hellish sorry, Sophie. If I hadn't resorted to caveman tactics it would never have happened.'

Sophie flushed and looked down at her hands. 'Rubbish. If you hadn't been there I'd have been in bed anyway, so I'd still have copped it when the window blew in.'

'The fact remains that if I hadn't hauled you upstairs at that particular juncture you wouldn't have been injured.' His voice was so bitter with self-loathing, Sophie tried to raise his spirits with a mischievous little smile.

'Oh, come on, Alexander. It does have a funny side. I thought the earth was supposed to move, not the sky fall in!'

Alexander's startled look warmed slowly to a smile. 'Does this mean you're not angry with me any more? You were fighting mad last night, and I still don't know why.'

She looked at him hard, but it was quite plain he meant what he said. 'Are you being entirely honest?'

He shrugged. 'It's obvious Delphine's at the bottom of it—God knows, she could hardly have materialised at a less opportune moment.' His eyes met hers very directly. 'But why were you so furious with *me,* Sophie? I had no idea she was back, I promise.'

'No,' agreed Sophie drily. 'I could see that.' She contemplated him thoughtfully for a moment or two, then gave him the details of Delphine's warning-off visit, and watched, fascinated, as Alexander's face, normally so inscrutable, darkened from incredulity to murderous fury by the end of her little tale.

'My God!' he said, seething. 'And you believed her?'

'She was flashing her engagement ring at me, Alexander. Why wouldn't I believe her?' Sophie looked down. 'Besides, I'd forgotten how beautiful she is. So had you, by the look on your face when she turned up in the Unicorn bar.'

Alexander put a hand under her chin and turned her face up to his. 'Sophie, I swear I made it crystal-clear to Delphine that everything was finished between us. My mistake was in telling her she could keep that confounded ring. She'd never given it back, of course, so I told her to sell it, do anything she liked with it. If I'd known what she had in mind, I'd have rammed the bloody thing down her throat.' He stroked her cheek. 'When she appeared out of the blue like that I could hardly believe her sheer brass-faced cheek.'

Sophie was beginning to feel better. 'I thought you were struck dumb by that incredible face of hers.'

Alexander's eyes lit suddenly with laughter. 'Turned to stone, you mean. Like one of those

Greeks faced with Medusa.'

'Then why did she come to warn me off, Alexander? She must have known I'd find out she was lying.'

He sighed heavily. 'Delphine's been spoiled all her life, given everything she wants simply because of the way she looks. Then suddenly she loses face twice in the space of a very short time, first with the job in the States, then with me. So she needed a whipping-boy. Someone she could vent her spite on.'

'And once again I was the nearest,' said Sophie wryly.

Alexander raised an eyebrow. 'Not at all. Delphine went berserk because I told her it was you I wanted to marry, not her.'

She stared at him in dismay. 'But that isn't true!'

'Oh, yes, it is.' He leaned closer. 'You know very well you're going to marry me, Sophie.'

She pushed him away, and shrank back against the sofa cushions. 'I know nothing of the kind.'

'At the very moment Delphine interrupted us you were about to make me a very personal request. Am I right?' Alexander's eyes were steely with determination. 'Do you deny it?'

'No, I don't. But asking you to—to take me to bed doesn't mean I want to *marry* you, Alexander.'

He jumped to his feet, raking a hand through his hair as he glared down at her. 'You mean I'm OK for a quick session in bed, but otherwise on my bike!'

Sophie's head was beginning to throb. 'I don't know why you're so angry. Isn't that precisely what you had in mind before the window fell in?'

His face hardened. 'It's true I wanted to make love to you. Enough to fight you tooth and nail to do so, for my sins. But only because I meant to show you it was you I wanted more than anything or anyone in the world, including Delphine. To make you see we belonged together, you and I, Sophie. For life.'

Sophie was quite unable to cope with this on top of the trauma of the night. 'Can we drop the subject for now, Alexander? My head's thumping so much I can't think.'

Alexander's tension drained from him, leaving him very pale, with a look of weariness on his face to match Sophie's. 'I'm sorry. I seem to keep on saying that, don't I?' He rubbed a hand over his face. 'I just felt I couldn't go on any longer without clearing things up between us.'

'Thank you for that.' Sophie gave him a tired smile. 'Come back when I've gathered my wandering wits together.'

Alexander looked morose. 'Whatever you say, Sophie. But in the meantime try to give my proposal some thought. Please.'

'It won't make any difference, Alexander,' she felt obliged to point out. 'I told Delphine yesterday that marriage had no place on my programme. I meant it.'

Alexander's eyes glittered angrily in his ashen face. 'I don't believe you.'

'That's your privilege, of course.' Sophie shrugged. 'Believe this, at least, Alexander. If I *were* marriage-inclined, you'd be the only husband

I'd want. But husbands rarely come as a single item. They're part of a package, along with children and cooking and laundry and housework. No novelty for me, any of it.'

'You haven't mentioned love.'

'Neither have you.'

There was a short, tense pause, while green eyes bored into brown, then Alexander turned away blindly and made for the door.

CHAPTER ELEVEN

SOPHIE was glad to spend the rest of the afternoon
in bed, utterly worn out one way and another, but,
deaf to Kate's entreaties, she insisted on getting up
for dinner, and came downstairs to a house filled
with flowers. There were carnations from Sam
Jefford, a great glowing sheaf of chrysanthemums
from Perry, and, last but by no means least, a very
delicate arrangement of white violets and greenery
from Julian Brett.

'Nice to be popular,' commented Dr Gordon.

'Must be easier ways to merit bouquets, Dad!'
Sophie smiled cheerfully, secretly disappointed
because none of the flowers were from Alexander.
Which, she told herself sternly, was silly. He'd
looked a lot worse than she did by the time he left.
Certainly in no condition to think about flowers or
anything else but getting himself home to bed.

Later in the evening there were several phone
calls from friends who'd heard about the accident,
including one from Sam Jefford, who was very
sympathetic, but sensibly brief. She was touched
by his concern, but a great deal less pleased when
the doorbell rang and Julian Brett was ushered in.
He told Sophie she looked quite dreadful, and
went on to hold forth interminably on the evils and
risks of girls living alone and unprotected. When

168

Sophie informed him he was mistaken, that in fact Alexander had been with her at the time, he looked deeply affronted, and only Perry's timely arrival prevented a further lecture. Julian approved of Perry even less than Alexander, and quickly took himself off, to Sophie's guilty relief.

'Right then, Perry,' she said urgently. 'How's the cottage?'

He cheered her up considerably by telling her that apart from a new window, and probably a new bedroom ceiling as well, Ilex Cottage was in reasonably good shape.

'Which is more than can be said for you, love,' he added. 'You look distinctly wan.'

'I feel wan!' Sophie grinned. 'So would you if a window had fallen on your head.'

Perry's blue eyes were quizzical. 'Lucky thing Alexander was on hand.'

Sophie flushed. 'Yes. Very.'

'Poor chap had a hell of a night. Once he knew you were all right he dashed back to Church Row to see if your neighbours were in need of help.'

Sophie put a hand to her mouth. 'My God, I never gave them a thought! Were they all right?'

'Startled by the commotion, and very worried about you, but otherwise unaffected.' Perry got up to go. 'Things better between you and Alexander now?'

'In a way.'

'Hm. Well, all I can say, love, is that Alexander was not exactly a ray of sunshine this afternoon.'

'This afternoon?' she said sharply. 'I thought he was going home to bed.'

'No, darling. He insisted on going back to Ilex
Cottage with me to see the damage for himself.
Then he bullied a glazier to replace the window at
once, and organised a decorator to see to the
plastering and paintwork in your bedroom. I rather
fancy Alexander thinks the cottage means more to
you than anything. Including him.' Perry bent to
kiss her colourless cheek. 'Mrs Rogers has
produced a niece who can fill in for you at the
office for a few days. So don't think about coming
back until you're well. Right?'

Sophie thanked Perry gratefully, then lay lost in
thought once he was gone. So Alexander had
checked over her cottage in person, after all; rather
like heaping coals of fire on her ungrateful head.

'Cecily's been on the phone,' said Kate, coming
in with a tea-tray. 'I said you were knee-deep in
visitors, and suggested she came over for lunch
tomorrow.'

Sophie thanked Kate affectionately, drank her
tea then went back to bed. Rest, she decided, was
essential one way and another, if she were to get
back to work as quickly as possible, or even muster
up sufficient stamina to hold her own against
Alexander when he resumed the battle over their
future relationship. *If* he renewed it.

Alexander made no move to do any such thing,
Sophie found, feeling distinctly anticlimactic when
his manner towards her was cheerfully friendly
during his subsequent visits. These were brief, and
no one would have suspected from his demeanour
that his feelings towards his sibling-by-marriage
were anything more than affectionate concern

about her health. The latter improved daily.
Sophie's temper did not. Her dressings gradually
diminished in size, the stitches were removed from
her scalp, the soreness and pain died away, and her
appetite returned, nurtured lovingly by Kate. Still
Alexander spent no more than a few minutes with
Sophie at any one time. Some days he was unable
to put in an appearance at all, and even when he
did he somehow contrived never to be alone with
her. Sophie began to wonder if the talk of marriage
had been a hallucination, born of trauma and
concussion. The Alexander who came with books
and records as presents for the invalid was more
fraternal towards her than her brothers themselves,
since the twins' concern was limited to a phone call
or two and an extremely vulgar get-well card.
Sophie looked forward to her return to work, since
it seemed likely she'd see more of Alexander at the
office than she did at home with her father and
Kate. But during the first few days back at her post
she saw nothing of him at all, since he was away,
and she was obliged to make do with second-hand
accounts of his movements from Perry. Alexander,
she concluded, had taken her at her word and
decided to drop the subject of marriage. Or any
other kind of relationship.

The prospect was so depressing that Sophie
called in the Unicorn on the Friday lunch time to
volunteer her services over the weekend, and the
Mitchells, once satisfied Sophie was fully
recovered, were gratifyingly eager to take
advantage of the offer for Saturday evening. In
spite of opposition from her father and Kate,

Sophie insisted on spending the night afterwards at
Ilex Cottage on her sitting-room couch, since the
bedroom was still recovering from the night of the
storm. For the time being Kate was driving her to
and from Deansbury each day, but Sophie had no
intention of involving either Kate or her father in
any social extras.

Dr Gordon took himself off for a rare round of
golf at the weekend and Sophie spent Saturday
morning shopping with Kate, then volunteered to
make lunch, so that it was Kate who went off to
answer the telephone when it rang.

'Alexander,' Kate mouthed silently, and whisked
herself upstairs out of earshot.

'Sophie? How are you after your week at the
office?'

Annoyed to find the mere sound of Alexander's
voice affected her knees so badly, Sophie was extra
cool with her assurances about her well-being.

'Then will you have dinner with me tonight,
Sophie?'

She breathed in deeply. 'Sorry. I can't.'

'Can't? Or won't?'

'I already have an engagement,' she snapped,
stung by the sarcasm in his voice. 'Not surprising,
really, Alexander. It *is* the weekend.'

'I've been away for a couple of days. As you well
know,' he added curtly.

'Yes, I do. Successful?'

'Never mind that.' Alexander sounded brusque
and impatient. 'Can't you put off whoever you're
tied up with tonight? I want to talk to you.'

'Sorry,' she cooed. 'Can't be done. Some other

time, perhaps.' She heard a loud click in her ear, then smiled, cat-like, as she put the phone down.

'You look very pleased with yourself,' observed Kate over lunch.

Sophie grinned. 'I am, rather. Alexander asked me out to dinner.'

Kate eyed her narrowly. 'I assume he wasn't overjoyed to learn you're working at the Unicorn.'

'I didn't tell him. He thinks I'm going out with someone else.'

Kate shook her head. 'I wish you two would sort yourselves out, you know. It's wearing to be in the same room with the pair of you these days.'

'You haven't been lately,' said Sophie tartly. 'Alexander's been conspicuous by his absence.'

'Ah! I see.'

Sophie scowled at her new stepmother blackly, then began to laugh. 'You think I'm behaving like a spoilt child.'

'No.' Kate smiled. 'Like a girl in love, Sophie.'

Saturday night was, not surprisingly, very busy at the Unicorn. Sophie was welcomed with open arms by the new girl who'd taken over behind the bar. Linda was tall and blonde and very good-natured, but, as she said to Sophie, she had only one pair of hands and feet, and even with mine host and his wife working at full stretch, extra help was a godsend.

For most of the evening Sophie coped very well, dealing pleasantly with the customers and doing her share of the chores. Then, towards nine, a lull enabled Frank Mitchell to go down to the cellar for more soft drinks, and Sophie to round up the empty glasses. The lounge bar was the haunt of smart young couples, except for one large table crammed with noisy young men celebrating the home win of the local rugby team. As Sophie collected a handful of tankards, the most presentable of the group caught her round the waist, grinning familiarly into her startled face.

'You're new, love. Haven't I seen you somewhere before?'

Loud brays of laughter from his companions greeted the hoary approach, and Sophie did her best to smile pleasantly as she removed herself smartly from the young man's grasp.

'Trouble?' asked Anna Mitchell, as Sophie returned to the bar.

'No. Harmless enough, I think.' But she was glad to take the landlady's advice and remain behind the bar, leaving Frank Mitchell to collect glasses from then on.

Her Lothario, however, was undeterred. On his way back from the men's cloakroom he elbowed himself a place at the bar and remained there, watching Sophie's every move during the time he took to dispose of three pints of beer.

'Creepy,' said Linda in an undertone. 'One of the Dawsons from Mile End House. Fancies his chance with the girls.'

'Not with this one!' Sophie tried to ignore the unswerving stare, but it was difficult, busy though she was. Then she tried moving to the other end of the bar, but her admirer promptly followed, thrusting to a point of vantage as near to her as he could get, waving a twenty-pound note under her nose.

'Give me a whisky this time, darling,' he said, smiling at Sophie with the confidence of someone who believed himself irresistible.

'Certainly, sir.' Sophie supplied the drink, took the note and gave him his change, counting it into his outstretched hand. Suddenly he caught her wrist.

'Can I drive you home later?'

Sophie shook her head, smiling pleasantly. 'Sorry.'

'Oh, come on, don't be shy.' He smiled cajolingly, his fingers tightening. 'Pretty girl like you shouldn't be shy.'

'Please excuse me—I have other customers to see to,' said Sophie, feeling her temper rise.

'S'all right with Frank. He knows me.' The man laughed. 'Everyone knows me. I'm Phil Dawson, from Mile End House.' It was an announcement expected to impress.

'How do you do?' Sophie pulled her hand away sharply, conscious of amused faces watching the little interplay, then hurried off, irritated. Her undismayed admirer stayed where he was, never taking his eyes off her, and refused to let anyone else serve him a drink.

'Humour him if you can,' said Frank Mitchell quietly. 'Don't worry. I'll see he doesn't get out of hand.'

Reluctantly Sophie supplied the persistent young man with a second whisky, and once more he captured her hand.

'You're cute,' he informed her.

'And you're beginning to bore me,' she retorted. 'Let go.'

'Now, now, don't be unfriendly, sweetheart.' He was very flushed by this time, with a dangerously belligerent look about him. 'Girls like me,' he bragged loudly.

'Not this one!' Sophie tugged angrily, but he hung on to her hand, his face turning ugly as he realised she meant what she said.

Suddenly a familiar hand shot from behind to close in a grip of iron on the unfortunate Mr Dawson's wrist, and Sophie stared up in dismay at the formidable sight of Alexander in a towering rage.

'Who the hell are you?' blustered her unwanted admirer.

'The lady's fiancé. Take your hands off her. Now!'

Any protest the importunate Phil Dawson had in mind died a very quick death as he saw the look in the eyes of Sophie's rescuer.

'Just a bit of fun,' he muttered, and retreated hastily, leaving Sophie to the full force of Alexander's icy displeasure.

'I've had a word with Frank Mitchell. You're coming with me. Now. Get your coat,' said Alexander very quietly.

Sophie opened her mouth to protest.

'If you don't,' he said, forestalling her, 'I shall come round there and carry you out bodily.'

It was patently clear Alexander meant what he said. Sophie took leave of the Mitchells and Linda, then collected her coat and followed Alexander to the car park at the back of the Unicorn. In fraught silence she slid into the car as he held the door open for her.

'You had no business to do that,' she said coldly, deciding to carry the war into the enemy's camp as he started the car.

'I disagree. Unless, of course, you enjoy being pawed by all and sundry.'

Sophie decided to ignore this. 'How did you know where I was?'

'I went to see Kate and your father.' Alexander gave her a cold, sidelong look. 'I learnt that this isn't the first time you've worked at the Unicorn. And that David is no happier about it than I am.'

'But he, of course, being a man of reason, realises I'm adult and able to do what I like with my life, whether it's working in a pub or living on my own.' Sophie stared stonily through the windscreen.

Alexander made no reply. He drove in taut silence, swiftly and skilfully, as always, until they reached Brading and the high hedges of Willow Reach. Sophie kept up her silence stubbornly as she slid out of the car, disdaining his helping hand as she stalked ahead of him.

'I thought you'd like to see the place now it's finished,' said Alexander neutrally, as he unlocked the door.

Sophie's anger began to recede almost as soon as she put foot inside the house. There was something in the atmosphere of Willow Reach which made her anger and resentment seem unnecessary, and almost against her will she felt her defiance dissolve. The peace and tranquillity of the house was a tangible thing, something she could almost reach out and touch as she walked with Alexander through the graceful, uncluttered rooms, gazing at the harmony their mutual blend of taste had achieved. She was shaken badly by a fierce pang of possessiveness, and subsided on one of the sofas in the drawing-room, a prey to emotions she shied from analysing.

'It's beautiful, Alexander. Perfect.'

He sat beside her, turning sardonic eyes on her pensive face. 'Beautiful, yes. Perfect, no.'

'Oh, I know it's not fully furnished yet——'

'I meant it's not a house for a man to live in alone. No, hear me,' he said, as Sophie would have spoken. 'It's strange,' he went on. 'I altered the Chantry for Delphine, because she thought it was so smart to turn an old house into the kind of showplace you see in magazines. Yet afterwards there was no mark of her personality there. Nor oddly enough, of me, although I'd lived there all my life and designed the alterations myself. In fact, when I visit Kate and David there now, it's *their* house already. So much so I might never have been there at all.'

'But *this* house is yours,' said Sophie. She twisted the gold signet ring on her little finger, not looking at him. 'This is your creation, isn't it? Your brain-child. The other occupants were almost like caretakers, in a way. Just keeping it ready for you to take over one day.'

Alexander nodded. 'Exactly. And the fact that you understand so well only underlines what I'm about to say.'

Sophie stiffened. 'Alexander——' she began, but he reached out and put a finger on her lips.

'Let me finish, Sophie. Please.'

She subsided, her pulse racing at his touch.

'Don't look so tense, Sophie,' he said gently. 'I just thought you'd like to know the house is haunted.'

'By the mistress of your Restoration courtier?'

'No. One can be haunted by events from the future, not just the past.' Alexander moved until he was near enough to take her hand. 'In this house I'm haunted by you, Sophie, by a vision of how it would be if we were here together, sharing our lives.' He took her by the shoulders, turning her towards him. 'We happen to have arrived at this juncture in the opposite direction from most people, Sophie. We've known each other so well all our lives, we never saw what was under our noses all the time.'

'How can I believe that when you almost married Delphine?' said Sophie urgently. 'And the "almost" bit is due to *her*—not you. If Terry Foyle hadn't arrived that day to tempt Delphine to the States, you'd be a much married man by now.'

'And regretting it.' A look of distaste shadowed Alexander's face, then he smiled. 'Funny, really. Terry Foyle, unknown to himself, will always have my undying gratitude.'

'If we—we did get married,' said Sophie with care, 'how do you know you might not repent in haste over me, too?'

Alexander drew her very gently into his arms.

'Because we've done all the other part, Sophie. We know each other better than some couples learn to do all their lives. You've worked with me, known me at my worst, God knows, and hopefully at my best, too.' He put a finger under her chin and lifted her face up to his. 'All that's left is to become lovers. Would that be so difficult?'

'You know only too well how easy it would be.' Sophie looked up into his intent face. 'Which leads me to ask for my own say, Alexander. Before you go any further I'd like to put forward a proposition of my own.'

Alexander looked rather as though she'd thrown a bucket of water in his face. 'What is it?' he asked warily.

Sophie took in a deep breath. 'You know how I feel about domesticity. I'm no career woman, I grant you that, but I enjoy my job and if I have to carry on with it all my working life I'll be perfectly happy. You see, now, for the first time ever, I've got a place of my own, a life of my own, with no one to consider but me. And I love it, Alexander.'

He jerked away, jumping to his feet. 'Then there's no more to be said.'

'No, wait! You hear me out this time.' Sophie hesitated, then blurted, 'Couldn't I just be your mistress, Alexander?'

He swung round in utter astonishment. 'My *what?*'

'Your mistress,' she said resolutely, feeling her colour rise. 'I mean, you could spend your evenings with me, or as many of them as you wanted. Nights, too, if you like. Weekends in

London, maybe, or even Paris. Holidays. That sort of thing.'

Alexander stared at her as though she'd lost her wits. He raked a hand through his hair, then his lips began to twitch uncontrollably and he dissolved into laughter.

Sophie glared at him. 'What's so funny?'

Alexander breathed deeply, trying hard to control himself. 'I had this vision of myself slinking up to your door to find you reclining on that chaise-longue in a—a négligé, is that right? All seduction and suspenders!' He bit his lip hard. 'My *mistress,* for God's sake! What put that idea in your head?'

'If you're going to make a great big joke about it——' she began huffily, and jumped up, but Alexander caught her, holding her loosely round the waist.

'Sorry. I couldn't help it, Sophie. It's such a preposterous idea.'

'Lots of people don't get married these days,' she said sulkily.

'But they usually live together, nitwit! A mistress is something a *married* man indulges himself in, darling. If he can afford it.'

They looked at each other in silence for a moment, while Sophie's flaring colour faded.

'I love you, Sophie,' said Alexander unsteadily. 'I want you here with me. Always. I don't relish the thought of snatched hours of illicit bliss, thank you just the same, bliss though they'd certainly be. I don't fancy sneaking along Church Row in the small hours, hoping Mrs Perkins wouldn't see me.

I want a wife. I want *you*.'

'But I had everything worked out so beautifully,' wailed Sophie in desperation. 'It all seemed to be *meant*. I mean, Gran finding me the cottage, the new Paget branch opening up in Arlesford just as the job with Sam Jefford fell through . . .' She trailed away, eyeing him with suspicion. 'That's a very odd look.'

Alexander's eyes flickered, then he sighed. 'Let's sit down, Sophie.'

She looked at him in alarm, but allowed him to settle her in the crook of his arm on the sofa again.

'Sophie, did you learn about my namesake in school?' he said unexpectedly.

Sophie frowned, surprised. 'Of course. Alexander the Great. Julian calls you that when he's feeling bitchy.'

Alexander snorted. 'He would! Anyway, I brought it up because I'm trying to explain something to you. If you remember, a certain Phrygian king by the name of Gordius tied a complicated knot no one could unravel, until Alexander came along with his sword and simply cut the Gordian knot in half.'

Sophie nodded, mystified. 'So?'

'I feel we've rather got ourselves tied up in the same sort of knot, so I'm going to wield a figurative sword to *un*tie it. In a way I've done it before on your behalf. You see I haven't always been wrapped up in my own problems, even during the time I was involved with Delphine. I knew better than anyone how much you longed to leave home like the boys. So when my tenants in Ilex Cottage left——'

'*Your* tenants?' Sophie's eyes opened wide.

'Yes. It belongs to me. So I told Cecily you could have it for a while. Until you got married.' His smile was rueful. 'Only I didn't realise at the time I meant until you were married to me.'

Sophie's eyes dulled to a forlorn, lost look. 'So Ilex Cottage was yours all the time.'

His arm tightened. 'There's a bit more, too. I'd better come clean and tell you one of the reasons I made Arlesford my choice for the branch office was so you could work for me there.'

'But—but I was all set to work for Sam Jefford!'

'I did a deal with him. If he told you the job was off, I'd put as much work his way as I could, on top of the branch office, the sale of your house, and so on.'

Sophie pushed away his arm and jumped to her feet, pacing back and forth in the space between the sofas. 'So,' she said tightly, 'all this new life of mine wasn't mine at all. I got it by courtesy of Alexander Paget.'

He nodded, his eyes shuttered. 'In a way. I wanted to keep you in my ken. Somewhere I could keep an eye on you.'

'Big Brother!' she said bitterly. 'As if I didn't have enough brothers of my own.'

Alexander rose to his feet and caught her by the hands. 'I'm not your brother, Sophie. I want to be your lover, your husband. *And,*' he added forcefully, 'contrary to your belief, it *is* possible for a man to be both.'

Sophie turned her head away sharply, trying to come to terms with the cold new light shining on her bid for independence. What a farce it had all been, she thought bitterly, her teeth sinking so hard into her bottom lip that they drew blood. At last she looked up into his watchful face, with a smile that stopped short of her eyes.

'All right, Alexander. You win. Now I think I'd like to go home, please.'

His eyes narrowed. 'You mean you *will* marry me?'

'I suppose so. If Ilex Cottage belongs to you, it's pretty pointless my staying there. I might as well move in here and let you rent it out again, save you some money. And since you're so set on a conventional arrangement, all right. Let's get married.'

Alexander pulled her into his arms. 'You haven't said anything about feelings, Sophie. I thought you'd be angry with me, God knows, but I'd prefer a tantrum to apathy. *Do* you love me?'

She shrugged. 'I'm not sure.'

'Then why the hell are you marrying me?'

'Because if I don't, I assume your fine Italian hand will be writing the script for the rest of my life anyway,' she cut back at him, suddenly fierce. 'Whatever I do, wherever I try to go—there you are, blocking my way. So to hell with it. Let's get married. I give in.'

Alexander flushed, then paled, his eyes glittering like a cat's in his set face, and suddenly he gave a smothered curse and took her by the hand, pulling her along with him as he strode from the room and up the stairs to the master bedroom at the front of the house.

'What are you going to do?' Sophie panted, as he kicked the door shut behind them. 'Careful—you'll mark the wood!'

'What do you think I'm going to do?' he said through clenched teeth. 'I'm sure as hell not marrying a female whose only reason for saying yes is because she's given up saying no. So I think I'll take advantage of your original offer. Once, anyway.'

'Not like this,' wailed Sophie miserably, as she found herself dumped in the middle of the bed. 'Please, Alexander!'

'Shut up.' And Alexander silenced her protests in the most effective way possible, stifling them with his mouth as he began removing her clothes.

'I don't——' she gasped, pushing at him.

'Yes, you do,' he said flatly, and began to caress her breasts, her stomach, moving to her thighs as his mouth left hers to rove all over her, everywhere, astounding her by its encroachment on parts of her she had never dreamed would be so clamorous in response. The audacity of his marauding tongue took her breath away, and she stiffened as it left her navel to move downwards.

'No!' she cried, rearing up, but he pushed her flat and parted her unwilling thighs to find the place that pulsed with response to his tongue.

'No!' she said hoarsely, almost sobbing, her head thrashing to and fro. 'No—no——' But the words ended in a choked, quavering moan as waves of hot, languorous sensation convulsed her body. Before she had time to recover Alexander moved swiftly, and almost before the throbbing had subsided he was over her and inside her and she gasped at their merging, her body rigid for a moment before it yielded. Abandoning all effort at resistance, Sophie clutched at Alexander as her one constant in an earthquake of new sensation as he swept her along on a mad, careering ride to the final glory they experienced almost in unison.

Afterwards they lay very still for a long, silent interval while their pulses steadied and their breathing slowed, and Sophie came to terms with a fact she'd suspected all along. It would be very nice indeed to be mistress to a lover of Alexander's calibre. After years of Julian's company it was reassuring to find that a man like Alexander could want her so badly.

'What are you thinking about?' asked Alexander at last, moving so that she fitted snugly against him.

'Julian.'

'*What?*' Alexander shot up in outrage, but she pulled him down to her again. He allowed her to soothe him, then turned her towards him so that they lay eye to eye, one of his legs thrown over hers in an intimacy which distracted Sophie very thoroughly from thoughts of any other man.

'I always thought Julian Brett's preference was not inclined in a feminine direction,' said Alexander bluntly. 'I could never see why you bothered with him.'

'Convenience. And I was his cover, I suppose.' Sophie smiled into the eyes so close to hers. 'Julian is one of those men who is just plain celibate, Alexander. Not gay. Once upon a time a man could be a bachelor without comment, but these days it's different. So we had a sort of tacit arrangement. He wined me and dined me fairly regularly. In return I had a man in my life I knew wouldn't get any ideas about marriage.'

'Like me.'

'Nobody's like you, Alexander. Mind you,' added Sophie, 'he did propose some sort of marriage when I told him I was moving away. Said I could move in with him and his mother—that I'd be company for her.'

Alexander shook with laughter against her. 'As proposals go, surely mine's more tempting than that.' He ran the tip of his finger over her lips and Sophie bit it gently.

'Very true. In fact——' She paused, wriggling even closer. 'I've changed my mind again about marriage.'

Alexander lay very still. 'You mean it's no now, not yes?'

'No, I mean it's yes now, not no.' Sophie giggled. 'If you see what I mean.'

'Elucidate,' he said sternly, then held her so tightly that Sophie was reassured enough to comply.

'Perhaps,' she said slowly, 'marriage to you wouldn't be so bad, after all.'

'Careful, Sophie. Much more flattery like that and I'll get above myself!'

She kicked his ankle. 'What I *meant* was that, here with you like this, I feel I could very much enjoy being married to you, Alexander.'

'Why, thank you, Sophie. Does that mean I pass muster as a lover?'

'As I've always said, Alexander, superior's the

word.' She thought for a moment. 'No. I've changed my mind. Incomparable is better.'

Alexander kissed her deeply, his hand moving down her spine to press her closer against him. He raised his head a fraction to smile into her eyes. 'A graceful compliment,' he whispered. 'Except that comparison isn't possible, is it, darling? I'm the first lover you've ever had.'

'True.'

'I'm going to be the first husband you've ever had, too. And the last. Agreed?' He kissed her hard. 'And I'll be a good husband, I promise.'

She chuckled. 'You'll be a *great* husband—Alexander!'

'No corny jokes, please!' He turned her over on her back and hung over her. 'But I've had a great idea.'

'Really?' she said, breathless.

'Since—for some reason—you appear to have changed your mind about marriage——'

'You seduced me into it!'

'Do you mind?'

'No.'

'Right. Now because, like my namesake, my strategy was so brilliant that you capitulated——'

'Is that what I've done?' She ran her hand down his thigh, and he breathed in sharply.

'More or less. To proceed, since you are now more amenable to the prospect of our legal union, I'm prepared to make concessions.'

'Such as?'

'I'm prepared to get someone to help you with the housework you detest so much, I'll even cook dinner myself sometimes—after all, the greatest chefs are men—ouch! Don't be so violent. Then, when we send the children——'

'What children?'

'Ours. I repeat, when our children go to school I'll persuade Kate to sew on their name tapes!' Alexander grinned down at her in such smug triumph that Sophie gave him a great dig in the ribs, whereupon he tickled her in retaliation and they collapsed together, helpless with laughter which gradually gave way to something very different as Alexander proceeded to demonstrate, beyond any last possible doubt Sophie might have harboured, how very superior a lover he could be when given the right and proper encouragement. If proper was the word.

Helen Brooks lives in Northamptonshire and is married with three children. As she is a committed Christian, busy housewife and mother, her spare time is at a premium but her hobbies include reading, swimming, gardening and walking her two energetic, inquisitive and very endearing young dogs.

Her long-cherished aspiration to write became a reality when she put pen to paper on reaching the age of forty, and sent the result off to Mills & Boon®. Since then, her twenty-eight novels have been published in over twelve different languages—including Taiwanese!

FIRE BENEATH THE ICE

by

HELEN BROOKS

CHAPTER ONE

'I HOPE you haven't got me another empty-headed little bimbo out there, Connolly, who is more interested in a chip in her nail varnish than getting on with the damn job.'

'Mr Strade—'

'I told you my requirements last night and I meant what I said. Grey hair, middle-aged, with nothing less than a first-class typing speed and skirts down to her ankles, OK?'

'Please, Mr Strade—'

Lydia found her mouth had fallen open in a little O of shocked surprise as she stood waiting in the outer office where Mr Connolly had positioned her thirty seconds before. He had smiled at her apologetically before scuttling into the inner sanctum of the chairman and managing director of Strade Engineering, motioning for her to stay where she was until he returned. He had obviously intended to shut the door, but it had opened the merest crack after he had closed it and now the conversation of the two men inside was clearly audible.

'You changed the agency?' the hard masculine voice continued grimly.

'Yes, Mr Strade.' She could just imagine Mr Connolly's thin, nervous face trying to smile. 'Of course. But you must understand that it was such short notice that most of their employees were already in a position.'

'And that means?'

'This lady is extremely capable, I do assure you, and

5

I'm sure she will meet all your work requirements admirably.' The nervous squeak wouldn't have convinced Lydia, and clearly Mr Strade was of the same opinion.

'She isn't a blonde-haired bombshell, is she?' the harsh voice asked tightly. 'It's going to be another few months before Mrs Havers comes back after this damn maternity leave, and already I've endured two females who were a darn sight more interested in the size of my bank balance than doing the job they were hired for. Short skirts and fluttering eyelashes have their time and place, but my office is not one of them. Are you sure this one isn't on the make?'

Enough was enough. The flood of anger that burnt hotly through Lydia's pale, creamy skin brought her small chin militantly upwards and made her deep brown eyes shoot sparks. Who on earth did this creep think he was? Robert Redford and Richard Gere rolled into one? She had pushed open the door and stepped into the huge plush room beyond before she had time to consider what she was going to say.

'Do excuse the interruption, gentlemen,' she said coolly, her eyes sweeping in magnificent disdain over the two men standing by the far window, 'but in view of your conversation, I hardly think there is any point in my waiting any longer. I'll see myself out.' The sunlight streaming in through the panoramic plate glass held the two men in silhouette, although one was clearly taller and broader than the other and it was to this figure that she addressed the last remark. 'Do have a good day, Mr Strade,' she finished with acid sweetness as she turned to leave.

'Stay exactly where you are.' She didn't even think about disobeying him; there was something in the deep voice that demanded and received acquiescence, although her chin raised itself another notch as she swung round to face the two men again. As they moved from the window and into focus she was aware of two thoughts striking her simultaneously, both of which were acutely unwelcome in the circumstances. One was that the tall figure just in front of Mr Connoly was hopping mad, if the scowl on his dark face was anything to go by, and the other? The other was that he was the most attractive man she had seen for a long time. She hadn't been far wrong with the Robert Redford and Richard Gere comparison, she thought weakly as he came to a halt just in front of her, his six-foot frame seeming to dwarf her slim, petite five feet four.

'Yes?' She raised her eyes to meet the arctic blue of his, her face straight. He had been rude, incredibly, un-forgivably rude, and if he thought she was going to crawl now he'd soon find out differently.

'What the hell do you mean by bursting into my office uninvited?' he asked cuttingly, his eyes moving to her ash-blonde hair, secured in a neat and demure French plait at the back of her head, with more than a touch of resigned contempt in the blue gaze.

'Blonde-haired bombshell'. The words spoken with such raw harshness came back to her. Well, she had blonde hair, that much was for sure, and she'd die before she apologised for the fact, especially to a male chau-vinist pig like this one.

'Don't be so ridiculous, Mr Strade,' she said coolly, blessing the impulse that had made her wear her best suit that morning instead of the usual blouse and pencil-slim skirt she favoured. The expensive material and beautiful cut of the suit always made her feel good, and she had felt, after the agency had rung, that she might need something of a boost if she was stepping into the domain of such an illustrious and well-known mogul as Strade of Strade Engineering. Little had she known then how right she was! 'I did not burst into your office, as you are well aware. The door was open and I had been asked to wait just outside, where every word of your conversation with Mr Connoly was received loud and clear. In view of the fact that I only qualify on one of the requirements you laid out in such graphic detail, I assumed there was no point in my continuing to wait.'

'And that is?' he asked coldly. The frown had died now, to be replaced by an expression of almost blank coolness.

'My typing speed.' It was hard work to keep her gaze from faltering from the rapier-sharp eyes, but she was determined to hang on in there. 'My hair is blonde, I am twenty-seven years of age and my skirt—' she glanced down for just a second to the tapered material that finished just below her knees '—is not ankle-length,' she finished tightly.

'No...' His eyes had followed hers and lingered for just a second on the length of slender leg encased in gossamer-thin stockings the skirt exposed. 'No, it isn't.' As the icy gaze met hers again she found it hard to stop a shiver from showing. There was a coldness in his eyes, his whole face, that was positively raw in its bleakness, turning the high, chiselled cheekbones and square, hard jaw into stone. He had to be the most detached, unapproachable man she had ever met in her whole life. And the two girls before her had made a pass at this block of ice? She'd like to shake their hands for sheer nerve.

'Goodbye, then, Mr Strade.' She hadn't even begun to turn this time when the frosty voice rang out again.

'*I* do the hiring and firing, and as yet I am not aware that either applies. You came for an interview and my time is valuable and not to be wasted. Sit down, Miss…?'

'I'd rather not.' She didn't know where this aplomb was coming from—perhaps the chill that was emanating from him was affecting her, because in all fairness she should feel grossly intimidated, but instead her cheeks were burning with rage. 'And it's Worth, *Mrs* Worth,' she finished with cold emphasis.

'You're married?' The relief on his face was transparent and added to Lydia's sense of outrage. What did he expect her to do, for goodness' sake? Leap over the desk and rip off his trousers at the slightest encouragement? The man's ego was jumbo-sized.

'Yes, but I really don't think—'

'Please sit down, Mrs Worth.' The transformation was sudden and breathtaking. What had been a block of stone metamorphosed instantly into the secretary's ideal of the perfect boss—smiling, handsome and exuding benevolence. 'We seem to have got off on the wrong foot, for which I accept the blame entirely.'

It was a twenty-four-carat smile, she had to give him that, Lydia thought weakly as she felt herself persuaded into the large, easy seat opposite the magnificent shiny desk in gleaming walnut. Mr Connoly still continued to hover anxiously at his managing director's side, his mild, watery eyes begging her to be reasonable.

'Could we put this unfortunate episode aside and begin anew?' The vivid blue eyes fastened on her again and she realised with a little jolt that they were still as hard as iron. She had read somewhere that the eyes were considered windows to the soul in some cultures, and if that were the case… The shiver returned tenfold. 'I don't know how much Mr Connoly has told you about the position, but my very able and efficient secretary is at present on maternity leave.' The harsh twist to his mouth as he spoke revealed his opinion of the poor woman's amazing audacity more eloquently than any words could have done. 'The agency we were with until yesterday provided...unsuitable replacements, and I do not have the time or the inclination to continue along that particular avenue.' His scathing comments on her predecessors returned with renewed vigour and she nodded non-committally as her mind raced.

'I want a secretary for the next few months who is prepared to work hard and be flexible when the occasion warrants it,' he continued coldly. 'Mrs Havers was forced to leave a month early due to some unforeseen difficulties, so I have been left in rather a vulnerable position, and I don't like that, Mrs Worth.' His smile was ironic. 'I don't like that at all.' She glanced again at the firm, cruel mouth and ruthless, handsome face and nodded mentally. She could believe that, very definitely. She didn't smile back.

'For the right person, the rewards will match the dedication I require,' he said quietly, after waiting a moment for her to speak, 'but you understand this is not a nine-to-five job.'

As Mr Connoly opened his mouth to speak, the other man glanced at him, motioning towards the door with a hard flick of his wrist. 'Coffee, I think, Ted? Perhaps you'd organise that?' he asked coldly.

'Certainly, certainly.' Mr Connoly fairly scampered across the room and out of the door, clearly glad to be out of a potentially difficult situation.

'Mr Strade, I don't think—'

He cut across her voice as though he hadn't heard her, his tone reasonable, but with that underlying thread of steel that made her hackles rise. 'The salary is not the usual agency rate, but if you accept the position you will earn every penny.' He mentioned a figure that made her eyes widen and her mouth open slightly before she closed it with a little snap. With that amount guaranteed even for two or three months, she could afford to redecorate Hannah's bedroom, turning it from a nursery into a little girl's room, and perhaps even lash out on a new carpet for the lounge—the other *was* threadbare. And definitely those outstanding bills wouldn't keep her awake any longer at night. But to work in close contact with this man each and every day? Could she endure it?

'Of course, you may feel that, with family commitments, you couldn't accept such a post if it was offered.'

'I'm sorry?' She raised her head from mental calculations of gas, electricity and water bills, realising she hadn't heard a word he'd said in the last thirty seconds.

'Your husband,' he said patiently, his face expressionless. 'Perhaps he would object to you working late or having to take off at short notice for a couple of days? It is not unusual for me to have to visit my subsidiaries at an hour's notice and, as I have branches in Scotland, Wales, Manchester and Ireland, it often necessitates an overnight stay. Some husbands would find this unacceptable.'

Now was the moment to tell him. She stared across the desk into the austere face opposite her, but images of pink frilly curtains and flowery bedspreads and Hannah's little face came between. If she told him she was a widow, she would be out of the door before she could say Jack Robinson, she thought frantically. He would think she was available, or at least that she thought *he* was available, she corrected mentally. And she knew that he was the last person on this earth she could harbour any romantic inclinations for, so where was the harm in a little unspoken deceit? And she wouldn't *actually* lie, not really. And she needed that money, desperately. The mortgage had been paid off after Matthew's death but the old, draughty terraced house ate gas and electricity, and the last three years had been an uphill struggle to survive on what she could earn. If her mother, herself a widow, hadn't insisted on helping out as unpaid child-minder, financial waters would have closed over her head more than once...

'Mrs Worth?' Now the hard, deep voice was clearly impatient. 'Would your husband find unsocial hours unacceptable?' he asked tightly.

'No.' She raised her head and stared him straight in the eye. 'No, he wouldn't,' she answered firmly.

'Good.' He settled back on the corner of the desk where he was perched, looking down at her. 'Then perhaps this might be the time for a short test of your skills. You do do shorthand as well as audio-typing?'

'Yes.' She slipped a hand down to her bag and brought out notebook and pencil. 'When you're ready.'

Half an hour later, as she presented a neatly typed, well-set out report in front of him, he glanced up from his desk, his eyes narrowed. 'Sit down, Mrs Worth.' He flicked through the pages quickly and nodded slowly. 'Excellent. The job is yours if you want it.'

'I...' *Did* she want it? She glanced down at his lowered head, noticing the gleam of red in his black hair—virile, thick, strong hair. Her stomach muscles clenched in an involuntary spasm she was at a loss to understand. No, she was suddenly quite sure she didn't want the job if it entailed being close to this man for a few hours every day, but she *did* want the money, No, not want, *need*.

'Well?' The icy blue gaze was suddenly fixed on her

flushed face and she took a deep silent breath as she struggled for composure.

'Thank you, Mr Strade,' she said levelly. 'I would like the job, please.'

'Good.' His eyes lowered to the papers on his desk that he had been studying when she had entered the room from the secretary's office just beyond. 'Go and get yourself a cup of coffee and a sandwich and make any phone calls you think necessary; you'll be working late tonight. I've a hell of a lot of work to catch up on.'

He hadn't asked if she had any children, she thought bemusedly as she left the room. Hadn't it occurred to him?

She had just reached the desk in the outer office when the buzzer on the intercom sounded stridently, making her jump a mile. 'Yes?' As she flicked the switch she was annoyed to find her voice a little breathless.

'I forgot to ask.' His voice was uncompromisingly severe. 'Are there any little Worths?' She knew what he wanted her answer to be, and it would be easy to lie, but somehow she couldn't deny Hannah's presence in her life, even if it meant losing this golden opportunity for the pair of them to get on their feet.

'Yes.' She kept her voice steady and clear. 'I have a daughter aged three, Mr Strade.'

'Oh.' She could tell he had expected a denial. 'You have an understanding child-minder?' he asked coolly.

'Hannah is looked after by my mother when I'm at work, and she is very flexible. The hours will be no problem.' She could feel her heart thudding as she waited for his reply. Suddenly the amount of money he was offering was desperately important. 'She's a widow and likes the company,' she added quietly.

'Be back in the office by twelve, Mrs Worth.' The

flick of a switch signalled the end of their conversation and she stared at the closed door of his office as her heartbeat returned to normal. He really was the original ice-man but... She sank down on the upholstered typist's chair at the smart desk as her thoughts raced on. He *had* given her a chance and she was honest enough to admit that quite a few men in his position would have hesitated in taking on a secretary with a young daughter in tow, however temporary the position, in view of the travelling and long hours the job entailed.

She was back in the outer office within half an hour of leaving it, after a brief explanatory phone call to her mother, who responded with maternal encouragement, after which Lydia gulped a hasty cup of coffee in the splendid canteen and decided against one of the delicious meals on offer. She bought a pack of ham sandwiches to eat later—she was far too nervous to eat anything now in spite of having skipped breakfast once the agency rang—and returned to the thickly carpeted, hushed opulence of the top floor. The grandeur of the huge building had begun to get through to her, and the fact that she was working for a multimillionaire who could buy and sell half of London if he so chose was more than a little awe-inspiring.

It wasn't that she didn't think she could handle the job, she thought feverishly as she opened the drawers of her desk to familiarise herself with the contents, it was just... Just what? she asked herself irritably. What on earth was the matter with her? Since Matthew's untimely death from undiagnosed genetic heart disease just a few weeks after Hannah was born, she had kept both herself and her tiny daughter, as well as running a home and coming to terms with the emotional package of grief and anger her loss had entailed. So why was she letting an ice-cold individual like Mr Strade get to her? It was ridiculous. *She* was ridiculous! She nodded mentally and took a few deep, calming breaths as she forced her heart-beat to behave. She was mature and sensible and per-fectly in control of her emotions and her life, not some giddy schoolgirl with no responsibilities and no brain.

'You're back already?' She came out of her reverie abruptly as a cool voice spoke from the doorway, and raised her eyes to meet the direct blue gaze trained on her face. 'Ready for work?'

'Of course, Mr Strade.' She smiled mechanically as she tried to keep her nervousness from showing. She could understand why those girls before her could have been initially attracted to him—he really was an absolute dish—but surely within ten minutes of meeting him those ice-blue eyes would have frozen over even the most ardent female heart? She had never met a less ap-proachable man in her life.

'Wolf.'

'What?' She forgot to be polite as she stared at him open-mouthed.

'We are going to be working in close contact for a ridiculous number of hours a day, so I suggest we drop the formality,' he said coolly. 'I understand your first name is Lydia?' She nodded weakly. 'And mine is Wolf.'

'It is...?' She really wasn't handling this very well, she thought miserably as she watched the hard mouth tighten at her reaction. It was perfectly clear he had had this conversation more times than he would have liked in his life, but with a Christian name like that it was hardly surprising! She stared at him as she tried to pull herself together. And when added to his appearance and whole demeanour—

'My father was a wild-life expert involved in an expedition studying the Canadian timber-wolf at the time of my birth,' he said coldly, after a few uncomfortable seconds had ticked by. 'Unfortunately he thought the name rather apt for his baby son and my mother did little to dissuade him.'

'Oh.' She blinked tensely. 'You haven't got a middle name, have you?' she asked tactlessly.

A glimmer of a smile touched the hard mouth for an instant as he turned away. 'Fortunately, no. I hardly dare think what that would have been. Now, if you'd care to bring your notebook…?'

What an incredibly stupid thing to say, Lydia, she berated herself fiercely as she followed him into the massive office a moment later. The little incident had been a perfect opportunity to impress him with her diplomacy and discreet delicacy, and all she had managed was, 'You haven't got a middle name, have you?' She cringed mentally.

'Do stop looking so tragic.'

'What?' For the second time in as many minutes, he took her completely by surprise and it showed.

'In spite of my name, I really don't eat little girls for breakfast, especially when they look like you,' he added surprisingly as the shuttered gaze passed remotely over her clear, creamy, translucent skin in which the dark brown of her heavily lashed eyes stood out in startling contrast to the ash-blonde of her hair. 'Your colouring is most unusual.'

'It's natural.' She raised a defensive hand to her hair, sensing criticism as her mind flew back to the remarks he had made on her predecessors.

'I'm sure it is,' he said gravely, without a glimmer of amusement in either his face or voice, although she felt, somehow, that that was exactly what he was feeling. 'Now, do you think you could relax a little? We've one hell of an afternoon in front of us and it would be a great help if you could ease up a little.'

She nodded tightly as anger replaced the nerves. He really did have the most colossal cheek! She wouldn't be feeling like this if he had been halfway to normal. Something of what she was thinking must have shown on her face because the quirk to his mouth was definitely wry as he lowered his gaze to the papers on his desk. 'Right, then, if you are ready?'

She was conscious, somewhere towards evening, of being utterly astounded at the speed and energy with which Wolf Strade devoured the workload in front of him, despite a hundred and one interruptions every two minutes and numerous telephone calls for which she, at least, was pathetically grateful. It gave her a chance to check her frantic shorthand and get her thoughts in order for the next barrage.

The September evening was growing dark outside when she walked dazedly from his office a few hours after entering it, with a small list of several items of correspondence he needed typing before she left. She sat down at her desk with a weary little plop and flexed her aching hand gently. He was some sort of a machine! She stared across at the closed door separating them, aware that her head was pounding, and a distinct feeling of nausea was reminding her that she hadn't eaten all day. Well, she had no time now: it was going to be at least another two hours before she could leave—

'Lydia?' The box on her desk crackled as it spoke her name abruptly. 'Order us both coffee and sandwiches and take a break for half an hour. You're no good to me looking like you did when you left this room.'

'I'm fine.' She glared at the inoffensive intercom as Wolf's last words made her cheeks burn. 'I can—'

'Do as you are told.' The tone was uncompromising. 'I rarely make suggestions—that was an order, in case you didn't recognise it.' Both the harshness of the deep voice and the authoritative arrogance made her hands clench at her sides as she struggled for composure, but it was a good few seconds before she could bring herself to reply. How was she going to stand working for this megalomaniac for five or six days, let alone five or six months?

'Very good, Mr Strade.' The use of his surname was deliberate and there was a blank silence for a moment before he spoke again.

'Did you come by car this morning?' he asked coldly.

She nearly said 'What?' for the third time that day and checked herself just in time. 'No, I didn't,' she said abruptly. 'I travelled by tube—it's not far.'

'Then when we're finished here you order a taxi. The name of the firm we use is under T in Mrs Havers's address-book in the left-hand drawer of the desk, and you charge to the firm's account, OK?'

'There's really no need—'

The deep, long-drawn out sigh cut short her protest. 'I might have known.' His voice was laconic and extremely sarcastic. 'Here was I thinking I'd found the perfect substitute secretary—pleasant to look at, highly efficient and utterly devoid of fanciful ideas.' By that she supposed he meant that with a husband and child in evidence he was safe, she thought furiously. 'But unless I'm very much mistaken, there is a strong streak of stubbornness in you, Mrs Lydia Worth. Would you really prefer to wander about London on your own late at night when you can be safely transported to your door?'

'I don't intend to wander anywhere,' she retorted tightly, 'but I am more than capable of getting home—'

'Order the taxi ten minutes before you think you've finished,' he said sharply, 'and I don't want to hear another word on the subject.' She heard him mutter something rude a moment before the click of the intercom signalled the conversation was at an end.

She wasn't going to be able to stand this. She shut her eyes for a second before lifting the internal phone to call down to the canteen for the coffee and sandwiches. He had to be the epitome of all the qualities she most disliked in the male of the species, he really did. It wasn't so much what he said but the way he said it most of the time—arrogance was far too weak a word to cover such cold, aggressive hostility. Was he like this all the time?

She was pondering exactly the same uncomfortable thought later that night as she lay in the peace and tranquillity of her bedroom with her head spinning from the impressions of the day. She had finished the work he wanted just before eight, presenting the neat pile of typewritten pages to him in fear and trepidation and waiting by the side of his desk while he checked them through.

'Excellent.' He had raised piercing blue eyes to the soft brown of hers. 'I can see we are going to get along fine, Lydia, despite a few hiccups. Have you ordered the taxi?' She had nodded reluctantly and his mouth had twitched as he lowered his eyes to his desk again. 'Good. Well I suggest you scoot off home to that husband of yours and reassure him that this won't happen every night. Goodnight.'

'Goodnight.' She had just reached the door when his voice had spoken her name again.

'And, Lydia?' She had turned to face him, her eyes

apprehensive. 'You really have done a magnificent job today, thank you.' And then he had smiled, really smiled, and she had almost reeled from the shock of it, from the transformation it had wrought on his whole face.

Had he smiled at those other girls like that? she asked herself as she flexed her toes in the warmth from the electric blanket—it was almost October now and had been a particularly cold autumn. If so, she could understand why they had been smitten. Not that it affected her like that, she assured herself hastily, definitely not. She knew what he was really like—cold, aloof, hard and quite inexorable, but nevertheless... The softening of the austere classical features would cause any female's heart to give a little jump.

Thank goodness she was immune. She nodded to herself firmly. He was pleased with her because she did her job well and was guaranteed not to get any romantic ideas about him. Well, that suited her just fine. She didn't need any complications in her life at the moment. Hannah more than filled any spare time she had. She turned over in the big double bed and pounded her pillow into shape with unnecessary vigour.

There had been the odd suitor since Matthew died, but none had remotely stirred her blood or her heart and she had never repeated any of the dates more than once. Perhaps she would never marry again, never find a man to replace Matthew? She shut her eyes and let her thoughts roam where they would.

She had known Matthew forever: they had grown up next door to each other from babies and she couldn't remember a time when she hadn't been going out with him. Marriage had been a natural progression. He was as familiar to her as her own skin, and life had been comfortable, peaceful and relaxed with him—no big highs, no desperate lows. Perfect. She curled into a little ball in the warmth of the bed. Their lovemaking had been gentle and infrequent, but that had suited both of them. They had been busy with their separate careers. She didn't believe in the sort of mindless passion one read about in books, anyway. She smiled whimsically in the darkness. Such emotion was a figment of writers' imaginations, poetic licence, and if it became a reality would probably prove to be unbearably uncomfortable.

The last three years had been a hard struggle, she reflected quietly, and painful at times, but she had managed to get through by her own determination and fortitude, finding within herself a tenacity she hadn't known she possessed. She had still been a child in many ways when Matthew died, protected and cocooned by circumstances and his love, but she had had to grow up very suddenly, and now her hard-won independence was precious, very precious.

She straightened in the bed, fingering her wedding-band as her thoughts wandered on. It hadn't occurred to her for a long time to take it off—in a way it was a solid link with Matthew that time couldn't erase—but when a friend had hinted she ought to think about doing that very thing, she had been shocked and horrified. Hannah deserved all her time and love for the next few years. Her daughter had been cruelly robbed of her natural father and no one, no one, could replace a father's love. She had seen too many situations where the children of a first marriage were subtly pushed aside as a new baby made an appearance. No. She wouldn't betray Matthew's memory or Hannah's trust by giving her anything less than her whole heart. Besides... She twisted restlessly in the bed. She had got used to being alone, to making her own decisions, *she had*. And everyone got lonely at times, even people who had been happily married for years.

No, everything was fine in her world, just fine. It didn't occur to her that this was the first time she had ever had to assure herself of the fact, which was probably just as well because sleep was a long time in coming. A certain hard, masculine face, with eyes the colour of a winter sky, kept getting annoyingly in the way.

CHAPTER TWO

LYDIA awoke very early the next morning, aware that she had been dreaming but unable to remember what about. But it had been a disturbing dream. She flicked her long blonde hair out of her eyes and glanced at the tiny alarm next to the bed. Five o'clock. Even Hannah wasn't stirring yet. She padded through to the small bedroom next to hers and stared down at the delicate baby face of her tiny daughter. She had been asleep when Lydia had got home the night before. She said a quick mental prayer for staunch grandmothers who insisted baby-sitting was a joy, but she had missed the night-time routine of bath and then story in bed with Hannah. She wished she could see more of Matthew in the minute features, but they were all her own. Everyone commented on the remarkable likeness between mother and daughter.

Within an hour, the instant Hannah opened huge, liquid brown eyes, in fact, the small house was a hive of activity, the normal morning routine of breakfast, shower and dressing taking all Lydia's concentration.

'You didn't kiss me night-night, Mummy.' Hannah's face was reproachful as she spooned cornflakes into her rosebud mouth. 'Gamma told the story all wrong.'

'Did she, darling?' Lydia stroked the top of the silky blonde head lovingly. 'You didn't tell her that, did you?'

'Course not.' Hannah was a true diplomat even at three. 'Are you going to pick me up from nursery today?'

'I doubt it, sweetheart.' Lydia knelt down by the breakfast stool and cupped the heart-shaped face in her hands. 'Did Grandma tell you about my job?'

'Uh-huh.' Hannah was distinctly disenchanted. 'But I want *you* to pick me up.'

'Well, this job is a bit different from my usual ones,' Lydia said carefully. 'The man I work for needs me to work much longer hours sometimes, but he is going to give me a lot of money if I do that. How about if we think of a new bedroom for you? You could choose the curtains and quilt and everything, even a new carpet if you want.'

'Really?' Hannah planted a swift milky kiss on her cheek. 'Can I have Pretty Pony, Mummy? Sophie has.' Sophie was her best friend at nursery and the two were inseparable most of the time.

'I should think so.' Lydia rose to look down at the small face smilingly. 'But you must promise to be good for Grandma when she picks you up and brings you home, even if I'm very late. I've only got the job for a little while, so we need to get as much money as we can for your room, don't we?'

'Yep.' Hannah obviously realised she was on to a good thing. 'Gamma says I'm her little angel,' she continued, fishing for praise which Lydia dutifully gave. 'Little angel' was pushing things a bit far, but then she had never wanted a placid child anyway.

She was in her office at just before nine after dropping Hannah off at the nursery, which unfortunately was in the opposite direction to the Strade office-block, and found Wolf was already at his desk, his black head bent over a long report as she tapped nervously at the interconnecting door. 'Come in, Lydia, don't stand on ceremony.' He didn't raise his head as he spoke and she wondered for an instant if he was telepathic as well. 'You can get straight on with that dictation from yesterday,' he said, after making a few notes in the margin before raising his head. 'I have an appointment at the other end of the city in an hour, so you should have a relatively undisturbed day.' He didn't smile.

The fine silk shirt he wore exactly matched the clear sapphire-blue of his eyes, she thought inconsequentially as she smiled and nodded her reply before leaving the room, and his aftershave— She caught her thoughts abruptly, annoyed at the way they were heading. His aftershave was *aftershave*, that was all, she told herself sharply as she sat down at her desk and pulled out her notebook. He had probably paid a fortune to get the sort of reaction her senses had made when the sensual, intoxicatingly masculine fragrance had reached her nose.

She worked steadily for the next half-hour, pausing as he left to take a note of where he could be reached, her face bland and polite as he rapped out the telephone number and name of the firm, his face preoccupied and his voice remote.

There were several interruptions during the morning, but none she couldn't handle, and after snatching a quick meal in the canteen at lunchtime she continued to work her way through the pages of dictation until three, when a courteous knock at her outer door interrupted her as she had almost completed the notes.

'Come in.' The polite smile on her face widened as the tall, good-looking man who had poked his head round the door spoke her name in surprise.

'Lydia? What on earth are you doing here?'

'Mike!' She felt inordinately pleased to see a friendly face in the huge, overwhelmingly decorous establishment. 'How nice to see you. I'd completely forgotten you work here.'

'You're not working for Wolf, are you?' He came fully into the room and walked over to her desk, his eyes bright with interest. Mike Wilson was the husband of one of her oldest friends, Anna, who had been a tower of strength to her when Matthew died, often arriving unannounced when she was feeling at her lowest pitch to whisk her out to lunch and provide a rock-like shoulder to cry on. Lydia didn't know Mike that well—usually the two women met during the day when the agency didn't have any work for Lydia, or at the weekend when Mike was playing his endless rounds of golf—but whenever they had met, Mike had seemed warm and pleasant, if slightly effusive.

'Temping.' She smiled up at him ruefully. 'The agency dropped me in the deep end this time, straight to the top.'

'I rather think that's a contradiction in terms, but I know what you mean.' Mike grinned sympathetically. 'Bit of a slave-driver, isn't he, from what I've heard?'

'I don't know really, I've only been here a day or so.' A little alarm bell, deep in the recess of her mind, tolled warningly. There had been something in his face, she couldn't quite define what, that had made the words more than what they seemed at face value and, ridiculously, she felt a surge of defensive loyalty to Wolf without knowing why.

'Well, this is a nice surprise.' He wandered round the side of her desk as he spoke, glancing idly at the papers lying on the top of it as he smiled down at her. 'Wait till I tell Anna.'

'How is she? I haven't seen her for a couple of weeks,' Lydia said uncomfortably, feeling she should cover the detailed report on an important contract that she had just completed and printed, but knowing that it would look as though she suspected him of being nosy.

'Fine, fine. You know Anna, nothing gets her down.' He gestured towards the door of Wolf's office, still with his eyes on her desk. 'I presume the great man is elsewhere?'

'Yes.' To her relief he moved round the front of the desk again and bent down with his elbows resting on the wood as he spoke quietly.

'Well, that being the case, could I make a suggestion, Lydia? Wolf is a little…difficult about his personal secretary fraternising with the mere workers.' There it was again, that faint caustic note. 'The reputable Mrs Havers was a positive iceberg. Have you met her?' Lydia shook her head silently. 'Well, you haven't missed anything,' he continued with a faint grin. 'Anyway, it might be better for you if Wolf doesn't know we're old friends. He wouldn't like it, and as you'll only be around for a short time it seems silly to make waves, don't you think?'

'Well, I—'

'It might make things a bit uncomfortable for me too,' Mike continued quietly. 'You never know how Wolf is going to jump on things like this.'

'Well, of course I don't want to do anything that might reflect on you, Mike,' Lydia said quickly. 'It's just that it seems…unnecessary.'

'It isn't, believe me.' He smiled quietly. 'Well, do we have a deal, then?'

'Well, I can't see it matters one way or the other, so I suppose it's all right,' she said hesitantly.

'Good girl.' His smile widened. 'And how about you and that delightful little daughter of yours coming to

Sunday lunch soon? I haven't seen her in months. I'll get Anna to ring you, shall I?'

'That would be nice, thank you.' She forced a smile.

'And don't forget, not a word about our little secret.' He leant across and kissed her lightly as he had done several times in the past, a social gesture, nothing more. 'Good afternoon.'

If the ceiling had suddenly fallen in on her Lydia couldn't have reacted more violently. She shot out of her chair, hand to mouth, as she stared at Wolf's dark countenance in the doorway. It was clear he had heard, and seen, more than enough. 'I—I didn't know you were back,' she stammered, aware she had gone a brilliant red.

'Obviously.' He eyed Mike coldly. 'I presume you are in these offices for a reason, Mike?'

Mike had recovered far more quickly than she had, thrusting his hands casually in his pockets as he faced Wolf with an easy grin. 'Just wanted a word with you about the figures for Kingston,' he said calmly, 'if it's convenient?'

'Perhaps later.' Wolf's narrowed gaze brushed Lydia's hot face before he gestured to the finished work on her desk. 'Bring that in, would you? I'll glance through it before I do anything else. I want some of those letters to go off tonight.' His voice was infinitely cold, and she shivered as she glanced at Mike before gathering the files together. 'I'll ring you if I have time today, Mike.' It was a dismissal, and Mike went without another word, not even glancing in Lydia's direction as he left.

She followed Wolf into his office and placed the work on his desk. 'You've been busy.' He was looking at the pile of correspondence as he spoke, but she felt the

words were the proverbial two-edged sword and remained silent. 'Sit down, Lydia.'

She sank into the chair facing his desk as he seated
himself without taking his eyes off her troubled face. 'I
didn't know you knew my financial director,' he said
slowly, his voice expressionless but as cold as ice. 'You
didn't mention it.'

She stared at him helplessly. What on earth was the
matter with the man? Why did it matter to him who she
knew anyway? 'I...' There was something so chilling in
his face that it was freezing her thoughts. 'I didn't know
I had to,' she said weakly, his aggressiveness making
her feel twice as guilty as she did already.

'How long have you known him?'

This was ridiculous, she thought frantically. Pull yourself together, Lydia, explain you are a friend of Anna's,
talk to the man. But she couldn't. Those ice-blue eyes
were totally unnerving and, when she thought back to
how the little tableau in the office must have seemed,
embarrassment sent its red fingers all over her face. 'I
don't know...' She tried desperately to think of how
long Anna and Mike had been married. 'I think— '

'No matter.' He straightened suddenly in his chair as
though he had just come to a decision, and she stared at
him, alarmed.

'Do you often wear your hair loose for the office?' he
asked coldly as his gaze moved to the soft, silky locks
lying in a shining veil across her shoulders.

'My hair?' She raised an unconscious hand to her
head as she stared back at him. What had her hair to do
with this?

'I prefer it tied back in the sort of style you wore
yesterday,' he said coolly. 'As my secretary you have a
certain reputation to maintain, and a neat, unassuming

appearance gives the sort of impression I like in my staff. There are always men who are inclined to stand and waste time by the desk of a pretty woman, given the slightest encouragement.'

She really couldn't believe what she was hearing. She stared at him open-mouthed as she wondered if what she had heard was what he had really said. 'Exactly what are you saying?' she asked, after a moment of stunned silence.

'I'm saying that I would prefer a more discreet hairstyle,' he said calmly as he picked up the phone that had begun to ring on his desk and gestured for her to leave. 'If you don't mind.'

There was nothing she could do but leave him to take the call, but as she returned to her own office her wits returned along with a flood of hot colour in her face. The cheek of it. The absolute cheek of it! Once that call ended she would tell him that she did mind, she minded very much, the arrogant, overbearing—

'Could I leave this with you for Mr Strade, please?' She came out of her silent fury to see one of the office juniors timidly holding out a large sealed envelope. 'It's from Mr Collins in Personnel.'

'Of course.' Lydia smiled at the nervous girl, who couldn't have been a day over sixteen, as she took a deep, silent breath. When that call ended, Wolf Strade, *when it ended*... But half an hour later she was still waiting, by which time her anger had cooled, along with her face, and reason had asserted itself. This was a golden opportunity to get on her feet financially, and if she had to put up with this unpleasant, unreasonable male chauvinist pig as the cloud on which the silver lining was placed, then so be it.

But surely he didn't expect to choose her clothes and

her hairstyle, did he? Even the reputable Mrs Havers couldn't have tolerated that, surely? She sat back in the chair with a puzzled little sigh. She didn't understand a thing about this man and, worse still, she didn't understand how he could get under her skin so badly. She had worked for more than a few awkward types in the last three years, but the most she had felt in the past was minor irritation accompanied occasionally by silent contempt for their crassness. But Wolf Strade... He was different. Totally different. And she had a good few months to get through yet. Could she do it? She frowned. Of course.

She thought of Hannah's bright little face as they had chatted about a Pretty Pony beanbag to match the rest of her proposed new bedroom, and sighed resignedly. But it wasn't going to be easy. She had the feeling Wolf Strade didn't like her much, even if he appreciated her attributes as a secretary. Still—she glared across at the closed door as a tiny flame of anger reignited—he shouldn't have given her the job, should he? She was blowed if she was going to be bullied into altering either her manner or her appearance to suit that pompous swine.

Nevertheless, the next morning she found herself fixing her long hair into a loose knot on the back of her head even as she told herself it was simply because it was less trouble that way. Wolf made no comment when she knocked and opened the door of his office to announce her arrival, wondering as she did so if he lived at the office. He was always around when she left at night and immersed in work when she arrived. She had been right. He *was* a machine.

'Could you work on these tapes before you do anything else?' he commanded abruptly as he handed her two audio-tapes from his desk. 'It's a report involving some complex financial data and I want it done immediately. And make sure you get the numbers right,' he added tersely.

'Of course, Mr Strade.' The tone and the name were a cold rebuke, and he raised his head abruptly to meet the dark, angry gleam in her eyes.

They stared at each other for a good thirty seconds before he surprised her utterly by leaning back in his chair and running his hand across his eyes with a weary gesture that spoke of utter exhaustion. 'I'm sorry, I sounded very rude.' The icy blue eyes were a little dazed, she realised suddenly, almost as though he hadn't slept. 'I've been here all night working on this damn mess. Why I employ an accounts department and do the work myself, I'll never know...'

'You've been here all night?' She saw the shirt was the same one he had worn the day before, but definitely the worse for wear, and the black stubble on his square chin made her heart give a solid little kick against her breasts before she could control it.

'Crazy, eh?' His smile was very boyish and rueful, and again her heart jerked uncomfortably. 'The graveyards are full of guys like me who can't let go of a problem until they've beaten it.'

'Or it beats them,' she added quietly.

'Yeah, maybe.' He settled back in the big black leather chair, stretching his hands above his head in a way that brought the muscled wall of his chest into stark prominence against the blue silk of his shirt. Some time during the night he had undone his tie and opened the first few buttons of his shirt, and now the sight of the dark, rough body-hair that covered his chest made her hands damp and her throat dry. What is the matter with me? she asked herself in disbelief. This wasn't sexual attraction, was it? She didn't fancy Wolf Strade of all people…did she? 'How about a strong cup of coffee, and then maybe I'll grab a couple of hours' sleep on the couch before the meeting at eleven?'

'Weak tea would be better if you're going to sleep,' she answered automatically as her gaze flicked to the large studio couch in a shadowed corner of the huge room. She didn't want to be here when he lay down on that thing. She didn't even try to analyse why.

'I said coffee.' The cold authority was back in his voice but she didn't mind; that other Wolf was too dangerous to contemplate. 'And strong,' he added warningly.

'Coming up.'

Thankfully he was still sitting in the chair when she returned with the coffee a few minutes later, and she hurried out of the room after depositing the cup in front of him without speaking, her cheeks flushed.

At a quarter to eleven she was just contemplating gathering every scrap of courage she possessed and venturing into his office to wake him, when the connecting door opened and he stood framed in the doorway, blinking a little in the harsh artificial light overhead. 'If anyone arrives early, sit them down out here until I buzz,' he said abruptly, his eyes red-rimmed. 'I'm just going for a wash and brush-up.'

'Where?' she squeaked nervously, having visions of her room filled to overflowing with irate managers as they waited and waited.

'The washroom next door.' He glanced at her in surprise. 'Didn't you know it was there for your use too? I keep a change of clothes in there for emergencies—you can do the same if you wish.'

'I don't think that will be necessary,' she said stiffly, 'and how could I know it was there if you didn't see fit to tell me?'

'By using your initiative?'he suggested coolly.

'My initiative?' All thoughts of Hannah's bedroom faded into insignificance. 'In the three days since I've worked for you I haven't had time to breathe, let alone go exploring this block of concrete.' She glared at him angrily. 'It's got nothing at all to do with initiative, Mr Strade.'

'I thought blondes were supposed to be cool and un-emotional,' he said drily, studying her angry face with a superior frown. 'Are you like this with your husband?'

'Mr Strade, I—' She stopped abruptly as hot colour flooded her pale, creamy skin in a hectic flush. She couldn't ever remember having a cross word with Matthew. Life had been a flat, tranquil sea with him, with the days stretching out before them, calm and un-troubled. In fact, until she had met Wolf Strade, she could have sworn on oath that she had the mildest of tempers.

'And the name's Wolf.' His voice disappeared as he stepped through the doorway, and as she sank back in her seat she was aware of feeling slightly disloyal to Matthew's memory without understanding why. She stared at her wedding-ring for a long painful moment and then turned resolutely to the word processor and began to work. These fluttery feelings of excitement and agitation were a direct result of her nerves coping with the unusual sensations of anger and irritation, that was all. *That was all.* And in view of the self-opinionated, downright arbitrary despot she had been thrust into con-tact with, it wasn't surprising either. She had never met anyone, male or female, who could make her so mad so quickly by doing so little. He was so cold, so self-contained. Didn't *anything* touch him?

At five to eleven he reappeared in the doorway restored to his usual immaculate self, black hair slicked back, face shaven and a fresh grey silk shirt replacing the blue of the day before. He looked gorgeous. She held his glance with a cold composure that was the best piece of acting she had ever done, and listened as he gave her a list of files he needed for the meeting. As she deposited them on his desk two minutes later she caught a whiff of his aftershave and despised herself for the way her stomach clenched in an involuntary response, but she was honest enough to admit there wasn't a thing she could do about it. For some strange reason her body was determined to be aroused by a man she both disliked and disapproved of. Did he know? She glanced at his bent head as he checked through the files, and her heart thudded against her chest. She would die if he did. Just die.

'Right.' As he raised his head she saw his face was preoccupied and distant, the ice-blue eyes cold and hooded as they met hers. 'I'd like you to sit in on this one, Lydia, and take notes, OK?' She nodded quietly as a rush of relief made her light-headed. He didn't know, and she would have to make darn sure he never suspected even for a second if she wanted to keep her job. Thank goodness she had said she was married; it would probably never even cross his mind that she was attracted to him in a physical sense. 'Record anything Mike Wilson says, incidentally.' He paused, and the handsome, cruel face hardened into stone. 'No matter how obtuse. OK?' He was watching her very closely and she felt a little shiver flicker down her spine.

'Why?' she asked carefully.

He shrugged slowly. 'You'll know soon enough, if my suspicions are right.' He lowered his head in dismissal.

At exactly eleven o'clock her office filled as though by magic, and as she ushered the group of men through she reflected, with wry uncomfortable humour, that Wolf had certainly got them well-trained. As the meeting progressed she didn't understand half of what she took down, but dutifully recorded everything in case she missed something vital.

It was a long day and an arduous one and, as she put the minutes of the meeting on Wolf's desk at just after six, she was conscious of an illogical, and quite unreasonable, sense of injustice that he should still appear cool and razor-sharp whereas she was visibly wilting.

'Your friend has been on the take.' It took a second for the words to register, spoken as they were in such a casual tone.

'Mike? No.' She raised shocked eyes to his. 'What are you going to do?' She somehow knew instantly it was true.

'It has already been done.' She looked away, her mouth unconsciously tightening at the flinty hardness in his face. 'You refuse any requests for references and refer any queries concerning him directly to me.'

'You've sacked him?' she asked with a horrified gasp.

'Too damn true.' He was flicking through the work she had just given him as he spoke, his head lowered. 'He'll be lucky if he gets a job sweeping the roads after I've finished with him.'

'But surely—?' She stopped abruptly as the ice-blue gaze switched to her face. This was awful, *awful*—poor Anna.

'Yes?' His tone was not encouraging.

'If it wasn't actually illegal...?' Her voice trailed away at the darkness in his face. 'I mean—'

'I know what you mean.' He shook his head tightly as he settled back in his chair, the razor-sharp eyes hard on her face. 'And, no, it wasn't "actually" illegal, not at this stage, but it would have been.' He eyed her grimly. 'You think I ought to have let the thing progress until I could throw a court case at him?'

'Of course not.' She flushed slightly at the hard scrutiny. 'But have you asked him why he did it?'

'I'm not interested in why,' he said coldly. 'He lied to me, that was his first big mistake, and then he thought an abject apology and a great deal of grovelling could extricate him from his foolishness. That was his second error of judgement.' He moved forward in the chair and lowered his gaze to the papers again. 'I won't tolerate being lied to, Lydia. I never have.'

'Oh.' She was glad he was looking downwards and missed the sudden surge of hot, guilty colour into her cheeks. 'Well, if there's nothing else, I'll say goodnight.'

'Wait a moment and I'll give you a lift home,' he said casually, still with his eyes on the papers in front of him. 'I'm dog-tired and enough is enough. The rest of this will wait.'

'There's no need.' She spoke so hastily that the words came out in a breathless rush. 'I don't want to take you out of your way and—'

'Get your coat.' It was as though she hadn't spoken.

'I...' She thought frantically for a cast-iron excuse to refuse the lift, but nothing came to mind, and as she stood hesitating in front of him he swept the papers into a neat pile and raised his head, his eyes blank.

'Well, go on,' he said irritably as he moved from the

desk towards the coat-stand in the corner of the room. 'I haven't got all night.'

She hesitated for one more moment and then turned quickly and sped into the outer office, her thoughts in turmoil. She didn't want a lift with him, she *didn't*, she thought, panic-stricken as she slipped into her coat and checked the word processor was switched off. How was she going to make conversation with this iceberg of a man on the way home, and what if he expected to be asked in? He wouldn't, though, of course he wouldn't— would he…? She shut her eyes for a moment and prayed for calm. But if he did, she could say her husband was at work, or away, or something. Her eyes snapped open as he appeared in the doorway, his big black overcoat and heavy, dark briefcase adding to the image of formidable imperiousness.

Why had she started this? she asked herself desperately. Why had she lied? A tremor raced through her as she remembered his face when he had spoken of Mike Wilson's deceit. She should have come out in the open, made her position as a widow clear, and then the ball would have been in his court. And she hadn't explained properly about Mike either.

'Ready?' He waved a dismissive hand towards the door and followed her out into the corridor, his face remote and withdrawn and his body straight. She glanced at him carefully as the lift took them swiftly downwards. She knew why she had lied. It was there in the almost tangible signals of dissociation his body was sending to hers, the total repudiation of any involvement, however slight, on a personal level. He wanted an efficient machine in his office. That was all. If she had said she was in effect single again… She nodded to herself mentally. She had done the only thing possible in the circumstances. And of course he wouldn't want to come in for coffee—one didn't fraternise with machines, after all.

'You seem to be settling in very well.'

It was as she opened her mouth to reply to the obviously forced cool pleasantry that the lift shuddered to a halt between floors, the momentary imbalance of the big box shaking her off her feet and throwing her against the solid bulk of his chest. His arms opened automatically to receive her as he in turn stumbled against the wall of the lift, and for a breath-stopping moment she was aware of being held in his arms, her face lifted up to his, for all the world like two lovers about to kiss as the lights flickered and dimmed.

'Are you all right?' Afterwards she realised he hadn't reacted as she would have imagined by pushing her impatiently, or even distastefully, away. In fact his arms tightened fractionally as he looked down into her frightened upturned face, in which the darkness of her eyes stood out like two velvet pools. 'Don't worry, lifts have a habit of playing silly devils,' he reassured her softly.

'Do they?' She tried to smile but the combination of her fear of plunging to her death trapped in this little metal box and, more especially, his closeness was making her feel as helpless as a child. Although certainly her body was reacting in a way that was definitely not child-like, she countered wryly as she carefully eased herself away from him. He was holding her loosely now, his hands under her elbows, but the smell and feel of him were all around her and they were…unsettling. And thrilling. Undeniably thrilling.

'You haven't hurt yourself?' For a split second she considered saying yes so that he would hold her a little longer, but that impulse alone was enough to shock her out of his hold as she shook her head, moving back a pace quickly.

What on earth's the matter with me? she asked herself weakly as he moved across the few feet of space and pressed the emergency button, his movements cool and controlled and his face expressionless. Is it sexual frustration? She shut her eyes briefly and prayed for the trembling that had taken over her limbs to still. But she didn't even have a sex drive, did she? Or not until three days ago, anyway.

'Claustrophobia.'

'What?' She opened startled eyes to see his face inches from her own again, and the next moment he had taken her into his arms, stroking her face comfortingly as he held her close against him.

'The panic you're feeling,' he said softly, his voice deep and low. He had seen her trembling and put it down to claustrophobia? She said a mental thank you to her guardian angel. 'It's perfectly natural and you'll be out of here in a few minutes. Just relax and let me take the load—you're doing fine.'

This wasn't helping, it definitely wasn't helping, she thought weakly as he enfolded her into him, wrapping his overcoat round her as he held her next to his heart. He thought she was scared to death but, instead of the biting scorn she would have expected, he was displaying a tenderness that was alarming. She was immensely glad a few seconds later when the emergency button buzzed loudly and the small intercom next to it crackled out the security guard's voice. 'Hello? Is anyone in there?'

'Rogers?' Wolf moved across to answer and Lydia leant limply against the wall of the lift, her heart thudding as she watched him. 'My secretary and I are in here. What the hell's happening?'

'I'm sorry, Mr Strade,' the male voice answered promptly, 'but there's some sort of a power-cut that's affected all this side of the road. I understand it's being dealt with as quickly as possible, but I'm afraid there's nothing we can do at the moment.'

'Brilliant.' He glanced across at her quickly before speaking again. 'Any idea how long before we're out?'

'Not long, sir.' There was a brief pause while they heard him talking to someone else. 'About twenty minutes or so at the most.'

'Right, keep me informed.'

As he turned to face her fully again she spoke quickly in case he thought he had to continue the role of comforter. 'I'm fine now, really.' She smiled brightly. 'It was just the suddenness of it all.'

'Good.' He clearly thought she was just trying to be brave, because the expression of gentle concern that was so surprising on the harsh features didn't lessen. 'Well, we may as well make ourselves comfortable while we wait. I suggest you take off your coat—it's already getting a little warm in here.'

'Right.' As she shrugged the jacket off her shoulders he moved quickly and drew it down her arms, his light touch burning her flesh as his fingers briefly made contact.

'Sit on this.' He made his own coat into a large cushion, crouching down as he plumped it into shape. As she sat down on the wad of material he gestured at his tie. 'Do you mind?' he asked mildly. 'I don't like these things at the best of times.'

'Of course not.' He stood up again, for which she was supremely grateful. The way the material of his trousers had moulded to his thighs had caused her breathing a few problems. He unbuttoned his jacket, revealing the grey silk shirt tucked into the flat waistband of his trousers, and then loosened his tie, undoing the first few buttons of his shirt. Somehow, in the close confines of the small lift, the action was painfully intimate, but for the life of her she couldn't draw her eyes away from his broad shoulders and muscled chest, the dark body-hair beneath the shirt causing hot colour to surge into her cheeks. Was he hairy all over? She shut her eyes against the thought.

'OK?' Her eyes snapped open to see him sitting against the opposite wall, his narrowed gaze fixed on her face. 'You look hot.'

'No, I'm absolutely fine.' She smiled brightly.

As she brushed a wisp of hair from her cheek his eyes followed the action, his gaze resting on the smooth blondeness of her hair. 'How did you come to get such unusual colouring?' he asked suddenly. 'Your hair is so fair and yet your eyes are almost black.'

'I don't know.' She tried for a casual smile—that piercing gaze was more than a little unnerving. 'Some errant gene, I suppose, but it must be a strong one. Hannah, my daughter, is exactly the same. Everyone says she is a carbon copy of me.'

'Do they?' There was something in his expression she couldn't read and it unnerved her still more. 'Your husband is a very lucky man to have two beautiful females to love,' he said, after a few strangely tense seconds had ticked by.

Lydia's stomach clenched and she looked away quickly, her eyes downcast. How could she reply to that? She took a long, hidden breath and prayed for calm. 'How long have we been in here now?' she asked tensely.

'About ten minutes.' He didn't glance at his watch as

he spoke; his gaze never left her face. 'Shut your eyes a moment and try to relax,' he added gently. 'Take a few deep breaths and regulate your breathing.' He thought there was a danger of her hyperventilating? Lydia thought weakly. How right he was, but not for the reason he imagined! Nevertheless, she did as he instructed, leaning back against the wall of the lift and shutting her eyes tight as she folded her arms protectively over her breasts. The dim light from the emergency batteries in the lift's back-up system produced a dull charcoal glow against her closed eyelids, and after a few seconds she heard Wolf's briefcase snap open and the rustle of papers.

He was going to work *now*? She opened incredulous eyes to see him crouched over a long report, a slight frown wrinkling his brow as he peered at the small figures in the shadowy gloom. He was unbelievable, quite unbelievable. Didn't he ever stop working? She smiled bemusedly.

'What?' She hadn't been aware that the blue eyes had flicked upwards, but now saw they were trained on her face.

'I'm sorry?' She was flustered and it showed.

'You were smiling, a Mona Lisa smile if I may say so,' he added softly. 'Why?'

'Oh, nothing, it was just—' She stopped abruptly as she wondered if she dared tell him. Oh, blow it, he *had* asked, after all. 'I was wondering if you ever stop working,' she said quietly, 'that's all.'

'Do I detect a note of disapproval?' he asked smoothly as he crouched back on his heels, the position emphasising strong muscled legs and hard inner thighs.

'Not really.' She smiled with what she hoped came

across as cool composure. 'I'm sure it needs your sort of dedication to stay at the top in this business—'

'You're right,' he interrupted expressionlessly, 'it does.' He stood up slowly, leaning back against the wall with his arms crossed and his eyes narrowed as he looked down at her. 'But that is only part of it. I like what I do, that's the bottom line.'

'Yes…' She shook her head slowly. 'But incidents like the Mike Wilson thing, don't they bother you at all?'

'Mike Wilson has been dealt with before he could do any damage,' he said coldly, 'and, more importantly, has been *seen* to be dealt with. He will serve as a timely example of what happens if anyone is stupid enough to try and cross me, so, if anything, I have gained, not lost, from the episode. That being the case, why should it bother me?'

She stared at him silently, shocked by the blatant ruthlessness his words revealed. 'But he has a wife and child,' she murmured, after a pregnant pause. 'You said yourself he'll never get another job—'

'That is his concern, not mine.' The handsome face was stony now. 'He had an excellent and extremely well-paid position with me, which he chose to put in jeopardy through his own greed. He has lived an executive life-style for several years, complete with large house, private schooling for his boy, all the trappings wealth brings, and that has been on the salary I have paid him. If you are asking me to feel guilty, forget it. I don't.' He eyed her grimly. 'Besides which, the Mike Wilsons of this world always get by,' he finished brusquely.

He was right. She had to admit there was more than a grain of truth in what he said, and he had had the option of giving Mike enough rope to hang himself but decided against it, and yet… She too rose, very slowly, to stand looking at him across the few feet of space. Did he have to be so cold, so remote, so untouched by it all? She doubted if he had any normal feelings at all or, if there were a few, they were deeply encased in solid ice. 'I can understand what you are saying but—' She stopped abruptly, not quite knowing how to continue. This was her boss, when all was said and done, her bread and butter, so to speak.

'But?' His expression was cynical and cold, and suddenly Lydia knew he was totally aware of her feelings about the matter and they didn't bother him an iota. He was a man who would always do exactly what *he* thought was right in any situation in which he found himself, and to hell with the rest of the world. Her own mouth hardened, but even as she opened it to speak the security guard's voice crackled over the intercom again.

'Mr Strade?'

'Yes?' Wolf's voice was clipped.

'Any minute now, sir. Are you all right in there?'

'Fine, Rogers.' He bent, stuffing the papers back in his briefcase and gesturing to her coat by her feet. 'I suggest you put that back on,' he said calmly as he reached across for his own. 'No doubt it'll strike cold once we're out of this sauna.'

At the same moment that the lights flooded back on the lift began to move, but in the same instant it jerked violently, throwing Lydia off her feet for the second time that night as it stopped again. And this time she *was* frightened, petrifyingly so. 'Wolf?' He had caught her as she fell, the momentum of her body and the bending position he had been in sending him to his knees and now she lay across his lap, her face uplifted and hair fanning out across his arm as the knot came loose. There was one split second, as she looked up into the hard, masculine face above her own, when she knew what was about to happen and felt the blood pound through her veins, her body beginning to quiver in anticipation. His eyes were bright and glittering as they stared down into the velvet brown depths of hers, the desire she could read so plainly in his dark face hot and hard and incredibly sensual.

He was going to kiss her. The thought exploded into her mind, and now little tremors of helpless excitement reached her toes and curled the small pads into the soles of her feet as she envisaged his mouth on hers. She could feel his heart pounding against the solid wall of his chest and the expensive, heady, totally masculine smell of him pervaded every nerve and tissue.

She wanted him to kiss her. She wanted it more than she had ever wanted anything in her life and, strangely, the thought didn't seem shocking as his arms tightened and his eyes narrowed into brilliant blue slits.

Wolf. She was never sure even afterwards if she said his name out loud or just breathed it in her soul as a silent, helpless plea, but just as she thought his dark head would lower to hers, that she would know what it was like to be kissed by this fierce, powerful, cold man, he moved her from him, his face stiffening with unconcealed disgust and his body rigid with control.

CHAPTER THREE

AS THE intercom coughed and spluttered, the sound seemed to explode into the deathly quiet of the tiny box and then Rogers's gruff voice spoke, his tone concerned. 'I'm sorry, Mr Strade, there seems to have been a minor hiccup. The circuit-breakers have tripped out due to their normal mode being broken, but it won't take me above five minutes to re-set them. Are you and the lady all right, sir?'

'Just get on with it, Rogers.' The security guard's voice had acted like a deluge of cold water, and immediately he had spoken, bringing the outside world into their small domain, an icy blankness had wiped all expression from Wolf's face. He helped her to her feet without speaking, his body stiff.

'Lydia?' She raised her hot face slowly, unable to take a verbal slap in the face after the contempt and scorn he had just shown so plainly, but she wouldn't blame him if he told her exactly what he thought. How could she have encouraged him like that? How could she? What on earth must he be thinking? She was supposed to be a married woman, after all, and she had practically begged— 'It won't be long and we'll be out of here, OK?'

'Yes.' Her voice was small and bewildered and the sound of it made the harsh, masculine face in front of her tighten savagely, the hard features setting into stone. She had lain there and asked him to make love to her. Her mind shouted the accusation at her. And he had

47

wanted to—well, what man wouldn't if it was offered so outrageously?

But he had had the moral strength to turn away, his disgust at her wantonness evident in every line of that handsome face. She couldn't bear this humiliation, she couldn't. The thoughts raced frantically through her mind as she tried desperately to pull herself together, fighting for the control that had seen her through so many difficulties and traumas in the last few years.

'I…' Her voice faltered and she took a deep breath before trying again. She had to retrieve this situation, dredge up some dignity from somewhere. 'I feel much better now, thank you, it was the panic…'

'Panic?' He looked at her blankly for a moment and then nodded slowly, his mouth tightening still more. 'You were scared to death, I know that, but I just want to say—'

'How long will it be before we are out?' She had seen his devastating brand of honesty once or twice in the three days she had worked for him, but she wished with all her heart he could let it slip just once. She couldn't talk about what had so nearly happened now, and if he tried to take the blame through perverse male pride it would make things ten times worse. A post-mortem at this moment was more than she could take.

He stared at her for a long, silent moment, the narrowed cold eyes tight on her face, and then took the cue she had given him with a cool equanimity that made her tangled thoughts seem even more confused. 'A couple of minutes more, no longer.'

She nodded weakly. Suddenly her safe, ordered little world had turned upside-down and she was stunned with the unexpectedness of it. The two or three minutes it took for the lift to resume its downward journey seemed like two or three hours, and for the whole time her heart was thudding against her breasts so hard it hurt. Not a word was spoken but the silence was deafening, banging against her ear-drums until she felt like screaming.

But nothing had *actually* happened. She forced herself to think logically, to apply reason to the shame and embarrassment. But he had known. He had known she wanted him to kiss her. What should she do? She glanced across at Wolf's stony face as he stood leaning against the far side of the lift, his eyes half closed and his body seemingly relaxed.

This time the lift started smoothly, gliding down to the ground floor and opening its doors with silky obedience. As she followed Wolf out to his Mercedes in its reserved spot just outside the main entrance, she contemplated, for a crazy moment, telling him the truth, but as he opened the passenger door of his car for her to enter one look at his dark face convinced her she didn't have the nerve. It might persuade him that he hadn't got a potential adulteress in his office, but if he knew she had deliberately misled him, secured the job on a whopper of a lie... And he hadn't liked her defence of Mike; that was most certainly another nail in her coffin. She swallowed painfully.

'Your address?' His tone was clipped and short, and after she had given it she slid into the beautiful Mercedes and sat huddled tensely in the seat as he joined her, his face cold.

'Could you try and relax a little?' They had been travelling in silence for some minutes and she started violently as his voice, abrupt and deep, sounded at her side. 'I'm beginning to feel like some sort of pervert with you sitting halfway up the window like that.'

'What?' As she glanced at the large area of vacant

space on the right-hand side of her seat, she realised she was indeed perched against the side of the car in a manner that he could well term insulting, and she slid quickly into the middle of the seat, her face flaming. Great. Now he'd think she was a split personality too! One minute a shameless temptress and the next the original shrinking violet. 'I'm sorry, I didn't realise.'

'I'm not sure if that makes it worse or better,' he said drily, with one swift, piercing glance at her red face. 'Look, I don't want anything to spoil our working relationship, Lydia—'

'It won't.' The reply was immediate as she cut off his voice. She couldn't talk about it, she just couldn't. Somehow the whole incident had opened up another side to him that had her tingling all over and, although the feeling wasn't unpleasant, in the circumstances it *was* intensely humiliating. He had rejected her with apparently the minimum of effort and that cool, devastatingly clear mind wasn't in the least affected. But she—she closed her eyes against her own weakness—she was aware of every tiny movement he made, of his strong, capable hands on the steering-wheel, his long, lean legs and powerful thighs...

'Good.' She felt his glance on her face again but didn't look at him.

'You turn right here.' She was unutterably thankful this nightmare journey would end soon. 'Then left at the corner.' He followed her instructions without speaking again, and when they drew up outside her house some minutes later she realised her hands were clenched together so tightly her fingers were numb.

'Thank you for the lift—' she began primly, fumbling for her handbag at her feet, but he had already opened his door, moving round the car and helping her out with

an old-fashioned courtesy that was all the more seduc-
tively attractive for being entirely natural. 'Thank you—'
she began again, only to be interrupted a second time as
Hannah's bright little voice called to her from the top
step seconds before her tiny daughter bounded across the
three or four feet of paved front garden and into her
arms. 'Mummeeee!' Hannah's voice was ecstatic. 'Mrs
Thomson next door says I can have one of her kittens
for my very own. Can I, Mummy? Can I?'

'This is Hannah.' She looked at Wolf warily over her
daughter's head and surprised a look in his eyes that she
couldn't quite fathom. Pain? Distress? Bitterness? Dislike? But then a shutter slid into place and the remote,
cool gaze was the one she knew. 'Hannah, this is Mr
Strade.'

'How do you do, Hannah?' he asked gravely, a smile
touching the hard features briefly.

'Lo.' Hannah smiled back as she twisted round in
Lydia's arms for a better view. 'My mummy works for
you, doesn't she?'

'Indeed she does.' He moved towards the car as he
spoke, clearly not wishing to prolong the moment, for
which Lydia was extremely thankful. The weight of her
lie had suddenly become like a noose round her neck.

'Do you like kittens?' Hannah was speaking directly
to Wolf, who paused with his hand on the car door.
'They're little cats,' she added helpfully.

'Hannah, Mr Strade has got to go,' Lydia said hastily
as her mother appeared in the lighted doorway to the
house. This was fast becoming too much.

'Yes, I like kittens.' He looked at Hannah as Lydia
held her close, their two heads touching as Hannah snuggled down in her mother's arms, and then raised a casual
hand to the figure in the doorway before sliding into the

interior of the car and starting the engine in the same movement.

'I like him.' As the car moved smoothly away Hannah waved vigorously, but the dark figure in the driving seat didn't respond. 'He's nice.'

'How do you know?' Lydia's mother asked smilingly as she joined them in the street, sharing a glance of amusement with Lydia over Hannah's head as they watched the tail-lights of the car disappear. 'You've only said hello to him.'

'He likes kittens.' That, as far as Hannah was concerned, was the end of the matter. 'And Mummy likes him, don't you, Mummy?'

Lydia smiled weakly. 'What's all this about Mrs Thomson and a kitten?' The diversion worked, but later that night, as she lay in bed with sleep a million miles away, Hannah's words came back to haunt her. *Did* she like him? She pictured the hard, handsome face and powerfully masculine body and a little shiver trickled down her spine, sensitising a hundred nerve-ends she had never known she had. 'Like' was not a word that applied to Wolf Strade somehow. One 'liked' neighbours or friends or the family doctor, but Wolf... She twisted in the big bed irritably. What on earth was she thinking about him for, anyway? He was her boss, that was all, a multimillionaire whose lifestyle was so at variance with hers they could have been on different planets. But he had wanted her... The thought was there before she could stop it and she sat up in bed jerkily, her face stricken.

'Oh, no, none of that, Lydia.' Her voice as she spoke into the dark room was tightly emphatic. 'You work for him, that's all, and the only reason he took you on in the first place was because he thought you were married and immune from any fancy ideas. Women chase him all the time, you *know* that, for goodness' sake.' But he *had* wanted her, the voice in her mind taunted quietly. She had read it in his eyes. It wouldn't mean a thing to a man like him, she answered silently, not a thing. In spite of the desire that had flared between them so swiftly, the wild hunger she had seen in his face, he had been able to push her aside without a qualm, although he must have sensed her surrender. Sensed it and shown his disgust at it too, the inexorable voice reminded her relentlessly. She groaned softly, the sound a little lost whimper in the emptiness of the silent room.

The next day was a Friday, and painful in the extreme as Lydia struggled to maintain a cool, efficient image while shrivelling up inside every time she glanced at Wolf's dark countenance, but after a normal family weekend Monday was easier and Tuesday more so. Wolf was his normal arrogant cold self, his blue eyes cool and remote if they caught hers, and gradually the incident in the lift became a little less stark as day followed hectic day. Once or twice she thought she caught him staring at her with an odd expression in the darkly lashed blue eyes, but his manner would change so swiftly when he caught her gaze that she told herself she was imagining things. And she *had* noticed he went to great pains not to touch her, even in the most abstract way, but then, he wasn't a physical man, she told herself uneasily…was he? Matthew hadn't been. She shook her head mentally at her naïveté where men were concerned, but then she had only ever known Matthew. The normal scenario of boy meets girl, the inevitable experimentation of life and love, had completely passed her by.

And she knew absolutely nothing about Wolf. This

fact was brought home forcibly on the day Hannah was to collect the kitten from Mrs Thomson, it now having reached the requisite age of eight weeks. She had arranged to leave an hour early in order to pick Hannah up herself from nursery, and was just finishing the final pages of a complex financial report when a cursory knock at her outer door interrupted her train of thought.

'Yes?' The door had opened even as she spoke and a heavy gust of expensive perfume drew her head upwards.

'Is he in?' The woman who had just sauntered into the room was tall, willowy and so beautiful that Lydia found herself gaping for a startled second before she collected herself.

'Yes...' She reached for the buzzer on her desk. 'Who shall I say—?'

'Don't bother with that thing.' The throaty, attractive voice was warm and confident and wide blue eyes gave her the once-over a moment before the woman opened the door to Wolf's office and stepped through.

'But you can't—' Lydia followed through the open door a second later, her face aghast, to find the woman leaning over Wolf's desk to deposit a fleeting kiss on his mouth before turning to survey her in the doorway.

'It's OK, Lydia.' Wolf didn't look particularly pleased at the intrusion, but neither was he displaying the sort of anger she had expected.

'I'm sorry—'

'Oh, Wolf is used to my barging in at any time of the night or day, aren't you, darling...?' A perfect little rotund bottom seated itself on the corner of his desk, the manoeuvre exposing a great deal of slim, tanned leg as smiling blue eyes wandered over Lydia in open appraisal. 'He's my mentor. Is that the appropriate word, darling?'

'That's enough, Elda.' Wolf smiled back at the beautiful brunette indulgently. 'And get off my damn desk.'

The brunette's thin but beautifully shaped mouth pouted in a little grimace as she did as she was told, her movements elegant and unhurried. Where did she get such amazing self-assurance? Lydia wondered as she turned to leave. But then perhaps it wasn't surprising really. Sleek dark hair cut in an expert feathery style to complement the graceful head and long neck, huge blue eyes and a perfect skin added up to an impressive whole, and her clothes weren't from the local high street either!

As she returned to her desk, shutting the door quietly and firmly behind her, she found to her dismay that she was shaking slightly. She sat down with a little plop and took a long deep breath, willing her heart to calm down. So he had a girlfriend? So what? Of course a man like him wouldn't be short of female company, she knew that, didn't she?

But what a girlfriend! The thought was painful. And it wasn't exactly that he had a girlfriend that was bothering her, but the way he had looked at Elda. She hadn't seen that gentle, soft look on his face before and it had hurt her. Why, she didn't know.

Their working routine had settled down into a pattern that, despite the odd panic here and there, was relatively straightforward, although she certainly couldn't have called Wolf Strade an easy man to work for. He was blunt to the point of rudeness on occasion but, she had to admit, the social standing of the recipient didn't affect his brusqueness at all. He was simply a man who suffered fools badly, be they kings or paupers.

The buzzer on her desk interrupted her train of

thought. 'Lydia? Could you arrange some coffee, please?' Wolf asked pleasantly.

'Certainly.'

She normally phoned down such requests but today she took the lift to the canteen herself. Somehow she didn't want to be in the office and, as she carried the tray in to Wolf ten minutes later, she knew why. There was something too cosy in his acceptance of Elda's easy intrusion.

'Cut along now, Lydia, and I hope all goes well with the kitten.' As Wolf gave one of his rare smiles Lydia saw Elda's blue eyes narrow in sudden sharp scrutiny.

'I'll just finish the last page of that report first.' She smiled with what she hoped was cool composure, nodded to Elda, who had now seated herself in the large easy chair opposite Wolf's desk, and walked quietly from the room, more shaken than she cared to admit. It was nothing to her who he saw in his private life, she told herself fiercely as she finished the report to the sound of occasional laughter from the connecting room, nothing at all.

Did he make long, passionate love to Elda? She didn't know where the thought came from, but it was enough to jerk her out of her seat as though she had been pricked with a pin. Of course he would, she answered herself irritably as she slipped into her jacket, her eyes stormy and her mouth unconsciously tight. A man like him didn't get to thirty-eight and remain single without perfecting his technique. And it would be *some* technique! She shut her eyes briefly and then resolutely turned her mind away from the dangerous path it was following. She was as bad as her predecessors. What had he called them? Oh, yes, empty-headed little bimbos. The chauvinistic phrase still had the power to make her mad. And *that* was the sort of man he was; she'd better remember it. He'd made it perfectly clear over the last few weeks that he viewed her in the same way as the office furniture, and it suited her just fine, *just fine*. Involvement with him, with any man, just wasn't on the cards.

'That's some frown.'

'What?' She hadn't heard him come into the room, but now she saw the connecting door was closed as he stood just in front of it, his eyes quizzical and his mouth straight.

'Is something wrong?' He leant against the door-jamb as he spoke, crossing his arms as he viewed her through narrowed eyes. 'You seem…disturbed.'

'Disturbed?' She was acutely aware of Elda in the next room and the sudden desire to hit him hard was as shocking as it was irrational.

'Lydia…' He paused as though he found it difficult to continue, but his voice was quite expressionless when he spoke. 'Is everything all right at home? I mean, are there any domestic difficulties that are worrying you, any problems?'

'Of course there aren't.' Her relief at his misinterpretation of her agitation was overwhelming. 'Everything's fine.' She dropped her eyes for a moment, her face flushing.

'Yes, it would be.' He stared at her for a long moment with expressionless eyes. 'He wouldn't be such a fool—' He stopped abruptly and moved to her desk, picking up the report she had finished. 'Goodnight, Lydia.' His voice was cold and abrupt and she stared at him for a moment, nonplussed by his coolness.

What had she done now? He turned and re-entered his office without looking at her again, a small muscle jumping in his jaw that convinced her she was right. She had done something to annoy him, but what? Suddenly she had the crazy impulse to fling open his door, march up to his desk and demand an explanation, but then a soft husky giggle from the inner room swamped her with cold reason. What was she thinking of, for goodness' sake? He hadn't said or done anything wrong, in fact he had shown concern, albeit frostily, that something was bothering her. And there was. She frowned helplessly at the shut door. But she couldn't put a name to it. All she knew was that from that moment in the lift she just couldn't view him in quite the same light. The incident had revealed a wildly passionate, sensual side to him that didn't fit in with the cold, intimidatingly intelligent individual of office hours and she wanted— She cut her thoughts abruptly. She didn't know *what* she wanted! Yes, she did—the safe, comfortable, ordinary existence she had always known without disturbing night-time dreams that made her feel shamefully wanton if she recalled even a part of them.

She rubbed her hand across her hot face and took a deep breath as she buttoned her jacket and checked the word processor was switched off. She should never have worked for him in the first place, never have got embroiled in the lie that had seemed to stretch and grow in the last few weeks. Wolf never referred directly to her private life but there had been one or two instances when a negative reaction, a reiteration of her husband's place in her life, more by what she had not said than what she had, had proved itself necessary.

Hannah was thrilled with the kitten, a tiny scrap of fur and eyes that she immediately named Tiger because of its markings, and Lydia let her stay up later than usual after tea, watching them both through the open kitchen door as she made up a little basket for the animal and arranged a litter-tray in an alcove near the back door. She had just ventured up the somewhat rickety step-ladder to reach a small dish on top of one of the kitchen cupboards that was just right for such a tiny scrap when the phone rang, making her jump. Whether she leant over too far or the step-ladder slipped she was never quite sure, but the next moment she was clutching frantically at thin air as she fell, landing with a bone-jarring thud on the kitchen floor as the step-ladder caught her a stunning blow across the head as it collapsed at her side.

'Mummy! Mummy!' Hannah's voice was shrill with panic as she ran into the kitchen, the kitten disappearing under a chair, its back arched in fright.

'It's all right, Hannah.' She wanted to be sick, desperately, but she fought it along with the rising tide of blackness that was threatening to take her over. She couldn't pass out, not when Hannah was alone like this. 'Answer the phone quickly, darling,' she mumbled through numb lips, 'it's probably Grandma. Tell her I've fallen down and need some help.'

'Oh, Mummy…' As large tears welled up in Hannah's big brown eyes, Lydia used all her strength to speak again.

'Answer the phone, Hannah, quickly.' It was their lifeline. '*Now*, darling.' And then the rushing in her ears became like an express train and darkness closed in, shutting out Hannah's sobs and her own frantic desperation.

She could only have lost consciousness for a few minutes, and as she struggled back out of the roaring blackness her first thought was for Hannah. She must have spoken her daughter's name because a little voice answered immediately by her side. 'Yes, Mummy?'

'Don't worry, darling.' As her eyes focused on the small face she lay for a few seconds, willing the faintness away, and then moved gingerly, pulling herself into a sitting position with her back against the line of cupboards. 'I'm all right, Hannah, I promise.' Hannah nodded tearfully but looked far from convinced, and as Lydia opened her arms dived into them like a tiny, frightened rabbit. 'Did you answer the phone?' Lydia asked weakly, relaxing again as the little head nodded an affirmative. Thank goodness. Help was on the way.

As she sat with Hannah in her arms she tested each part of her body slowly and was relieved to find nothing seemed to be broken, although everything was hurting. How could she have been so stupid? She shut her eyes helplessly. She was usually so careful, so cautious.

After a few minutes Tiger's striped head peered warily round the kitchen door, only to disappear abruptly again as the front doorbell rang stridently. 'That will be Grandma.' Why hadn't her mother used her key? she thought wearily as she struggled painfully to her feet, Hannah trotting along by her side like a scared puppy.

She could feel each step in her head as she walked slowly to the door, and the short journey took all her concentration. She hadn't been aware her head had bled, but just as she reached the door she saw her white blouse was smudged with red, and as she raised her hand to her brow it came away sticky. Great, just great. If her mother hadn't panicked already she would throw a blue fit at the sight of blood. But it wasn't her mother who faced her as she opened the door.

'What the hell…?'

The shock of seeing Wolf on her doorstep was almost too much, and as she swayed he caught her arm firmly before bending slightly and whisking her up into his arms. It was only a step through the minute hall into the small but cosy lounge, and the open door at the far end which led into the kitchen was wide open, the stepladder bearing evidence of the accident. 'I'm all right, really…' she murmured faintly as he deposited her with startling gentleness into the depths of the sofa.

The expression on his face told her how stupid her words had sounded in the circumstances, and he knelt down at her side before turning to speak to Hannah who was standing just behind them, her eyes wide and her face tear-smudged. 'Are you OK, sweet-pea?' She had never heard him speak in that tender tone of voice before and it did something to her heart that was almost painful. As Hannah nodded uncertainly he reached out an arm and drew the small child close, hugging her reassuringly before speaking again. 'Your mummy is going to be fine. She's just bumped her head a little, like you bump your knees if you fall over. Understand?' The small nod carried more assurance this time.

'That *is* all you've done?' He turned back to Lydia suddenly. 'No broken bones, no sprains?'

'I don't think so.' She tried to smile but the effort was too much. 'I've just got this awful headache.'

'How awful?' he asked grimly as his gaze took in her cloudy eyes and trembling mouth. 'Did you pass out?'

She nodded, but the action caused such excruciating pain that she gasped out loud, the whiteness of her face standing out in stark contrast to the blood on her forehead.

'Where's your husband? Matthew, isn't it?'

As Hannah opened her mouth Lydia jumped in first, her voice high with strain. 'Hannah, go and get ready for bed, darling. Just pop into your nightie, we'll have a wash in the morning.' The kitten made a cautious reappearance as she spoke, its bright green eyes enormous in the delicate face. 'I'll bring Tiger in to stay goodnight when you're in bed.' That did the trick, and as Hannah's feet disappeared up the stairs Wolf stood up slowly, his eyes concerned as he quietly glanced round the room.

'What's going on, Lydia?' She stared up at him, quite unable to speak. 'He's not living here, is he?' It was a statement rather than a question, and with the sick pounding in her head a lowering of her eyes was all she could manage. She ought to explain, she told herself weakly, now was the perfect opportunity and he wouldn't be too mad, would he? Not with her like this? But somehow, as he stood in front of her, his face uncharacteristically gentle and his eyes warm, she couldn't bring herself to speak, to see his expression change from one of tender concern to hard condemnation of her deceit. 'I thought something was wrong for the last week or two,' he said almost to himself. 'I should have guessed, especially with the kitten. That was to take Hannah's mind off it?' She stared at him, frozen in mind and body as she realised he thought Matthew had just recently left her. She couldn't let this continue, it was too awful, but as she opened her mouth to explain he knelt at her side again, his face rueful. 'Hell, there couldn't be a worse time for twenty questions, could there? Just relax, Lydia, I'm going to phone a doctor to check out that bump on your head—'

'No!' She caught hold of his arm. 'I'm OK, really, I don't want any fuss. Please, Wolf—'

'Lydia, you are going to see a doctor.' His eyes lingered on the gash on her forehead again. 'It's just a surface wound, but you may have concussion—'

'My mother will be here shortly and she'll stay the night.' She was gabbling, but she had to get him out of here before her mother arrived or Hannah came back and said something that would betray her.

'She knows?' he asked quietly, indicating her head.

'She phoned just as it happened. Hannah told her.'

'I think that was me.' He stared at her with brooding eyes. 'I was ringing to ask if you could come in a few minutes early to do a short prefix on that report. When Hannah answered the phone and said you'd fallen and needed help, I came straight here. Fortunately I hadn't left the office, so I was on the doorstep, so to speak.' He leant forward and stroked a strand of hair off her face as he spoke, his flesh warm and firm. She felt the contact in every nerve of her body.

'You were very quick,' she managed faintly.

'Tell me about it.' He smiled a crooked smile that would have made her weak at the knees if she wasn't already. 'Fortunately I didn't meet a police car on the way.'

Was this the icy, distant individual she knew? she asked herself unbelievingly. The aloof, cold tycoon who had everyone jumping through hoops at the office, including her?

'Now, first things first.' He eyed her consideringly as he stood up, shrugging his big black overcoat off his shoulders and slinging it on a nearby chair as he strode into her small, gleaming kitchen and lifted the stepladder off the floor. 'I'm going to clean you up a bit and then ring my own doctor—' As she made an exclamation of protest he raised an authoritative hand. 'He's an old friend too and won't mind taking a look at you as a personal favour. Then, if we need to contact your mother, we will, otherwise...' He glanced across at her as he filled a basin with warm water as though he administered first aid to concussed secretaries every day.

'You can ring her in the morning,' he finished quietly. 'I guess she has been pretty upset by…what's happened, too?' The brief pause made her blush scarlet. She had to say something, she had to, even if he was furious—

'Mummeee.' Hannah's voice was a plaintive wail, and as Lydia made to rise Wolf gestured her back on the sofa sharply. 'Lie there and don't move,' he said firmly. 'Where's the damn cat?' As he whisked Tiger up in the palm of one hand Lydia struggled into a sitting position despite his ferocious glare.

'I need to say goodnight to her, reassure her.' She gulped deep in her throat as the room waved and spun. 'Please, Wolf, she'll be awake all night—'

'I'll carry you and the moggy, then.' He plonked Tiger in her arms and, as before, picked her up as though she weighed no more than a feather. It was a bit of a struggle up the narrow stairs, but she was oblivious to his careful manoeuvring. She could feel his heart beating steadily through his shirt, his jacket having been discarded along with his coat, could feel his arms strong and hard as they cradled her to him, see his dark face inches from her own and the smell of him… It was all around her, making her dizzy with an intoxicating delight that was more dangerous than any concussion.

I don't believe this is happening, she thought helplessly as he carried her into Hannah's small bedroom, depositing her and the kitten on the side of the bed, and waiting in silence while she cuddled her daughter and settled her down. 'Mummy needs a rest now, sweet-pea.' She rose as he spoke; she didn't think she could stand a repeat journey in his arms, but he frowned at her grimly before indicating Tiger. 'Hold that.' She did as she was told, and the next moment was being carried from the bedroom despite murmured protests. 'Shut up,

Lydia.' He felt, rather than saw, his way downstairs and once in the lounge proceeded to bathe her head, very gently, before phoning the doctor. That accomplished, he disappeared into the kitchen again and re-emerged with two cups of strong sweet tea.

She was mesmerised by the unusual and dangerously sweet feeling of being looked after for once, and petrified that he would begin to ask questions about Matthew now they were alone. He didn't. He talked softly and inconsequentially about a hundred and one things until the doctor arrived. Wolf let him into the lounge and watched silently while his friend examined her head and established the facts.

'Nothing to worry about, but I'd like you to take it easy for the next day or two.' The good-looking, warm-eyed man smiled down at her gently. 'You're going to feel a trifle sore in the morning, with a head that will be worse than any hang-over you've ever had.'

'I've never had one,' she replied honestly.

'Is that so?' The professional smile faltered just a little and then recovered magnificently. 'I wish I could say the same. I'd rather there was someone around for the next twenty-four hours to keep an eye on you. Is there someone—?'

'I'll sort it, Andrew,' Wolf had cut in before she could open her mouth. 'She won't be alone.'

'Right.' Andrew smiled at her again before leaving the room with Wolf, and she heard the two of them talking quietly in the tiny hall before the front door opened and closed.

'I hope that sofa is comfortable.' As he re-entered the room she saw he had pulled his tie loose again, and despised herself for the way the fact registered hot and warm in her lower stomach.

'What?' She stared at him bewilderedly.

'The sofa.' He smiled slowly. 'If I'm going to spend the night on it I'd prefer a bit of comfort.'

'You can't.' The reply was instinctive, and as his face closed against her she desperately tried to take away the sharpness in her reaction. 'Please, we have to phone my mother,' she gabbled quickly. 'She would never forgive me if I didn't let her know the situation, Wolf, believe me, and she's used to sleeping over the odd night.' He couldn't sleep here, he just couldn't; the idea was somehow totally immoral.

'You don't think it would be kinder to let her have a good night's sleep and phone in the morning?' His voice was expressionless and cool, his eyes hooded.

'No.' She was quite unaware of how frightened her voice sounded. 'If you could ring her and explain? I know she'd want to come over.'

'The number?' His voice was curt, but softened considerably as he talked with her mother for a few moments, his tone reassuring.

'I'll stay until she arrives.' She didn't want him to but didn't dare object, and as he walked over to the chair opposite her and seated himself comfortably in its depths, crossing one muscled leg over the other as he leant back and surveyed her through narrowed eyes, she felt her nerves jump painfully.

'Is it true you've never had a hang-over?' he asked suddenly, his voice quiet. He could believe it, he thought tightly. That air of shy vulnerability, the almost tangible innocence— He caught himself abruptly. But she wasn't, was she? There was living proof upstairs of the fact that she was a married woman who knew the facts of life, and that day in the lift... He felt the hardening in his loins that always accompanied the memory, despite his

efforts to erase it. She had melted for him. And Mike
Wilson... Exactly how well did she know him? And was
it merely coincidence that she had arrived in his office
or—? He stopped his thoughts grimly. Hell, this
wouldn't do him any good, he'd better get out of here
as soon as he could...

'I don't drink.' She looked tired and bruised and he
didn't like the way it touched him. 'I don't like the
taste,' she admitted quietly, her voice soft and shaky.

'You don't?' He adjusted his position in the chair and
noticed the way her body tensed. He made her nervous.
Or was it that she was frightened of men in general?
Had this husband of hers abused her? He was surprised
at the murderous rage the thought provoked. He definitely needed to get out of here...

'You'd better get to bed,' he said abruptly as he rose
and took the two empty cups into the kitchen. 'Your
mother will be here in a couple of minutes or so. I'll let
her in and then disappear. Can you manage the stairs or
shall I help you?' His voice was suddenly brusque and
distant.

'I'll be fine,' she said quietly.

'OK. Goodnight, Lydia.' It was a clear dismissal.

Now what? she thought, as hurt mingled with anger.
Suddenly he was the ice-man again, infinitely cold. She
rose slowly and walked hesitantly to the kitchen where
he was rinsing the cups under the tap. 'Thank you,
Wolf.'

'For what?' He turned, his big body taut and his face
cool, and she shrugged helplessly, finding words difficult.

'For coming round, for helping.'

'Forget it.' He smiled, but it didn't reach his eyes. 'I'd
do the same for anyone. Take a couple of days off and

I'll see you next week, OK?' He turned away, his body tense.

She stared at him a moment longer and then nodded quietly before turning and leaving the room, but the big body didn't move until he heard her footsteps upstairs, and then he leant against the sink with his arms out-stretched as he forced his body to relax. Dammit, he didn't need this. If there was one thing he didn't need it was this.

It was some minutes later when Lydia heard the sound of her mother's key in the lock and then her voice talk-ing with Wolf briefly, and again her stomach clenched with nerves.

As she heard the front door quietly close and then the sound of his car starting in the street below Lydia twisted miserably in the big bed. Her head was pounding in spite of the pills the doctor had given her and her whole body felt as though a herd of cows had been trampling on it, but the weight of her conscience made the physical af-flictions unimportant. *She should have told him.* She curled up into a small ball as her mind ground on. Some-how this thing seemed to have snowballed and it was all her fault. Hot tears pricked against the back of her eyes and she sniffed disconsolately. He had been so kind in spite of the fact that he had obviously wanted to be else-where. She remembered his stony face in the kitchen and sighed wretchedly. She'd ruined his evening… Had he been going to see Elda? The thought brought her abruptly upwards in the bed and a flash of hot pain speared her brain as her mother tapped carefully on the bedroom door.

'How are you feeling?'

'More embarrassed than anything at causing such a fuss,' Lydia replied quietly. 'Thanks for coming, Mum.'

They talked for a few moments before her mother went downstairs to make herself a cup of cocoa, and then she was alone with her thoughts again, thoughts she just couldn't control. Thoughts that centred around the feel of his body as he had carried her close to him, his strong muscled arms and broad chest... She closed her eyes tightly and prayed for control, but it was difficult with the smell of his aftershave still clinging to her hair where she had rested her head against his face. And he was probably with Elda now.

At that thought the tears that had been held at bay by sheer will-power began to trickle from beneath her closed eyelids, soon to become a flood and then the flood a torrent. She should never have gone to work for him, it just wasn't working out. He had been so strange to-night: helping her, taking care of things, but overall that sense of cool aloofness, of cold reserve was what she remembered most, despite his gentleness. He had helped her because it had been the right thing to do in his eyes, that was all. She felt suddenly that he didn't even like her very much. And if she told him Matthew had been dead for three years? That she had deliberately misled him in order to secure the job as his secretary? She cringed mentally. He'd be absolutely livid and rightly so. Her mouth twisted in self-contempt. What was that ditty she'd learnt at Hannah's age? 'Oh, what a tangled web we weave when first we practise to deceive.' She hadn't known how true it was, she reflected miserably.

She pictured his face, eyes blazing and mouth tight with rage, and knew she didn't have the courage to tell him the truth. It was her last coherent thought before sleep overcame her.

CHAPTER FOUR

'LYDIA?' As she heard Wolf's deep voice on the other end of the phone she forced herself to take a steadying breath before she attempted to reply.

'Yes?' She didn't acknowledge that she recognised his voice; she couldn't, somehow.

'It's Wolf.' The tone was pleasant and cool, with just the right amount of polite concern that was fitting for an employer to an employee. 'I trust you're feeling considerably better this morning? I expected your mother to answer the phone.'

'I'm fine, thank you.' She didn't mention she had persuaded her mother to leave once breakfast was over. Wolf was the type of man to whom twenty-four hours meant twenty-four hours, and she had the feeling he wouldn't be too pleased at her flouting the doctor's advice, but years ago, just after Matthew's death, the two women had decided that if their close relationship was going to hold fast it was necessary that each understood they had to lead totally independent lives while still being available for each other when the need arose. Today was her mother's bridge morning and there was no good reason why she should miss a little event she looked forward to all week. 'It was good of you to help out last night,' she added carefully.

'No problem.' There was a brief pause. 'I'll see you on Monday morning, then.'

'I could come in tomorrow if you like, there's no—'

'Monday morning.' His voice was abrupt, and for an

instant she pictured him at his desk, hard blue eyes narrowed and mouth straight. Her heart did a strange little somersault and she bit on her lower lip hard. The man seemed to get under her skin with no effort and it was most disconcerting, especially as she didn't affect him at all. 'There is absolutely no point in you pushing yourself when it isn't necessary,' he continued calmly. 'It might mean you have to have more time off in the long run.'

'I suppose so,' she agreed quietly. 'It's just that there are one or two important items of correspondence I was going to do first thing. That addition to the report, for instance—'

'It's already been dealt with.' His tone was not unkind but it brought home to her how little he really needed her. Anyone would do. Any reasonably capable secretary. She felt her heart thud painfully. For goodness' sake pull yourself together and stop being so pathetic, Lydia, she told herself angrily.

'Is there—?' He stopped abruptly and then continued in an almost expressionless voice. 'Is there anything you need over the weekend? Anything you'd like me to drop in?'

If only he was offering because he cared in some way rather than through a sense of duty, she thought painfully. But he had made it perfectly clear the last few minutes he was in the house that she was at best an irritation, at worst a burden. She wouldn't ask him for a thing.

'No, thank you.' She tried to sound as impersonal and brisk as she could, considering the sound of his voice was sending her insides whirling. 'Everything's under control.'

'I'm sure it is.' His voice was dry now and very distant. 'You are a very independent lady, aren't you?'

'Am I?' There was a note of surprise in her voice. 'I suppose I am,' she added quietly, unsure of how to react.

'Very independent and very single-minded,' the sardonic voice continued. 'A formidable combination, if I may say so. Goodbye, Lydia.'

'Goodbye,' she said quietly, unaware of the forlorn note in her soft voice. There was a split second of hesitation and then the phone was replaced at the other end, leaving her with a monotonous buzz to say the call had ended.

The weekend dragged by on leaden feet, but then it seemed as though Monday morning had arrived too fast as she got ready for work, her stomach churning. She pulled a few strands of her hair forward, cutting it in a soft fringe to hide the cut on her forehead, and outwardly at least no sign of the accident was showing as she walked into the office later. Inwardly the whole incident, or more correctly Wolf's part in it, had affected her far more than she cared to admit. Hannah had plagued her all weekend with requests to see 'the nice man' again, and in the finish she had had to be uncharacteristically sharp with her small daughter to get her to stop, which had then resulted in a massive guilt session.

All in all, everything seems wrong, she thought silently as she hung her coat carefully in the corner of the room, but for no good reason. Or nothing she cared to explore, anyway.

'Good morning.' She hadn't heard the connecting door open, but now as she swung round it was to find Wolf framed in the doorway of his room, a polite smile stitched on an otherwise cold face. 'Fully recovered?' he asked coolly.

'Yes, thank you,' she nodded quickly, annoyed to find she had blushed scarlet and that her pulses had leapt so violently at the sight of him that her heart had run away like an express train. 'Is there anything urgent you'd like me to attend to first?'

'Plenty.' He nodded drily towards her in-tray in which several tapes lay, before turning into his own office and shutting the door. She stared after him as a little curl of angry irritation snaked a path into her mind. So. That was how things stood: no softening of the rigid ice-cool image, nothing approaching even the mildest form of friendship. Fine, just fine. She wasn't here to make friends, after all, she was here to do a job. And she'd make sure he found no fault with her work.

The thought carried her furiously through the day on such a burst of adrenalin that she accomplished an exorbitant amount of work before replacing the cover on her word processor just after five. Wolf had spoken, when necessary, in polite monosyllables which she had answered in like vein, and it wasn't until she was waiting for the tube among a crowd of London commuters that she realised a tension headache was drumming away at the back of her eyes. 'Is it worth it?' she murmured faintly to herself as she rubbed a tired hand across her eyes, opening them to find a portly, well-dressed businessman surveying her with distinct apprehension before edging away down the platform a little. Talking to herself out loud! This was all she needed. But perhaps tomorrow would be better.

It wasn't, nor the next day, nor the next. For some reason the cool, careful formality with which Wolf had always treated her had turned into a cold abruptness that she was at a loss to understand. She hadn't *meant* to fall off the darn ladder! She found herself gnawing at the thought in her lunch-hour on the Friday as she did some shopping, wandering round the large supermarket close to Wolf's office-block without seeing the well-stocked shelves in front of her. Was he mad because she'd interfered with his precious work schedule? But she'd caught up that first day, or very nearly. And she would have come in before Monday if he hadn't vetoed it so firmly. He had to be the most impossible, awkward, intractable man...

She returned to the office with an empty shopping-basket and a deep frown to find Wolf's door firmly shut and that unmistakable throaty giggle deep inside. Elda. The sinking feeling in the pit of her stomach that went hand in hand with the name did an immediate nose-dive. The elegant brunette had already rung twice this week. What on earth did she want, anyway? As if you didn't know, she told herself grimly as she started work again, tapping the silent computer keys with unnecessary vigour. As if you didn't know...

'Lydia, I'm just popping out for a quick lunch— Are you all right?' Wolf stopped dead in the middle of her office with Elda hanging on his arm, and she hastily tried to school her features into something approaching normality. But somehow, as they had left his room, she'd had the strangest feeling that someone had punched her hard in the stomach.

'Of course.' She smiled stiffly but it was the best she could do. 'Have a good lunch.'

'Elda, I'll be down in a moment.' As Wolf disentangled himself from Elda's grasp Lydia saw the beautiful brunette's fine, pencil-thin eyebrows raise themselves a fraction, the blue eyes narrowing thoughtfully before she walked out of the office, shutting the door quietly behind her.

'Something's happened, hasn't it? Is it Matthew?' Wolf moved to stand just in front of her and for a moment the desire to stand up and hit him hard across the face was so strong she could actually taste it. How dared he stand there and pretend he had any interest in her situation one way or the other? How dared he! One minute he had Elda hanging on his arm like a limpet and the next— The flood of unreasonable, unjust rage was immediately swamped by cold hard reason. He was her *boss*, for goodness' sake. Of course he would care that she might be less than the perfectly efficient, one hundred percent operational machine he was used to. The thought didn't help.

'It's nothing.' Her smile was brittle and the sharp blue eyes watching her narrowed thoughtfully. 'It won't affect my work and—'

'Damn your work!' The words were an explosion and for a moment the stillness that followed was absolute. 'Lydia, do you need someone to talk to? I mean—' He stopped abruptly and seemed to collect himself before continuing. 'There are counselling places for situations like this. Have you considered—?'

'I don't want to talk to anyone.' She lowered her head as she spoke—that blue gaze was unnerving—and missed the tiny instinctive movement he took towards her before it was firmly checked. He thought she was cracking up, was that it?

'I see.' There was a moment of silence and then he spoke again, his words bringing her head sharply upwards, her eyes angry. 'Have you considered Hannah in all this? It might be a form of indulgence to try and get through by yourself.'

He did think she was cracking up, she thought tersely. He didn't credit her with any guts at all.

'I always put Hannah first in everything I do.' She glared at him furiously even as she acknowledged that from his viewpoint it was a reasonable comment. She had to tell him. Now. Before she lost her nerve. 'Actually there is something I have to tell you—'

'Wolf, the taxi's waiting.' The words died on her lips as Elda's dark head peered round the door. 'I'm sorry, but I really can't be late for that appointment at two...' The big blue eyes were prettily penitent.

For a moment Lydia thought Wolf was going to snap at the lovely brunette as his head swung round and his eyes narrowed into slits of ice, but then he took a deep breath, that iron control she had seen so often in the last few weeks springing into place, and when he spoke his voice was pleasant, if cool. 'OK, Elda, don't fret.' He moved across and took the other woman's arm, gently turning her round and out of the doorway. 'I'll be back at two,' he said over his shoulder to Lydia. 'We'll continue this conversation then.' The door shut with a firm, cool click.

Over my dead body. She stared at the closed door bleakly. Definitely over my dead body. The moment had come and gone and she just wouldn't have the courage to admit the truth with no lead-in. Besides which, what if he should subsequently ask why she had been looking so wretched when he and Elda had left his office? What could she say then? That she was jealous? The thought shocked her into an immediate denial. She wasn't. Of course she wasn't. How could she be jealous of someone she didn't even like? She bit her lip hard. She might find him physically attractive but that was all, and no doubt there were hundreds of men who were just as attractive but normal human beings as well. Not blocks of ice. And he *had* wanted an efficient, capable secretary for a few months. Which she was. That was all that mattered to him. She sank back in her seat despondently. So why did she feel so horribly guilty?

When Wolf returned just before two she lowered her head immediately to her work after a cursory good afternoon, her cheeks flushing scarlet, hoping he'd let the matter drop.

'I'd like a word in my office, please, Lydia.'

She didn't move as he strode across the room but as he opened his door she spoke quickly, her voice steady. 'If it's about what was said earlier, I'd rather not.' She raised her head slowly.

He turned with his hand on the door-handle, his big body taut and straight and his eyes cold. 'What was said earlier? I wasn't aware anything *was* said. That is precisely—'

'And I think it's best that way. I'm sorry.' A faint trace of Elda's heavy, musky perfume had come into the room with him and that, combined with the oblique sarcasm in his dark voice, strengthened her resolve.

'I see.' He eyed her grimly. 'And if I think differently?'

She stared at him, faintly nonplussed. 'Well, why should you?' She gestured towards the word processor in front of her. 'My work isn't suffering and my private life is my own concern. I only work here and that's temporary—'

'I'm well aware of that!' The words had been a sharp bark and his eyes glittered dangerously for one long moment before she saw him take an almost visible control on his temper. 'You do understand I can't afford your concentration to be anything less than one hundred per cent?' he asked stiffly, after a long taut moment of silence.

'Yes.' She stared up at him, trying to keep calm. 'And I've already said that my work isn't suffering.'

'I heard you.' He glared at her as though she had just admitted to some heinous crime. 'But would you accept that you aren't the best judge of that at the moment?' He raised his hand as she went to reply, his face autocratic. 'It is well known that a marriage breakdown causes the sort of stress that is only a little less than a bereavement. You might feel you're coping fine, but surely to talk to someone else, an independent stranger if you like, wouldn't do any harm? If only to find out exactly what you do want.'

'There is no need.' She called on every shred of willpower she possessed and managed a bright, dismissive smile which in the face of his dark frown was Oscarwinning stuff. 'I've told you I'm all right and I am—Hannah too. I've been used to coping with things on my own for some time now.' That much at least was true. 'The last few weeks haven't changed anything.'

He opened his mouth to reply just as the telephone rang shrilly by her side, and never had she been more pleased at an interruption. She whisked it up before he could say a word, her face as blank as she could make it. 'Good afternoon. Mr Strade's secretary speaking.'

'Is he there?' The husky female voice didn't bother to identify itself but it didn't matter. Lydia would have recognised it anywhere. 'I've left my gloves in his office.'

'It's Elda.' She raised cool eyes to his. 'Missing gloves?' He swore, softly but vehemently, and strode into his office.

Wonderful. She sat quite still as the heavy thudding of her heart began to settle. Absolutely wonderful. No amount of money was worth this.

The rest of the afternoon passed in comparative peace for the simple reason that Wolf didn't step out of his office once and she didn't venture in. At exactly five o'clock she slipped the cover on the word processor and left an impressive pile of finished work at the side of it. She was going home now and nothing was going to stop her. She'd had enough. He'd probably berate her on Monday because she hadn't taken the work in but she couldn't, she just couldn't. She needed at least forty-eight hours to charge up her batteries before she faced him again.

The lift doors were just closing when she heard his voice. 'Hold it.'

It was reflex action that made her keep the doors open for him, but as he stepped into the lift with a brief nod of thanks she wished she hadn't. He was dressed in a black dinner-jacket, the dusky red shirt and silk bow tie enhancing his tanned skin and black hair, and the superb cut of the jacket making his broad shoulders even broader. He looked devastating. Devastating and over-whelmingly attractive, and she felt her knees grow weak. This wasn't fair, it just wasn't fair. Damn that little washroom. 'Thanks.' She noticed he was still carrying his briefcase despite the evening wear, and suddenly the remembrance of the last time she had been in a lift with him turned her face crimson. 'I'm already late,' he added with a slight frown.

'Going somewhere nice?' She forced the words through numb lips and was surprised at how normal her voice sounded. What was happening to her? She didn't want to feel like this; it was making a mockery of everything she had thought she was.

'A somewhat boring reception.' He smiled briefly. 'But then to the opera, so the whole evening won't be a total disaster.' He glanced at his watch before speaking again. 'I can drop you off on the way—it's in the right direction.'

'There's no need—'

The blue eyes fastened on her, a dark, satirical gleam in their depths, and her voice trailed away. 'I can drop you off on the way,' he repeated quietly, his voice silky with an underlying thread of iron.

A gust of rain, the drops needle-sharp and icy, met their faces as they left the warmth of the building, and as Lydia slid into Wolf's Mercedes she was aware of a small feeling of relief that she hadn't got to fight her way home with the rest of the commuters on such a filthy night. It vanished instantly as he joined her in the car, the enclosed confines of the beautiful vehicle bringing him much too close for comfort. She glanced at him under her eyelashes as he manoeuvred into a place in the fast-flowing traffic. The dark hair was slicked back and he looked as though he'd just shaved; who had he gone to so much trouble for? She was immediately furious with herself for thinking such a thing. It was none of her business, and what did it matter? He was just her boss, after all.

He drove swiftly and competently through the cold London night as the rain beat a steady tattoo on the windscreen, the wipers labouring to clear the window at times as sudden squalls threw gusts of hail in their path. The silence between them lengthened but she felt quite unable to break it, and he seemed to be in a world of his own, his eyes concentrating on the road ahead and his mouth tight and grim.

'Thank you.' As they drew up outside her house she turned to him, forcing a smile on her face. 'I hope you have a good time tonight.'

'I will.' He didn't smile back. 'It's guaranteed.'

'Guaranteed?' And then the penny dropped. 'Oh, it's someone special, then?' Elda. She might have known.

'Someone…' His eyes narrowed as if in puzzlement and then cleared abruptly. 'Not exactly, Lydia, no. But the company I shall be with know how to enjoy themselves. That is a prerequisite if they expect me to attend.'

She stared at him, her eyes darkening at the harshness in his tone. He sounded angry with her, and after the miserable week she'd had she fired back without stopping to consider her words. 'By company I take it you mean women?' She raised her chin as she met the ice-blue gaze head on.

'If I had meant women I would have said so,' he said coldly, 'but, as it happens, I do expect my female companions to be good company, yes. When I acquire a good suit I don't mind going to some lengths to make sure the measurements are right and the cloth suitable, and I pay for the best, but having done all that I expect it to be on time, precisely to my requirements and prepared to fit me exactly.'

She couldn't believe her ears. '*A suit*?' The rain still continued to drum down on the roof of the car but neither of them was aware of the outside world as they faced each other like two gladiators about to enter the ring. 'We're talking about a man and woman relationship here, not a cut-and-dried purchase of an expendable item.'

'Isn't it the same thing?' His face and voice were perfectly expressionless but the piercing eyes were watching her intently, their blueness as sharp as glass.

'Are you telling me…?' Her voice faltered. He couldn't be saying what she thought he was saying. Not a man like him. Handsome, inordinately wealthy, with the world, or his own part of it at least, at his feet. It was ludicrous. 'Are you saying you pay for your women?' she asked faintly.

'Of course not.' He was instantly and angrily scathing. 'Not in the way you mean.' He eyed her sardonically, his lip curling at her confusion. 'But what I *do* mean is that the females of my acquaintance expect to be wined and dined in some…comfort, escorted to all the right places—you know the routine.'

'I don't, actually.' She was sitting very straight in her seat now, her cheeks fiery but her eyes steady as they watched his face. 'And I'm very glad I don't.'

'Oh, come on, Lydia,' he drawled lazily, with a small, mocking smile that didn't reach his eyes. 'You are a very beautiful and desirable woman and I'm sure you must have had lots of men-friends before you married your husband. Are you telling me you didn't get the most out of them you could?'

'Now, just hang on a minute,' she interrupted frostily as a flood of burning hot rage swept through her small frame. 'Just hang on a darn minute! Don't you dare make assumptions about me, Wolf Strade.' She forgot he was her boss, forgot all the normal social niceties such a relationship warranted, as her eyes filled with rage and her body became as taut as a bow. 'Matthew was my first and only boyfriend, as it happened. We grew up together from children, and if you expect me to apologise for that you've got another think coming.'

'Lydia—'

But she was in no mood to listen and swept on, her next words hardening the face that had softened at her admission. 'It sounds to me as if you get exactly what you deserve in your relationships. If all you're interested in is someone to grace your table and your bed, a live

doll with the right connections, not to mention proportions— '

'I merely choose women of like mind,' he interrupted
coldly, 'who are happy with no commitment, no ties.'

'No, you don't.' He stiffened at the challenge, but she
was too angry to notice. 'You *choose* women who are
shallow and materialistic, who have no real values.
That's what you do.' Her eyes were flashing fire. 'Your
earlier comments when you lumped the whole female
sex together in one greedy package prove that! And what
on earth is with this "choosing" idea, anyway? Women
aren't clothes that you can select at will and wear for a
time before you dispose of them—not *real* women. But
if you only shop in the tinsel and glitter department that
is all you're going to see, isn't it? A real relationship
isn't a matter of choosing in the way you mean, with
one person selecting another like a lump of meat.'

'You're being ridiculous.' His voice was deadly cold.

'You didn't like it when I thought you paid for your
women, but really that's exactly what you do,' she said
slowly. 'All the time. Not with money, nothing as crude
as that, but with the places you take them so they can
be seen, the presents and attention they take as their
right, even your performance in bed. You pay, Wolf.
Don't fool yourself.' She stared him straight in the eyes,
her cheeks scarlet.

'My *performance* in bed?' He hadn't liked that last
bit, she could tell from the way his face hardened almost
savagely. 'So you think I give a performance, do you?'

As he leant over her the warm, clean fragrance of his
skin mingled with the intoxicating sensuality of his aftershave and she felt her senses begin to spin even before
his mouth came down on hers. She had expected anger,
violence, but the moment his lips touched hers she real-

ised this was a deliberate assault on her senses, a subtle form of punishment for her condemning words but one she was powerless to resist. The kiss was more teasing than penetrating…at first. She could have moved away—he wasn't holding her, after all, his mouth just lightly resting on hers—but it wasn't until much later that she realised the idea had never even occurred to her. And then the kiss became more demanding, his tongue exploring the soft contours of her lips and mouth and causing tiny helpless shivers to shudder down her spine. She had never guessed it could be like this… The same emotions she had felt that day in the lift returned to torment her. She was twenty-seven years of age, had a small daughter who was all her own, and yet it was as though she had never been kissed before in her life. The thought had the power to jerk her away from Wolf as though she had been burnt. How could she betray Matthew's memory like that? And with a man like Wolf Strade? And especially after what he had just said?

'Lydia—'

As she wrenched open the door and stumbled out of the car she heard him call to her, but she sped across the street and up the steps to the house without a backward glance, thrusting her key into the lock and almost falling into the small hall as though it were a real wolf that was after her, fangs open for the kill and hard yellow eyes dilated.

How had that happened? She looked dazedly into the small mirror in the bathroom some minutes later, after a furious bout of weeping, and sniffed dismally. Hannah would be home soon. She had gone to tea with Sophie, and Sophie's mother was dropping her home just after half past six. She had to pull herself together and act normally. She'd think about this later.

But when later came, in the quiet and solitude of her lonely bed, she was no nearer to an answer. All she knew was that from the moment she had laid eyes on Wolf Strade her world had turned upside-down, and her with it. She wasn't the person she had known for twenty-seven years; there was some other being working there inside her skin. A passionate, tempestuous, strange being with hidden desires and cravings that the old Lydia found more than a little shocking. It didn't help that the rest of the female population seemed to find him equally attractive. She remembered a conversation she had overheard the week before when she had been sitting quietly in the canteen one lunchtime. Two of the junior secretaries had been seated at a table just round the corner from her, and although she wasn't visible to their gaze every word they had spoken had registered loud and clear.

'He's such an out-and-out dish.' A deep sigh had followed the statement, along with the sound of chairs being pulled out, and Lydia had grimaced sympathetically for whoever had spoken. They'd certainly got it bad! There had been a wealth of hunger in the female voice. Boyfriend trouble, perhaps?

'I know.' The other girl had added her sigh. 'But there's no way he'd look at me or you, Carol.'

'Well, I can dream, can't I?' the first voice had said, a little indignantly.

'By all means, dream on, but as far as I know he's never dated an employee—not his style.'

'Well, with the women he can have at his beck and call, it's not to be wondered at, is it?' the said Carol had replied tersely. 'Did you see that photo in the paper a few months back. ''Wolf Strade and friend'', the caption said. Some friend! With a figure like she'd got I bet they

didn't play ludo all night.' A small, suggestive giggle
had followed.

'*Carol*!'

'Well… It makes me mad. Why can't men see that
ordinary working girls can be fun too?' Carol had said
petulantly.

'You're getting positively sour in your old age,' the
other voice had said laughingly. 'And anyway, he'd be
too much for you to handle. He was married once, you
know, and since then he's had more women than I've
had hot dinners, if only a quarter of the rumours about
him are true.'

'Oh, they'd be true,' Carol had sighed resignedly.
'You've only to look into those beautiful blue eyes to
know they'd be true, and frankly I'd be prepared to let
him teach me anything, *anything* he knows.'

Lydia had left the canteen at that point but the
women's conversation had stayed with her all day, try
as she might to dismiss it from her mind, and even now
she could remember every word. It was stupid and irrational and quite out of character, but she had felt like
slapping both of them, and that had horrified her almost
as much as the fact that she had sat and listened to a
private conversation. *Had* he been married? she wondered fretfully. And, if so, how had it ended and where
was his ex now? What was the matter with her? She
shook herself angrily. It was none of her business, *it
wasn't*.

But *why* had he kissed her? She twisted restlessly in
the big bed. Did he think she was easy, like some of the
other women who threw themselves at him so blatantly?
Well, she'd hardly done anything to dissuade him from
such a line of thought, she reminded herself miserably.

She had returned the kiss until the very last moment.

She knew it and he would have known it. He hadn't been holding her, trapping her in any way; she had been perfectly free to move away if she'd so wished. But she hadn't! The thought brought on a fresh deluge of humiliation and she sat up to punch her pillows violently into shape.

This couldn't continue. She'd be a nervous wreck if she worked for him much longer. The thought gathered steam as she lay there in the soft darkness, and by the time she drifted into a restless, troubled sleep her mind was made up.

She was leaving Strade Engineering and she would tell him so first thing on Monday morning. Desperate situations needed desperate measures, and right now that was exactly how she felt—desperate.

CHAPTER FIVE

LYDIA dressed very carefully for work the following Monday, choosing a demure high-necked blouse in pale coffee and a calf-length full skirt in a darker shade, securing her hair in a tight French plait that she fixed with grim fierceness, and allowing herself just the merest touch of eyeshadow on her wide eyelids. There. She checked herself in the mirror just before she left to take Hannah to nursery. He couldn't say there was the remotest suggestion of a come-on in this chaste ensemble. She had tormented herself all weekend with the thought that she might have encouraged him in some way, although in all honesty she couldn't see how. But she intended to be all cool efficiency this morning, composed and calm when she told him she would be leaving at the end of the week. Her stomach turned over at the thought. Stop it, she told herself silently. Wolf Strade will be like a shadowy dream in a few months, an indistinct, vague phantom relegated firmly to the past.

The vague phantom was prowling about her office when she arrived some time later, a sheaf of papers in his hand and a ferocious scowl on his face. 'I've been here all weekend.' He glared at her as if it were her fault. 'Those fools in my Scotland office have nearly lost us the biggest order we've ever had through sheer incompetence. Can you be ready to leave in a couple of hours?'

'Leave?' She stared at him as though he were mad.

'For Scotland.' He gestured irritably as though she

were being deliberately obtuse. 'If I don't salvage this thing now, in the next twenty-four hours, I can kiss over five million pounds goodbye.'

It was an unfortunate choice of words, but even as she felt her cheeks burn she saw the import of the phrase hadn't registered with him at all. He was in business mode, all his energies concentrated on the job in hand and it was unlikely that he even remembered Friday evening. And for this she had been devastated all weekend? She glared back at him now as her thoughts brought sparks to her eyes. 'What time do you want to go?'

'Lunchtime.'

'Right.'

He hadn't even noticed her abruptness, she thought painfully as he strode back into his office, growling instructions about the pile of papers on her desk as he went. He was impossible. Absolutely impossible.

She phoned her mother, who assured her she would love to take care of Hannah for a few days, phoned the nursery to say she would be dropping in a little later to explain things to Hannah and say goodbye, and then worked frantically on the more urgent correspondence before taking it, and a cup of black coffee, in to him mid-morning. He was sitting at his desk as she entered the room, and looked tired to death.

'Coffee?' She indicated the cup as she placed the papers in front of him. 'You look as if you need it.'

'I don't know if I can pull this one round, Lydia.'

No. As she stared at his face, uncharacteristically doubtful and faintly boyish, she felt her heart thud painfully. Don't do this to me. Not now. Fury, temper, irritability she could cope with, but not this weariness that was putting a grey tinge of exhaustion on the handsome face and made her want to gather him up in her arms and kiss all the anxiety away. Against that her heart had no defence at all.

'You're tired,' she said as matter-of-factly as she could, considering she was aching to give more than verbal reassurance. 'How much sleep have you had in the last forty-eight hours, anyway?' she added reprovingly.

'Sleep?' He looked up at her as though she were talking a foreign language. 'I've cat-napped once or twice, I think.'

'And food?' She stared down at him severely. 'Have you eaten?'

'Some sandwiches some time yesterday.' He had been sipping the coffee as they talked and already a tinge of the old mordant note was back in his voice. 'And don't fuss, woman. I can't stand fussing.' He eyed her sardonically.

'Nevertheless, you need someone to keep an eye on you.' She smiled in what she hoped was a cool, secretarial way, but he didn't smile back as he looked up at her, the piercing eyes suddenly very clear and blue.

'No, I don't.' They both knew he was answering the light comment with more seriousness than it had warranted. 'Some people aren't meant to form bonds, Lydia, not even in the mildest sense. They walk through life alone because they are a danger to themselves and other people if they don't.'

'Do you think so?' She didn't know how to reply, what to say, and was floundering badly.

'I know so.' He looked at her for one more long moment and then lowered his head to the papers. 'Believe me, I *do* know so.'

'Oh.' As she stood looking down at his bent head an almost irrepressible urge to ask more, to delve deeper, brought her lips firmly clamping shut. She was his temporary secretary, that was all, and he had just reminded her of it in the nicest way he could. Take it on board and be smart, she told herself silently, protect yourself. For all you know he is probably still in love with his ex-wife, despite all those other women.

'I'd like to say goodbye to Hannah before I leave for Scotland,' she said, after a few seconds of absolute silence. 'And of course I shall need to collect some clothes and things. How long do you think we'll be away?'

'Two or three days, four at the most.' He looked up and she saw his face was the old expressionless mask again, withdrawn and remote. 'And of course you must see Hannah. The flight is booked for two this afternoon but we need to be at the airport a little earlier. If you want to scoot off now and see to things, I'll pick you up just before one.'

She nodded and left the office without another word, but just as she was preparing to leave she picked up the internal phone on impulse and ordered a hot meal from the canteen to be brought up immediately. He might call it fussing, he might call it a lot worse, but he couldn't carry on at this pace without burning himself out. And she didn't want that. She checked the weakness quickly in her mind but it was no good. She was concerned about him even as she told herself it was foolish.

By half-past twelve she was packed and scribbling a short list of notes to her mother as she sat with a cup of coffee on the occasional table beside her and Tiger purring contentedly on her lap. Her mother had offered to stay at Lydia's house in order that Hannah's routine was interrupted as little as possible so there was little to organise. Hannah herself had accepted the news quite stoically in spite of it being the first time they had been parted since she was born. Several of her friends' parents were often away on business so the idea was not new to her, besides which the present Lydia had mentioned would be brought on her return had been a definite plus.

As Lydia glanced at the small suitcase by the door her lip curled in wry self-mockery. Dashing off to Scotland with him was a little different from her plans of the weekend! She shook her head at her own weakness. But she couldn't let him down in an emergency. There was time to tell him she intended to leave later, once they were back in London again.

His authoritative knock just before one set the butterflies whizzing frantically in her stomach and she took a long deep breath as she opened the door. 'Hi.' Was it her imagination or was he faintly sheepish? she asked herself silently as he walked through and picked up the small suitcase. 'Thanks for ordering the meal.' He put the suitcase down again and turned to face her, his eyes wary. 'And I never said I appreciate you responding so well to the emergency.'

'It comes with the job.' She hoped she looked cool and composed because she certainly didn't feel it. He seemed to have more personality changes in the space of an hour than the rest of the people she knew put together. 'You did warn me I might have to take off at a minute's notice at my interview,' she said lightly.

'Nevertheless, it was good of you.' He looked so gorgeous as he dominated her small lounge that she felt the blood positively pounding through her veins. 'Thank you.'

'No problem.' She smiled carefully.

'Did Hannah take the news of the trip OK?' he asked quietly as he looked at her steadily through clear silver-blue eyes.

'Fine.' She smiled carefully again, aiming for lightness. 'My mother is very good with her, they get on like a house on fire, so I never need to worry if I can't be with her.'

'That's good.' He eyed her soberly. 'It must be reassuring for you to know she's in good hands.'

'It is.' She glanced at him, faintly puzzled. It was almost as though he was hesitating about something, but perhaps it was her imagination. She certainly couldn't trust her feelings around this man, that was for sure. 'There's no one like your own mother, after all.'

'I should imagine not.' The words were faintly enigmatic but she sensed he hadn't meant them to be.

'Do your parents live close by?' she asked quietly, feeling as though she was treading on thin ice. It would have been a normal, polite pleasantry with most people, but with Wolf the normal wasn't, somehow.

'My mother died in an accident when I was about eighteen months old, so unfortunately I can't remember anything of her,' he answered shortly, 'and my father lives in New Zealand. We communicate regularly, he's a great guy, but due to the distance we only meet a few times a year.' He shrugged dismissively.

'Oh…' Her tender heart was touched and it showed. 'That's a shame.' His face closed immediately, his mouth straightening.

'I've never looked at it that way.' It was a definite snub, but in view of the fact that he had just told her he'd lost his mother at such an early age, she found it washed over her head.

'Well, I would.' She looked him straight in the face now. 'I think families are important.'

'Do you?' He smiled slightly at her vehemence and she saw the hard face relax slightly. 'Well, I suppose

I'm not the best judge of that. My mother was killed on an expedition my father had organised, and I think he always felt the fault was his. They were very much in love and it took him many years to get over her death. In the meantime I was cared for by a nanny and various servants in whatever country we happened to be in until I went to boarding-school in England at the age of eight. I never really got to know my father until just a few years ago when—' He stopped abruptly. 'When I was passing through a bad time,' he finished shortly. 'He was a tower of strength and we found we had more in common than we thought.'

'You must have travelled extensively, then, when you were younger?' She felt the personal revelations were alien to him and sat uncomfortably on his shoulders, and aimed at lightening the mood.

'And how.' He grinned suddenly and, as before, it did something to her heart that was acutely uncomfortable. 'But it had its advantages although I didn't appreciate them at the time. I can speak fluent French, German, Italian and Greek and have a smattering of several other languages, all directly attributable to my nomadic beginnings. Once I was taught languages officially at school I found I had absorbed far more in my early years than I had known.'

'That's good.' It hurt her, far, far more than it should have done, that he hadn't had a mother's love. Ridiculous, and he would be furious if he knew what she was thinking, but the thought of the boy Wolf being cared for by paid employees hit a nerve inside her that was distinctly painful.

'Did you enjoy school?' she asked as she slipped into her jacket, keeping her voice casual. He mustn't guess that these tiny glimpses into his personal life were of intense interest.

'Yes, I did, actually.' There was a note of surprise in his voice as though he imagined he shouldn't have. 'Most of the other boys were always aching to get home and see their folks, but as that didn't apply to me I found school life fulfilling and interesting. My father sent me to a good school and always provided the cash for any activities I wanted to take up.'

'Did he?' But he wasn't around, she thought painfully, for the childish confidences and sharing of troubles that were so important in adolescence. He had had to cope alone.

'What about you?' He smiled down at her and her heart flipped over. 'The regulation two-point-four family?' he asked teasingly.

'Almost.' She smiled back carefully. 'My parents just had me and the dog. They wanted more children but somehow, after me, it just didn't happen. Then Dad died when I was twelve and I guess from that point Matthew took over looking after me. He was brilliant to me and Mum,' she finished flatly. 'I'll never forget that.'

'Of course you won't.' His voice had stiffened but she didn't notice as she reached for her handbag. As she turned to him again he gestured towards a large framed photograph of herself and Matthew that she kept on a small coffee-table under the window at one end of the room. She had felt in the early days that it was important for Hannah to see and recognise her father as much as possible as she would never see him again, and the idea had worked well. When asked by another child at nursery why her Daddy never came to pick her up, Hannah answered quite cheerfully and without a moment's hesitation that her Daddy was in heaven and liked toast and marmalade for breakfast.

'Where did she get that last bit from?' the teacher who had reported the children's conversation had asked Lydia when she had arrived to pick Hannah up in the evening.

'That's *her* favourite breakfast,' Lydia had replied quietly, her eyes warm as she had watched her small daughter playing with a group of friends. She was secure and happy and contented. Matthew couldn't have wished for more. She hadn't failed him.

'Lydia?' She was brought back to the present with a jolt as she realised Wolf was looking straight at her, his mouth tight. 'Have you seen him recently?'

'Seen him…?' The suddenness of the question flummoxed her completely. 'Matthew? No…'

'And is there any chance of the two of you getting back together again?' he asked, still in the strange, blank, hard voice as he watched her tightly through cool blue eyes.

'Wolf—'

'Just answer yes or no, Lydia.' His eyes were totally expressionless and as blue as a summer sky. 'Is there a chance?'

'No.' She took a deep breath. 'But—'

'We've got to go.' He picked up the suitcase and strode to the door, waiting for her to precede him. 'We're going to cut it fine and we need to be on that flight.'

He had known she was going to talk about Matthew and he hadn't wanted her to, but why not? Lydia asked herself bemusedly as she walked out into the street to see a taxi-cab waiting patiently. Why ask her about him like that if he didn't want her to explain? But then he wouldn't want to get involved, would he? His earlier words about relationships flooded her mind. If he could ascertain that his temporary secretary wasn't likely to have any difficult emotional outbursts that might affect her capability, if he could be reasonably sure that the estranged husband wasn't likely to cause problems with his efficient machine... That was all he was interested in, after all. The grey day outside suddenly seemed a shade greyer. But why had he kissed her? Once seated in the taxi Wolf sat staring silently out of the window and she glanced at the hard profile under her lashes. He was an enigma. She felt a moment of deep and painful confusion. She had never met anyone she understood less.

Once the formalities were completed they were settled comfortably on the plane and she couldn't fault Wolf's courtesy in the way he treated her but...it was so cold. Chillingly so.

And in the taxi, the departure lounge, and now here on the plane, he was so very careful not to touch her, to make sure that not a part of his body came into contact with hers.

'Wolf?' She touched his arm to get his attention and felt powerful muscles tense under her hand. 'Have I done something to annoy you? Recently, that is...' She smiled carefully as she kept her voice light. Observation of this man over the last few weeks had shown her that any display of emotion, however slight, was met with an expressionless mask.

'Annoy?' He turned to her, his face cool and hard and his mouth cynical as he prepared to make an easy rejoinder, but as he did so blue eyes met soft, velvety brown ones and the words seemed to die in his throat as their gaze joined and held. She could feel herself begin to drown in the silver-blue sea of his eyes as time hung suspended in a sapphire mist, the thud of her heart and pounding of the blood through her veins the only things that convinced her this was happening. And then his face came slowly closer, as though something outside himself had control over his actions, and his warm lips brushed tantalisingly over her half-open mouth, their touch provocative. 'So soft and beautiful...' She could barely hear the murmured words, and the next instant he had settled back into his own seat, his eyes shadowed and unfathomable. 'You haven't annoyed me, Lydia.' She had forgotten her original question and blinked at him in surprise before she pulled herself together. He was dangerous. Oh, he was so, so dangerous.

'Good.' She smiled brightly and forced herself to reach forward and select a magazine from the pile the efficient blonde stewardess had brought her a few minutes before. 'That's all right, then.' She hoped the trembling that had spread into every fibre of her body wasn't visible to those sharp, ice-blue eyes but as she glanced at him, the brittle smile held in place by sheer will-power, she saw he was reaching for his briefcase, his face distant and preoccupied as though he had forgotten her already. She knew a moment's deep and humiliating chagrin at how easily he dismissed her, before a fierce flare of pride brought her chin upwards. The light caress didn't mean anything to her either, *it didn't*. She wouldn't let it.

They were met at the airport by Wolf's general manager of the Scottish branch, a tall, good-looking man called Douglas Webb, who immediately began to apologise, once introductions were over, for the imminent catastrophe.

'Calm yourself, Doug.' Wolf's attitude surprised Lydia. She had expected tight rage or the icy-cold, biting condemnation he was so good at, but as the three of them walked towards the waiting car his face was cool but friendly, his voice even. 'It's not a *fait accompli* yet, by a long way.'

'If you want my resignation—'

'Of course I don't want your resignation,' Wolf responded with his usual acerbity. 'What I *want* is for the two of us to work together and get out of this mess. I had copies of the costings and production dates too, Doug, and I didn't pick it up either, although the way the facts were buried it isn't surprising. You trusted Mike Wilson to give you the correct data—hell, *I* trusted him! It looks like we've all been had,' he finished grimly, his mouth hard.

'I heard you got rid of him.' The other man's voice was almost faint with relief. Lydia guessed he had not expected his chairman to be so reasonable.

'A little too late, by the look of it.' Wolf slanted a sideways look at Lydia's face as they reached the car, and as their eyes met she flushed slightly, remembering her earlier protestations that he was being too hard on Mike. If this important deal was lost through Mike Wilson's dishonesty, even a prison sentence didn't seem too severe. She still found it hard to take in that Anna's husband was little more than a crook.

'Why did he do it?' Doug Webb asked. 'I mean, he had everything going for him—'

'Filthy lucre.' Wolf's voice was grim. 'He got greedy.'

They drove straight to the office and spent several hours there, and by seven o'clock in the evening Lydia was again reflecting that Wolf Strade was an extraordinary man. In spite of practically no sleep in the last forty-eight hours, his mind was still razor-sharp, the intimidating intelligence and hard practical business acumen unaffected. The air had become electric as soon as he had walked through the door of Strade Engineering Scotland, his employees almost falling over themselves to be helpful, although Lydia noticed that one or two of the younger females seemed to have more than work on their minds if their furtive, hungry glances were anything to go by. Several frankly envious and one or two downright hostile pairs of eyes had met hers through the course of the afternoon, although Wolf seemed totally unaware of the admiration coming his way, his whole concentration fixed on the job in hand. He had sent Doug, and the remnants of his staff who were still around, home just before seven with his customary authority, sweeping aside their offers to stay still later and ordering a management meeting for eight o'clock the next morning.

At half-past seven he threw a sheaf of papers he had been reading on to his desk and stretched noisily. 'Right, that's it for tonight. Food, I think?'

'Is there a chance I could wash and change first?' Lydia asked carefully.

'Yes, there's a chance you could wash and change first,' he mimicked mockingly, his deep voice taking on her wary, careful tone. 'You don't have to tread on eggshells, Lydia, despite the circumstances. I'm a big boy now. I can take adversity in my stride.'

'You couldn't this morning.' She had answered before she had time to think. 'You nearly bit my head off.'

'Ah, well, this morning...' He settled back in his chair, the big powerful body stretching slightly and causing her heartbeat to race a little faster. 'This morning I was still trying to come to terms with the fact that I should have noticed this mess arriving weeks ago.'

'But you couldn't have, no one could—' she began in surprise, only to come to an abrupt halt as he interrupted her, his voice wry.

'I didn't get where I am today without doing just that,' he said slowly, his eyes wandering lazily over her flushed face and the silky tendrils of hair that had worked loose to curl about her face during the course of the afternoon. 'But unfortunately I have had other things on my mind the last few weeks. A distraction,' he added enigmatically.

'Oh, I see.' Elda, no doubt, she thought testily as she wrenched her gaze from his and began to tidy her desk in a corner of the room. Distraction was a novel way of putting it.

'I doubt it.' She didn't look up as he spoke but continued to put the desk in order, switching off the lamp and pushing her chair into place as she stood up. 'I doubt it very much. You really are as innocent as you seem aren't you, Lydia?' he added suddenly.

'What?' Now her gaze did meet his, her eyes wide with shock. She wasn't innocent, there was Hannah—

'I've met sixteen-year-old schoolgirls who were more worldly-wise than you,' he said softly. 'In fact, one or two of my friends have teenage daughters who are worrying them to death. But you... You're just too vulnerable for your own good.'

'Vulnerable?' She reared up as though he had just hit her, and to her it seemed as though he had, at least verbally. He was telling her she was naïve, unable to cope with life, was that it? She stared at him, hurt beyond measure. He thought she was some pathetic creature who was utterly gullible and simple, bare of any sophistication or elegance at all? Not like Elda. Oh, no, she thought painfully. *Definitely* not like Elda. 'I hardly think so,' she said stiffly. 'I do have a daughter, Wolf, and I'm a very good mother.'

'I'm sure you are,' he agreed immediately, 'but that doesn't even touch on what we're talking about. How long did you go out with Matthew before you married him?' he asked abruptly, his eyes searching her flushed face.

'How long?' She stared at him with wide eyes as she struggled to keep the hurt and humiliation from showing. 'It wasn't like that, not with Matthew and me. I'd always known him, you see, we grew up together—'

'But from when you became sexually aware of each other,' he insisted softly. 'How long?'

Sexually aware? she thought faintly as she blushed hotly, her eyes dropping from his. How could she answer that? Had she ever been sexually aware of Matthew? She remembered her wedding-night and their confused fumblings, and the warmth in her cheeks burnt hotter. She hadn't liked that side of married life at first, but Matthew had been gentle and undemanding, and although their lovemaking had been infrequent she hadn't found it disagreeable. But she had never found him sexually attractive. The sudden knowledge was the worst sort of betrayal of his memory, and she closed her eyes tightly against it before she opened them to face Wolf again. She would have to think about this later. It was too much to absorb now with Wolf watching her with those piercingly intuitive eyes.

'We got engaged when I was eighteen and married on my twenty-first birthday,' she said flatly, 'and I don't want to discuss this any more.' She faced him tensely, unaware that the play of emotion across her sensitive, expressive face had intrigued the man in front of her more than he would have thought possible.

He caught himself abruptly. What the hell was he doing asking her personal questions, anyway? He was too old and too wise, far, far too wise, to play with fire.

'Neither do I.' He smiled coolly, a remote, imperturbable expression settling on the hard features that suggested they had been discussing something of no more interest than the weather. 'But I *am* hungry. How about if we make for the hotel, have a wash and brush-up and use their excellent restaurant? Sound good?' he asked lightly.

'It sounds lovely.' She used all her reserves of will-power and smiled with polite enthusiasm.

She'd got some guts. He stared at her for one more moment before rising and collecting both their coats from the coat-stand in the corner of the room. Something had bothered her more than a little, for a few seconds there she had looked devastated, and yet she was handling it with the sort of bravery he suspected was an integral part of the woman. Damn! He closed his mind off with ruthless determination. She was just a female like any other. *Like any other*.

The company car that Wolf was using during his visit ate up the twenty or so miles to the hotel with consummate ease, but Lydia was so tense she wouldn't have noticed if they had been bumping along in an old jalopy. She tried to keep her mind from returning to the conversation with Wolf, but it was no good. She had to face it, she thought suddenly. Had to accept that what she had thought was a perfect marriage hadn't been. I'm sorry, Matthew. She closed her eyes against the darkness outside the windows that reflected the void in her heart. But she *had* loved him, she had. She hugged the thought fiercely to her. He had been so gentle, so kind, protecting her from anything that might harm her... She sat up suddenly as her mind travelled ruthlessly on. More like an older brother. And he had treated her most of the time like a beloved little sister, spoiling her, preventing any contact from the outside world that might disturb her. They had loved each other, genuinely, but…a vital ingredient that she had seen in some other relationships had definitely been missing. Physical attraction, desire, lust, call it what you would. They hadn't had it. She hadn't even had a personal knowledge of that emotion until—until this man seated next to her with the ice-cold eyes and even colder heart had swept into her life. But she was aware of it now. And she wished with all her heart she wasn't. It was making her exactly what he had accused her of being—vulnerable.

'Here we are.' As they drew into a wide, tree-lined drive she saw a blaze of lights in the distance and saw what appeared to be a small castle, complete with turrets and lit with powerful floodlights. 'Our hotel.'

'This is our hotel?' She turned to the hard profile in amazement. 'But it's absolutely beautiful.'

He smiled as he drew the car to a halt in the car-park to one side of the wide stone steps. 'There are plenty of buildings in Scotland like this, but it is impressive, isn't it?' he agreed lazily. 'The food's excellent.'

She stared at him for a spilt second, noting the easy careless smile and cool composure. He had turned her world upside-down, brought things to light he had had no right to reveal, insinuated she was naïve and pathetic among other things and… And he had the nerve to be totally untouched. She hated him. She really hated him. She turned and stared out of the window in despair. She had been a fool to come.

'Don't you like it?' The deep male voice next to her had a note of almost comical amazement.

'What?' She turned to look into his dark face.

'The hotel.' He gestured towards the building as she turned to him. 'You're glaring at it as though it's Wormwood Scrubs,' he added sarcastically, his voice dry.

'I've never seen Wormwood Scrubs, or any other prison for that matter,' she said haughtily. 'And of course I like it. It's absolutely beautiful.' She glared at him angrily.

'Then why the ferocious frown?' he asked wryly.

'Wolf, you have the right to object if I'm not concentrating at work, you even think you have the right to "suggest" how I wear my hair in the office,' she continued coldly, 'but one thing you do not have the right to is my thoughts. They, at least, are all my own and I have no intention of sharing them with you or anyone else.' She stared at him crossly.

'I see.' He settled back a little further in his seat and she waited for the explosion. It didn't come. Instead he surprised her utterly by reaching forward, after a long moment of studying her angry eyes, and cupping her face between his large hands. 'You have to be the most beautiful lady I have met in my life,' he said quietly, 'as well as the most enchanting. Look at the sky.'

'The sky?' She was beginning to feel she was caught up in one of those awful plays that appeared now and again on television with no beginning and no end and utter confusion all the way through. 'What—?'

'Wait.' He had left his seat and walked round to her door before she could move, helping her out of the car and then slipping his arm round her waist as he turned her head upwards towards the black, velvety sky overhead. The night was icy-cold, with the smell of frost in the clear dry air, and the dark blanket overhead was pierced with a hundred tiny twinkling stars in which the clear orb of the moon sat in silent splendour as it surveyed the world beneath. 'The sky.' He had pulled her back against him so his body was the length of hers, his chin resting in the pale silk of her hair and his arms holding her securely against his hard frame. She didn't see the sky. Every part of her was vitally aware of the powerful male body behind her, the smell and feel of him sending a million tiny signals to nerve-endings she had never known she possessed. 'Beautiful, isn't it?' he asked softly.

'Yes.' She had begun to tremble, but for the life of her she couldn't control the faint tremors. All she wanted, more than anything else in life, was for him to kiss her. And then he did just that.

'You're cold.' He had noticed the shaking she couldn't hide and turned her round to face him, pulling her hard into him as his mouth took hers in a kiss that curled her toes. His mouth was urgent and hungry as they stood there in the shadowed darkness, the crisp clean air and faint smell of winter adding a poignancy to the moment that stayed with her for a long time afterwards. 'Lydia…' His voice was a groan, almost a tortured sound in the still air, but in the next instant she was free as he moved her from him, his breathing harsh and ragged as he stared down into her face. 'This is ridiculous, you know that, madness…'

She couldn't move, couldn't say anything, although she wanted to. All she *could* do was to stare up into his dark, handsome face and wonder how she was going to get through the rest of her life after she said goodbye to this man. And it was imperative she said goodbye, and soon. This dark force, this overwhelming attraction that drew her to him like a moth to a flame would destroy

her peace of mind forever if she wasn't careful. He
wanted a brief dalliance, a temporary affair at the most,
the sort of game he was used to and enjoyed. And she
wanted… She stepped back from him so sharply that she
almost fell. She wanted nothing. *Nothing*. She wouldn't
let it be any other way. If she wasn't strong now she
would regret it the rest of her life.

'Shall we go in?' Her voice was as flat as she could
make it, but nevertheless she heard the little tremor in
its depths and hoped he didn't.

'In?' He had been staring at her, his eyes hungry on
her mouth and his face dark with desire.

'In to the hotel,' she said carefully. 'It's cold out here.'
It was true, the air was cold with a biting quality all of
its own, but the chill that was emanating from deep inside her was far more wintry than anything Mother
Nature could dredge up. He wanted her for one thing
and one thing only. He hadn't even tried to pretend otherwise. And she felt vulnerable here, in this bleak, beautiful part of Scotland with its majestic beauty and harsh,
untamed mountains. He was too seductive, too powerful,
too fascinating…

'Of course.' He instantly slipped back into business
mode, his face straightening into its habitual handsome
mask that revealed little and his eyes veiled. 'You must
be freezing.' She was, but the weather had little to do
with it.

He tucked her case under one arm, holding his with
the same hand, and took her elbow in his other hand,
and she felt the contact like an electric shock. His touch
was light, but it burnt through her clothing like fire, each
nerve vitally aware of his closeness. Idiot, *idiot*, she cau-
tioned herself as they walked towards the main door, but
it didn't help. He only had to touch her and she turned

to jelly. So she had to make sure he touched her as little as possible. It was up to her. But it was going to be hard. She glanced at his cold, handsome face from under her eyelashes. Very hard.

CHAPTER SIX

THE interior of the hotel was even more impressive than the outside, and as they entered the sumptuous lobby a bellboy moved forward instantly to relieve Wolf of the suitcases at the same moment as the receptionist glanced up from her desk, the practised, cool smile warming considerably as her eyes fastened on Wolf's tall frame.

'Mr Strade.' The smile warmed to gas mark nine. 'We've been expecting you, sir. Your usual suite is ready.'

'Good.' Wolf's smile was polite but not particularly enthusiastic, but it didn't seem to cool the girl's interest an iota, if the bright gleam in her eyes was anything to go by.

'Would you prefer dinner upstairs, sir, or in the restaurant?' The receptionist's hard blue eyes flicked over Lydia briefly. 'Your usual table has been reserved in case you chose to dine there.' She smiled up at him warmly.

'The restaurant, I think.' He turned to Lydia with dark eyebrows raised. 'Would you prefer to eat there?'

'I…' She pulled herself together with considerable effort as her mind raced. What was this about a suite? And where was her room? And she definitely *would* prefer to eat in the restaurant, surrounded by plenty of other people. 'The restaurant.' She smiled with her mouth as her eyes narrowed. He didn't think she was sharing… Of course he didn't. He couldn't. Could he?

He could. 'Come along.' As the bellboy took the key

and picked up the suitcases again, Wolf led her towards the lift.

'Where's my key?'

'What?'

She came to a halt just outside the lift and, as Wolf saw the expression on her face, he indicated for the bell-boy to go ahead. 'We'll be up in a moment.'

As the lift doors closed on the young man's studiously blank face, Lydia glared up at Wolf, her eyes darkening to coal-black ebony. 'My key. Where is it?' she asked tightly.

'You don't need a key.' His voice was completely expressionless. 'I have the key to the suite of which your room is one of two bedrooms.'

'You've reserved a suite?' She was trying to keep her voice low, but anger was throbbing through every word and she was fighting a losing battle. 'A suite?' she repeated furiously.

'Yes, Lydia, a suite.' His tone was infinitely patient now, his manner that of a responsible adult dealing with a difficult and troublesome child, which in the circumstances was calculatedly insulting. She glared at him angrily.

'Well, you can just unreserve it,' she said tightly. 'I want my own room.'

'You've got your own room.' His eyes narrowed on her flushed face. 'In the suite.'

'There is no way I'm staying here in a suite with you,' she said tensely. 'I want my own room with my own key.'

'Dammit, Lydia!' The cool control was slipping, she noticed interestedly as he took her arm and roughly pulled her out of the way of an elderly couple who had come to stand just behind them, patiently waiting for the lift, the woman's face bright with interest as she caught the last part of their exchange. 'What the hell do you expect me to do, leap on you in the middle of the night?' he asked curtly.

'I want my own room,' she repeated resolutely. 'I never dreamt—'

'For crying out loud, woman...' He shut his eyes briefly and then glared at her in exasperation. 'I always have the suite when I stay here, and knowing that it had two bedrooms I obviously assumed—'

'I know what you *assumed*,' she said tightly.

'I don't believe I'm having this conversation.' He appeared, for once, completely out of his depth, and then as the lift doors opened she felt a gentle tap on her shoulder.

'Excuse me, dear.' The little old lady was standing behind her, her husband watching anxiously from inside the lift as she reached forward and murmured conspiratorially in Lydia's ear in a stage whisper that was clearly audible to Wolf, 'You stick to your guns, my dear. There is too much of this free love these days— '

'Right. That's it.' As Wolf took Lydia's arm and marched her the few feet into the lift, the woman's husband made a swift exit to join his wife, taking her arm and walking swiftly in the opposite direction. 'You are going to come up with me, inspect this damn suite and then see you've got nothing to worry about,' Wolf said furiously as the lift took them effortlessly upwards. 'Dammit all, Lydia, every other woman of my acquaintance would be mad if I *hadn't* booked a suite—'

'I'm fully aware of that,' she said icily as she forced herself not to wilt under his temper. 'And I am not "every other woman".' The phrase had cut through her heart like a knife.

'Tell me about it.' He shook his head slightly as he leant against the side of the lift and watched her with eyes that softened suddenly as they ran over her flushed stiff face and tremulous mouth. 'I haven't been in such a crazy situation since I was eighteen and out on a date in my first car when I really *did* run out of petrol. I seem to remember there was an interfering old busybody about then too, in the first car that came by. My girlfriend disappeared with her and that was the end of that.' He eyed her mockingly as she glanced at him once quickly before fixing her gaze somewhere over his left shoulder. 'I'm really not some sort of sex-crazed animal, you know,' he drawled slowly as the lift drew smoothly to a halt. 'I don't know what impression you've picked up or what little stories or gossip you've been listening to, but I'm not completely without sensitivity.'

'Just morals.' She didn't know what made her say it, perhaps it was the easy mockery in his voice and face when she was as tense as a coiled spring, but once out the words couldn't be retrieved and she stared at him aghast as the handsome face hardened into stone-cold granite and his eyes took on the texture of polished glass.

'I'm going to do us both a favour and pretend I didn't hear that.' She found herself ignominiously frog-marched out of the lift into a small corridor before she could protest. The bellboy had opened the door and placed their suitcases inside and at their approach he prepared to leave, pocketing the folded note that Wolf slipped him with a beaming smile which faded some-what as he glanced at their grim faces.

'I'm sorry, Wolf.' As soon as the door had closed she launched into an apology before she lost her nerve. 'That was a rotten thing to say and without foundation. I don't know anything about you—'

'No, you don't.' His face had relaxed at her words but now he walked across to the drinks cabinet in the far corner of the beautiful lounge, gesturing for her to be seated on the massive corner unit that wound round a large open fireplace in which several logs crackled. 'What would you like to drink?' he asked coolly.

'I don't—' She stopped abruptly. She didn't really drink, Matthew had never approved of alcohol and she wasn't keen on the taste, but she needed something to relax her a little if she was going to get through the rest of the evening without shattering into a hundred tiny pieces. 'Sherry, please,' she answered stiffly.

He poured himself a stiff whisky and brought both glasses over to the settee where she was perched nervously. 'Come here.' He placed the drinks on the coffee-table and took her hand, drawing her up and across the room to a door at the far end. 'This would be your room. It has its own ensuite bathroom, so you needn't emerge until you are fully dressed, with your coat on if you wish.' He eyed her wickedly as she blushed a deep scarlet. The room was huge and very luxurious in soft shades of gold and red, an open door in one wall revealing a magnificent bathroom complete with sunken bath and the biggest shower cabinet she had ever seen. 'There is another bedroom for me, again with bathroom,' he continued blandly as he gestured for her to precede him out of the room, 'and you will notice you can lock your door from the inside. I could perhaps arrange for a bolt to be fitted if you're a little nervous?'

'I'm sure that won't be necessary,' she said tightly as she walked back over to the fire with burning cheeks. He was loving this, just loving it, but then she had made the most colossal fool of herself. Why, oh, why hadn't she waited and made sure of the facts before launching in with the veiled accusations? But he had just seemed so sure of himself, so in control, as though he had done this a thousand times before. And he probably had. She glanced at him now as he sat down beside her and reached for his drink. With a thousand different women. Her heart pounded violently. And that was what had made her so mad. The self-knowledge was a bitter pill to swallow.

'I'll carry your suitcase through in a moment and you can freshen up a little before we go down to dinner.' He glanced at her now and she felt her pulse leap at his closeness. She could cope with him in an office situation, just, but this was too informal, too intimate. 'That is, if you're staying?' he added softly, with one raised eyebrow.

'Of course I'm staying.' She reached for her glass with a jerky hand and swallowed half the sherry in one gulp. She would have liked to edge down the settee a little but didn't dare. The evening was enough of a disaster as it was without adding to her crimes. 'I misread the situation before,' she added, as coolly as she could.

'That you did,' he agreed gravely, but with an underlying throb of amusement in his voice that added to the heat in her cheeks. She swallowed the rest of the sherry without even realising what she was doing, and he took the empty glass and silently refilled it, sitting down next to her again with a little sigh. 'It's been a hell of a day, hasn't it?' He stretched out his long legs as he spoke and she nodded a reply as she watched him through her lashes. He had leant back against the settee, closing his eyes, the glass of whisky held loosely in one hand, and she couldn't believe what the casual pose was doing to her hormones, the ones she hadn't known she had until

recently. He had to be the most sexy, flagrantly masculine, attractive man she had ever met in her whole—

'Would you like to phone and see how Hannah is?'

She jumped so violently as he spoke that the rest of
her sherry, which fortunately wasn't much as she had
been sipping it unknowingly as she watched him, disappeared down the front of her blouse. Hannah. She felt
a moment's deep and piercing guilt. Here she was, sitting positively ogling this man, lusting after him, and
she hadn't given her daughter a thought. 'Yes, yes I
would. Where…?'

'Over there.' He gestured to the phone with one hand
as his eyes narrowed on her flustered face. 'And relax,
Lydia. This is supposed to be the time of the day when
you *relax*,' he added grimly, frowning slightly.

She spared him a cool smile as she rose hastily and
walked across to the phone. If he'd read her thoughts…
She felt her heart leap against her ribcage. But he
couldn't. Thank goodness. A fragile defence but better
than nothing.

Hannah was fine, and after a brief conversation with
her mother she turned to face Wolf again with a composure that was hard-won. 'I'll just change…' She indicated her stained blouse and he rose immediately, carrying her case into her room without speaking and
leaving quietly, closing the door behind him.

She sank down on one of the large twin beds once
she was alone, and willed her racing thoughts to slow
down. She had to pull herself together: this just wouldn't
do. She was acting like a teenager on her first date, for
goodness' sake. She lay back on the soft cover for a
moment and shut her eyes. But then, this was probably
how people *did* feel on a date—she wouldn't know,
would she? There had only ever been Matthew, after all,

and he had always been as familiar as her own skin. She sat up abruptly and shook her head at her thoughts. Anyway, this *wasn't* a date, first or otherwise. She was going to have dinner with her boss on what was a brief business trip, and that was that. She reached for her case and began to unpack quickly. But that kiss… She made an exclamation of annoyance at herself out loud. That kiss had happened because he was trying it on to see how she would respond. It was as simple as that. She might be unworldly in his eyes, vulnerable even, but even she knew that most men were capable of sleeping with a woman without it meaning a thing. And he had already admitted that emotional ties, even the vaguest sort of involvement, were not his style. She bit her lip hard. He probably thought that if she had recently separated she would be missing that particular…ingredient of married life. Even that he would be doing her a favour? She reared up at the thought, and stalked into the bathroom as though Wolf himself had voiced it.

When she emerged from her room some fifteen minutes later Wolf was waiting for her, his eyes lazy as they wandered over the smart but feminine soft wool dress in pale cream, and ultra-slender high-heeled shoes in the same shade. She had chosen the outfit because the dress gave her poise and confidence and the shoes an extra two inches in height. She had the feeling she would need all the help she could get tonight. One look at his dark face confirmed the thought.

'You look beautiful, Lydia,' he said softly, 'but perhaps a more casual hairstyle?' he suggested blandly.

She touched the tight knot at the back of her head that she had purposely strained every last hair into, and smiled brightly, her eyes expressionless. 'I don't think so.' She fiddled with the clasp of her bag so that she

could let her eyes drop from his—that clear blue gaze
was a little disconcerting. 'This is a working trip, after
all.'

'Of course.' There was something in his voice she
couldn't quite place, but when she glanced at him
quickly the hard, male face was cool and cynical, his
eyes hooded. 'Ever the perfect secretary. But you do
allow yourself to eat, I trust?' He moved across and
opened the door into the corridor, waving her through
with a mocking flourish. As she passed she felt his hand
on the clasp at the back of her head but was too late to
do anything about it as her hair swung in a soft silky
veil to frame her face and shoulders. 'That's better.'
There was immense satisfaction in the arrogant male
voice as he glanced down into her angry eyes. 'Far more
comfortable,' he added lazily.

'I thought you insisted that your employees dressed
and behaved discreetly?' she said tightly, as the words
he had spoken that day weeks ago came back to her.

'I have nothing at all against your being discreet,
Lydia.' He smiled slowly. 'Far from it.' She glared at
him in reply and the smile deepened. 'But surely you
understand part of being a good secretary is to keep your
boss happy?' It was such an outrageous line that she
couldn't formulate an adequately scathing rejoinder before the lift glided upwards and the doors opened, but
as she walked past him, head held high, her eyes flashed
fire.

The dining-room appeared full as they entered, the
tables all at a discreet distance from each other, with
subdued lighting and beautiful furnishings adding to the
general air of unashamed opulence. A waiter appeared
as though by magic at Wolf's shoulder and seemed to
know instantly who he was, ushering them both to a

perfectly positioned table for two in an elegant alcove
where they could see everything but remain relatively
unobserved themselves.

'Could you bring us a bottle of my usual champagne?'
As the waiter handed them two large, heavily embossed
menus he nodded immediately, his face deferential.

'There's one on ice now, Mr Strade,' he said quietly.

Lydia saw him raise his hand to someone just outside
her line of vision and within seconds an ice-bucket complete with vintage Bollinger was placed in front of them.
She might have known. An expression of distaste flickered across her face for a brief moment. Was he treated
with this ingratiating respect that bordered on reverence
everywhere he went? No wonder the man's ego was
jumbo-sized. She glanced up to find the vivid blue eyes
tight on her face, their depths intuitive. 'Don't frown,'
he said drily.

She opened her mouth to protest that she wasn't, but
then realised she was and shut it again abruptly.

'And I can't help it if money talks, it's the way of the
world.' The hard gaze moved over her pink cheeks
slowly. 'With most people, that is… Now, what would
you like to eat?' he asked smoothly.

She glanced at the menu apprehensively. Was it going
to be one of those ultra-sophisticated non-readable items
in French? There were several languages, but thankfully
English was one of them, and she was able to select the
first and main course without any difficulty, which Wolf
duly relayed to the waiter once he returned after a discreet interval. As he did so she glanced carefully round
the room. It must cost a king's fortune to eat in a place
like this if the clientele were anything to go by.

'How was Hannah?'

Her eyes snapped back to his and she saw he was surveying her thoughtfully, his gaze narrowed.

'Fine, thank you, she's very adaptable,' she said carefully.

'She seemed a plucky, sensible little kid on the night of the accident,' he agreed quietly. 'You must love her very much.'

'Yes, I do.' She smiled warmly as she pictured her daughter's bright little face. 'You were very good with her that night, Wolf, especially for a confirmed bachelor,' she finished lightly, and then was suddenly conscious as she looked into his face that a mask of ice had frozen over the hard features.

'My daughter was the same age when she was killed.' The words hung in the air, stark and raw, and for a moment Lydia stared at him helplessly, her mouth half-open.

'Wolf—'

'It was a long time ago, Lydia, buried in the past now.'

It didn't look as though it was buried, she thought with stunned horror as her wide eyes took in his taut mouth and haunted eyes. 'My wife and daughter were involved in a car accident eight years ago and both killed instantly,' he continued expressionlessly, his voice flat. 'From that point on it seemed…logical to concentrate on my work and keep emotional strings to the minimum.'

'I didn't know…' She tried to think of something comforting to say, something uplifting, but her mind was completely blank with the shock of what she had just heard. His wife was dead and they'd had a child? *A child*?

'There is no reason why you should.' He poured them both a glass of champagne as he spoke, his movements perfectly controlled and calm although Lydia knew, somehow, that despite appearances he wasn't feeling like that inside. 'As I said, it was a long time ago.' He smiled, but it didn't reach the beautiful blue eyes. 'Life goes on.'

'I'm so sorry, Wolf.' Her eyes were luminous with unshed tears; she actually felt the pain he must have suffered, and as he gazed into her white face he was completely still for a moment before gesturing abruptly, his voice suddenly harsh.

'No need.' He picked up her glass and placed it in her hand, his face suddenly closed and cold. 'Have a sip of champagne, it's rather good.'

She drank automatically, the clean, cold, sparkling liquid barely registering on her senses as she struggled to absorb the enormity of what he had told her, and when she put down her glass she was surprised to find it was empty and that her head felt a little muzzy. Two glasses of sherry and now champagne on an empty stomach, she thought suddenly. She really mustn't drink another thing tonight.

Wolf's revelation seemed to have robbed her mind of any normal conversation. She wanted to ask him a hundred questions, not one of which was possible, and to follow with light chit-chat after such a disclosure would have been the height of callous insensitivity. She stared at him now as she searched for something, anything, to say. He was sitting in apparent easy contemplation of his fellow diners, big body relaxed and lazy and his gaze indolent as it flicked round the massive, dimly lit room. He seemed at ease with himself and the world in general, but Lydia was beginning to understand that outward appearances were subtly misleading with this man. What went on behind that closed, shuttered mind was his busi-

ness and his alone. He let very little of himself be seen.
It was unnerving, to say the least.

'I shouldn't have told you,' he said suddenly.

'What?' As the blue eyes fastened on her face she
hadn't had time to school her expression into what he
would want to see.

'About Carrie and my wife—I shouldn't have told
you.' He shook his head slowly as he looked into the
dark depths of her eyes. 'It's upset you and now you
feel sorry for me. Is that about right?' he asked grimly.

She was aware she had to answer carefully, very carefully, if he wasn't to clam up for good. 'I'm sorry that
someone as young as Hannah didn't have the chance to
grow up,' she said slowly, 'very sorry. I think if I feel
grief for anyone it's for her.' She mustn't show him pity,
he would abhor it, but it was hard when every soft female instinct in her body wanted to comfort and reassure.

He held her gaze for a long, considering moment before sighing softly as he leant back in his seat, his face
suddenly open again. 'That's exactly what tormented
me,' he said quietly, his eyes looking inward to something only he could see. 'She had the whole of her life
before her.'

'Perhaps she's spending it in a better place.' His eyes
moved to focus on her again, their sapphire light piercing.

'Do you believe that?' he asked quietly.

'Yes.' She returned his look bravely, without waver-
ing. 'In the case of children, I do believe it.'

'I'd like to.' His voice held unutterable sadness.

As the waiter appeared at their side with the first
course, the shutter came down again and she realised the
brief moment of intimacy was over. As she ate the best

prawn cocktail she had ever tasted in her life she realised
they hadn't discussed his wife at all, and yet he must
have been devastated at her death too. How long had
they been married? What was her name? What had she
looked like? A thousand little questions buzzed at her
mind but she resolutely forced them into her subcon-
scious.

At some time in the last few minutes Wolf had refilled
her glass and again she took a sip almost automatically.
He was such an enigma, this man. How could anyone,
anyone at all, walk a solitary path through life? It was…
unnatural.

The trout, when it arrived, was excellent, served with
baby new potatoes and a selection of vegetables that
positively melted in the mouth but, delicious as the food
was, Lydia found she was eating almost mechanically.
The picture she had had of Wolf in her mind, the picture
he had deliberately painted for her and everyone else,
didn't fit with this new side to him and it unnerved her.

She glanced across the table at him now and found he
was watching her, his blue eyes piercingly fixed on her
face. 'Are you enjoying the meal?' He smiled lazily, but
the sapphire depths shaded by their thick black lashes
didn't flicker. 'It's Scottish trout, of course.'

'It's wonderful.' She smiled back carefully, her mind
anywhere but on the food. 'But I suppose you're used
to eating like this all the time.'

'Is that what you suppose?' His voice wasn't unfriendly but definitely dry. 'You see me as a high-flying
socialite, is that it?'

'No—' She stopped abruptly as she saw the glimmer
of amusement in the dark face watching hers. 'Not exactly,' she finished weakly.

'I have a house in London close to Hyde Park, with

a garden that persists in rebelling against all efforts to control it,' he said quietly, his eyes slumberous now as they stroked over her pale skin. 'My housekeeper lives in…with her husband,' he added wickedly, as though she had voiced the suspicion that immediately sprang most unfairly to life. 'The house is an indulgence for a man living alone, but I loathe flats and, contrary to your suppositions, I much prefer eating at home, although I have to admit I rarely get the chance. I have two dogs and two cats inherited from my married years, all of which are geriatrics with enough idiosyncrasies to fill a book. Anything else you'd like to know?' he added blandly.

'I wasn't prying,' she objected indignantly as hot colour flooded her face.

'Weren't you?' He eyed her lazily. 'How disappointing.'

She stared at him without speaking, for the simple reason that she couldn't think of a word to say.

'I have a house in Madeira where I try to escape for at least a month every summer to recharge my batteries,' he continued in the same quiet voice, 'although unfortunately it does have a telephone which I am seriously thinking of having taken out. Last year was a series of interruptions. Every time I stretched out by the pool to take in a few rays, the damn thing went crazy.'

'Oh…' The thought of him barely clothed made her hot. And weak. Definitely, deliciously weak.

'And that's about it in a nutshell.' He spread his hands wide and leant back in his chair as the waiter came to remove their plates. 'Any surprises?' he asked expressionlessly.

'Not really.' She was lying. She had seen him in a smart bachelor flat that was elegant and impersonal and never, never in her wildest dreams had she imagined him bothering with any pets. 'What are the animals' names?'

'The dogs are retrievers, Honey and Muffin, and the cats are Meenie and Mo. So there you are, you know it all now.' He smiled dismissively. 'And how about dessert? The strawberry pancakes are especially good.'

'Lovely, thank you.' The change of subject was sudden and intentional and it hurt. His face was guarded now, his eyes hooded, and she sensed he regretted the brief intimacy had happened. She was just a ship that had passed, or was passing, in the night. She mustn't forget that.

The rest of the evening passed in a haze of good food and light conversation, with Wolf acting as the perfect dinner companion, and although she knew it was an act, that he had deliberately set out to charm and entertain her on a superficial level, nevertheless she found she was enjoying herself immensely. He was devastatingly witty and unashamedly wicked, his sense of humour in perfect tune with hers. They sat for some time over coffee and brandy, the latter accepted by her without a qualm as the soft, rosy glow of the evening lowered all her defences, and it was with a real sense of loss that the realisation the evening had finished washed over her. She couldn't remember enjoying herself more.

'Would you like more coffee in our suite?' Wolf asked quietly as he moved back her chair and took her arm as they left the restaurant, his hand firm and warm on her flesh.

'Oh, no, thank you, I shall never get to sleep as it is,' she answered dreamily, her face upraised to his as she replied, and her hair silky-soft and pale as it framed her flushed skin and sparkling eyes.

'I have a perfect remedy for sleeplesness.' The deep

voice was faintly mocking and definitely sensual, and as she met the narrowed eyes in which a small blue flame flickered her heart began to pound with a mixture of excitement and nervous anticipation.

She wanted to sleep with him. The thought was both shocking and intoxicating. She remembered the embraces she had shared with Matthew in those years that seemed so long ago, the lukewarm intimacy and careful, gentle familiarity that had nevertheless produced Hannah, and imagined what lovemaking with Wolf would mean. The blood ran through her veins like liquid fire and she felt a tightness in her lower stomach that caused her to stumble slightly. The hard hand on her arm checked the movement instantly and he drew her protectively into his side as they entered the lift, his body supportive.

'I forgot you don't drink.' His eyes smiled down at her but his mouth was sensual, and his lips lightly stroked her forehead as he folded her into his arms in the seclusion of the snug little box. 'Do you still love him Lydia?' She froze as his voice murmured the words in her ear, but he moved her slightly from him so he could see her face and she saw his eyes were determined. 'Do you?'

'Not in the way you mean.' It was the truth, and carried an unmistakable genuineness, but his mouth still tightened at her reply.

'What the hell am I supposed to read into that?' he asked grimly, and then as she opened her mouth to tell him the whole of it, that she had been without Matthew for three years, that she was a widow, he put his finger on her lips and pulled her roughly against him again. 'No, don't answer that. I'd rather not know.'

'But, Wolf—'

'I said no.' As he took her mouth it was almost as though there was pain in his desire, his lips hard against hers, savage even, but then, as the lift drew smoothly to a halt and the doors opened, he lifted his head and scooped her into his arms, carrying her across the few feet of corridor and setting her down with one arm tightly round her waist as he unlocked the door.

'Wolf—'

'No—don't talk, don't think. For once just do what you want to do.' He drew her inside and immediately kissed her again, his hands running over her back in a soft feathery caress that brought a million nerve-endings into glorious life. 'And you want to make love with me, don't you?' He touched her aching breasts lightly. 'Don't you, Lydia?' he persisted softly.

'I can't—'

'Yes, you can.' As his hands shaped the fullness of her breasts through the soft material of the wool dress she felt flames of fire wherever he touched, her arousal immediate. She couldn't believe the way her body re-acted to his; nothing in life so far had prepared her for the onslaught of fierce physical desire that coursed through her small frame, leaving her trembling and shak-ing in his arms.

He began to explore her mouth with experienced, teas-ing caresses, his lips and tongue first soft and light, then hard and thrusting until she felt a heat rising inside her that had to have release. His mouth wandered to her ears, her throat, finding secret erotic places that had her moan-ing in his arms as the warmth of his lips worked a magic she found it impossible to resist. He was good, much, much too good at this.

She found she was clinging to his hard-muscled shoul-ders as much for support as the pleasure of having his powerful body beneath her hands, the smell and taste of him all-encompassing. And he was making no attempt to hide his reaction to their lovemaking, his desire urgent and unashamed and his arousal obvious as he moulded her into the length of his lean, muscled body. There was something breathtakingly satisfying in knowing that she could make this tough, fascinatingly masculine man want her so badly. The knowledge was dangerously erotic, heady.

'I need you, Lydia. I'm sleeping, eating, living you…' His breath was warm and clean against her throat as he covered her skin in tiny, passionate kisses in between each word. 'It's driving me crazy.' She melted against him, unable to stand any longer, and as he lowered her gently on to the thick carpet she felt his hands slide up the satin-smooth skin of her legs. 'I want you and you want me; it's as simple as that.'

As simple as that? She twisted under him, moving to the side and then away as she scrambled to her feet, her heart pounding. Simple, like with all those other women? A sating of bodily need, a physical release? What was she doing? *What was she doing*?

'No.' She stared at him, her eyes huge pools of tortured darkness in the pale delicacy of her face, her lips trembling. 'I can't…'

'Lydia—' As he took a step towards her, his body as taut as a rod and his face working with a hundred different emotions, she backed from him desperately, her hand to her mouth. He stopped instantly. 'Don't look like that, I'm not going to hurt you,' he said furiously, his eyes bleak.

Hurt her? She felt a moment's hysteria before she brought it sharply under control. He had the power to destroy her, never mind hurt her. 'Leave me alone.' She backed from him across the room. 'I can't be what you want me to be, I can't just…' She waved her hand feverishly in the air. 'It has to mean something. I'm sorry.' She felt the handle of her door beneath her fingers and turned to stumble through, her eyes streaming with tears, blind and deaf to everything but her own humiliation, shame and misery. How could she have come so close to betraying herself like that? So close to sleeping with him when she knew it would mean less than nothing to him, merely another in the long line of temporary diversions, a physical sating of the senses that would be forgotten as soon as the bodily need was eased. He had *told* her what he wanted in his relationships, he had spelled it out loud and clear. She had no excuses, none at all.

As the door closed behind her Wolf stood exactly where she had left him, his mouth a white slash in the hard line of his jaw. 'It has to mean something.' He drove his clenched fist against the palm of his hand, his face savage. And it clearly wouldn't with him. And why? Because she still loved that damn fool who had walked out on her, on her and the young child who was Lydia in miniature. This had to be the ultimate irony in his life so far. But now he knew exactly where he stood. He strode across the room and poured himself another half-tumbler of whisky, taking the bottle with him as he walked into his bedroom and shutting the door with a savage kick.

CHAPTER SEVEN

WHEN Lydia awoke the next morning it was to heavy, driving rain against the bedroom window, and as she glanced at her tiny travel alarm the illuminated dial told her it was half-past five. That meant she had had precisely three hours' sleep after hours of heart-searching following the disastrous confrontation with Wolf. Her heart thudded as she remembered the whole catastrophic finish to the evening in its entirety. It was all very well to blame the alcohol, the seductive surroundings, even him, but... She shook her head slowly as she climbed wearily out of bed and padded across to the bathroom. She'd wanted him to make love to her and then she had chickened out. He must think she was the worst sort of tease. The tears started again and she brushed them aside angrily. Useless to say that she hadn't been thinking straight, that for once in her life she had gone with her feelings and not her head. She'd made a hopeless mess of the whole thing and she wouldn't blame him if he packed her straight back to London this morning. And how was she going to face him, anyway? She shut her eyes tightly as she let the warm, cleansing flow of the shower ease away some of the aches of a restless night. She could just imagine the cool mockery and veiled contempt with which he would meet her this morning.

When she did meet him at seven o'clock, for breakfast served in their suite, his face was completely expressionless. 'Good morning.' He nodded to her as she left her room, face burning and head held high. She wanted to sink through the carpet but forced herself to join him at the small dining-table to one side of the full-length window. 'The waiter has just brought the food up.' He indicated the beautifully laid out breakfast complete with a small posy of yellow and white daisies in the centre of the table. 'Would you like to help yourself?' he asked flatly.

'Thank you.' If she ate anything it would choke her, she thought painfully, but then as she saw his full plate and the way he seemed to be eating with every appearance of enjoyment, a perverse pride made her select a more than adequate meal. Each mouthful was an endurance test but she managed to clear her plate. It didn't help that the whole meal was eaten in absolute silence, Wolf remote and sombre behind his newspaper. But she hadn't met the cool and cynical mockery she had expected. She glanced up now as she finished her coffee. She didn't understand him at all. Suddenly the newspaper lowered and a pair of very blue and very clear eyes met hers. 'It's going to be a hard day,' he said slowly, 'and a long one.'

'Yes, I suppose it is,' she agreed quietly.

'So the first thing I would like to do is apologise for last night.' As she opened her mouth to speak he raised his hand quickly, his face dark and severe. 'No, hear me out, Lydia, please. The second is to say it was not my intention to take advantage of you—'

'I wasn't drunk,' she protested weakly. She hadn't expected him to behave like this: she had expected rage, contempt, cold mockery—

'I'm aware of that.' He smiled grimly. 'But you aren't used to alcohol, by your own admission, and you had drunk enough to feel…a little reckless? I misunderstood the situation and thought—' He stopped abruptly and her face flamed still further. She knew *exactly* what he had thought and she couldn't blame him at all. It had been her body giving the 'go' signals there, and she knew it.

'It was my fault, Wolf,' she said bleakly. 'I don't know what came over me.' Liar. *He* had come over her, the little voice in her mind sniped immediately.

'Well, don't let's argue the finer points.' He rose from the table as he spoke and held out his hand, his eyes veiled. 'Suffice to say we both know where we stand and perhaps we could leave it at that? This project we're involved in is important to me, Lydia, damn important, and I don't want any outside difficulties or tension to deflect our concentration.' His voice was expressionless and cold.

'Of course.' She had never felt so miserable in her life, she thought desperately as she smiled brightly and nodded her agreement. She had been right; she wasn't even a serious consideration in his life. He could dismiss her without a second thought as a write-off. She took his outstretched hand as he helped her up from the table, and let go immediately as the warmth of his flesh sent a shiver down her spine. 'I'll just get my things,' she said quickly.

It had stopped raining as they left the hotel and a weak November sun had lit the grey-blue sky with streaks of gold. The hotel was just past a small village, screened by trees and set back from the main road, and as they drove out of the beautifully tended grounds she glanced in the distance to where craggy mountain peaks of red sandstone and granite topped with white quartzite towered over wild hills dotted with grazing sheep.

'It's lovely in the summer.' He had followed her eyes to the harsh, haunting beauty of the bare hills. 'A sea of heather colours the fells purple, and the contrasts of shades have to be seen to be believed.'

'I can imagine.' She nodded stiffly. How could he talk so normally, how *could* he? 'But it's beautiful now in its own way,' she said quietly, forcing herself to make conversation.

'Yes, it is.' The big, powerful car drove swiftly past the tiny village of whitewashed houses and carved gravestones in the ancient churchyard, reaching within minutes the main road which was the fastest route to Inverness, where Wolf's factory was situated. Lydia tried to relax on the short journey to the office, but it was difficult with his big, aggressively male body so close to hers and the scent of him teasing her nostrils. In spite of every effort to the contrary, she kept remembering how it had felt to be in his arms last night. It was everything she had imagined and more. She kicked herself mentally, hard. Stop it, Lydia, she told herself sternly, you're being ridiculous. But, ridiculous or not, her body continued to play tricks on her all the way to Strade Engineering Scotland, and she was immeasurably thankful when the Rover drew to a halt in front of the offices. Never had a journey seemed so long.

The day proved every bit as arduous as Wolf had suspected, but by late afternoon the onerous hours of hard labour had paid off. The contract was saved, albeit with a few concessions. 'I didn't think you'd pull it off, Wolf.' Doug Webb ran a weary hand over his face as he spoke, his eyes red-rimmed. Wolf on the other hand looked every bit as fresh and razor-sharp as when he had stridden into the office first thing that morning, barking orders and setting the place scuttling.

'Piece of cake.' Wolf grinned at the other man with sardonically raised eyebrows, and Lydia felt an emotion shoot through her that caused her breath to stop in her throat. Just physical attraction, she told herself sharply as she tidied the last of the papers on her desk. The fact that he had just looked like a proud schoolboy receiving a hard-won accolade had *not* stirred her heart an iota. She did *not* feel tenderness or warmth towards this man, she did not.

'Hell!' Doug suddenly clapped his hand to the side of his head. 'I was supposed to ask you this morning—' He stopped abruptly. 'Sue'll kill me.'

'She will?' If Lydia had been looking she would have seen Wolf's easy expression stiffen somewhat. 'What's wrong?'

'I was to let her know before lunchtime if you couldn't make it for dinner tonight,' Doug admitted shamefacedly. 'You and Lydia, that is. Otherwise she was going to go ahead with a dinner for four. You know how Sue loves entertaining.'

'Yes.' This time a certain inflexion in Wolf's voice caught Lydia's ear and she glanced up to see the habitual expression of cool remoteness had settled over the hard features. 'Well, we were going to enjoy a quiet meal at the hotel, but you'd better ring Sue and let her know what time to expect us,' Wolf said with neutral politeness.

As soon as they drew up at Doug Webb's smart, detached house the door opened, and a tall elegant woman positioned herself in the lighted doorway, arms stretched out in dramatic welcome. 'Wolf, how lovely. And you must be Lydia.' As they reached her side the slim brunette arched pencil-slim eyebrows as she let her wide, green-flecked eyes wander over Wolf's bland face. 'You look wonderful, Wolf, it's just not fair that men improve with the years, is it...?'

Lydia found her mouth had fallen open as she preceded Wolf into the house, his hand in the small of her back. Doug's wife was not at all what she had expected and seemed very familiar with Wolf for one of his employees' wives. She glanced at the other woman in the bright artificial light in the hall and felt her heart sink as she noticed the tall, model-slim figure and expensive immaculate dress that draped over the beautiful frame beneath it as though it had been sewn on. Her own skirt and blouse were fine for the office, smart and prudently formal, but hopelessly inadequate for an evening out, besides which, after the sort of day they had been engaged in, she felt sticky and crumpled and drab.

'Do come through.' Sue took her arm as Doug divested them of their coats, and Lydia saw that the lovely face was expertly made-up, her long thick dark hair arranged in an upswept style that lent emphasis to the slender long neck and graceful shoulders. 'You must be absolutely dying for a drink,' she said languidly.

'Lydia doesn't drink.' Wolf's voice cut in behind her before she could reply, and she felt herself stiffen at the expressionless tone. Was he being sarcastic, mocking, after last night, or merely trying to be helpful? She couldn't see his face, and turned as they entered the lounge, but the bland cool features were giving nothing away, his eyes remote and distant as she searched his face.

'Don't you?' Sue's voice expressed utter amazement, with a subtle hint of disapproval at her crassness. 'Well, we've got tonic or bitter lemon or things like that.' She smiled at Lydia with her mouth as her eyes swept coldly over her face and figure with exacting thoroughness.

'There's some freshly squeezed orange in the fridge.' Doug indicated for them to be seated as he spoke.

'That would be lovely.' Lydia forced a smile at his cheerful face gratefully.

'Well, you see to that and I'll look after Wolf,' Sue smiled sweetly. 'Whisky on the rocks, as usual?'

'Please.' Wolf didn't return the lovely brunette's smile but Lydia didn't notice; she was trying to absorb and understand the messages her brain was giving her. There was something wrong, something not quite…nice here.

As Wolf seated himself beside her on the beautifully upholstered settee she glanced round the large room warily. Everything was of the very best. Wolf obviously paid his employees well. She noticed a photograph of two snub-nosed, brown-haired children in a corner of the room, and spoke impulsively as Sue handed Wolf his drink. 'What lovely children. How old are they?'

'Geraldine is seven and Geoffrey is eight. They are Doug's children from his first marriage.' The green eyes flicked uninterestedly over the photograph. 'They live with their mother,' she added coldly.

'Oh, I see.' Lydia sought for something to say—the brunette's tone had almost been a snub. 'Do you have any children?' she asked politely, trying to stifle her dislike.

'No.' Hard green eyes met hers. 'I still work now and again, so it's impractical.'

'Sue is a model.' Doug had joined them, handing Lydia her drink with a quick glance at his wife. 'She feels being pregnant would put her out of action too long, besides which, she doesn't really like children. Do you, darling?' It was obviously a sore point, and Lydia felt herself flush at her inadvertent gaffe, but Sue seemed quite unaffected, throwing her husband a cold glance of distaste as she agreed with him.

'No, I don't.' She smiled coolly at Lydia. 'Deadly for the figure.'

As the evening progressed Lydia felt more and more uncomfortable. Apart from the first few moments, the social repartee had been light and amusing; Sue was a sparkling hostess and Doug was droll and humorous, but under the surface polish of well-bred refinement she sensed a whole host of different emotions bubbling and simmering with puzzling ferocity.

Wolf was his normal cool, cynical self, adding the odd bite of mordant humour which Sue in particular seemed to appreciate thoroughly, but then she seemed to appreciate thoroughly everything about Wolf, Lydia thought testily as the brunette made yet another outrageous bid for his attention, the third in as many minutes. It was obvious and embarrassing, and yet Doug seemed quite relaxed, jovial, even.

Suddenly the beautiful brunette's attention turned to Lydia, her eyes as hard as glass as she looked into her face. 'Is that a wedding-ring I see?' She glanced pointedly at Lydia's left hand. 'You're married?'

'Separated.' Wolf had answered before she could speak, his tone infinitely cold.

'Oh, what a shame…' The narrowed blue eyes flickered a moment. Wolf had made it perfectly plain that further questions would be an intrusion, but his hostess chose to ignore the warning. 'Had you been married long?' she asked silkily.

'I got married when I was twenty-one.' This time Lydia forestalled Wolf. The look on his face indicated that his reply wouldn't have been conducive to harmonious relations.

'Any children?' the smooth voice persisted.

'Sue...' Doug spoke quickly, with a meaningful glance at Wolf's dark face.

'A little girl.' Lydia smiled brightly. 'She's three now and absolutely gorgeous.'

'Is she?' It was clear the last thing Sue wanted to talk about was Lydia's child, so for that very reason Lydia detailed Hannah's life from birth to present and the diversion worked as she had thought it would. Immediately Lydia paused for breath Sue launched into a description of her latest modelling assignment with great gusto, and as the other three listened patiently Lydia caught Wolf's eye. He winked, slowly and very sardonically, before turning away. He had recognised the manoeuvre and given her due acclamation. She quickly checked the surge of pleasure she felt. Careful, Lydia, careful, she told herself silently. It doesn't mean a thing.

All in all she felt overwhelming relief when Wolf glanced pointedly at his watch as they finished dinner and made their apologies. 'It's been a long day,' he drawled lazily as Sue pouted in his direction. 'We're all dead on our feet.'

'A quick coffee, then?' Sue smiled beguilingly. 'It's ready and will keep you awake on the drive back to the hotel.'

Wolf raised enquiring eyebrows at Lydia and, much as she would have liked to shake her head and agree they go immediately, she found herself politely acceding to just one cup. It seemed unnecessarily rude not to.

'Come and help me, Lydia,' Sue invited surprisingly. 'Many hands make light work, and all that.'

Once in the huge fitted kitchen, that was the ultimate in elegance, Sue shut the door carefully, her eyes narrowed as she turned to Lydia and indicated the tray and cups and saucers on the work-surface. 'Have you known

Wolf long?' She removed the aromatic pot of coffee from its stand and waited while Lydia set the tray.

'Not really.' Lydia felt the hairs on the back of her neck prickle as though in warning of a confrontation, but told herself she was imagining things. 'His secretary is on maternity leave and I'm standing in for her,' she explained quietly.

'Really…?' Sue stood back a pace and surveyed Lydia's blonde beauty through half closed eyes. 'You aren't the normal sort of office girl, are you?' It was meant to insult, and Lydia stared back steadily as she felt herself stiffen in readiness for the attack. Their glances held for a long moment and Sue was the first to look away, a sudden flush of colour flaring across the high cheekbones.

'There has been a steady stream of young hopefuls in Wolf's life since Miranda died,' the hard voice continued nastily as Sue walked across to a cupboard at the far end of the kitchen. 'You know he was married, of course?' she added as she suddenly swung round to face Lydia, eyes narrowed like a beautiful cat about to pounce.

'Of course.' Whatever impulse had made Wolf share the confidence she blessed tenfold. Sue had obviously hoped and expected it would be a shock. 'The accident must have been a shock for everyone,' she said expressionlessly.

'The women absolutely adore him, you know.' Sue clearly wasn't going to be deflected from her chosen form of attack. 'Well, it isn't surprising, is it? He has to be the most gorgeous man in the whole of London.'

'Well, as his secretary, my job is to organise and help as far as I can in the office,' Lydia said calmly, keeping her temper in check with considerable effort. The woman was a monster.

'Oh, of course…' The words were delivered in such a way as to make them a subtle insult. 'His secretary…' Sue turned and extracted some fresh napkins from the well-stocked cupboard, her movements graceful and cool. She really was elegance personified, Lydia thought dispassionately as she watched the regal brunette carefully, and she had never met anyone she liked less.

She waited quietly for the next attack and it wasn't long in coming as Sue walked over to the tray, slinging the napkins carelessly by the side of the expensive bone china.

'I was his wife's best friend, you know.' She had obviously changed the direction of the assault, Lydia thought warily as Sue spoke again. 'We were both models, of course, and quite inseparable when Miranda married Wolf. She was just so beautiful, everyone adored her.'

'Did they?' Lydia prayed for composure as she watched the other woman open a box of after-dinner mints and place them on the tray. She didn't want to hear any of this, but she had the feeling there was no escape.

'He was just so devastated after the accident, I was *so* glad I was around.' Sue turned hard green eyes on Lydia's pale face. 'To help…you know.' She smoothed her dress suggestively.

Oh, she knew all right, Lydia thought painfully as the green eyes narrowed into feline slits in which the meaning was unmistakable. Suddenly a whole host of little incidents that had bothered her all night fell into place. 'I'm sure your friend would have been very grateful,'

Lydia said coolly, with biting scorn. 'Shall I carry the tray through?'

'And we're still such *good* friends.' Sue's face was poisonous with a mixture of dislike and virulent maliciousness. 'Doug got this job on my recommendation,' she added meaningfully.

'Did he?' Lydia had had enough. She took hold of the tray and walked across the room. 'Well, your husband is very good at his job, so I understand, Mrs Webb, and I'm sure he got the position because Wolf knew he could do the job, not because you were available to sleep with the boss.' She flicked open the door-handle with her hip, almost dropping the tray in the process, and stalked into the lounge with her head held high.

The next few minutes were painful in the extreme. Lydia sat in regal silence, sipping her coffee without looking to left or right, aware of Sue's tight-lipped face as she made desultory conversation with the two men, although it was obvious her heart wasn't in it. Wolf's razor-sharp gaze had flashed over Lydia's face more than once, but she was determined not to give him the chance to enquire what was wrong until they were in the car. And then she'd let him have it. Hot and strong. Her lip curled as she thought of the implications of what Sue had revealed. He'd slept with his wife's best friend for nothing more than sexual gratification, that much was obvious, and then secured her husband a post in his firm. It stank. Whatever way you looked at it, it stank. Was he still sleeping with her when he felt like it? Well, he'd said he wanted relationships with no ties, and what better way to ensure that than to have an obedient husband to take charge when he felt he'd had enough? Her eyes flashed over Doug and she saw he was looking at her with a faintly bewildered expression in the blue eyes. It was awful. Poor Doug. A flood of self-righteous anger added to the sense of outrage. Whatever his first wife had been like, she couldn't be worse than Sue.

They left the house shortly afterwards, Sue effusive in her goodbye embrace with Wolf and stiffly rigid with Lydia.

Once in the car Wolf turned to her, his eyes silver in the dim moonlight trickling in through the car window. 'OK, let's have it.' The deep voice was dry but not unfriendly. 'Obviously Sue's got under your skin in some way? She has a knack of offending practically every woman she comes into contact with.' The conciliatory note was the last straw.

'I can't imagine why.' She glared at him angrily, her eyes black with furious rage. 'But apparently that wasn't the case with your wife? I understand the two were great friends.'

They had been travelling along the neat, newly made road that led on to the small private estate in which Doug's house was situated, but now Wolf turned into a bus pull-in, parking the car with cool controlled movements and turning to her once the engine had died.

'Sue knew Miranda, yes,' he said with studied calm, his eyes stroking over her hot cheeks and glittering eyes. 'Great friends is probably a bit strong, but I think they got on OK.'

'And Sue was so comforting after the accident.' She knew she was going to regret this, but somehow, after all that had gone before, it had to come out.

'Was she?' He eyed her grimly. 'I take it that should mean something?'

'Well, it clearly didn't to you.' How could he be so icy cold, so calm?

'Lydia…' He paused and settled himself further into

the seat, studying her through narrowed eyes. 'Would you like to tell me exactly what the hell you're talking about?'

'I'm *talking* about sleeping with your wife's best friend and then giving her husband a job to keep her available,' she said scathingly.

'*What*?' The word was a pistol-shot in the close confines of the car but his face had frozen, the lines round his mouth and eyes standing out in startling contrast to the rest of his tanned skin. And as she looked into his face, into the icy blue eyes, she knew she had made a terrible mistake.

'Sue said—'

'I don't care what the hell Sue said,' he snarled softly. 'Surely it didn't take you above one minute to see the sort of woman she is? She's rotten, Lydia, right through. Life has soured her to the point where she is no good to herself or anyone else. She makes Doug's life hell.' He took a deep breath and then spoke more softly, but still with a cold, deadly intensity that frightened her half to death. 'I knew her long before I met Miranda, when she was just seventeen and I was nineteen, and for a time we had some fun together. Then she got on to the model circuit and everything changed. She changed. But we still moved in the same set and when Miranda came along…' He shrugged tightly. 'I guess they had the work in common. She married Doug three years ago when the modelling contracts began to dry up, and when he lost his job eighteen months ago she suggested I give him an interview. *Suggested*. That's all. Doug got the job on his excellent capabilities. He knows that and I know it and, for the record, Sue knows it too,' he added grimly.

'Wolf—'

'Doug is not just an employee, he's a friend,' he

growled softly. She shrank back against the cushioned seat and he gave a small, mirthless smile. 'I've never raised a hand in anger to a woman before but you, Lydia, you push me to the limit. Have I cross-questioned you about Mike Wilson? Have I? And I had every right, believe me, but I tried to believe—' He stopped abruptly. 'Oh, to hell with it.'

Mike Wilson? she thought helplessly. What had he got to do anything? What was he thinking about her? 'Wolf, I don't understand—'

'What do you see when you look at me?' He cut into her voice savagely, his face ruthless. 'Some creature from the pit with horns and a forked tail? Do you seriously think I would employ a man, a good, honest man, for the sole purpose of sleeping with his wife when I felt the need? I haven't touched Sue in eighteen years, although for the whole of that time she's made it very clear she was ready and willing, even before Miranda died.' He gave her a last scathing glance of biting disgust and turned the ignition key, his face white.

They drove back to the hotel in absolute silence, and mercifully Lydia was numb with shock. She realised she had played right into Sue's hands. Somehow the tall brunette had sensed the attraction between Wolf and his secretary and had been determined to destroy what she didn't quite understand. And Lydia had believed her, or *tried* to believe her. The thought pierced the numbness as they reached the hotel grounds. She had wanted to believe the worst of Wolf, needed to; it had been protection against this deadly, overwhelming attraction that made her putty in his hands. If she could despise him, work up some disdain and scorn for the man she thought he was, it would have been a defence against her own feelings for him. Because, although she knew he didn't want any lasting commitment with a woman, although she knew his heart, if he had one, was as cold as ice, everything in her wanted to throw herself at his feet. And *that* had been what she was fighting, not him.

'Goodnight, Lydia.' He left her immediately they entered the suite, without giving her a chance to say anything, walking into his bedroom and shutting the door with a dismissive controlled click. She would have preferred he slam it hard. At least that way it would have shown he had some feeling about her left. She stood in the lounge for a few seconds more, her head whirling, and then went to her own room on leaden feet.

Well, she had what she wanted now. She stared at her reflection in the full-length mirror, misty through her tears. He would leave her alone. She had killed even that strange animal passion he had felt for her. She hugged herself tightly round the waist, the image in the mirror blurring still more. So why didn't she feel relieved, comforted, reassured? Why did she feel as though the world, her world, had just shattered into a million tiny, sharp, piercing little pieces?

CHAPTER EIGHT

SURPRISINGLY, when she surfaced from a thick, deep, heavy sleep the next morning, she realised she had slept the night away. A combination of mental and physical exhaustion along with practically no rest the night before had worked like a powerful sleeping-draught in spite of her overwhelming misery. She glanced at the clock and then looked again more sharply. Ten o'clock? It couldn't be saying ten o'clock? She leant closer and heard the steady rhythmic tick. She must have slept through the alarm at half-past six. She turned the small clock upside-down and saw to her dismay she hadn't set it the night before. Damn! She leapt out of bed with her heart pounding. What would Wolf think? Why hadn't he called her, knocked on the door? Where was he?

She hastily pulled her silk dressing-gown over the matching pale blue nightie and felt for her fluffy mules under the bed, catching sight of her ruffled reflection in the mirror as she did so. She looked a mess but she hadn't got time to worry about that now. Was Wolf at the office? She'd have to ring—this was awful.

She wrenched open her door and had taken two or three steps into the lounge before she realised Wolf was sitting at the table in a replay of the previous morning, newspaper open, table full, and a steaming cup of black coffee in front of him. 'Good morning.' The newspaper lowered, and just for an instant she saw surprise at her attire flash across the hard, handsome face before the blank mask settled again. 'The waiter's just left. Did he wake you?'

'No… Yes… I don't know…' She stared at him as she struggled to compose her racing thoughts. 'I didn't know you were here, it's so late…' She glanced desperately towards the phone. 'I was going to ring you at the office.'

'And now there's no need.' The dark voice was quite expressionless, his whole manner one of cool, reserved control and careful politeness, but she sensed somehow that below the surface it was a different story. The black eyebrows rose a fraction as his blue eyes wandered over her ruffled hair and sleep-flushed face. 'I had a mental picture of what you would look like in the morning and I'm not disappointed.' She stared at him helplessly, quite unable to move, let alone reply, and after a long moment the newspaper was raised again. 'Why don't you sit down and have some coffee now you're out here?' It was obvious and reasonable and she couldn't think of a reason not to, so she walked gingerly across to the table, pulling the belt of the dressing-gown still tighter round her slim waist as she slipped into a vacant chair.

'There's toast and preserves and a variety of cooked dishes under the covers,' the cool voice behind the newspaper said. 'I ordered enough for two in case you joined me.'

'I'm sorry I'm so late,' she said stiffly to the black and white print. 'I forgot to set my alarm—'

'No problem.' The newspaper crackled a bit but still remained in place. 'Relax and enjoy a leisurely breakfast—you earned it yesterday.'

Yesterday? For a moment she thought he was being sarcastic about the dreadful, ill-fated evening, and then reason asserted itself. He was referring to the long day's work. Of course he was. She brushed a silky strand of hair off her face. Somehow yesterday had narrowed down to several catastrophic hours as far as she was concerned.

She must look awful. She touched her hair tentatively. No make-up, and she hadn't even brushed her hair before she had raced out here. She shut her eyes for an instant in exasperation at her impulsiveness and then opened them to pour herself a cup of black coffee. She usually had it white but she needed all the undiluted caffeine she could get this morning—that stimulating alkaloid had better work, and fast. To sit here and eat breakfast with him was bad enough, but with him fully dressed and looking as delicious as ever, and her barely decent... She sighed deeply.

'Now what?' As the newspaper lowered her heartbeat increased tenfold. Freshly shaven and with his still-damp hair slicked back he was just too—too much.

'Sorry?' she gazed at him warily, noting the absence of a jacket. The pale grey shirt sat on the big broad shoulders like an advertisement for its brand name, and the carelessly knotted silk tie matched perfectly. It wasn't fair that one man should have so much going for him.

'The big sigh?' He eyed her sardonically. 'I would have thought you'd be starving this morning. Sue's food may be gourmet style but she serves the sort of portions that she and the rest of her model-friends eat. Hardly satisfying or even remotely adequate. Now, stop contemplating the food and eat it instead.' The newspaper was raised again, leaving her staring at it open-mouthed.

She hadn't dreamt that disastrous finish to the evening, had she? It *had* actually happened? She remembered the black rage on his face and the icy fury that had turned the silver-blue eyes into pinpoints of steel, and shivered suddenly. But this morning he was so… reasonable. What was going on?

'You'll be seeing Hannah later,' the disembodied voice said after a moment or two. 'We're catching the two-thirty plane to London.'

'Oh, right,' she responded weakly.

'We could have stayed another day but Doug can see to the odds and ends now, and there's a previous appointment at five I'd like to keep if I can. Perhaps you'd take most of the papers back to the office for me?' he asked quietly.

'Of course.' A previous appointment? There was some inflexion in his voice, just something, that told her it wasn't a business appointment. Elda? The beautiful brunette's name flashed into her mind and she felt the piece of toast in her mouth turn to cotton wool. Of course it would be Elda and why shouldn't it be? He was a free agent, unattached and fancy-free. He could see exactly who he liked. The pain in her chest deepened. The corrosive scene last night, her awful accusations he could dismiss as unimportant this morning, because *she* was unimportant. When would she learn? When would she ever learn?

She finished the slice of toast quickly and stood up, her voice cool and flat even as she trembled inside. 'I'll go and have a bath, if that's all right?' she asked quietly.

'Fine.' His eyes had narrowed at her tone but he made no other comment. 'I'd like to leave here at twelve and call in the office for a few minutes, OK?'

'I'll be ready.' She walked with as much dignity as she could muster into her room, and when she joined him just before twelve she was the epitome of the perfect secretary—immaculate, cool, with not a hair out of place and a remote, businesslike expression tightening her delicate features. Never again would she betray any emotion to this man, *never*. Her back stiffened with conviction. Once back in London she would give a week's notice and then that would be that. She ignored with ruthless determination the jerk her heart gave at the thought.

Doug was waiting for them at the office, a good-natured, warm smile on his face and his manner easy. It only took one glance for Lydia to realise that Sue hadn't told him what had passed between them the night before. Whatever excuse she had made for the obvious tension, it wasn't the real one. How could some men be so blind where the female of the species was concerned? she asked herself in amazement. Sue was the original barracuda, in fact she made the large voracious hunter seem like a sweet little goldfish, but Doug obviously loved her in spite of the fact that she didn't even like his children. Men were different creatures, she thought faintly, aliens... She glanced at Wolf's hard, cold face silently. Definitely aliens. And she had given this particular alien far too much power where she was concerned.

'Well, all's well that ends well?' Doug grinned cheerfully as they finished checking the last of the figures and gave them to his secretary to fax through. 'Next time you come down I hope you can stay longer, Wolf—perhaps we could put you up? I know Sue would like that.'

Lydia glanced sharply at Doug's smiling face to see if there was an edge beneath the apparent goodwill but no, his face expressed nothing but what his words indicated.

'Thanks, Doug.' Wolf's voice was bland and dry in the extreme. 'But it's probably better if I'm independent.

I often work until late in the night and I wouldn't want to keep you up.'

'Well, the offer's always open.' The other man seemed totally oblivious to Wolf's cynical glance at Lydia and her burning cheeks.

Once back in the privacy of the car, Wolf eyed Lydia sardonically as he started the engine. 'Trusting soul, isn't he?' The deep voice was bland and cool. 'Unlike some.'

'If that means me, I think you're being most unfair.' She glared at him angrily. 'I've said I'm sorry for misunderstanding things and I am, but surely you can see how things looked from my side? Sue virtually told me—' She stopped abruptly. 'Well, you know what she hinted at,' she finished helplessly.

'And how readily you believed her.' There was a note in his voice she couldn't place. If she hadn't known it was impossible, she would almost have thought it was pain. The journey home was tight with tension, the air electric. Wolf seemed to have disappeared into a world of his own, his face withdrawn and cold and his body taut, but she barely noticed; her whole being was eaten up with misery. She knew she had to leave this man, and fast, but the thought made her sick with pain. It was ridiculous, crazy, but somehow the idea of never seeing him again had got all out of proportion in her mind. She didn't understand it, or herself, but it was a fact.

Once back in London he settled her in a taxi-cab with a pile of papers to drop off at the office. 'I wanted to talk to you today, but the timing was all wrong.' His face was stiff as he surveyed her through the window. 'There's something I need to discuss with you in some depth, something you need to understand, but it can't be rushed.'

'I'm sure tomorrow will do.' She forced herself to

smile brightly. 'You mustn't be late for your appointment.'

'No…' He straightened and stood back from the taxi and just for a moment, an insane moment, he seemed vulnerable and strangely alone among the crowds thronging the terminal, his eyes bleak and uncertain as they held hers. She felt herself leaning forward instinctively but then the taxi moved off and the moment was lost. She sank back against the upholstered seat that smelt vaguely of leather and smoke as her heart thudded its beat violently against her chest. She really must be losing her reason. If the taxi hadn't chosen that second to move away she would have made the most colossal fool of herself for the second time in twenty-four hours. What would she have said to him? She didn't know. What she *did* know was that her hand had been moving to reach out to his. She shut her eyes tightly. He would probably have ignored it with that icy-cold disdain he was so good at or, worse, made a cool cynical remark that would have cut her in two. She had to leave him. *No*. She corrected herself firmly. She had to leave Strade Engineering's employ, that was all it meant. That was all it had to mean.

She dropped her suitcase off at home before continuing in the taxi to the office, where she worked furiously until just on five, when she left on the dot. She wasn't normally time-conscious, just the opposite in fact, but the thought of being around when Wolf returned fresh from Elda's arms was too much. OK, so she had been wrong about Sue, she told herself bleakly as the tube carried her swiftly homewards, but Elda still remained. And it was worse, somehow, that Elda was so inoffensive—likeable even. If she had been another Sue, hard and patently selfish, Lydia could have dismissed her as

just another jet-setter out for kicks, but Elda was…nice.
And Wolf displayed a gentleness with her that seemed
to belie his earlier comments on his attitude to his
women. But perhaps this appointment had nothing to do
with Elda? The hope died as quickly as it was born.
Somehow a primitive instinct that was irrefragable told
her it had.

Hannah's welcome was ecstatic, and for an hour or
so the ache in her heart eased as she played with her
daughter before getting tea. The trip had been hectic and
not conducive to shopping, but she had found the perfect
present in the airport shop, a delicate gold chain with a
tiny little engraved locket that she knew Hannah would
love. Matthew had bought Lydia a similar, much larger
one on her eighteenth birthday, which had always held
untold fascination for her daughter, and now Hannah insisted on keeping hers on as they went upstairs for her
evening bath. As she soaped the tiny wriggling body,
responding to a long, involved story Hannah was telling
her about an incident at nursery, the phone began to ring
downstairs.

'Oh, Mummeee…' Hannah's pouting lower lip and
disappointed face as she made to lift her out of the bath
halted her in her tracks. The phone continued relentlessly. What if it was Wolf? Her stomach lurched helplessly. Well, what if it was? She turned back to Hannah
with a reassuring smile.

'Five more minutes and that's all.' If it was Wolf, *if*,
he could always phone back later, and why would it be
him, anyway? She was beginning to get into the realms
of fantasy with this thing, she thought testily. All that
had happened, the bare unadulterated fact, was that he
had been tempted to indulge in a brief convenient affair
with his temporary secretary, and when she had refused

had accepted the rebuff with the minimum of emotion. He was probably quite relieved, her mind ground on ruthlessly. Once the initial passion had been sated she would have become the proverbial millstone round his neck. He knew, and she knew, that she just wasn't his type. Naïve, inexperienced, unsophisticated? Probably, she thought grimly. But if there was a choice of remaining as she was or becoming like one of the women he usually enjoyed, she knew she had had no alternative but to act as she had. To do otherwise would have been emotional suicide.

She had just settled herself in front of the television later that evening, Tiger a warm bundle of purring fur on her lap, when the telephone rang again.

'Lydia?' Ridiculous, stupid, but at the sound of his deep, silky voice her oxygen-level took a nosedive. 'Is this a good moment?' the dark voice asked carefully.

'A good moment?' She tried valiantly to pull herself together and act like a responsible, mature adult.

'I wanted to talk to you.' There was a brief pause, and just for a moment she felt he was finding this conversation as nerve-racking as she was, but that was crazy. 'I'd prefer it be somewhere private, not the office.' This time the pause was longer. 'Are you free now if I come round?'

'But—' She stopped abruptly and took a long, deep shuddering breath. What did he want to come round for? The answer registered in every nerve of her body and scared her half to death. She *wanted* him to come round, to make love to her...

'Can you give me some idea of what it's about?' she asked faintly. Did he think that her rage over Sue had indicated she was jealous? That she wanted him? That her 'no' had been a subtle come-on? Perhaps he wasn't

used to being refused, and that apparent calm and cold
acceptance of her rebuff had merely hidden a ruthless
determination to get his own way?

'You know,' he said quietly. 'This attraction between
us.'

'Oh.' His very control was intimidating. He was so
much in command of every situation, the master of his
own emotions and everyone else's. Suddenly she had to
ask, and she knew she wouldn't be able to do it if he
stood before her in the flesh. 'That appointment tonight?'
She shut her eyes tightly. 'Was it with Elda?' she asked
bleakly.

'How did you know?' He sounded surprised, nothing
more. No guilt. No shame.

How did she know? The pain that shot through her
whole being was shattering. She knew because her love
for him had sensitised her to every little thing about him.
She knew the look on his face when he thought of Elda,
the tone of his voice. She knew so many things about
him she had never consciously realised before. Because
she loved him. The knowledge had been there with her
for weeks but she had been too busy fighting it to let it
get through to her brain. She loved him in a way she
had never loved Matthew. In a way he had told her he
was incapable of and didn't want.

'I don't think it would be a good idea for you to come
round, Wolf.' There was a small, blank silence and she
forced herself to continue. 'Elda wouldn't like it,' she
said painfully.

'Elda?' The name was a small explosion. 'What the
hell has Elda got to do with it?'

'Not a lot, probably.' Her heart was pounding so hard
against her ribcage she was sure he could hear it. 'Let's
just say she's an illustration of the case-history.'

'Lydia, I'm sure that this is making sense to one of us, but it sure isn't me.' She heard a deep, indrawn breath and then his voice spoke again more quietly. 'I'm coming round—'

'No!' For a moment she felt a flash of emotion that was close to hatred. 'Perhaps Elda can stand knowing she is just one in a long line of brief liaisons, perhaps she even really wants it that way, I don't know. What I do know is that I have no intention of being her replacement.' This time the silence on the end of the phone was absolute. And then shockingly, unbelievably, the line went dead. He'd hung up on her. She gazed at the inoffensive piece of plastic in her hands for a full minute before replacing the receiver slowly. He hadn't tried to cajole, reassure, bully... He'd just simply hung up on her. The rejection was a stunning slap in the face. He couldn't have made it plainer how little she mattered.

She began to pace the lounge, Tiger staring up at her with wide, disapproving green eyes as she walked to and fro in an agony of bitter pain. Well, what had she expected? she asked herself wildly. Protestations of undying love? A declaration of a change of heart? An announcement that he had discovered she was the one true love of his life and that he was prepared to give up all for her? She laughed bitterly, that sound a cracked, dry exclamation of pain in the quiet room. She *had* harboured such stupidly romantic hopes in the secret recesses of her heart, she admitted to herself grimly, even if she hadn't acknowledged them to herself. And now she had got exactly what she deserved. She clenched her hands together and forced herself to sit down on the settee. He had lost a wife and daughter and his heart had died with them. End of story.

The sharp, angry knocking on her door a few minutes

later took no account of a small child sleeping. *He had come to see her.* As she stumbled forwards she wasn't sure if it was anger, pain, relief or wild exhilaration that had turned her legs to water, but as she flung open the door, to reveal Wolf dark and scowling on the doorstep, she knew the main component of her emotion was burning rage. Rage that he could put her through this, rage that she meant so little in comparison to what she felt for him, rage at Elda and the hundred and one others like her—

'Elda is the wife of my best friend.' As she automatically tried to close the door, stunned at the outrageous lie, he thrust his foot in the space and jerked the handle out of her hand. 'Oh, no, you're going to listen, listen to every damn word I want to say.' The words were low and furious and all the more deadly for being spoken in a quiet, controlled hiss. 'I don't know what this husband of yours has done to you to make you so distrustful of the male gender, but I sure as hell intend to find out.' She found herself manhandled back into the lounge and sank down on to the settee as her legs refused to support her another moment.

'Elda is Andrew's wife—the doctor I called out to you when you hurt your head?' She nodded helplessly as he stood in front of her, magnificent and frightening in his black rage. 'I've known them both since university and there has never been a couple more deeply in love,' he continued grimly, his eyes lethal. 'But Elda can't have children, or to be more precise she can't carry a baby more than twelve weeks. It's been miscarriage after miscarriage, I've lost count, and since the last one a year ago she's got it into her head that Andrew is going to leave her for someone else who can give him children. *I* know that it's the last thing on Andrew's mind, *he's* nearly been going insane trying to convince her that he loves her more than any desire for procreation, but six months ago she tried to kill herself and things got really heavy for a time. She can talk to me, she trusts me.' He eyed her condemningly as he said the last three words. 'And Andrew and I both thought it was better than a psychiatrist, so I've been there for her—for them both.'

'And the appointment?' she asked through numb lips.

'Elda's going to America,' he stated expressionlessly. 'A colleague of Andrew's suggested a doctor who is unparalleled in his work for childless couples, added to which we all thought the change would do her good. The thing is an obsession now, which she has seen at last. She is a lovely lady and I hated to see her so messed up.' He eyed her grimly. 'That is the truth, Lydia, take it or leave it. Andrew is going to join her out there in a couple of weeks when the initial tests have been completed, but he wanted me to turn up before she left as a surprise. She left on the seven o'clock flight,' he added flatly.

'I see.' Totally inadequate, but she couldn't think, let alone speak. 'I'm sorry,' she said weakly.

'So...' He looked down at her, his eyes hooded. 'Do you believe me? Really believe me?'

'Of course I believe you.' If she had been looking at him she would have seen the hard face soften at her total acceptance of the ignominious position she had placed herself in. 'It was just after all you'd said—' She stopped abruptly. This was her fault. She'd jumped to all sorts of conclusions without any real knowledge of the facts, and she couldn't blame him, not even indirectly. Oh... She bit on her lower lip painfully. What an utter fool she'd made of herself. 'I'm sorry,' she said again, her voice wretched.

'I haven't looked at another woman since the first day I set eyes on you.' The deep softness in his voice brought her head jerking up, her eyes wide as they met his. 'If that helps at all? Not that there was a steady stream before that, I might add.' He smiled slowly. 'Your faith in my prowess in that direction is more than a little touching.'

'Wolf—'

'I need to talk to you, Lydia. I should have done it weeks ago but I wasn't ready, you weren't. I knew you were hurting and I wasn't sure if your marriage was really over. Added to which—' He stopped abruptly. 'Dammit, woman, don't look at me like that, I can't think straight,' he said thickly.

'Wolf...' His name was a plea for understanding.

As he reached for her a little movement behind him caught Lydia's eye. 'Hannah?' Wolf turned in the same instant and they both surveyed the tiny pink and white angel standing in the doorway with sleep-smudged eyes and silky blonde hair, a battered teddy bear tucked under one arm. It was a picture guaranteed to win first place in anyone's affections, and as Lydia moved towards her daughter Wolf crouched down, his eyes soft as they looked gently into the small face in front of him.

'Bad dream?' It hurt her unbearably to see him like that, to understand what memories it must bring back to him of his own daughter, but as he held out his arms to Hannah and she climbed into them Lydia only saw a quiet tenderness in the hard male features that wrenched at her heart.

'You woke me up.' Hannah spoke fearlessly into the dark, handsome face in front of her. 'You're very noisy.'

'I'm sorry.' His face was rueful as he glanced at Lydia over her daughter's fair head.

'That's all right.' Hannah snuggled contentedly in his arms. 'I like you. I asked my mummy when you were coming to see us again,' she continued happily.

'And what did your mummy say?' he murmured quietly.

'She said you were too busy.' Hannah moved back an inch and surveyed him thoughtfully. 'But you aren't, are you?'

'No.' He smiled suddenly. 'I'm not at all busy, Hannah. Now…' He glanced at Lydia again, his eyes enquiring. 'If I'm the one who woke you up, how about if I put you back to bed—yes?'

'Yes, please.' Hannah was clearly enchanted by the thought, brown eyes dark with satisfaction.

'Perhaps your mummy will make me a cup of coffee while I do so?' Lydia nodded weakly. This was all too much. Wolf here in her small home, acting as though he had always been here. Her heart jumped into her mouth. Acting as though he *liked* being here.

It was some ten minutes later before she heard his footsteps on the stairs and she had no premonition of what was coming. She turned as he entered the room and then shrank back against the wall as she saw his face.

'Why, Lydia?' His voice was a low snarl and the dark colour burning the high cheekbones spoke of furious, contained rage. 'Why the fairy-tale?'

'What?' And then she realised, far, far too late, what Hannah had innocently revealed to the big, powerful man in front of her.

'He's dead, isn't he? He's been dead years.' His voice was raw and brutal and savage. 'I've suffered the torments of the damned for weeks, called myself every kind of swine for my baser urges regarding you, and all the time…' He was breathing hard and deep. 'I was burning up inside for days when you first came to work for me, and that day in the lift…' He shook his head angrily. 'I loathed myself afterwards, couldn't believe I'd fallen so hard, and then when I found out he'd left you, that there was a chance you were free—'

'I wanted to explain,' she said desperately. 'I tried—'

'But not *too* hard.' The icy, cynical voice was scathing. 'It gave you some sort of kick, did it? To see me making a total fool of myself?'

'It wasn't like that—'

'Who else knows?' He glared at her furiously. 'Mike, of course, he'd just love this. And the typing-pool? And the cleaners?'

'No, believe me, Wolf, it's not like that. I didn't try to make you look a fool—'

'But you succeeded.' His voice was as hard as steel, the man who had been in the room ten minutes before now seeming a figment of her imagination. 'For the first time in years I wanted to be with someone because of who they were, or who I thought they were,' he finished cuttingly. 'And however I tried to fight it the feeling got stronger and stronger. But you were so naïve, so pure, so untouchable.' The harsh bark didn't resemble a laugh in any way. 'Oh, you're good, baby, I have to give you that. You're the best.' He raked his hand through his hair wildly, his eyes narrowed slits of cold ice. This was worse than anything she could have imagined. She stared at him with great bruised eyes as he verbally ripped her apart.

'How long was the charade going to continue?' he asked icily. 'I knew I should have followed my head and not my heart after I'd seen you with Mike that day. It was all too pat, too convenient. And I *heard* him warning you to keep quiet! Hell, I don't believe all this! You dared to lecture me on my lifestyle when all the time—'

'It wasn't like that. You're making it sound as if I planned it all,' she protested desperately.

'Oh, and it just happened?' he asked bitterly. 'You told me a pack of lies, Lydia, admit it.'

'But—'

'Admit it,' he said ruthlessly.

'Yes, I lied.' She stared at him wildly, her eyes hunted. 'But Mike is nothing to do with this, I hardly know him. I lied to get the job and it didn't seem important at first. Not at first—'

'And later?' he asked grimly.

'Later…' Her voice trailed away. How could she explain later? How could she tell him that she had used her supposed husband as a defence against her own feelings for him and the attraction she knew he felt for her, albeit only physical? That she hadn't dared to let him know she was free because she would have been unable to resist him, but that in her case it wouldn't have just been a giving of her body. She would have given her mind, her soul, everything. She loved him. But he would have used her and walked away. *He would.* 'I knew you just wanted a brief affair,' she said bleakly.

'You knew?' He eyed her with such coldness that she felt the chill of it freeze her blood. 'The hell you did.'

'You told me you steered clear of any involvement, that you chose your women as much for that as anything else,' she said hotly. 'You can't deny that. You wanted physical satisfaction, maybe some fun—'

'Don't tell me what I wanted,' he growled furiously. 'So this is all my fault? Is that what you're saying?'

'No!' Her voice was too shrill, and she checked it quickly. Hannah arriving back on the scene would be the final straw. 'But you didn't tell me anything, *talk* to me—'

'I talked to you more than I've talked to anyone in years,' he said angrily. 'I felt as if I was treading on eggshells half the time but I tried—' He stopped abruptly. 'Hell, what am I defending myself for? Even if you'd dug a hole for yourself there were times you could have told me, you know that.'

'Yes, I know.' Her misery seemed to make him more angry.

'So why the hell didn't you? Because you liked having me on a string?' He eyed her coldly. 'Well?' he barked suddenly. 'Answer me.'

'What do you want me to say?' She knew she was losing the last thread of control but her temper had risen to match his. He was seeing this all his own way, he wasn't even trying to acknowledge the position he had put her in at the beginning of their relationship and, whatever he said, he *hadn't* talked to her, not really. If anyone had been kept at arm's length it was her! 'Just tell me and I'll say it. That's all you want, after all, isn't it—obedient little female puppets to jerk to your string? The great Wolf Strade, cold and unapproachable, making everyone tremble if they come within a hundred yards of you! You don't know the meaning of love and commitment and normal life. You're so caught up in your own little world. You talk about poor Elda being obsessed? Well, at least she is obsessed with something positive, a desire for her own child with the man she loves. You're just obsessed with emptiness—'

'Have you quite finished?' He was glaring at her, hands folded across his chest and his big body as taut as an iron rod.

'No.' She stared back defiantly, but the rage was beginning to die and a wave of agony take its place. This was the death-knell of all her secret hopes and desires. He would never forgive her for the things she had said, even if he could have forgiven her for the lies and deceit regarding Matthew. 'It's about time you listened to someone else for a change.'

'Is it, indeed?' The rigid control was slipping, she could see it in the burning fury in the piercing blue eyes. 'But perhaps I don't want to listen to you, Lydia, perhaps I want to do something quite different.'

'Don't you come near me.' As he took a step towards her she backed away, her hand to her mouth.

'Don't come near you?' He laughed bitterly. 'But why shouldn't I? You aren't a distressed young wife, forsaken by her childhood sweetheart, are you? Far from it.' He seemed beside himself with rage. 'What *exactly* you are I haven't the faintest idea and frankly I don't care. You are here now and so am I. That's all that matters.'

He walked back to the door and shut it, sliding a chair against it before turning and walking over to her again. She was standing straight and erect now, determined not to flinch before him. 'If I start to make love to you it won't be rape, you know that.' His face was hard and cold as he surveyed her insolently from head to toe, his eyes burning into her flesh wherever they touched. 'You want me, Lydia, you can't deny that.' She had given his pride a body-blow, she reflected silently as she saw the mask of arrogant hauteur that clothed the handsome, harsh features. 'I've waited longer for you than I've ever waited for a woman before, and enough is enough.'

If he took her like this, by force, he would never forgive himself. The knowledge was there inside her. It would poison the rest of his life with an insidious toxic contamination that he wouldn't be able to overcome. He was a proud man but he wasn't sufficiently egocentric to excuse this outrage, once the furious rage and bitterness had died.

'Yes, I want you.' She faced him, trembling and soft now, her eyes holding his, open and bare. 'I want you because I love you, Wolf, and you're right, it wouldn't be rape.'

'You love me?' He shook his head angrily, his voice gritty. 'I've been told that before too.'

'I don't doubt it.' She stared back at him, conscious that she was laying herself wide open to the worst sort of pain and rejection. 'But not by me. I do love you, whether you believe it or not,' she said quietly.

'I don't.' But his eyes were stricken as they held hers. 'I don't believe love is an emotion that really exists.'

'Yes, you do,' she said softly.

'No.' He shook his head blindly, his eyes hardening. 'Sex, lust, desire, those things are real and powerful and honest. You can dress them up as love but the end result is the same.'

'Which is?'

'This.' His mouth was angry and harsh as it ravaged hers, his arms like bands of steel as he held her so closely into his hard frame that she could feel his heart pounding like a sledge-hammer against the wall of his chest. She didn't try to fight him, she was intuitive enough to know that any movement of her body would send them over the edge into brutal passion, and she had to convince him that her feeling for him was more than blind desire. He probably wouldn't, couldn't, accept her love for him, but he had to know that in that alone she was different from all the rest. If she succumbed now, gave in to the fiery heat and sweet sensation that his nearness produced, she would become just another name in his little black book. But it was hard, doubly so because she had no inner conviction that she could penetrate that cold, dark, outer shell to the real man she had glimpsed fleetingly. Maybe, if she hadn't lied, if he had taken the step of trusting her…?

The feel and taste and intoxicating smell of him was becoming more than she could deny. She felt a moment's panic at her weakness, at the vulnerability her love for him had exposed. He would explain away her response as animal desire, she knew that, but it was becoming harder to remain cold and unresponsive in his arms.

His mouth had become more coaxing now, persuasive, moving to her throat and still lower in burning-hot, feathery kisses that lit little chills of fire wherever they touched. She moaned slightly, the sound escaping her lips in spite of herself, and heard a low growl of answering passion in the big body trapping hers. He was hugely aroused against her softness, his mouth ravaging the soft silky swell of her breasts as her blouse fell open under his insistent fingers.

She wasn't going to be able to stop this. As her hands moved up to his back, the hard swell of powerful muscles clenching as he felt her touch, she knew she was lost. She loved him too much…

The thought brought a little sob to her lips. Too much to reach him. She began to shake helplessly, the knowledge that she had capitulated swept away by a feverish hunger to become as one with this strange, cold man who had captured her heart and her mind and turned her body into liquid heat. 'My love, my love…' She wasn't aware she had murmured out loud, wasn't aware of the tears dampening her face, but suddenly he pushed her from him with a groan that seemed wrenched out of the very depths of his body, and as she sank to the carpet, her legs refusing to support her, he stepped back a pace as though from something repugnant.

'You see?' He was panting hard, his face dark and ravaged by an emotion that caused the breath to constrict in her throat. He hated her. He was looking at her as though he hated her. 'Do you?' he demanded savagely. 'It all comes down to this, nothing more. You're no different from the rest.'

She stared up at him silently, her eyes wide and luminous like the beautiful eyes of a wounded doe.

'You lied to me.' The words were torn out of him. 'I don't know who you are.'

'I'm sorry—'

'And that makes it better?' He glared at her ruthlessly. 'Sex is the only real thing between a man and a woman and I'm going to prove that to you now.'

'No.' Her voice was very soft. 'If we make love it will be just that on my side, Wolf, love. From almost the first day of meeting you I couldn't understand why I felt like I did. I fought it, I admit it. I felt I'd betrayed Matthew, let him down in the worst way possible because what I'd felt for him didn't even begin to compare with the emotions you called forth. I called it physical desire too.' She stared at him, a touch of bitterness in her face now. 'But it is much, much more than that with me. I know you're incapable of loving a woman again, but it doesn't seem to make any difference. I can't kill this feeling however much I try.'

'You loved Matthew—'

'Yes, I did.' She raised her chin slightly, unaware that her blouse was still open, her body revealed in all its softness, and that the gesture of brave confrontation combined with the vulnerability her body presented hit him like a physical blow, causing his face to whiten.

'I loved him very much, but not in the way I love you. The love I had for him was undemanding, gentle. He'd always been there and I think we both misunderstood what we felt. He was an only child and so was I. Our love was more that of siblings, brother and sister, but neither of us realised it.'

'You expect me to believe that?' he bit out harshly.

'No.' She held his glance painfully. 'I don't suppose you'll believe anything I say.'

'Dead right.' His eyes narrowed on her face. 'Hell, you aren't worth this.' His voice cracked and he turned on his heel in the same instant, flinging the chair aside with a viciousness that frightened her and banging the door behind him as he strode into the dark street.

It was some time before the stillness of the house reached her bruised, aching senses, but then she rose slowly from the floor, her movements dull and sluggish and her face as white as a sheet. The tears had gone, burnt up in the fierce pain that had cauterised her mind so that all that was left was a numb, anaesthetising blankness. She had told him, laid her heart bare before him, exposed her love in all its fragility, and he had ground it under his heel.

She locked the front door automatically, her limbs heavy and leaden and her mouth swollen and bruised with the evidence of his lovemaking, and climbed the stairs slowly, her movements automatic. She had ruined everything, any chance they might have had. It was all her fault.

Mercifully sleep came immediately—a thick, empty blanket in which there was no feeling, no pulse, no life.

CHAPTER NINE

WHEN Lydia awoke to the insistent ringing of the alarm the next morning the merciful covering had been lifted and the wound was exposed in all its raw agony. Somehow she got Hannah to nursery, returning home in a daze of pain and grief to an endless post-mortem that produced nothing but guilt and regret.

She *had* lied to him. She shut her eyes tightly in an agony of remorse. Knowing that it was the one thing he wouldn't tolerate. And what a lie. She shook her head desperately against the sight of his face in those last few moments before he had left. There was nothing she could do, no way back. It was the ultimate betrayal.

The hours slipped by somehow; she was hardly aware of their passing although she forced herself to eat a sandwich and drink a cup of coffee at lunchtime. She couldn't afford to indulge her misery at the cost of Hannah's peace of mind, and if she became ill it would only be her daughter who would suffer.

She paced endlessly up and down the small lounge after lunch. Tiger had made one or two tentative attempts to sit on her lap in the morning, but had now retired under the settee for sanctuary, watching her carefully with big saucer-wide eyes, clearly thinking she had gone mad. She couldn't blame him. She hadn't been reasoning like a sane woman lately. Why, oh, why hadn't she told

Wolf about Matthew long before this? There had been so many opportunities…

She stifled a sob as she drove her fist into her mouth with a hard groan. And all this with Mike. He had obviously suspected she was in league with Anna's husband, at least initially. She should have given him a straightforward explanation after that very first incident, but she had been so horribly embarrassed it had been easier to push it to the back of her mind. 'Coward, coward, coward…' She looked out of the window bleakly. She wouldn't have thought a human heart could stand pain like this and not shatter.

Her mother phoned at two, her voice anxious. 'Lydia? Are you ill, darling? I phoned your office to see how Hannah liked her present, but there was another woman there. What's wrong?'

So he hadn't wasted any time in securing her replacement. Her heart jerked and thudded painfully. He hadn't even waited to see if she would go back. She clenched her teeth against the anguish. But of course he had known she wouldn't go back—how could she after the things they had said to each other?

'I'm OK, Mum, just seem to have gone down with one of these viruses.' She spoke carefully, making her voice as blank as she could. 'Not enough to knock me off my feet but enough to make concentrating at a word processor impossible.'

'Do you want me to come round? Fetch Hannah? Anything?'

'No, no, thanks. Everything's under control. A few days at home and I'll be fine, and I don't want you to catch anything.' She forced a modicum of warmth into her voice. 'Forty-eight hours and I'll be as right as rain.' As right as rain? What a stupid banality, she thought bitterly.

'Are you sure?' Her mother was unusually persistent. 'I'm not stupid, Lydia, and I *am* your mother. It isn't anything to do with that man, is it? Wolf Strade?'

'That man'? For a moment Lydia felt a flood of wild hysterical laughter well up inside. 'That man' had effectively battered through all her defences and shattered the self-esteem of the last few years into fragments. It was *everything* to do with him. And still she loved him more than life. She took a deep breath. 'No, of course not.' There was a pregnant silence on the other end of the phone that lengthened. It was an attribute of her mother's that she could be scathingly disbelieving without saying a word. 'Well, perhaps it is, but I can't talk about it now. Another time,' she added desperately.

'You know best.' Her mother's voice was disapproving but resigned. 'Well, if you're sure I can't help in any way... Give me a call if you change your mind.'

'I will. Thanks, Mum.'

'Goodbye, Lydia.'

'You know best.' Her mother's words taunted her after she had replaced the receiver. But she didn't, did she? She didn't know anything any more.

She thought about how he had come to the house, his explanation regarding Elda. So he was free...at the moment. Perhaps it would have been better to take the brief affair he had wanted? At least that way she would have had memories, if nothing else. Now there was just an empty void where her heart should have been.

And Wolf? Her heart thudded as she pictured him in

his office, barking orders at the new secretary and immersed in work as usual. It wouldn't take him long to forget she even existed—if he still remembered, that was.

She ignored the doorbell at first. She needed time to pull herself together before she collected Hannah, and a door-to-door salesman was the last person she felt like coping with right now. They were renowned in this district and normally she could remain polite and firm, but today she wouldn't be responsible for her actions if they tried a hard sell. In fact the urge to bite and scream and kick at something, anything, was shockingly fierce. But they were persistent. She'd give them that. After a full minute of the bell ringing, with the sort of offensive determination that hit a raw spot deep inside, she suddenly leapt up and flew to the door, wrenching it open with a ferocious scowl that froze as Wolf removed his hand from the button.

'Hello.' He made no attempt to move.

'Hello.' She didn't either.

They stared at each other in silence for taut seconds before she forced words through her numb lips. 'I thought you were at the office.' It was inane, but his appearance following so closely behind her thoughts was shattering.

'The office?' She could have said the moon from the blankness in his deep voice. 'No. I haven't been to the office today.'

'Oh.'

He looked terrible. And gorgeous. He hadn't shaved and the black shadow on his chin gave a whole new meaning to the attraction of designer stubble. A flood of emotion surged into her chest, constricting breath and sending red-hot tears pricking painfully behind her eyelids. She stepped back quickly, petrified he'd notice. He hated emotion, she knew that.

'I—' He cleared his throat and tried again. 'I would like to come in, but if you don't want me to I understand. I guess after last night I'm the last person in the world you want to see.'

Wrong, wrong, wrong, she thought dazedly. Utterly and totally wrong. 'You look as if you could do with a coffee,' she said weakly as she waved him into the house.

'No. It's not coffee I need.' He followed her as far as the lounge doorway and then stood leaning against it, hands thrust deeply into his pockets and his eyes narrowed and piercingly blue as he watched her turn round and face him.

He was everything she had ever wanted in a man. The knowledge pierced her soul with fire. And he could have been hers, for a time at least, but she had thrown it all away. Her throat felt like sandpaper and she knew in a minute she was going to burst into tears, which would probably be the final straw for him. She didn't know why he was here but she did know emotional scenes weren't his style.

'What I *need* is to talk to you, explain—' He stopped abruptly and she knew the words weren't coming easily to him, that he found this baring of his soul distasteful.

'It's all right—'

'No, it's *not* all right!' The rigid control faltered and slipped, and for a moment the harsh intensity that flared in the tormented blue eyes caused her breath to stop. 'Dammit! It's anything but.'

He took a long deep pull of air but the mask was severely out of place now, his face naked and open for the first time she could remember. However could she have imagined he was unemotional? she asked herself faintly as fierce hunger, anger and burning contempt washed over his face in scorching savagery. He must hate her. To look at her like this he must hate her.

She backed from him, her hand to her mouth and her eyes wide with a painful suffering she couldn't hide. 'Please go. This won't do any good—'

'I'm not going to hurt you.' He swore softly as he saw the agony in her face. 'Dammit, Lydia, stop looking at me like that. I have to explain to you, you have to understand at least.'

'I do.' She forced herself to walk as far as the settee and sank down on it, her legs trembling. 'I know I lied to you and you must hate me for it, but please, I can't take much more—'

'But you have to understand *why*—'

'I don't care why!' Suddenly she was screaming at him as her nerves finally snapped. 'I don't care, do you hear? You think I'm deceitful and treacherous and dishonest, you've told me that. You think I wanted to make a fool of—' The lump of lead in her chest choked her voice, and as he made a move towards her she shot bolt-upright, her eyes flashing and her face as white as a sheet. 'Don't you touch me. Don't you dare to touch me. And I'm not going to cry, so don't worry. I just want you to go.'

'No.' It was a small word but coated in steel. 'Not till I've talked to you, properly, without any dramatics.'

Dramatics? He dared to call this bitter grief that was tearing her apart 'dramatics'? His words acted like a deluge of icy water, restoring control and freezing her heart. 'Then talk,' she said flatly as she faced him with her hands clenched into fists at her side. 'If that's what you want.'

'It is.' He shook his head slightly, although his eyes never left hers. 'I've got no right to be here, I know that, not after last night and the things I said, but I need to explain things just once before I get out of your life for good.'

She sat down then. The thought of Wolf being out of her life for good took her legs from under her.

'I was going to talk to you in Scotland but—' He stopped abruptly.

'But?' she asked wearily.

'But I chickened out, lost my nerve.' She stared at him, her eyes portraying her shock, and he laughed harshly, the sound a low, raw wound of pain and contempt. 'Surprised? I don't blame you. Doesn't quite fit in with the macho image, does it? The wolf who walks alone?' The self-derision was so scathingly bitter she could only watch him numbly as he began to pace the room, his hands clenching and unclenching at his sides.

'I told you my wife and child died eight years ago,' he said harshly, 'but there was something else, something I didn't tell you. They were killed on an icy country road driving into town to see a pantomime just before Christmas. An articulated lorry jack-knifed on a patch of black ice and they were killed instantly.'

'Wolf—' He raised his hand at her anguished voice, and now she saw his eyes were steady.

'The reason they were there, the reason they died all alone in a piece of twisted metal, was because I had a big contract going through that I considered more important than my family,' he continued tightly. 'I had arranged to be home in time to take them myself, but when a few problems delayed things I rang Miranda and told her to take Carrie in her car and I'd meet her there. I left nearly half an hour later. I knew I'd miss the first part, but what the hell? It was only a two-bit pantomime, wasn't it? No influential contacts present, no high-fliers to clinch a deal with.' The pain and disgust in his voice were almost more than she could bear. She was seeing the real Wolf now, the man behind the mask, and it was agonising.

'I saw the police cars first, then a fire engine and a couple of ambulances...' His eyes focused on her, black with pain. 'There was nothing anyone could do. The car was mangled beyond recognition but, in one of those quirks of fate, the number-plate had been ripped off and was found intact at the side of the road. Funny thing...' He stared at her blindly. 'I couldn't believe it when the policeman told me the number, and yet I'd known the first moment I saw the road was blocked. I'd known.'

'But you didn't know the accident was going to happen,' she said softly as the tears streamed down her face. 'It was a million to one chance, one of those things against which there would have been no protection even if you had been driving. You do see that, don't you?'

'Maybe.' He raked back his hair savagely. 'Maybe not, we'll never know.' He continued the pacing again, his face grey. 'After the funeral I guess I went crazy for a time. I sure can't remember much about the weeks that followed, anyway. I think they're blanked forever. Dad came over and took me off somewhere, a log cabin in the depths of the Lake District with the snow up to the windows. I think he saved my sanity.' He stopped and turned to her, his eyes focusing on her white face. 'And then one day I wanted to go back. The house was weird, empty, and I began to sort Miranda's things—it was as if it was happening in a film to someone else. But I couldn't go into Carrie's room.' He stopped and she saw moisture glitter bright for a moment in the vivid blue eyes before it was blinked harshly away. 'I never did go into her room again, perhaps I should have. Anyway...' He continued the pacing again, his big body seeming to fill the small room, 'I found letters, addresses, even little gifts among Miranda's things. She'd been having a string of affairs from the first year we were married, before too, maybe. I don't know. Some of the letters were...disgustingly intimate. I sat and read them all, every one, and then I left the house and never went back. I had the site bulldozed within weeks.' He laughed harshly, the sound raw in the stillness. 'Half a million lost in a futile gesture, but I didn't care. I still don't.'

He stopped, turning to look out of the window with his back towards her. 'I couldn't believe I'd lived with someone, shared my life and my bed with them, and not known them. None of it had been real—the love, the sharing, the laughter. Oh, we used to have rows, mainly about my work, which I could understand. She was frustrated being at home with a child and I wasn't home enough—the isolation used to drive her mad.'

She waited, hardly daring to breathe as he paused. 'The worst thing, the worst thing of all was that I couldn't let myself think of Carrie for a time after that. She and Miranda were somehow linked together and I had to blank them both to survive. It got better...' He turned to face her now, taking a deep hard breath. 'It had to,' he said simply.

She rose slowly and walked over to him, putting her small hands against his chest as she looked up into his ravaged face. 'I don't know what to say,' she said softly. 'I thought it was bad with Matthew, the grief, the anger, but I couldn't have got through what you did.'

'Yes, you would have done.' He had tensed at her touch but made no effort to touch her, his body taut and still as he looked down at her. 'You've got more guts than any other lady I know.'

'Wolf—'

'You've got to hear it all, Lydia.' He moved away as though her close proximity hurt him, and she stood bereft, her heart thudding. Was he going to tell her all this and then leave? He was capable of it, she knew that, and she had no idea where all this was leading.

'I was in a mess for a long, long time, poison to myself and everyone else,' he continued grimly. 'Truth became an obsession with me, as did the conviction that I could never trust another woman—they were good for one thing and one thing only.' She flinched and he nodded slowly. 'That's how it was, Lydia, I'm not going to dress it up with fancy words and phrases. I had affairs with women who knew the score, were free and wanted a good time. There are plenty about,' he added cynically. 'Then one day a blonde fireball stormed into my office and put me in my place more effectively than it has ever been done before.'

'It's been done before?' she asked, in a voice she had trouble keeping steady.

'Well, no…' His face relaxed for a moment. 'I've never been any good at taking criticism, believe it or not.'

'I do.' She didn't know if she could take much more of this without breaking down completely, she really didn't.

'And I thought, this one actually says it as it is.' His voice held the note of amazement he must have felt at the time. 'No beating about the bush, no flannel, straight for the jugular. And then…' He stopped now and his eyes held hers steadily. 'And then I came into the office and found you in a huddle with the guy I *knew* was pulling a fast one.'

'Mike was—'

'No, I don't want to know.' He held her glance firmly. 'Whatever it is, I know you weren't involved with him now.'

'How?' she asked faintly.

'Because last night I walked the streets for hours and finally listened to my heart for the first time in years,' he said slowly. 'I used to do it all the time once, before—' He stopped. 'And then I lost the knack—'

'Whether you want to hear it or not, Mike is the husband of a close friend of mine,' she said quickly as he paused for breath. 'I'd forgotten he worked for you and then he came in the office and asked me to keep quiet about it, said you didn't like your secretary to be friendly with the other employees—'

'He's a cute one.' He looked at her wryly. 'And you were worried how he'd survive after he left my employ? The guy will be the next prime minister.'

'Wolf, I'm so sorry—'

'I love you, Lydia.' There was all the emotion she could ever have wanted in his face, and as her heart began thudding she watched the ice-blue eyes mist over. 'I mean I *really* love you. Not a for-the-time-being love. I've loved you from the minute I set eyes on you, can you believe that?' he asked, with a shred of desperation in his voice.

She tried to smile, but as her mouth quivered he moved across the short space separating them and pulled her into him, his body shaking almost as violently as hers.

'I don't deserve to ask but I'm going to anyway. Last night—last night you told me you cared. Have I destroyed that? Can you forgive me?'

'Me forgive you?' Her voice was muffled against his hard chest but it felt so good, so good, she would never have believed how good. 'But I've lied to you, it was all my fault—'

'No.' He moved her into the circle of his arms, staring down at her mouth. 'I put you in an impossible position from the word go, I realised that last night as I roamed the city. You have Hannah to support, this house... What the hell were you supposed to do?'

'But I shouldn't have lied.' She stared up at him weakly. 'And you were right, there were lots of times I could have told you about Matthew—'

'I don't care about Matthew.' His hand traced the line of her lips as his eyes devoured her. 'I don't care about any damn thing except you. I treated you badly when you first came to work for me, I know that, but I was despising myself for the way I felt when I knew you were married, and I wasn't sure how Mike fitted into the scheme of things. I wanted you, you'll never know how much I wanted you. The number of times I wanted to lay you out on that office floor—' He shut his eyes for a second. 'And I kept telling myself it was a physical hunger, nothing more, nothing unusual. I was angry you were married, but relieved too. It took the ball out of my court—*fait accompli*.'

She was still holding back, she didn't know why. It was too much, she couldn't take it in. He loved her? But all the time he had been so cold, so aloof...

'And then I found out he'd left. It scared the hell out of me. I didn't sleep for nights. I knew a brief affair wasn't possible, you weren't that sort of woman and my feelings were too deep and dangerous for that anyway, but if I let you in, just the tiniest bit, I was vulnerable again like the rest of the suckers out there. I couldn't take it, Lydia.'

'But you were so cold, so full of contempt,' she murmured softly. She wanted to believe him, oh, she did, but after what he'd been through, how did he *know* this was real for him?

'Aimed mainly at myself,' he said grimly as though he could read her mind. 'I tried to keep you at a distance but it wasn't working. You were everything I wanted in a woman—soft, gentle, innocent, and yet with a determination and an honesty that—'

'Don't.' She flinched at the last words, her face changing.

'You are honest, Lydia.' He cupped her face in his hands. 'I want to kiss you, but if I do I shan't be able to think any more, to convince you, and I need to convince you, don't I? I can see it in your eyes. Have I hurt you too much? I tried to convince myself yesterday that I needn't take the cataclysmic step, that you were just like Miranda, saying one thing and living a lie. But I couldn't. I've never loved anyone like I love you and I never shall again. You have my heart, Lydia. It isn't much of a gift and you deserve better, but it is wholly yours.'

'Kiss me.' She reached up to him, her heart in her eyes. 'Kiss me. I don't want to talk any more.'

'Lydia…' His voice was a groan, and as he took her mouth she became mindless beneath his, her body fluid and soft as his hands moved down her body in a passionate caress. Her arms clung round his neck as they swayed together in an agony of love, their mouths fusing in an endless kiss that was pure sensation. 'I love you, Lydia, for pity's sake say you'll marry me. Nothing else will do. I want to love you, take care of you, protect you, be a father to Hannah. I want everything, all of it, all of you. Hell—' he moved her slightly from him to look into her starry eyes '—say something, woman, you're torturing me.'

'Love me.' She breathed in the smell of him as she clung to the hard-muscled body, her mind spinning. 'Love me now.'

'No.' He moved her to arm's length now, his eyes steady. 'I want an answer in cold blood, not the heat of the moment. I want to hear you say you love me.'

'I do.' She stared at his dark, handsome face as her

head cleared, and then drew back a little, a touching uncertainty in her face. This was too sudden. Too great a change-about. 'What if you change your mind, if it begins to go wrong?' she asked faintly.

'Do you love me?' he persisted grimly.

'More than life.'

'Then we'll discuss it going wrong on our twenty-fifth wedding anniversary,' he said, his voice thick now as his hand traced one swollen nipple through the soft silk of her blouse. 'That should give us enough time to consider if we've done the right thing.'

And then there was nothing but fiery, heady pleasure as his mouth fastened on hers again, the kiss deepening to a primitive assault on her senses that was an act of possession in itself. She moaned softly in her throat, lost in a mounting exultation that he loved her. *He loved her*.

EPILOGUE

'WELL, Mrs Strade?' Lydia stretched languorously as a possessive, skilled hand stroked her dreamily out of sleep before it settled on one firm, full breast as its partner continued its erotic assault on her body. 'Fifteen years to go.'

'What?' She opened drowsy eyes to find Wolf propped on one elbow as he surveyed her through those silver-blue eyes that she had once imagined were as cold as ice. There was fire beneath the ice, she knew that now, and she also knew it was just for her.

He moved slightly, pulling her more beneath him, and as she felt one hard-muscled leg on hers, the body-hair furry against her softness, her body responded as it always did. 'Only another fifteen years to go before you tell me if I'm to get my marching orders.' The hard, chiselled face was tender and warm as he looked down into her sleep-flushed face, and the curling hair on his chest tickled her breasts as he bent to deposit a swift kiss on her mouth before resuming his original position. 'Don't tell me you've forgotten this is our tenth wedding-anniversary?' he asked softly.

'Of course I haven't.' Her indignation was lost under his mouth as it swooped down in hard passion now and took possession of hers, turning her bones to water as it did its devastating work on her senses.

'You're nice to wake up to, Mrs Strade.' He ran a

slow, satisfied finger over her curves, leaving a trail of fire in its wake. 'And nice to go to sleep with, and nice—'

'Oh, you!' She flicked him laughingly on one muscled shoulder as she thought again how lucky she was to have this man for her own.

'And you adore me, don't you…?' He kissed her throat lingeringly. 'So I'll take my present now.' He raised his head again and looked down into her flushed face, his eyes hot and the firm mouth she had thought so severe smiling with sensual anticipation. She shivered delightedly.

'Your present?' She arched provocatively beneath him, deliberately misunderstanding him. 'I might not have bought you a present.'

'Oh, you have.' He drew back the dark red sheet and feasted his eyes on her pale, slim body spread out to his gaze. 'And it's tasty, very tasty.'

'Wolf…' She giggled as he eyed her wickedly, his mouth curving in the boyish grin that was so at odds with the hard, male face. 'What about the children? I have to—'

'You don't have to do anything but please me.' The arrogance was intentional and satisfied. 'You know how Hannah enjoys the infants—let her have her moment of fun with them before the day begins.'

'But—' The protest was lost as he drew her against him, the feel of his magnificent body sending all lucid thought out of her head. It still amazed her, this passion that was a white-hot flame every time he touched her. Playful, tender, fierce, lusty—however he made love to her the result was the same, a total melting of her body

in a wave of overwhelming pleasure that left no room
for anything else.

She wouldn't have believed a man's body could work
such magic on her senses, but since that very first time,
when he had possessed her so completely the rest of the
world had shattered into a million pieces, the mere feel
of him was enough to set her body tingling. He was a
devastating lover. She opened her eyes now as his dark
head bent to her breasts, their peaks already swollen and
ripe in anticipation of his caress.

And an incredible father. James had been born five
years after their marriage—Wolf had insisted he wanted
a few years to enjoy her and get to know Hannah before
they had children of their own—with Edward following
a year later and little Jane Carrie eighteen months after
that.

He had never shown any partiality towards his own
children at the cost of Hannah, indeed he seemed to have
a special relationship with Matthew's daughter that his
own children couldn't touch. Hannah had healed his
stark grief over his first daughter in a way Lydia could
never have hoped to do, accepting Wolf totally from the
first moment and showering him with childish love and
affection, clearly delighted with her 'new daddy'. She
was nearly fourteen now and breathtakingly lovely, and
the other children adored their big sister as she did them.

'Wolf?' She raised his head upwards as she slid down
the bed a little to meet his face. 'I have got a present
for you, you know.'

'As I expected, wench.' He took the delay in their
lovemaking with indulgent good humour, knowing she
wouldn't be able to resist him for long.

'I'm just not sure if you'll really like it.' She was still holding his face, wedged as she was under his body, and he smiled slowly, his eyes slumberous.

'I'll like it.' He moved his body slightly and she gasped with pleasure. 'Well?' He moved on to his elbows and looked down at her, his eyes narrowed.

'The thing is, I've given you similar ones before.'

'You have?'

'But this is a little different.' He smiled at her teasing and did something with his hands that had her breathing more quickly as shivers of sensation flickered over her body. 'It comes in pairs.'

'Pairs?' Now she had all his attention as he rolled to one side, his face straightening. 'You aren't saying…?'

'Twins.' She grinned at him happily. 'It was confirmed yesterday.'

'Twins.' He shut his eyes for a moment and then gave a laugh of sheer delight. 'Twins.' He sat up in the bed looking ridiculously pleased with himself before his expression altered. 'And you're all right?' She loved him for the immediate concern.

'Of course.' She placed a satisfied hand over the faint mound of her stomach. 'Or I will be when you give me *my* present.'

'I'll just get it—' As he went to move from the bed she caught his arm indignantly. 'Wolf!'

'You know I love you?' He fell back against her with a low chuckle. 'Really love you?' Now his eyes were serious and his mouth was tender with something that caught at her heartstrings. 'You are my sun, moon and stars, my darling, the air I breathe and my life-blood…'

'As you are mine.'

He took her mouth in a long, passionate kiss that awakened both their bodies anew to the delights to come, and then, as his mouth began an erotic downward spiral over her satin-smooth flesh, she shut her eyes as she murmured his name.

'My darling, my own Wolf…'

And then words weren't necessary as he took her with him into the heights.

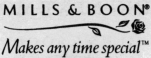

MILLS & BOON®

Makes any time special™

Bestselling themed romances brought back to you by popular demand

Each month By Request brings you three full-length novels in one beautiful volume featuring the best of the best.

So if you missed a favourite Romance the first time around, here is your chance to relive the magic from some of our most popular authors.

Look out for

Mothers-To-Be

in November 1999

featuring Jessica Steele, Catherine George and Helen Brooks

COMING NEXT MONTH

MILLS & BOON®

Presents...™

MARRIAGE ULTIMATUM by *Lindsay Armstrong*

Neve couldn't work out why Rob Stowe was suddenly insisting upon marrying her, or whether she should even say 'yes' when the mother of his child was still so much in evidence!

MISTRESS BY ARRANGEMENT by *Helen Bianchin*

Nikos Alessandros needed a social hostess and Michelle needed a male companion to deter an unwanted suitor. A convenient affair—if they can keep their passions in check!

BARTALDI'S BRIDE by *Sara Craven*

Guido Bartaldi had obviously decided upon his reluctant ward as his wife. When Clare accepted a position with him she began to suspect that Guido had an entirely different set of intentions!

BOUGHT: ONE HUSBAND by *Diana Hamilton*

In her innocence Alissa offered to pay Jethro Cole to marry her, to comply with the conditions of her uncle's will. In fact Jethro was a millionaire intent on making Alissa his own.

Available from 5th November 1999

Available at most branches of WH Smith, Tesco, Martins, Borders, Easons, Volume One/James Thin and most good paperback bookshops

COMING NEXT MONTH

MILLS & BOON®
Presents...™

THE SOCIETY GROOM *by Mary Lyons*
(Society Weddings)

Once, they'd had a passionate affair. When they met again at a society wedding Olivia thought she'd lost all interest in Dominic FitzCharles—until he made a surprise announcement...

SLADE BARON'S BRIDE *by Sandra Marton*
(The Barons)

When Lara Stevens met Slade Baron an overnight flight delay led to a tempting invitation. Who would Lara hurt if she accepted? He wanted her and she wanted...a baby.

GIBSON'S GIRL *by Anne McAllister*

Gibson was fascinated by the shy and beautiful Chloe. Should he seduce her? Gib was tempted. Should she resist him? Chloe had to. Eventually it became a question of who was seducing whom!

MARRIAGE ON TRIAL *by Lee Wilkinson*

Elizabeth had insisted on an annulment - and disappeared from Quinn's life. Now he'd tracked her down and claimed she was still his wife. Did he really love her, or did he want revenge?

Available from 5th November 1999

COMING NEXT MONTH

MILLS & BOON®

Enchanted™

ONE MOTHER WANTED by Jeanne Allan

Allie and Zane had once loved each other intensely. When they meet again and Allie offers to marry Zane so that he can win custody of his daughter, hope springs eternal. Can he now make Allie his wife for real?

SUBSTITUTE FATHER by Janelle Denison

Lauren's goal is to help an orphaned boy meet his hero, Rafe Dalton. Rafe isn't ready to be a hero but Lauren hopes that when he opens his heart to the boy he'll also find room for her!

TO TAME A BRIDE by Susan Fox

(Rebel Brides)

Lincoln is the first man to ever stand up to Maddie St. John. He also discovers that beneath her prickly pride is a vulnerable woman. Could Lincoln be the man to tame her?

RICO'S SECRET CHILD by Lucy Gordon

Julie is shocked to find that her new boss is the man she left eight years ago. Rico is as tender-hearted as he once was. Is now the time to tell him the truth about why she left?

Available from 5th November 1999

Available at most branches of WH Smith, Tesco, Martins,
Borders, Easons, Volume One/James Thin
and most good paperback bookshops

COMING NEXT MONTH

MILLS & BOON®

Enchanted™

THE CONVENIENT FIANCÉE by Jessica Hart

Polly was glad to do her friend Simon a favour and act as his fiancée. Then they found something new in common—chemistry. There was only one obstacle to a *real* engagement—Simon's real fiancée.

BRIDEGROOM ON APPROVAL by Day Leclaire

(Fairytale Weddings)

Hanna went to the ball to bring home a husband—on a trial only basis. Marco had been looking for a business deal, until he saw Hanna! They were married by midnight but he still had to convince her this marriage could last a lifetime.

THE BOSS'S BRIDE by Emma Richmond

Claris knew that acting as stand-in-mum to her boss's baby god-son would be challenging. Yet she and Adam were developing a taste for parenting, and for each other, and beginning to wonder what would happen when the baby went home to his mum and dad.

HUSBAND POTENTIAL by Rebecca Winters

Fran didn't want a husband and Andre didn't want a wife. To keep the undeniable sense of intimacy between them under control, Andre feigned unavailability. Would Fran feel so safe when Andre revealed he had husband potential after all?

Available from 5th November 1999

This month's
irresistible novels from

TEMPTATION®

CONSTANT CRAVING by Tori Carrington

Eva Burgess was pregnant and she needed a husband—at least whilst she made a visit to her old-fashioned family! So she asked her new colleague Adam Grayson to play along. What she didn't know was that Adam was already working undercover—to investigate her!

STILL HITCHED, COWBOY by Leandra Logan

Mail Order Men

Letters arrived by the sackful in response to Matt Colter's ad for a wife, but he took his time choosing. And just as he'd settled on a candidate, his *first* wife, Jenna turned up. She was still sexy, still trouble. And much to Matt's annoyance—still hitched. *To him!*

STUCK WITH YOU by Vicki Lewis Thompson

Wyatt Logan was not at all pleased at being stuck in an empty house with a stranger—at least not at first. But trapped by the snow, he and Charity Webster were looking for ways to keep warm. And there was a lot to be said for body heat...

TANTALIZING by Lori Foster

Blaze

Josie Jackson didn't expect to like Nick Harris! She'd been set up by her sister, a situation that usually led to disaster. But instead of the world's most boring man, Josie found the sexiest man alive. And instead of a blind date from hell, she was heading for a night of passion.

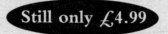
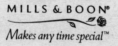

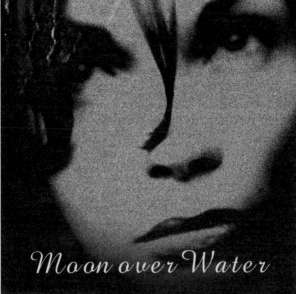